THE SOUND OF DREAMS

Baron's attention was drawn to the young couple seated no more than fifteen feet from him. It was their laughter, soft and rippling, that burned through his memory banks. A boy and a girl in their late teens sat opposite each other holding hands across a small table. Two cups of tortufo sat untouched between them. It was immediately apparent the delicacy wasn't the cause of their enjoyment.

Baron couldn't hear a word of their conversation, but their laughter was an enjoyment of each other's presence—filled with love and happiness, enriched with hidden promises . . .

Baron shivered, recognizing something that could be shared only by the young in love. It was the sound of dreams!

THE SOUND OF DREAMS

HERMAN WEISS

AVON
PUBLISHERS OF BARD, CAMELOT AND DISCUS BOOKS

THE SOUND OF DREAMS is an original publication of Avon Books. This work has never before appeared in book form.

AVON BOOKS
A division of
The Hearst Corporation
959 Eighth Avenue
New York, New York 10019

First Avon Printing, March, 1981

AVON TRADEMARK REG. U.S. PAT. OFF. AND IN
OTHER COUNTRIES, MARCA REGISTRADA, HECHO EN
U.S.A.

Printed in the U.S.A.

For Ruth

From whom I heard the true sound of dreams

CHAPTER 1

Rome—September 1973

The *pensione* occupied the top three floors of an old *palazzo*, its balconies and rooftop garden terrace offering an exhilarating panorama of Rome. One floor below the rooftop restaurant, Rick Baron gazed about his room desultorily, his mind too preoccupied to study its handsome antique furnishings. The sole appeal of his particular *pensione* rested in its secluded location, high on a hill just beyond the Colosseum. He stared at his unopened luggage with unseeing eyes. Friends had suggested the Excelsior or the Ambasciatori on the Via Veneto, but his mood didn't call for consorting with fellow Americans. The cynicism following him aboard the plane had dissipated long before his arrival, but there was still no desire to share his bittersweet remembrances of wartime Rome. His only other two visits since then—the latter over ten years ago for the Pope's coronation—were just long enough to complete his assignments, some thirty hours combined.

Strangely enough, it was at Verdi's suggestion that he was here. Baron smiled wanly. He hadn't thought of Joe Green, his partner, as Verdi for over twenty years. "Why not, Rick?" he had urged. "You've got ten days for play before we meet in Israel. Why not visit the old haunts where we had the only pleasant time of the whole god-

1

dam war? You especially lived with those memories for a long time—I know damn well you haven't forgotten them entirely!"

Baron sighed heavily and stepped out onto the balcony.

The narrow street lay eight stories below, but Baron's eyes were drawn to the Colosseum, the ancient structure visible a short distance away across the rooftops. His lips compressed, he leaned on the stone railing. Twenty-nine years ago, he thought with a sad expression, he had just turned twenty. He rubbed the stubble on his chin. The memories were distant, but at least they were no longer bitter.

As his tired eyes stared dreamily across the red-tiled rooftops, the half-forgotten memories returned with a clarity that made him wince. It had been some time since he had last thought of Eleanora, but now there she was in his mind's eye—Eleanora, seventeen-year-old Eleanora with the flashing blue eyes and jet-black hair. They had met after the third day of the Allied occupation. Before that, on June 4, 1944, "All Roads Lead to Rome" had literally come true.

After clearing out the enemy from Albano on the morning of the fourth, the bulk of Combat Command A moved northwest along Highway 7 toward Rome. The Germans, however, stubbornly delayed their advance with mines, demolitions, and an antitank force. It would be late in the evening before the Tiber would be reached.

At twilight, the lead tanks from Company H of the thirteenth Armored Regiment crossed the city limits on Highway 6. A few minutes later the first two were knocked out by antitank fire. Their advance stymied, reconnaissance scrambled through side roads in search of a route flanking the roadblock. American tanks followed and squeezed through narrow streets to Via Prenestina where they encountered fleeing German tanks. At sunset, advance patrols entered Rome proper through the Porta Maggiore wall. From the south, other units pushed through Porta San Giovanni and Porta San Paolo.

While two tank companies took positions along the Tiber amid masses of deliriously cheering Italians other units found it almost impossible to move between Rome's trolley cars and the joyous crowd. Signal Corps photographers stood up in jeeps, trying to get shots in the fading light. The scene was one vast panorama of a mob welcoming them as liberators rather than conquerors. In minutes, every American jeep and staff car was filled with flowers. Women swarmed about, kissing and hugging everyone including the infantry pacing the slowed tanks. Tired "dogfaces" grinned from ear to ear, reveling in the unexpected respite from war. American flags were suddenly as abundant as the Italian ones.

As far as the Roman citizens were concerned, the war had come to a close, and they had been liberated by the Allied Armies.

Baron straightened from the railing, his eyes fixed momentarily on the statued rooftop of the Basilica de San Giovanni and then Route 7 running beyond. "Crap!" he exclaimed aloud, aroused from his reverie. "Forget the damn war! That isn't the reason for this return to Rome!" Annoyed with himself, he went back into the room.

Thirty minutes later, freshly shaven and wearing a dark-blue blazer with an open-collar shirt, he stood undecided at the intersection of Via Cavour and Via Dei Fori Imperiali. Absentmindedly he had left behind his map of Rome. Across the way behind the parked, motorized three-wheeled *gelato* stands, the exhumed remains of the Roman Forum lay exposed. He glanced at it impassively and then looked back at the Colosseum, which he had circumvented without inspection. A thin smile appeared on Baron's face as he recalled Joe Green's remark upon first sighting the massive relic—"Well, there's one ruin they can't blame on us!"

Baron stood there for a few minutes, contemplating his next move while idly watching Fiats turn corners with tires screeching. As he looked upward at a sullen gray sky that matched his attitude, his stomach emitted a slow growl. He glanced at his watch and frowned. Eight A.M.? His expression softened as he set the Omega ahead to two o'clock, Roman time.

Although a lifetime of air travel had left him with little appetite for plane fare, he had eaten even less than usual on this trip. He forced a smile, realizing that his worldliness had vanished with the anticipation of revisiting the city where he had met Eleanora. Eleanora, his first love and his only true love.

3

After the war he had free-lanced for *Life* and *Look*, then joined Joe Green again in partnership. Baron even had two photodocumentaries published. How many women had he had in the interim? he wondered. He shook his head. Nothing ever resembled the two months he shared in Rome with Eleanora. A heavy sigh followed his thoughts. It was so long ago, and yet the memory lingered.

A narrow street ran off the Imperiali to his right, bordering the ancient ruins of Foro Traiano. Giving it a glance, he crossed over and continued north. He had no particular destination in mind—yet he did walk in a specific direction.

He waved away two hawkers selling slides of Rome and reached into his pocket for his Caminetto and pipe tobacco. Well, I've changed, he thought, holding his butane lighter to the bowl of his pipe. Three decades may not be much to Rome, but it could be half a lifetime for me. He fingered his thick, graying mustache reflectively. Directly across the busy, noisy *piazza* stood the Palazzo Venezia, its small balcony unchanged—except for the missing figure of Il Duce. Baron could easily visualize the tank units and staff cars converging upon the square amidst the wildly cheering throngs. To his left on the far side of the *piazza* stood the massive Monumento Vittorio Emanuele II Monument. The grime-filled indentations and crevices on its walls made the bleached carvings appear grotesque and bizarre. Baron smiled wryly. He still thought of it as a contemporary relic rather than a monument to past history. The graffiti on its base denouncing Nixon, Kissinger, and the Vietnam war didn't help it much.

Standing there, Baron abruptly decided he'd had enough of reminiscing. Walking briskly, he squeezed through the impatient cars waiting for a traffic light to change. He tarried only a moment at the Via Del Corso to bring his memory into focus and then continued along Corso Vittorio Emanuele with confidence.

When the sun suddenly broke through the gray overcast covering Piazza Navona, it seemed to be mocking Baron. He stared at the Bernini fountain with misty eyes, unable to cope with his emotions. Taking a deep swallow, he tried to master his thoughts. Was it merely a nostalgic yearning, or was it possible that he was still in love with

4

a seventeen-year-old girl who was actually nothing but a twenty-nine-year-old memory? Fighting the lump in his throat, he quickly relit his briar and stuck it into his mouth.

He selected a cloth-covered table beneath the awning of the Ristorante Tre Scalini, his chair angled so that he could view the fountain. Pulling out his wallet, he removed an old, worn photograph. It had been trimmed to fit the wallet. Twenty-year-old Sergeant Rick Baron was leaning backward, holding a protective arm across his face to imitate one of the four statues of the Bernini fountain. The young girl beside him was laughing in pure enjoyment.

Baron stared at it, his composure somewhat ruffled. He could still see her long black hair and those luminous eyes that always seemed to have a permanent sparkle. He blinked his eyes and put the picture away hurriedly, no longer needing the snapshot to bring back her image. The all-too-familiar surroundings were vivid enough to facilitate all recollections.

"Signore?"

Startled, Baron looked up to see the waiter at his side. A menu was slid across the table. *"Grazie,"* he murmured sheepishly.

He chewed his lip as he studied the menu. What would be the most appropriate entree to go with his reflections into the past? His eyes narrowed, then brightened. Of course! What else, but *tortellini?* It had been their favorite pasta. His smile was telling; he knew full well that he was playing games with himself.

He sighed wistfully and signaled for the waiter. *"Tortellini, vino bianco—piccolo."*

The waiter nodded, *"Si*—small bottle."

Baron smiled. The waiter's accented English was better than his own lame Italian.

The restaurant was quiet, although about one-third full. In the *piazza,* strollers—mostly late season tourists—moved about slowly along the granite surface until they reached the fountain. There, the shutterbugs took over.

In spite of himself, Baron searched each passing face wondering what he expected to find. The young Eleanora who he had loved existed no longer. For all he knew, she could have died many years ago. He recalled his anguish

5

upon returning to the States, unable to contact her. The girl he had loved vanished without a trace. It was as if she had never existed; the Red Cross and the Italian authorities could supply no information. "Address Unknown" kept coming back from all sources he tried. Anguish followed his anxiety—then bitterness. For months he had speculated on all the possible reasons she could have had for not contacting him. She had his parents' address. Had she deserted him for another? Without even a "Dear John" letter? No, he had decided, it was unthinkable after what they had shared. Dismissing one ugly thought, it was soon replaced with another. She had perished in the war, and the thought of her lying in an unmarked grave was more than he could bear. He never returned to Italy to search for her; he never wanted to know. It was better to have the memories remain untouched.

Baron, still young but no longer naive at the war's end, enrolled in the Columbia School of Journalism together with Joe Green under the GI Bill. Acquiring a '40 Dodge, they installed a short-wave radio and, when time permitted, occasionally followed the police calls. Green had purchased an Anniversary Graphic, and Baron added a flash attachment to the Leica from Italy. With this equipment, they found their own assignments through the radio—fires, riots, even murders. Baron made his first ten dollars from a magazine with a photograph of a drunk asleep on the front steps of a rooming house, the sign behind the prone figure reading, "Rooms For Rent—Cheap."

While still students, their work was getting recognition. But the work routine they had incorporated into their studies was interrupted by Mindy, a vivacious, statuesque blond who modeled for a commercial studio. Upon graduation, Green had married Mindy but failed to get Baron interested in a joint venture in a commercial studio.

On the loose with a Master's degree in journalism added to his wartime background, Baron was eagerly sought after by various publications.

His international reputation grew with his photographic essays of the Korean War. However, somewhat lonely upon his return from the Pacific, Baron needed close ties and accepted Joe Green's offer. With television in its embryonic stage the venture was a success from the start with Joe Green acquiring all the commercials they could handle.

Nevertheless, consumed with an innate wanderlust, Baron could not confine himself to studio work and continued to free-lance occasionally. Joe rarely accompanied Baron on his jaunts. In the one serious altercation between the two close friends upon Baron's return from an African uprising, Joe accused him of harboring a death wish.

"Why the hell can't you settle down and get married, Rick?"

Baron tried to laugh it off. "Why—you got another Mindy for me like yours?"

Joe Green looked him in the eyes. "When are you going to forget Italy? She's gone, Rick! Whether she's dead or alive, she's still gone!" Baron had stalked out in anger, returning several days later to apologize.

As the years passed, there were other women in Baron's life, but except for one, he never considered marriage. She was slim and dark-haired, and had revived the diminished memory of his first love. However, the marriage was a mistake because he had wanted her to be someone she was not. It was short-lived, and he vowed never to try it again. Many women sought him out, drawn by his professional reputation and his attractiveness, but he never allowed an affair to become serious again.

Time was not an absolute healer; his scars remained. Although the torch had been extinguished, occasionally in a despondent mood his memories of his first love would emerge, becoming fainter each time.

As time progressed, so did his talents and reputation. Two of his books were made into movies. He shied away from Hollywood, though, refusing screenwriting offers. He had no desire to be under the dominion of a studio. Although the movies were financially rewarding for him, he remained aloof and shunned publicity. His friendships were private and discreet; his only family was Joe, Mindy, and their two sons.

Baron had returned from Vietnam recently with a weariness that he had never experienced before. "There's a book in this," he told Joe, "if I can get it published."

7

Joe eyed him with concern. "Rick, don't you think it's about time you started taking it easy?"

Baron shrugged off the question, too weary to argue. Instead, he asked, "What about the contract for the Israeli documentary over the Jewish holidays?"

"A piece of cake," was Joe's quick reply. The ever-present cigar twisted in his mouth. "What I had in mind was for you to take a ten-day vacation in Italy before we meet in Israel."

Baron returned his gaze shrewdly, then smiled amusedly. "Why not! It's been a long time."

A sound reached out to him, drifting slowly at first, then growing stronger. It sent a cold shiver down his spine. His forehead beaded with sweat, he stood up abruptly and glanced apprehensively toward the source of the sound.

Adjoining the Ristorante Tre Scalini was their own *gelateria*. The outdoor tables were in the sun and only two were occupied. A middle-aged couple sat in the far corner, but Baron's attention was drawn to the young couple seated no more than fifteen feet from him. It was the sound of their laughter, soft and rippling, that burned through his memory. In their late teens, they sat opposite each other, holding hands across the small table, two cups of *tortufo* lying untouched between them.

Baron couldn't hear a word of their conversation, but their laughter indicated their deep enjoyment of each other's presence; it was filled with love and happiness, enriched with unspoken promises. . . .

Baron shivered, recognizing it as something that could be shared only by the young in love. It was the sound of dreams!

He dropped back into his chair and leaned on his elbows. How could that scene be so real after all those years? It was as if he were watching himself with Lee. . . . He hadn't thought of her as Lee since his anguish over her had turned to anger; she had become Eleanora again. Lee was someone he had loved; Eleanora was merely another faithless girl.

The waiter's return broke the spell. He set down the plate of *tortellini* before Baron and then opened the bottle of Frascati.

After his departure, Baron stared at the ringlets of

meat-filled pasta. Outwardly, there was no display of emotion, but there was a heaviness within. He had shed his tears many years ago; there were none left. He chewed thoughtfully. Lifting the glass of wine to his lips, he took a sip and stared out beyond the horizon of rooftops. His thoughts flew south, beyond the Colosseum—to another day, another year, another time. . . .

CHAPTER 2

Rome—June 1944

Charred German tanks, half-tracks, and overturned vehicles were tankdozed off the road to make way for the Fifth Army advancing on Rome. White tapes marked the areas cleared of mines.

On Route 7, Sergeant Rick Baron's jeep crawled along behind the slow-moving Shermans and half-tracks. Clouds of dust mixed with the heat and the stink of the dead in the bordering fields. Holding his nose and breathing through his mouth, he glanced at his driver, Corporal Joe Green, who was emulating his gesture. Silently they watched the medics gather bodies and line them up in the weeds beside the road while other masked soldiers shoveled decaying scraps of the dead into the earth. Hardened dogfaces riding troop carriers watched impassively without comment. They were all weary, just hoping Rome would be an open city. Less than twenty miles to go.

Their complacency was shattered by the whoosh of an approaching shell. It burst in the fields, a hundred yards off its closest target. The column halted abruptly, and the troops scrambled for the tall weeds off the road. A second salvo caught a tank, setting it ablaze. The men inside fled through the turret; one man, bloody and unconscious, had to be lifted out. A tank commander ran up, shouting orders for it to be shoved off the road. A second later,

11

hearing the whoosh of another shell, he dropped to the cobblestone surface. A machine gun sputtered bullets over his head at the same time.

A short distance away, Baron lifted his head.

"Well, I'll be damned!" he spit out, "the stupid Krauts!"

Less than fifty yards away behind the shell of a concrete farmhouse stood a small structure, not much larger than a telephone booth. He cupped his hands and shouted to the tank captain. "It's the craphouse! He's in the craphouse!"

On his elbows, the captain nodded. He looked up into the slits of the nearest tank. "Get that fuckin' shithouse!" he screamed.

The Sherman lumbered across the field, mashing up the dead bodies of two German soldiers and unconscionably bulling through the outhouse.

Farther up the road there were loud explosions, then suddenly no more shelling. The German 88s had been spotted and knocked out. As cheers broke out, one dogface stood on top of a tank and threw a kiss. *"Roma!* Here we come!" Whistles and shouting greeted his remark.

An angry major drove up alongside of the tank captain. "What the hell's holding up this column?" he rasped.

The captain saluted. "Nothing, sir. Nothing right now. We're on our way."

"Well, then, get their asses moving!" he roared. "I don't want this division to be the last one into Rome!"

"Yes, sir!" The captain saluted sharply and waved the column on angrily.

Another jeep pulled up alongside Sergeant Baron's. A lieutenant and a war correspondent were in the jeep. The reporter, carrying a machine gun, got out and climbed into Baron's jeep.

"This is Timino," said the lieutenant. "Get him into Rome." He disregarded Baron's perplexity. "Have you got all your equipment? I want pictures." Timino smiled benevolently to the two men, but said nothing.

Baron rubbed his stubbly chin in bewilderment. "Yes, sir. Right now?"

The lieutenant's face hardened. "You're damn right—I mean *right now!* You're not waiting for the column." He paused, then added brusquely, "When you're through, return to field headquarters for reassignment."

Corporal Green yanked the gearshift and shot past the

slow-moving column. Baron glanced at him with weary eyes. "What the hell you mad about?"

"Reassignment—that's what! We been at it since Anzio. They forgot about us?"

When Timino laughed, Baron turned sharply. Cramped sideways in the rear seat, the reporter waved a hand. "Relax, Sergeant. By tomorrow you'll be stationed in Rome with the Allied Army of Occupation."

"Scuttlebutt!" Green said cynically. "I've been hearin' that from half the regiment."

Baron said nothing, studying the reporter. He must know something, he wouldn't be so loose with his talk, Baron thought. Timino couldn't be more than thirty, he guessed. He glanced at the submachine gun in his lap. "You know how to handle that?" he asked casually.

"You can bet your life on it."

Baron nodded. He'd already met a couple of newsmen carrying side arms. "We may have to," he commented dryly. "All we've got between us is two side arms." He straightened in his seat and pulled out his pistol. He checked the clip and returned it to the holster.

Timino stared at the backs of the two men, then leaned toward them. "For two kids, I hear you've been doing a sensational job with your cameras."

"Terrific—" Green retorted, "you offering us a raise?"

The reporter leaned back; he had committed an egregious error. They couldn't have been over twenty, but the war had hardened them beyond their years. They were no longer kids.

Baron's thoughts shifted with the remark. When had he been a kid? After high school graduation, instead of waiting for the draft to shunt him anywhere it pleased, he had enlisted in the signal corps. His parents had taken it badly. And mom—he scratched an eyebrow—they never told him of her illness. He had just come through Anzio without a scratch when he was notified of her death.

He reached into a pocket and pulled out a cigarette, then leaned into the dashboard to light it.

"I'm out, Sarge," Green said. "Got an extra one?"

Baron handed over the lit cigarette and took out another.

Timino swore under his breath. There was no excuse for a reporter being careless with words. There were no kids left in the service. He had already seen hundreds who had become so inured to killing, death, and destruction that it made him wonder what would become of them in peacetime.

The corporal shot by the column. All the traffic was going in one direction—toward Rome. Emotionlessly Baron glanced at each military vehicle they passed. He scratched at his chest suddenly and swore. Could he ever use a bath! The day before they had come through Velletri, through dust, heat and the destruction.

Apparently with a distorted sense of humor, Timino laughed. He tapped Baron on the shoulder gently. "I'll make a deal with you, Sergeant. I've been assigned to the Plaza Hotel. Get me there within a half-hour and you can have the first bath."

Baron made a face. "What about the Germans?"

"Reconnaissance says they're moving out north of the city. Rome's going to be an open city."

Baron turned to Green. "What the hell you waiting for, Corporal?"

The corporal needed no prodding. The jeep leaped over the cobblestones and bounced up the road. Timino had to hold on to keep from being thrown out. A GI riding atop a tank shouted, "Ride 'em, cowboy!" From another came, "Save some of them Eye-tie broads for us, Sarge!"

Baron winced inwardly. No one in his outfit suspected that he was still a virgin. But there was no time to let that thought linger now. He held out his hand for Green to slow down. The column had come to a halt. Baron stood up.

"What is it?" Timino asked impatiently. "Mines?" There was no shooting.

Baron kept staring, then a surprised look crept on to his face. He scratched his jaw and turned toward his passenger. "You better stand up and take a look—there, at two o'clock. It's another one of our divisions coming into Route 7."

Timino unhooked a pair of binoculars and focused it on the intersection about two hundred yards up the road.

"Shit!" Timino spit. "They're all racing to get into Rome first!"

"Are you seeing what I am?" Baron asked.

Timino was aware that the sergeant was smiling for the first time since they had met. "You're damn right! They're

14

having an argument over who has the right of way." With the binoculars he scanned the horizon to their left. "Say, Sergeant, if you can manage a left onto that crossroad . . ."

Green brought the jeep to a halt, waiting for further instructions.

Baron frowned. "Then, what? We don't have a single map."

Timino smiled. "We don't need one. I know Rome like the back of my hand. I lived there back in '39. That road leads into the old Appian Way."

"We might not be any better off," Baron countered. "We're liable to run into the British sector."

"It's worth taking the chance, Sergeant. We're not making any headway here."

Baron studied the crossroad and the surrounding terrain. With his mind suddenly made up, he sat down abruptly. He whispered to Green, then reached down for his camera case. Green squeezed the jeep ahead and crossed the road until he reached a burned-out Tiger tank twenty yards from the intersection on the left shoulder. Green stopped behind the tank. Baron leaped out, carrying an Anniversary Graphic. Leaning his elbows on the tank, he checked the lens and shutter setting. Focusing on infinity, he took two shots of the right of way dispute. Getting back into the jeep, he ordered Green to cut across the field.

Timino chuckled as he scribbled in a notebook. "You'll never see those pictures in print."

"Maybe not," Baron replied, changing the filmpack, "but I'm sure someone at headquarters will save it for his memoirs."

Green raced down the road, leaving a dust storm behind them. Just as they reached the Via Appia Antica, they could see the dust cloud of the British First Division racing up from the south. "Let's go," Baron prodded. "They're liable to mistake us for the enemy." The jeep spun onto the ancient highway and bounced along the uneven surface of dirt and paving stones.

Passing ancient ruins, Baron eyed the relics of past glories with seeming interest, but without comment.

When the road surface changed to cobblestones and asphalt, Timino leaned forward. "In another minute or so we should be reaching the Tomba di Cecilia Metella. It'll be on our right. You can't miss it—it's a cylindrical."

15

"Never mind the tour," Baron interrupted sharply. "Just keep your eyes peeled for snipers. This may have been a road of peace for the old Roman conquerors, but I doubt that the 'master race' would respect the old custom."

The correspondent eyed Baron without replying, spontaneously reassessing his original evaluation of the man. He was certainly cool, but by no means detached. With the man's apparent knowledge of Roman history, he wondered whether the sergeant was experiencing any inner excitement as they passed the ancient ruins.

They reached the tomb, and the reporter was still studying Baron. Was the sergeant searching for snipers or was he considering the russet-colored stone structure? The corporal gave it a glance, then continued to stare ahead.

"What else do you know about the Appian Way?" he asked Baron.

With one last, lingering look at the tomb, Baron turned to Timino. "After a victorious foreign war, the Roman army always entered Rome by this route. That's why they called it the road of peace. This is also the road on which Saint Peter supposedly met Christ and asked, 'Domine, quo vadis?' St. Peter, fleeing Rome at the time, returned to be martyred."

The reporter nodded, satisfied with his reassessment. Again, he scribbled into his notebook. "Were you ever in Italy before, Sergeant?"

A cryptic smile appeared. "Nope . . ." He stopped speaking when Green tapped his knee.

"We got company, Sarge." He slowed the jeep.

About two hundred yards ahead a vehicle had wheeled onto the Via Appia Antica from a side road, a dust storm trailing in its wake.

Baron spun around in his seat, but Timino already had the binoculars trained on the unexpected intruder.

The correspondent gave a soft whistle. "It's a German staff car with four men in it."

Baron hit Green's thigh. "Step on it, Corporal. Pull alongside them." He barked to Timino, "Get that gun up. I'll take it if it bothers you."

"No sweat, Sergeant. I can handle it."

Baron had his side arm leveled on the driver as they pulled alongside the Germans. He waved them off the road onto the shoulder. From the back seat two officers shouted harshly in German but made no other offensive move.

"Do you understand their lingo, Timino? What are they complaining about? They're still alive."

Timino's eyes opened wide. "You're not going to believe it. They're complaining because we're keeping them from reaching their regiment."

A hard look came into Baron's eyes. "Now ain't that too bad!" To Green he said, "Get their guns."

The German officers continued to grumble as the corporal collected their Lugers. They had no other weapons. Baron heard Geneva in their remonstrations and guessed the rest.

"Crap! They're lucky we don't wipe them out."

"Hold it, Sergeant," Timino blustered. "I won't be a party to anything like that."

A slight grin appeared. "Don't worry. I have no intention of emulating the Nazis. Ask them where the Via Tasso is."

At the mention of the Via Tasso, the four Germans became silent. The driver looked terrified.

Timino looked grim. He realized the sergeant was Jewish. "I know where it is." He glanced at Baron. "What are you going to do with them?"

"Leave them for the British. They're not far behind us." He smiled again. "But first, take your gun and blow out all their tires."

The reporter breathed a sigh of relief once they were on their way again, wondering whether the sergeant would have done the same thing if he had not been along.

It was late afternoon when they reached the Porta San Sebastiano. The cobblestone road led right through the pockmarked granite Appian Gate. Considering that it dated back to the fifth century, the single fornix was holding up well.

"Now, what?" Green queried. "Where do we go from here?"

"Straight ahead," Timino said. "As I remember, the Colosseum can't be more than a couple of miles."

They continued unimpeded with a strange silence. They did not see a single figure or face until they reached the Viale Aventino Di S. Gregorio, a wide boulevard that led right to the Colosseum which was now in view.

17

"Well, I'll be damned!" Green muttered. "We're really in Rome!"

Baron, noting the frightened faces peering from windows across the way, rasped, "Watch those damn windows!"

Timino directed them to turn right and then left at the Colosseum. "Too damned quiet!" muttered Baron as they rode down the Via Dei Fori Imperiali.

The reporter laughed. "What the hell do you expect? The Germans are fleeing the city—they don't know we're Americans."

They drove past the Forum into the Piazza Venezia. It was empty. "Hey, Sarge," the corporal murmured, "I feel like there's a million eyes watching us."

The reporter pointed out Corso Umberto Primo. It was a narrow street, and they could see a tie-up ahead.

"Hold it here," Baron ordered. "Those are Germans retreating."

They had come upon the rear of a German regiment leaving Rome in defeat. A couple of soldiers turned and looked back at them without expression. One could see at a glance that they were a defeated lot. Baron motioned the jeep forward slowly. The Germans, still carrying their rifles, glanced at them desultorily.

Behind their jeep, the city suddenly came alive. The Romans emerged from buildings and jeered the Germans. Two women walked out of a doorway to the side of the slow-moving jeep. *"Americano!"* they cried out ecstatically. Immediately they were forced to stop, surrounded by wildly cheering Romans. More people appeared, throwing flowers into the jeep and offering bottles of wine.

Amid the confusion, Green turned to Timino. "You sure you got that scuttlebutt right? We're going to *stay* in Rome? Man, oh, man!" he gurgled.

Timino and Baron weren't able to answer. They were besieged by young women hugging and kissing them.

Green was laughing uproariously. "What a war this has turned into!"

Timino couldn't help noticing how Baron, the tough young sergeant, was blushing. Baron was trying to get his attention. "Cripes, Timino, where the hell is that hotel you're assigned to?" And to Green he muttered, "Put down that bottle before you get plastered."

"Just ahead," Timino gushed. "Gun the engine, they'll make way." In Italian he shouted to the crowd, "The Americans are coming in behind us."

"Viva, Viva Americano!" the shouts came from all over. Some people rushed back to the Piazza Venezia while others trailed the Germans, taunting and jeering them venomously.

When the jeep pulled up onto the sidewalk in front of the Plaza, Timino jumped out. Baron handed the Graphic to Green. "Get some shots of the Germans." Baron got out the Bolex movie camera. "Better open your lens, corporal, this street is in too much shadow."

"Don't leave your car," Timino warned. "It'll be stripped if you do." He reached for his duffel bag and added, "Give me five minutes."

As good as his word, the reporter returned in five minutes but wearing a frown. When Baron looked at him questioningly, he shrugged. "So I'm not the first correspondent in. Mike Chinigo and Michael Stern already registered."

"C'est la guerre," Baron quipped.

The reporter smiled. Thank God, the sergeant was showing some signs of being human. "But I still owe you two guys a shower."

"Forget it, we've got work to do."

"Nothing doing," Timino insisted. "I've taken a suite. The water may not be hot, but at least it's water."

Green scratched his chest. "What the hell, Sarge—just another half-hour?"

Fifteen minutes later Baron returned from the hotel. He jerked a thumb toward the hotel entrance. "All yours, Joe. Fifteen minutes—sharp!" He got into the jeep as Green let out a joyful whoop.

Baron leaned back, stretching his legs. Cold water or not, it sure felt good to be clean again. The silt of Velletri and the Albano hills were no longer with him. He felt the stubble of his unshaven chin and glanced at his watch. Don't take too long, Joe, he thought. When alone, the formalities of rank were dropped and Baron and Green were on a first-name basis.

Although Rick Baron and Joe Green lived no more than three miles apart in Brooklyn, it took the war and North Africa to introduce them to each other. Since then, an unspoken bond had developed between them. That

19

bond grew stronger on the bloody beachhead at Anzio where, in the first few hours, their combat had been confined to shooting with a camera. Their friendship solidified during the next few weeks as they pushed through valleys and over hills, chasing the enemy. Although they had been issued side arms, they picked up rifles along the way to stay alive. They learned to work as a team, covering each other as they "shot" men in action.

The individual was as important as a single straw pulled from a broom, they discovered. Viewing the corpses left behind, the waste and futility of war hardened them and made them cynical. Inevitably the devastation in each village and town influenced their endeavors. They took more and more pictures of the ravages of war and the people caught up in the maelstrom.

Eventually their work caught the attention of the company commander. Baron stood stiffly at attention before a makeshift desk where a spread of eight-by-ten black and white glossies lay in front of the Colonel. "You're a Signal Corps photographer," said the Colonel in a stern voice, "not an editorial reporter."

"I thought this to be part of the overall war scene, sir," Baron replied resolutely.

The colonel lifted his head, his eyes glaring. "Don't be flippant with me, Sergeant!"

"Sorry, sir." Baron began to sweat. "Sir, I meant no . . ."

"How old are you, Sergeant?"

"Twenty, sir."

The Colonel pursed his lips, his eyes softening almost imperceptibly. His rank did not permit any displays of weakness or emotion. "Very well, you know your job. From now on, leave such subjects for the magazines."

After Baron was dismissed, the Colonel swept the photos into a pile. About to tear them in half, he stopped suddenly. The top photo held his attention. It showed a white-haired woman, her head bowed, squatting on a step leading to a stone doorway. The doorway was all that remained of a razed farmhouse. The Colonel blew out air between his teeth, then slid all the photos into his briefcase.

Joe Green handed a slip of paper to Baron as he slid

behind the wheel of the jeep. "Timino sent it, Rick. What's with this Via Tasso?"

Baron's eyes narrowed. "It's Gestapo headquarters."

The corporal gave him an oblique stare. "I hope you're not thinking of busting . . ."

Baron waved a hand. "Forget it for now. Since we're staying, it can hold off till tomorrow. Right now, there's probably nothing left except painful memories." He folded the paper and stuck it in his pocket. "C'mon, Joe, get going. I can hear the half-tracks back in the *piazza*."

They turned right at the next corner, trying to find their way back. Soon they were lost; none of the narrow streets ran in a straight line. Adding to their confusion, they were besieged by the happy, cheering Romans.

"Dammit, Rick," Joe groaned. "I can hear the Shermans, but I can't tell where they're coming from."

The jeep was again littered with flowers. A dozen bottles of wine were at Baron's feet. Baron stood up and shouted to the crowd, *"Piazza—Piazza Venezia? Dove?"*

From a doorway, a tall, dark youth pushed his way through the crowd to the jeep. He sat on a front fender and shouted at the mob. He looked back at Green and waved him forward. The mob finally made way before the youth's persistent shouting. After a few yards he jumped off the fender and got into the back of the jeep. Baron turned to him.

"Parla Lei inglese?"

"Si," he said, grinning. "I speak good English. Next corner, *a destra.*"

Baron studied him in silence. When the youth held on as the jeep turned the corner, Baron's left hand darted for the pistol bulging beneath the boy's jacket. The boy released his grip on the jeep, grabbing for Baron's arm but falling backward instead. He shouted at Baron.

"No, no, *Americano!* I am partisan—*Ebreo!*" His eyes were pleading. "Do you not understand? *Ebreo?*"

"What the hell's going on?" Green interjected. He glanced at the Luger in Baron's hand. "Take it easy, Rick. He may be telling the truth."

Baron nodded, studying the Italian youth. The boy's fright was genuine. "Say something in Hebrew."

The Italian youth spoke quickly in a strange tongue.

Green laughed. "Give him back his gun, Rick. He is speaking Hebrew. That's more than we can do."

Baron relented, releasing a smile. He pointed to Green and then to himself. *"Ebreo*—both of us." He glanced at the Luger once more, then returned it to its owner.

Baron's smile broadened. He didn't expect the Italian to know Hebrew. He didn't know it himself. He noted the boy's olive complexion and asked, "Your name, what's your name?"

"Moscati, Enzo Moscati."

Baron pointed to himself. "Rick Baron." He tapped Joe Green's shoulder. "Joe Green—*Giuseppe Verdi.*"

Moscati grinned, his features expressive. He leaned forward, grasping their shoulders. *"Mondo bello!"* he yelled.

A semicircle of jeeps, staff cars, half-tracks and Shermans faced the Palazzo Venezia. A hysterical, cheering mob surrounded the vehicles. Hundreds of Romans had come out to welcome their liberators. Knowing that the Germans were gone, they demonstrated their feelings with ecstatic joy. Baron and Green snapped photographs of the troops and the Romans from every angle. There was flag waving, the snake dancing with GIs wearing looted medieval helmets. Young girls embraced the GIs and poured them wine by the gallon.

The scene was the same on every road leading into Rome. The crowds swallowed up each contingent, causing massive traffic jams and unwittingly holding up the chase for the Germans.

Standing atop an M4 Sherman tank, Baron focused the 16mm Bolex on a British tank force stalled on the Via Teatro Marcello. Hearing the film run out on his last roll, he gave a weary sigh and sat down heavily. The sun was fading, anyway, he thought with a dour expression. A corporal climbed out from the bowels of the tank and joined him. Glancing at the boisterous mob, he remarked: "You'd never think they lost the war, wouldja?"

"Who said they lost?" Baron replied dryly. "They're alive."

"Sarge, go back and take a look at what we left of Valmontone this morning."

Baron remained silent, but his heart said dead cities could be rebuilt—but not dead people.

Seconds later, an odd expression crept onto his face. As he sat there, his eyes following the dancing, he felt as if he was witnessing the unfolding of a Hollywood plot. What fools they were! He noted the men in different uniforms accepting the embraces of the willing young women while others joined in the snake dancing. He felt like shouting what are you doing? You're trained for destroying and killing, not celebrating! The war isn't over for you! What are you celebrating?

His expression betrayed him. The corporal shook his shoulder. "You all right, Sarge? You look like you hate the world."

Baron's smile was weak. "Yeah, sure. I was just thinking that this carnival has to end soon."

The corporal sprung to his feet. "You know, you're right, Sarge. It's about time I got into the action before it's too late." He slid forward and jumped to the ground. Immediately, an attractive young woman hooked her arm into his.

"Good luck, corporal," Baron said to him. "Stay in one piece."

The corporal grinned. "That depends on how much time they give us."

Baron smiled in spite of himself. He got up and searched for Green. He gave up after a few minutes; to single out anyone in that mob was impossible.

It took him fifteen minutes to conquer the thirty yards back to where they had left the jeep at the head of the Via Del Corso. To his surprise Moscati was still there, running a comb through his sleek black hair. Baron studied him, trying not to show his annoyance. All he needed now was an Italian Jew. . . . He stopped in the middle of his thought, shoved his helmet back, and pursed his lips. A guilty conscience pursued him. Why the hell did he join up before the draft called him? Patriotic duty alone? Bullshit! He knew damn well it was a combination of many things. His parents had lost all their relatives in Hungary and Austria to that madman in Germany. Did they die in the name of patriotism? They weren't even soldiers.

Altering his expression, he nodded to Moscati and got into the jeep. Why the hell was he thinking of Moscati as a kid? He couldn't have been more than a couple of years younger than himself—and he surely knew how to use that Luger.

"Seen the corporal at all?" he asked phlegmatically.

The boy shook his head, smiling.

Baron settled into the seat and removed his helmet. In

the act of wiping his face, he suddenly realized that Moscati was the first foreign Jew he had met overseas. Giving him a sidelong glance, it struck him that Moscati looked no worse than any other Italian. Baron remembered that he had yet to see a concentration camp set aside solely for Jews. Were they all dead or just in hiding? He shook his head morosely. Via Tasso, a Nazi chamber of horrors, was mentioned to him by a war correspondent. The same correspondent told him how the Nazis had gathered up more than a thousand Jews in Rome on one Sabbath morning—to be exterminated at a concentration camp in Austria.

He sighed deeply. Self-preservation never allowed time to lament for the dead. Only when he had time to think, did it creep into his consciousness. On such occasions, if possible, he would seek out Chaplain Leveron to say a Kaddish for his mother. But otherwise, he refused to allow his conscience to dominate his life. There were just too many dead. Human life had become expendable in the taking of a piece of real estate. Life had become meaningless when he had first witnessed the incineration of a German tank by a GI flame thrower. They had never known or seen the men within. A foot soldier nearby, noting the look of horror on Baron's face, merely smiled. "Do unto others before they do it to you," he simply said.

"Back already?" Green interjected into Baron's thoughts.

"Yeah," Baron replied, expressionless. "Out of film."

Green gave him a curious look. Rick was becoming moodier with each passing day. Have to keep an eye on him, he thought. He forced a smile. "What now, Rick—back to headquarters?"

Moscati became excited. "No, no! You must see Tempio Maggiore!" Noting their puzzled looks, he quickly added, "The synagogue, you must see synagogue!"

When Baron remained silent, Green spoke up. "I think we ought to, Rick."

Baron nodded as if deep in thought. "Got any packs left?"

Green turned and leaned into the back of the jeep. Opening a case at Moscati's feet, he said: "Only one, but the thirty-five's got a roll of Kodachrome in it."

"Any flashbulbs? It's getting dark."

"Some, but not enough for all the exposures."

24

"Okay, let's get going."

The traffic was breaking up, and the lumbering tanks were on the move again. Moscati directed them forward, then to an alley to their left. It was so narrow two jeeps could barely fit side by side. They had entered the ghetto. Green drove through twisting lanes until they crossed Via Del Portico. He pulled over on Via Del Tempio, a short distance from the synagogue, unable to penetrate the huge crowd celebrating in the street.

Baron gaped at them with confused emotions. There was a lump in his throat. The scene was like nothing he'd ever seen. Their jeep was surrounded. Men and women, young and old, all had tears of joy in their eyes. The men wore prayer shawls and skullcaps; were voicing prayers aloud. An old woman squeezed into the jeep and grabbed Baron's hand to kiss it, then pulled out a necklace with a *mezuzah* attached and dangled it in front of him to kiss it. He complied, unable to speak. For the first time in his life, he was witnessing the old-world Jew—the people from whom his roots were derived.

Out of the corner of an eye, Rick saw Joe focusing the Kodak Ektra. Quickly regaining his composure, he ordered him to put it away.

Baron's trained eye needed no equipment to record the images before him. He noted the cheap, coarse material worn by the elders and the tears of joy falling from tired, suffering eyes.

Suddenly, he became aware of a strange murmuring that was growing louder. The people about him swarmed toward the temple to join others already congregated there. Unexpectedly, a great uproar split the air, followed by cheering and wailing. Baron and Green stood up in the seats, sensing they were about to witness something monumental. Baron's heart was pounding.

Moscati, extremely excited, grabbed Baron's shoulder with one hand and pointed with the other. "Look—" he said with great emotion, "the great doors of the Tempio Maggiore are opening. They have broken the Nazi seals."

Baron felt a cold shiver run down his spine. The mere opening of doors allowed their hopes to live again. He noticed American and British officers entering the synagogue with the others.

Moscati tapped his shoulder again. "You want to see temple? I stay with jeep. Nobody steal."

Baron frowned and shook his head. "No, we'll leave the celebration for them now. They waited long enough. Tomorrow's another day."

Moscati grinned. "You stay in Rome?"

Seated again, Baron turned to the boy. "Yes, but tell me something. The temple seems to be in good condition. Why didn't the Nazis destroy it?"

The grin disappeared. "The Nazis tear up all *torahs* and steal all old books. They take all gold and jewelry from us, too."

"Yes," Baron persisted, "but why didn't they burn the temple? They did it everywhere else."

"Rome eternal city, religious city to everybody. Nazis afraid of Pope." Moscati saw their perplexity. "Pope afraid also—that's why he kept quiet so long. Pope also afraid of Communists, so he stay in middle of the road." He tilted his chin with a sagacious expression. "You know the church hide Jews from the Germans? I live in church for one month, then I join partisans."

Despite his age, Moscati had already lived a lifetime of danger and suffering. It was then that Baron realized that it was Moscati's boyishness that made him think of him as a kid. Even when angry or frightened, Moscati was quick to smile.

Baron twisted in his seat at the sound of shuffling feet. Two old women, their backs bent with age, approached the jeep on Green's side. The black cloths in their hands were opened to display cheap jewelry for sale. Baron took one hard look and couldn't take it. He ordered Green to check the knapsack and give them whatever rations they had. To their astonishment, the American soldier handed over four cans of C-rations. With their *grazies* lingering in his ears, Baron ordered Green to take off. He'd had enough of the ghetto for one day.

He spoke irascibly to Moscati. "Where can we dump you?"

Moscati understood Baron's behavior. "You should not blame them, Signor Sergeant. If they want to be Jew, they must live this way. Jews live here in the ghetto before Christ. Some of these people afraid to leave ghetto. They never see outside world. Some go Trastevere, but it not much better there. Others go away, forgetting they are Jews."

Baron considered what he was saying, but it didn't al-

26

ter his thinking. Why were they so damned submissive? Even before the Nazis, they were always being subjugated and doing nothing about it. Where were the descendants of King David who fought the enemies of Israel? There were plenty of bigots at home in the USA, but you could still stand up and make something of yourself. With that thought, he softened. It wasn't quite true. There were ghettos at home, but they were of the people's own making. A hardness set in his jaw. If he came out of this alive, he would make his presence felt when he got home— Jew or not. To accomplish this, all he would need would be a camera and typewriter.

Green pulled up at the end of Via Del Tempio. The *lungotevere* ran right and left along the Tiber. American engineers were still removing demolition packs from the bridges as the military vehicles crossed.

"Now what?" Green asked, looking from Baron to Moscati.

"Where you want to go?" Moscati asked expectantly.

Baron was looking at the synagogue with the people crowding the open doors. It was getting dark, and the liturgical chanting could be heard faintly.

"How can we get to Route 7, Appia Nuova, and where can we drop you?" Baron asked Moscati.

The boy's eyes sparkled. "I show you, I go to Appia Nuova."

They made a sharp left and darted past a British tank heading north. A friendly shout greeted them, "Hey, Yanks, how are the lassies?" Green held up a hand, making a circle with his thumb and forefinger.

Baron shook his head without comment. Sex was the most commonly discussed topic in the armed forces. Each platoon, it seemed, managed to have at least one boastful Lothario. Essentially a loner, Baron would reply when questioned that he never carried his testimonials with him. As the jeep swung around the ancient Teatro Marcello, Baron gave it a brief, unseeing glance. His thoughts drifting home.

To sum up Baron's preadolescent life, one word sufficed —sheltered. As the only child of deeply religious immigrant parents, he had always lived with a constant awareness of religion and conscience. His first frustrations came in high school. A better than average athlete, he was nevertheless unable to compete because too many sport-

27

ing events were held on Saturday, the day of rest. He was confined to intramural sports and other activities. The school photography club soon outweighed his previous desires. Whenever possible he roamed the city, snapping candid shots of people in all walks of life. Having no interest in landscape or nature photography, he preferred to capture the illusive thoughts of people in their eyes and their expressions. His photos depicting love, hate, happiness, sadness—all the ills and expectations of man. For Rick, there was a different story behind each pair of eyes.

This eventually led him to a new frustration. Rhoda, a Gentile girl in the club, invaded his privacy. With her precocious green eyes and long brown hair reaching down to her shoulders, she insisted on accompanying him on his jaunts about the city. Annoyed at first, he finally gave in to her persistence. He told himself his refusal wasn't because he was unsociable. But who needed help taking pictures?

It took him only two days to realize that her interests didn't lie in photography. She could never just stroll; she always had to hook her arm into his. Although extremely uncomfortable, he never shunned her moves, fearing that he would seem prudish in her eyes. But he wasn't just embarrassed whenever her hip rubbed against his. Aroused and confused, he asked himself naively, Why me? To his chagrin, the answer was soon revealed.

It was the final day of the school term, the last evening he could use the 35mm Argus before returning it to the photography club. Rhoda, sitting on the grass a few yards off the path, watched Rick as he caught an old couple staring into a glorious sunset. Few people were left in the park. Rhoda licked her lips seemingly with anticipation, then called for him to join her.

Rick nodded, sensing a different quality in her voice. He took his time putting the camera back into the gadget bag. What's with this girl, anyway? he thought. She'd been hinting around for days that he should take her out on a date. He rarely dated, and the only restaurant he frequented was a kosher deli and it was doubtful she would like that.

When she insisted that he sit beside her, he did so reluctantly. Grudgingly, he admitted to himself that it was nice being there with the smell of fresh grass and the sunset, but she still made him nervous.

"Aren't you tired, lugging that bag around all day?"

Again, he was aware of a strange, husky quality in her voice. "You catching a cold?" he asked, frowning.

"Cold? No, of course not. I'm just breathless from all the walking." Grabbing his hand, she suddenly cupped it over her left breast. "Can you feel it? My heart beating?"

He froze, afraid to move his fingers, his face burning. He waited a few seconds before taking his hand away. "Could you feel it, Rick?" she continued with an assumed innocence. He merely nodded in silence.

Her next move stunned him. Leaning toward him she kissed his cheek, and simultaneously grabbed him between his thighs. All he could feel was her fingers fondling him. Yanking her hand away he got to his feet, his body quivering with anger and excitement.

"What the hell's the matter with you?" he exploded. "Are you crazy or something?"

She seemed unperturbed. "Oh c'mon, Rick." Then she pouted. "Don't be such a spoilsport. All I wanted to do was feel a Jewish one—I never have before."

Rick turned away. Although angry, he was aroused and too embarrassed to face her.

"Don't be angry, Rick," she said coquettishly. "You can touch me, if you want. I don't mind."

"Americanos, you like to buy good camera? I have Leica. I sell cheap."

Moscati's interjection into Baron's daydream caught him off balance. Disregarding Green's look of distrust, Baron twisted in the seat to face the boy.

"What model? What condition? And how much?"

The boy ran his finger across his lower teeth, eyeing them speculatively. "You have *Americano* cigarettes?" When Baron nodded. *"Due . . ."* Moscati held out his hands about a foot apart, trying to find the right word.

"Two cartons?" Baron supplied.

"Si, cartons. *Due* cartons and I give you Leica." When Moscati noted the looks of suspicion, he quickly added, "The Leica, she is good. I let you try."

Baron nodded in silence. For two cartons, what could he lose?

As they approached the San Giovanni Gate, the darkness failed to hide the bombed-out apartment houses along the way. The outskirts of Rome had taken a brutal beating. Along the road, an endless line of American vehicles moved steadily into the city.

Shortly after passing the Aurelian Wall, Moscati signaled for Green to pull over. Except for the jeep's headlights, there were no lights. Baron turned questioningly. Moscati's expression displayed more than a little concern. *"Per favore,* wait for me. *Cinque minuto*—five minutes." His look was pleading.

Baron squinted at his watch. "Okay, five minutes but no more. Understand?"

The boy nodded and leaped from the jeep. They heard his running footsteps disappear into an alleyway.

"What the hell are we waiting for, Rick? You don't really expect him to come back, do you?" Green was impatient.

Baron had never owned a decent camera in his life. He wasn't about to pass this one up, no matter how slight the chance.

"I promised him five minutes. We'll wait."

Green shrugged helplessly and watched the GIs marching in.

Five minutes later Baron, looking disgusted because of his own gullibility, told Green to take off. Just then they heard running footsteps. Baron quickly reached for his side arm. A breathless Moscati appeared. His hands were empty.

"Well?" Baron stated impatiently.

"Nobody there . . ." Moscati sputtered between breaths. "The *signora* say Eleanora go home to Trastevere. She have Leica."

Green was ready to leave. "Well, Rick, that about does it. His girl's taken off with the camera. It was a good try."

"No, no," Moscati pleaded. "Eleanora no steal. She no *Ebreo,* but she good girl. For many weeks she hide me from the Germans in her house." He gripped Baron's arm. *"Domani*—tomorrow morning. I be in Piazza Navona. You find me. I be there with Leica and Eleanora. You meet her. She not like other girls. She fight Germans and *fascisti."*

Baron frowned. Perhaps because Moscati was Jewish, he felt he had to believe him.

Moscati sensed his distrust. "I no fool *Ebreo Americano.* I be near Bernini fountain. You see."

They took off with Moscati's *grazies* echoing in their

ears. Green shook his head. "I may be wrong, Rick, but I hope he's not pimping."

Baron made no comment. Green gave him a sidelong glance; he worried about Rick. "Something bothering you, Rick?"

With a heavy sigh, Baron expressed his annoyance. "Stop worrying about me! I was thinking of the girl—what's her name—Eleanora? I think you're wrong about her."

"Yeah! How so?"

"It's pretty obvious to me he's in love with her—and probably she with him."

Green snorted. "How do you figure that?" The corporal continued to prod the sergeant into conversation; any subject would suffice if it would alter his cynical moroseness. "You got that impression in a second, huh?"

"C'mon, Joe." Green smiled when he heard Baron using his first name again. "She may have had reasons for fighting the Germans and the fascists, but why should a Christian protect a Jew from them?"

Green tried not to show his elation with Baron's concern. "All right, so now you're a psychologist. You telling me that love conquers all?"

Baron glanced at him sharply, recognizing that he was being baited. "Listen, Joe, if you're gonna pull that crap about me needing a dame . . ."

Green put up his hands protectively in mock terror. "Awright, massa, please don't beat me!"

"Shit!" Baron blurted without anger. They understood each other too well. "C'mon, get this heap moving!" Slumping into the seat and stretching out his legs, his thoughts reverted to Moscati and the girl. A Jewish boy in love with a Christian girl? Incredible! And she puts her life on the line for him? Even more incredible! He made a face thinking about it. "Crap!" he spit out irascibly.

Green heard but ignored him, sensing Rick's turmoil. That boy's got to loosen up, he said to himself, got to get rid of all the old-world inhibitions. It's about time he realized the wrath of God wouldn't be inflicted upon him just because he didn't follow all the rules. Green also noticed that although he resented the insanity of war, on occasion Rick still demanded or even craved revenge without conscience.

"Okay, Joe," Baron interjected suddenly, "what's going on? I can hear the gears in your head turning."

Well, I'll be damned! Joe said to himself. Now we're reading each other's thoughts. He chuckled, somewhat pleased. "I was just thinking of Rome. Can you imagine? No more combat for a while. Take a sniff—no cordite stink! Everything will be different—even the people."

Without remarking Baron pulled out a cigarette and lit up. Seeing Green's smile he lit another and handed it over. Baron remained silent; he pondered a Christian girl helping a Jew.

It was three days before Baron would make it to Piazza Navona. He and Green were assigned to a building formerly used by the Gestapo on a street running off the Via Veneto. The lab alone took two days to put into a semblance of working order. Nevertheless, the entire three days proved to be a liberal education for Baron, taxing his emotions and his beliefs.

Captain Leveron, the Jewish chaplain, unexpectedly showed up for dinner on the second evening and sat with Green and Baron. Afterward he invited them to accompany him on a walk about town. Green was on duty, but Baron accepted. Baron was comfortable with him. He had discovered many weeks ago that Rabbi Leveron had a special way of dealing with the problems of young men in war.

It was just beginning to get dark, but the prostitutes were already in evidence. One GI claimed it only cost him twelve cents, another said a pack of Chesterfields was all you needed for a piece of tail. On hearing this, Green had asked, "A pack of cigarettes? Was she worth it?" The GI grinned. "Are you kiddin'? This dame was smokin' at both ends."

Baron was surprised when the chaplain headed away from the Via Veneto. He glanced at him questioningly. "I just want to show you something, Sergeant." The chaplain pointed toward a building down the street on the opposite side.

It was an ancient monastery enclosed by a protective wall. Baron examined the Gothic architecture for a few seconds, then shrugged. "So," he said dryly, "if you've seen one, you've seen them all. What's so special with this one?"

The chaplain knew how to play a scene to its fullest. He pulled out his tobacco pouch and straight-stemmed pipe. After filling the briar, he held a match to it, waiting for Baron to face him. "This monastery is special," he said finally. "I know you'll find this difficult to believe, Sergeant, but it was a way station for foreign Jews on the run and Italian Jews in hiding. There were literally thousands who came through here safely. While many were given new identities to protect them from the Nazis, other remained sheltered in monasteries and seminaries throughout Rome." He stopped to relight his pipe, searching Baron's face in the light of the match. Baron remained silent. Chaplain Leveron shook his head. "Still find it difficult to accept the fact that the world may not be altogether uncivilized?"

Baron ran a hand through his tousled hair, then scratched the back of his ear. "Rabbi . . . are you teaching or preaching right now?"

The chaplain smiled, placing a hand on Baron's shoulder. "You might say both, but at least you get my point."

"I get the point all right. But how do you explain it? Guilty conscience?"

The chaplain pondered the question. "No, not really. I don't doubt for one minute that racial prejudice existed here as elsewhere, but the Italians never had a so-called 'Jewish problem.' The Jews never made up more than one percent of the population."

Baron made a face. "And what about the Fascists?"

"This may surprise you, Sergeant, but there were many members of the Jewish community who were also held in high esteem by the Fascist Party."

Baron became irritated. "Rabbi, this makes no sense at all."

"True. None of it makes sense—the war, the persecution. But you should understand that while the Fascists were a menace to the people in general, they weren't a peril to the Jews until they joined with the Nazis after the Italian surrender."

Baron nodded. He'd known all this, but it was still hard to swallow. He spoke gratingly, his voice filled with bitterness. "And why were our people like sheep? Why did they just accept their fate without fighting back? Take that Sabbath morning back in October, when the Nazis gathered up more than a thousand Jews," Baron's eyes glared into the chaplain's, "why wasn't a single finger raised in re-

33

taliation? Not by a Jew, not by a Gentile—not even by the Pope who remained silent through it all!" He paused, regaining control but continuing sarcastically, "After all, isn't Rome the holy city—the city that respects all religions?"

Chaplain Leveron didn't reply immediately. Whatever the motive was behind the Pope's silence, that was for history to judge. His concerns were with the present and the future. With practiced patience, he waited for Baron's fury to subside.

"Sergeant, don't let your bitterness blind you to whatever goodness is left in this world. Where do you think our people were hiding during the German occupation? I've already told you about the monasteries and churches, but what about the homes of Christian friends! Yes—even though you may find it difficult to believe—it all started on the very day the Nazi trucks pulled into the ghetto."

With an abrupt change in manner, the chaplain smiled tolerantly and looked at Baron as a father would. Baron grumbled to himself.

"C'mon, Sergeant, can't you feel it? We're in the midst of world changes right now. Yesterday morning all restrictions against Italian Jews were abolished. This morning we invaded Normandy. You can see the importance of these actions in every face in Rome."

Baron's features softened, but he remained silent.

The chaplain used the end of a wooden match to clean his pipe, his brow furrowed deep in thought. The sergeant was a tough case. Secretly he suspected that Baron was subconsciously suffering from a guilt complex caused by the partial loss of his Jewish identity since entering the service. Unconsciously, he was blaming the European Jewish community for his dilemma.

"Baron, you been out of that lab yet?"

Baron looked up. "No, why do you ask?"

"How'd you like a couple of days leave? I think I could arrange it. It would do you some good. You could see the sights and meet the people. I know you'd find Rome a most interesting city."

A boyish smile appeared on Baron's face. This was not the look of a hardened military man. His first thought was that he still might find Moscati and get that Leica. The Piazza Navona had a reputation for being the mecca for black marketeers. He was sure Moscati would be there. His second thought of Joe Green.

"How about Verdi, uh, Corporal Joe Green?"

The Piazza Navona, a Baroque square built on the ruins of the Stadium of the Emperor Domitian, held no surprises for Baron at first sighting. It was like everything else in Rome. Originally, chariot races were held here for the entertainment of ancient Rome. Later the entire area was flooded and mock naval battles were staged. Eventually that phase of Roman history passed, and the stadium was filled in and built up to its present level. Now outdoor cafés bordered the square, facing the fountains of Bernini and Borromini in tranquility.

Of particular interest to Baron was Bernini's Fountain of the Four Rivers, dating from the seventeenth century. In silence, Baron and Green studied the reclining marble figures surrounding the Egyptian obelisk, forgetting for a few moments their reason for being there.

A few moments was all they were permitted. The street urchins besieged them like flies, begging or offering to sell them rings and cheap jewelry, which they guaranteed was "real gold, Joe, stolen right from the Nazis." As far as they were concerned, all Americans in uniform were either "Joe" or "Yankee." One eight-year-old tried to sell Green some pornographic pictures. He shooed them all away. To him, these kids were simply too streetwise. He shook his head in disbelief as they shouted epithets in Italian moving away to accost other strolling GIs.

Before either Baron or Green could reply, they heard their names called out. A figure standing beside a table at one of the outdoor cafes was waving wildly, bidding them to join him.

They were greeted like long lost brothers by Moscati with vigorous pumping of the hands and backslapping. He invited them to share a bottle of wine with him.

The usual aloofness Baron reserved for strangers dissipated with Moscati's ingenuous manner. He smiled and shrugged, saying, "Why not?" Sitting down, Green removed the heavy gadget bag from his shoulder and placed it on the floor between his legs.

Moscati watched him, then spoke softly, "You bring cigarettes?"

Baron nodded. "And you have the camera with you?"

Moscati's eyes widened expressively. "No—I not bring. I not know you coming. I think you maybe go north with army." He smiled suddenly. "But I still have camera."

Noticing their impatient looks, he quickly pulled up the sleeve of his jacket. He had a choice of three wrist watches, all reading half past noon. "Eleanora be home soon." He looked up. "You have jeep?"

Baron nodded, pointing to the far end of the square. "It's waiting there."

Moscati was alarmed. "You leave jeep alone?"

Verdi grinned and reached down into the gadget bag, pulling out a cloth-wrapped object. He showed the jeep's distributor cap to Moscati. "We've already been warned, Enzo. We also paid a kid fifty lire to watch it."

The Italian shook his head. "I hope he's watching the tires. They worth a lot of lire in the black market."

Baron made a face. "You don't seem to be doing too badly yourself."

Moscati was quick to defend himself. Pulling back his other sleeve, he displayed more wrist watches. "All watches come from my papa's store in Milano. Friends bring them here for me to sell. *Americano* make dollar in Roma 100 lire—in Milano it only twenty lire. Black market now big business in Roma." He seemed to sadden with Baron's distrust. He jerked a thumb at a couple walking by, an Italian girl hanging onto a GI. There were quite a number of similar pairs walking about. "You think she like GI?" He blew out air between his teeth. "She hungry! GI bring food, she go to bed with him."

Baron finished his glass of wine in silence, his features softening. "All right," he said, getting to his feet abruptly, "so where do we go from here?"

Moscati regarded Baron with a bewildered expression. This *Ebreo Americano* GI is one tough soldier, he said to himself, but he could be a good friend also. "Trastevere —we go now."

They had to wade through a congestion of bicycles to get to the jeep, which was being guarded by a ten-year-old sitting behind the wheel with his arms folded.

"Just like the centurions of old," Baron quipped. He handed the boy a lire note.

The boy held the money in a tight fist and said, "Signor Joe, you got cigarette?"

Baron glanced at Moscati. "He's gotta be kidding."

36

Moscati whispered to the boy. The boy shrugged his shoulders, leaped from the jeep, and took off for the square with a wave of his hand.

"Just like that," Green remarked. "What the hell did you say to him? In the *piazza*, the kids gave us a lot of trouble."

Moscati looked from Green to Baron, his dark eyes growing serious. "I tell him not to be greedy—or he kill goose with golden eggs."

Baron reacted. "And you say this to our face? Is this how you operate?"

"Si!" Moscati grinned suddenly. "I tell you because you my friends." He saw their looks of perplexity. "If I no be here, you give boy cigarette. He ask for 'nother and you give. He ask for more, you give whole pack to get rid of him." He shook his head, still smiling. *"Americano* GI's too easy. Yankee soldiers got too much money and much food. More food than Italian people. Cigarettes like money now—they buy food in black market."

Baron sighed. They'd already been lectured on the black market. The ration cards issued to the Italians barely bought ten percent of their needs. Two cartons of black market cigarettes was more than equal to a Roman worker's weekly pay. It took three dollars to buy either a pound of coffee or five pounds of sugar. Baron and Green had been cautioned to watch their jeep because a used tire equaled six months wages to a Roman.

With Moscati eagerly giving directions, they crossed Ponte Garibaldi in a few minutes. Baron noted the synagogue to their left, but said nothing as they entered the Viale Di Trastevere, a wide boulevard that briefly reminded him of New York's Lower East Side. Peddlers with pushcarts lined the sidewalks in front of a variety of stores, selling all kinds of jewelry and trinkets.

"Here," Moscati offered, "many Jews—but more Christians. Not so bad like ghetto. Here Christians hide many Jews. They share ration cards with us when Nazis here."

Baron nodded in silence, but Green asked, "How the hell did you manage to stay alive?"

The Italian grinned. "I join partisan group. We steal from the Nazi camps. Eleanora, too! Her papa partisan leader, the Germans kill him. He die in Via Tasso one week before *Americano* come. Now only Eleanora and her mama left. I live with them."

Moscati forestalled any further comment as he directed Green to turn right, which then brought them into another world. The street was so narrow and winding that the buildings seemed to converge over them. It was like riding through a canyon. People emerged from doorways on the road. There were no other cars but people on foot and bicycles jammed the street. Green drove slowly, intermittently blowing the horn, which drew angry comments from some. Moscati stood up and gestured wildly in response. Baron was enjoying the scene.

"Nothing like this at home, eh, Rick?" Green remarked.

"You can say that again," Baron blurted out, before bursting into laughter.

When Green started howling with laughter, a bewildered Moscati leaned forward. "Why you fellas laugh?"

Green stopped the jeep, unable to see through his tears. They laughed even harder with Moscati's bewilderment.

Finally Baron, wiping at his eyes, said, "Enzo, I don't even know how to explain."

Also settling down, Green glanced at Baron. In all the weeks they had been together, this was the first time he had ever seen his friend really laugh. A pleasant feeling spread over him as he observed Rick loosen up.

The apartment consisted of three rooms: a kitchen, a living room, a bedroom and a small bathroom off the kitchen.

Eleanora was pouting. Sitting at the kitchen table with her elbows resting on a spotless white tablecloth and a cold untouched sandwich before her, she stared at the yellowing walls. She was working only two days a week but was already frustrated with her job. Everyone who entered the dress shop seemed to want to buy *until* you mentioned the price. Who had the money? Only the *Americano*. And they weren't buying dresses.

Just thinking of the Americans brought a frown. She couldn't understand how soldiers could have so much money. Everyone knew soldiers were poorly paid. She shook her head defiantly. And why were they so cocky? she wondered. Did they think a whistle was really a proper introduction? Her deep blue eyes flashed for an instant. Did they think all Italian girls were prostitutes?

Two sudden, shrill whistles broke her reflections. Enzo. She moved quickly across the kitchen and into the living room. Pushing open the windows, she leaned over the sill and peered down to the *piazza* below.

"Pazzo!" she exclaimed, spying Enzo with two *Americano* soldiers. She noted his wide smile as he waved to her, realizing immediately that he was going to bring them up to the apartment.

"Mama mia!" she ejaculated in exasperation. She glanced about the room, at the faded wallpaper, at the worn furniture, at the drape that concealed Enzo's cot. Despite her consternation, she held a hand to her face, feeling a wave of excitement overtake her. They would be the first Americans.

Hearing Enzo on the stairs—he always took them two at a time—she ran into the kitchen, grabbed the untouched sandwich, and hastily threw it into the refrigerator that did not work. Next, she darted into the bedroom, stood before an old triple-mirrored vanity, and began brushing her hair. Her face devoid of makeup, she pinched her cheeks and bit her lips to bring some color.

The door sprang open and Moscati rushed in. He shouted for Eleanora when he found the kitchen empty. From the bedroom, she answered in Italian.

Baron and Green, who had been following Moscati cautiously now entered the kitchen hesitantly. He welcomed them in and waved them into the living room, pointing to the sofa.

"Sit, sit," he said animatedly. *"Uno minuto,* Eleanora be here." He scratched his head impatiently. "Some wine? You like some wine?"

Baron showed signs of unrest. "Look, Enzo, we didn't come here to impose upon you. The camera is all we're interested in." He looked to Green for help. Green grinned and shrugged. Seeming to enjoy the situation he made himself comfortable on the bumpy sofa.

Baron frowned disapprovingly. "Don't get too comfortable, Joe. We're not staying that long." He then became aware of the girl standing in the doorway, regarding him with an innocent expression.

So, she thought, these are Enzo's American friends. The one standing seems so nervous.

This is the Christian girl that worked with the partisans,

Baron thought. The one that took in Enzo and hid him from the Nazis.

As if anticipating his thoughts, Moscati pointed to the drape at the side of the room. "My bed behind there. Eleanora share bedroom with her mama."

Baron nodded, gazing at the Italian girl. Her jet-black hair was shoulder length and her eyes were the deepest blue he had ever seen. She was strangely disconcerting to him. He couldn't keep from staring at her. Petite and much too lean, he thought. Her mouth was small and compressed as she bit into her lip. Her eyes seemed to be holding a secret, daring him to share it. Unable to control himself, he felt his face turning crimson.

Eleanora smiled, she couldn't help it. A shy American? She didn't think it possible. *"Buon giorno,"* she said to Baron. *"Prego, si accomodi."*

Baron, now flustered, looked to Moscati.

Moscati gestured with both hands, displaying annoyance with the girl. *"Inglese, Eleanora, inglese!"*

She laughed cheerfully and said, "Please, sit down, *signore.*"

Her English was perfect with only the barest trace of an accent. Hearing her laugh and seeing her eyes sparkle Baron was dumbfounded and intrigued. Finally, somewhat embarrassed he managed to sit down next to Green who regarded him curiously.

"The camera, Enzo, the camera," Baron mustered, clearing his throat.

"Leica?" she asked. When he nodded, she pursed her lips. *"Per due* cartons?" When he nodded again, she rolled her eyes and left the room.

Green's knee rubbed against Baron's, signaling, "I told you so" to him out of the corner of his mouth. Baron muttered, "Shut up, Joe."

Baron knew that two cartons for the camera was a ridiculous price. He was prepared to give more, depending on the condition and the model.

Except for a few scratches, the Leica was in topnotch shape. At home, it would have sold for a couple of hundred dollars at least. Baron felt like he was stealing it.

"Five cartons, Enzo. You can have five cartons." He disregarded Green's sudden movement. "I'll have to owe you a couple—we only brought three with us." It was a bargain, even at black market prices, but now he felt a little better about it. The leather case alone was worth a carton.

Baron hid his elation well, but if Moscati was such a wheeler-dealer, he thought, why did he make such an inane offer in the first place. The F3.5 Zeiss Tessar lens by itself made the transaction unbelievable. And yet Moscati's face expressed pure pleasure.

"Vino, Eleanora, bring vino!"

Baron got to his feet in a hurry. "No, no. How about letting us treat you to lunch to seal the bargain?" He noted the looks of surprise. "You can pick the restaurant since we still don't know our way around yet."

Eleanora's immediate reaction was pure delight. Baron felt a warm glow within him, not quite understanding why.

Green, still seated, watched his friend silently. This was something he had never seen in Rick before. Always a loner, Rick had never been even slightly gregarious. Not having known Rick back in the States, he wondered whether this was a new role or an old one reassumed. Getting to his feet, Green glanced at the Italian girl, studied her face and her expression—then understood. He didn't have to search Rick's face; he knew what he'd find. The light would be in Rick's eyes, no doubt. Green turned away, rolling his eyes. Oh, brother! he thought. She must have recognized that Rick was ripe for the picking.

He moved to the window and looked down to the *piazza* where Moscati's Roman legion was guarding their jeep. His thoughts, however, remained on his own pal. Rick was not made of the same stuff he was. Rick was too easy a mark for this girl. She was playing it cute, but moving in fast, he thought.

While still in high school, Joe Green drove his own Lincoln Zephyr. Although it wasn't new—there were no new cars after Pearl Harbor—he managed very well on his "A" ration card. How much gas did you need to find a good parking spot? Coming from a wealthy family, he'd always had anything he wanted, and what's more he'd known how to handle it. Unlike Rick, his background wasn't heavily religious. Although almost a year younger than Rick, with confidence that was far beyond his years, he had taken it upon himself to be Rick's keeper.

Musing a moment longer on his suspicions of Rick's

virginity, he smiled to himself. Hell! What's the problem! There always has to be a first time, he thought.

Baron studied the menu, scratched his jaw, then looked to the others. "What do you recommend?" he asked. The Americans had been warned to stay away from the local meat. That reminder brought a smile. Before entering the service, he had never eaten food that wasn't kosher. He scanned the menu again and asked, "What's *tortellini?*"

"Stick to the pasta," said Green pointedly.

Moscati corrected him. "It is pasta, but perhaps you would like plain pasta better—not with meat." He glanced at Eleanora. "Someday when we get meat, Eleanora make for us. Nobody make *tortellini* like Eleanora."

Baron had been careful to avoid her eyes. Now he looked at her, wanting to speak but finding himself tongue-tied. He turned away and glanced about the restaurant.

It was a small room with just six tables, all of which were occupied. The frescoed walls, somewhat faded, depicted scenes of an ancient Roman court. The place had seen better days; the linen though worn was spotless and there were fresh flowers in a small chipped vase.

Enzo ordered *manicotti* for everyone and a bottle of wine. When Baron asked for coffee, Enzo shook his head. "You can have *cappuccino* without *zucchero*—sugar. But, Americano coffee . . ." he shrugged helplessly. "This not like America."

Baron pursed his lips, deep in thought. The mess sergeant was Jewish, he could deal with him. He felt his temples pounding before he spoke and didn't dare look at Eleanora.

"Enzo—if you don't think this is too presumptuous of me—I can get Eleanora some canned meat, flour, coffee, and sugar." When he saw their looks of amazement, he quickly added, "And no catches."

Green shaded his eyes, hiding his thoughts: For a guy that never bothered with girls, he sure as hell was moving fast.

For the first time, Enzo's eyes showed suspicion. He glanced from Baron to Eleanora. She looked puzzled but not suspicious.

42

"*Signore,* why you want to do this?" she asked innocently, sensing that he was somehow not like other Americans.

Green leaned back in his seat. "Yes, *signore,* tell me also why you do this," he mimicked. "As if I didn't know," he added under his breath.

Baron centered his attention upon Eleanora, pretending not to notice Green's sarcasm. "Enzo says you make the best *tortellini.* I'd like to see him eat his words."

Eleanora gazed at him quizzically. In one respect, she had found all Americans alike—aggressive and self-assured. "*Signore,* you make joke." Her lips broadened into a smile. "*Si*—and perhaps you and your friend would like to be our guests?"

Moscati was strangely silent.

Baron, aware of the change in Moscati, stifled his glee. "By the way," he asked, "you two . . . you're not engaged or something?"

Moscati seemed not to understand, but Eleanora laughed. "Engaged?" She pinched Moscati's cheek playfully. "No, *signore,* we are just good friends."

Moscati shrugged. "*Si*—just good friends." But his dark eyes belied that simple admission; his hope had always been to be much more than good friends.

After a mere three weeks, the war with all its madness no longer existed for Rick and Eleanora. It had all begun innocently enough with holding hands, but a mutual yearning enticed the initial stages of sex exploration.

Their opportunity came one afternoon when Rick was delivering his usual supply of food to her flat. Some coffee, some sugar, and a half-gallon jar of chicken livers. The mess sergeant always sold the livers because the GIs never ate it. Whenever Rick brought meat, Eleanora or her mama would cook it immediately, giving whatever surplus there was to their neighbors. With electricity for the refrigerator available only three hours each night, there was no other choice.

After letting him in, Eleanora locked the door as he placed the food on the table. She was unusually silent as she took the jar and put it into the refrigerator. Rick gaped at her. "Lee, it's uncooked . . ."

She turned and stared at him. "It will keep for a few minutes," she simply said.

A single step brought them together. With his lips upon hers, she took his hand and slipped it into her blouse. His lips moved to her cheek and then to her neck as she unbuttoned her blouse.

Rick lifted his head. "God, Lee," he mustered hoarsely. "We can't . . . we just can't . . ."

She uttered not a word, but took his hand, instead led him into the bedroom. Moving to the window, she drew the blackout curtains. The darkness seemed to fill them with eagerness.

Lee—she loved the shortened name he had given her —had realized early in their relationship that her feelings for him would soon get out of hand if she allowed it to continue. She fought with herself, knowing that nothing could ever come from it. Not only was he a foreigner "visiting" their land, but he was a Jew besides. Yet when they were together, everything was forgotten—religion, the war, its desolation and destruction nonexistent.

Mama was suspicious of him. If she was at home when he arrived with food, she would glance at him searchingly, refusing to acknowledge the look of innocent purity about him. "Only a priest has such a look, not a soldier," she would insist.

Lee realized their game of kiss, touch, and feel couldn't continue; they were both drowning in frustration. But she also recognized the fact that he wouldn't be the one to force the issue. The initiative must be hers, either stop seeing him or . . .

There was no turning back now. Their nakedness created sensations neither one had ever imagined. His lips were hot on her throat, and her feelings were wanton. The insides of her thighs were on fire as his hand caressed her flesh. A moan escaped when his fingers discovered her virginity. She ground her lip into his.

Rick lay at her side, overwhelmed by his own inexperience. He had never felt such humiliation. Should he get his handkerchief or a towel? His efforts had been ineffectual it seemed. He had left her wet, sticky, and unsatisfied—he had tried but failed to penetrate.

Lee's hand was on his chest, stroking him gently with patient understanding. She craved him with an intensity that made her want to scream. Her hand slid from his chest down to his genitals. She felt it stiffen. A friend's hysterical confession came into her mind. "Madonna, how

44

it hurt the first time." With her other hand, she rubbed her own wetness and then reached for him.

The pain was excruciating, but she accepted it hedonistically. Feeling his response as she moved rhythmically and slowly, the sheer ecstasy of loving him outweighed any restraint. Her hands were strong behind him as she squeezed and moved. "Oh, Lord!" she heard him moan between gasps. Their movements became convulsive.

Guilt feelings possessed Eleanora for a few moments. She was no longer mama's little girl—she was no longer a girl. She was different now. There was a brief yearning to recross the bridge just traversed. But she knew that was impossible. Her soul was not hers alone anymore. She buried her head into Rick's neck.

Rick's mind was filled with confused and troubled thoughts. Spinning onto the Via Del Tritone, he almost ran down a pedestrian. He shouted a *"scusi"* to the man's epithets and tossed him a pack of cigarettes. Instantly, he realized it was a stupid gesture. God! What a world could allow you to justify your sins with a pack of cigarettes?

Nearing the Piazza Barberini, he became aware of the GIs waiting in line for their turns at the brothel located behind one of the shops. His attempt to smile was forced as guilt encompassed him. Why, he asked himself, why did he feel this way? He was not like them—he was different. Lee was different. She was *Lee,* a girl like no other girl he had ever known. What they had shared transcended physical passion.

He circled Bernini's Fountain of the Triton, carefully avoiding the bike riders as he turned onto the Via Veneto. A smile appeared suddenly. Why should he be troubled? When they were together, nothing else existed. Their religions didn't matter. All that mattered was their love for each other. That love gave them the capability to cope with any strange element in their lives.

He smiled more broadly. Didn't she refuse to allow him to go through the Arch of Titus? Almost at the end of the Via Sacra, the ancient Roman road running through the Forum, that arch had been standing since the first century. Lee had pointed out the bas-reliefs that depicted the capture and enslavement of the Jews in Jerusalem. No

Jew has ever knowingly walked through the arch, she explained.

After parking the jeep in the courtyard behind the lab, Rick sat motionless. In a thousand years, he would have never thought it possible for him to get involved with a Gentile girl. Suddenly he wondered what Chaplain Leveron would have to say. He made a face. It wasn't necessary to wonder.

He tapped his fingers nervously on the steering wheel, thinking of home. Dad would be a problem, a big problem, he realized. He would have to write and try to make him understand. Sighing deeply, he finally got out of the jeep.

The courtyard was decorated with roses growing along one wall. He sniffed and thought he could bring her some tomorrow. She loved fresh flowers.

The chances were good, he thought to himself hopefully, that he would remain in Rome for the duration of the war. What could possibly go wrong?

CHAPTER 3

Rome—September 1973

Baron suddenly felt old, his mind reliving thirty-year-old events. Why am I here? he asked himself with a slight shrug of his shoulders. Yet, within himself, he truly understood why. There was no denying the warm glow that he felt with the remembrance of their escapades. No woman since was as appealing or as exciting as Lee—or for that matter, as loving. An audible sigh escaped. Whose fault was it? When had he ever allowed any woman the chance to compete with his career?

Standing a few feet from the Bernini fountain, his eyes left the reclining stone figure to stare vacantly at a Coca-Cola can, floating in the pool of water. They would often meet at this fountain, whenever the jeep wasn't available from the motor pool. From here they would go on their aimless walks about the ancient city, arm in arm, oblivious of all else.

He grimaced, his expression sorrowful. She had to be dead; he just couldn't conceive of her being unfaithful to him. Again he sighed. There simply was no answer.

Suddenly a tap on his shoulder startled him. He turned sharply.

An elderly couple confronted him, the man holding a camera. "You look like an American. Would you mind taking our picture?" The man smiled apologetically. "Me

47

and the missis has to have one together or nobody'll believe we were here together."

Baron took the camera and stepped back.

"You know where the shutter is?" the man asked.

Baron smiled. It was an inexpensive Instamatic. "I think I can find it." After he took the picture, the couple thanked him and departed.

At the far end of the *piazza,* Baron turned for one last look. There were no GIs about anymore and no kid hustlers to bother them. He gave a halfhearted salute and departed.

Baron found his way easily to the Corso Vittorio Emanuele, then turned into the Via Arenula. He thought of crossing the Ponte Garibaldi into the Trastevere section, but then decided there was no point to it. What would that accomplish?

The memories were vivid once again. He entered a narrow, curving alley, which led him through the ghetto toward the Via Del Tempio and the synagogue.

It was still there, just as he had seen it last—the pink and gray stone facade with the Ten Commandments staring down from beneath the blue dome. For some reason it brought back Chaplain Leveron to mind.

Chaplain Leveron was against the idea of marriage from the very first. "It simply couldn't work," he had persisted, "you're not the type to alienate yourself from your religious background."

Baron winced, recalling how he had almost begged the Chaplain to marry them. He and Joe had suddenly been reassigned to a cinematography unit on the Arno front. He had only one day left to be with Lee. The Chaplain adamantly refused to speak to the CO on his behalf, pointing out they were both underage. Angered, Baron replied tartly, "Too young to marry, but not too young to die!" The Chaplain remained steadfast. "You have no choice but to wait for war's end. Some laws cannot be broken. If fate decrees that you marry each other, it will happen." Baron had wondered whether Leveron was speaking as a captain in the U.S. Army or as a Rabbi.

That night, sitting in the jeep parked in the *piazza* below her apartment, words of comfort were difficult. He held Lee in his arms, trying in vain to stop her sobbing. "You must wait, Lee. The war will end—I'll come back for you."

Baron turned away from the synagogue. In his mind's eye, he could still see the tears streaming down her cheeks. He lingered a few moments longer to refill his Caminetto and light up, her image persisting. They had known each other for a mere two months, yet the scenes were becoming more vivid with each new site revisited.

He started commiserating with himself near the two-thousand-year-old Teatro Marcello. What had he lost? His life had been full, and with the exception of the Greens, there were no ties or responsibilities. His perpetual traveling made it impossible to maintain a permanent relationship with any woman. He wondered if Lee would have been able to accept it. But would he have chosen that life if he had not lost her?

Although extremely annoyed with himself, reaching the end of the ancient theatre, his eyes glanced to his left and beyond a slight ramp that led to the Gate of Octavia. Without bothering to investigate, he recalled the fish market just inside the arch and the Piazza delle Azimelle as the Square of the Matzoh Bakers was called. A cold shiver ran down his back as he recalled when he and Joe had walked through the ghetto with Chaplain Leveron. The buildings were stained and decaying—so were the people, it had seemed to Baron.

The chaplain was a learned man, and it was from him that Baron and Joe Green had learned much of the Jewish history of ancient Rome. The Porticus of Octavia was the very site where nineteen centuries ago the emperor sat on an ivory bench on a raised platform, welcoming Vespasian and his son Titus back from the wars in Judea. Jerusalem had been sacked and looted, the temple destroyed. The victorious armies had returned with Jewish slaves and riches such as Rome had never seen, among them a solid gold table and a candelabrum so huge it took eight men to carry.

The Octavian Gate dated back to the second century B.C., but it wasn't until the year 1555 A.D. that it became one of the two entrances into the Jewish Ghetto walled in by the Pope. In 1848, another Pope had the wall torn down.

Baron sighed. Nowhere in the western world was there more Jewish history. He glanced at the people walking by unconcernedly, saw their faces—some smiling, some tired and worn, but all totally oblivious to the ancient history surrounding them. Each generation was concerned only with their present welfare. You fools! he thought bitterly, you don't even know that Jews had more freedom in Rome under Julius Caesar than at any time in Italian history. There were laws protecting the more than 50,000 Jews, their temples, and their belief in monotheism.

Baron fiddled with the pipe, a sense of guilt suddenly obsessing him. Who was he to talk to? Since the war, he hadn't been much of a practicing Jew. There was no sense trying to rationalize his reasons. They were illogical, and he knew it.

He glanced at his watch—five o'clock already. Ignoring the blaring horns, he scampered across the road and moved energetically past the massive Emanuele monument.

There were a number of *gelati* wagons parked alongside of the Roman Forum. He waited his turn behind the many tourists and purchased a Coke, carrying it to the wall overlooking the ruins. Spread out before him were the remains of past glories, the scarred arches and broken, scattered columns. To his right, near the road dissecting the Forum from the Capitoline Hill, only three columns remained of the Temple of Vespasian. His eyes followed the Via Sacra to where the Temple of the Vestal Virgins had stood, remembering Lee pointing it out hesitantly. The penalty for Vestal Virgins who lost their chastity was to be buried alive. The memory brought a whimsical smile. And then, he remembered something else.

Discarding the empty Coke can, he moved briskly along the wall, his eyes for the first time shedding their sadness. In a small building, he paid the few lire required to walk down into the Forum. Reaching the ancient paving stones of the Via Sacra, he turned sharply to his left and proceeded along the uneven path. There was no stopping until he reached his target—the Arch of Titus, the arch which had stood for sixteen centuries without a Jew passing under it.

Baron studied the mocking bas-reliefs on the walls that depicted the enslaved Jews carrying the gold candelabrum while the Roman armies sacked the holy city. He tarried only a few moments, then calmly walked through the archway.

It was more than just a personal triumph. He now joined the thousands of Jews who had marched through this same arch on the night Israel had declared its freedom.

50

Panting from the excitement, he managed a smile. Turning around, he stared through the archway and viewed the Forum in its entire length. As he stood there, curious thoughts intertwined.

He was gazing at the remains of a dead society. Nothing remained of the magnificent temples and palaces except for worn marble and granite columns and tired arches on resurrected foundations. It was all ancient history, he thought, and should have no meaning for him in the present. And yet suddenly, he realized that he loved Rome and its gesticulating inhabitants. War had forced upon him the need to be loved, and he had found it here in this ancient city. For two months, at least, he had shared his love with a seventeen-year-old Italian girl.

He stood there, his spirit tranquil, looking through the arch, picturing himself and Lee strolling along the Via Sacra. It was all a fantasy—a beautiful fantasy. It was time to put it to rest and move on.

He started through the lofty archway once again but stopped on impulse. He gazed up at the adornments. His lips moved. "Titus, you bastard, *veni, vidi, vici!*"

Back at the *pensione,* he rented a Lancia. After dinner at a restaurant just off the Via Veneto, a place recommended by friends, he planned to take in the sights of Rome before he left. In the morning, he would make an early start for Venice.

The streets had been washed clean, and a brisk freshness lingered in the air. Baron glanced up and down the almost deserted street as the porter placed his one piece of luggage into the rented Lancia. He pressed a 500 lire note into the waiting hand of the porter and slipped behind the wheel. On the seat beside him, he placed the one camera he had brought with him—an old Leica 35mm, 1940 vintage, the leather case stained and well-used.

As the sun intermittently broke through the fast-moving cloud formations, he reached into the inside pocket of his windbreaker for his sunglasses. His clear brown eyes had a look of anticipation, the sadness of the previous day having departed. He glanced into the rearview mirror, adjusting it to look at himself. His full head of wavy hair was well-groomed, and he smiled with satisfaction. In a good humor, he traced the lines beneath his eyes with his finger. "Forget it, brother—you can't hide it."

After resetting the mirror, he unfolded a road map and studied it for a few seconds. Leaving it open beside him, he adjusted his seat until his 5'11", 180-pound frame was comfortable. Turning the ignition, he gunned the engine for a few seconds, then moved away from the curb.

Three cups of *cappuccino* and a croissant had sufficed for breakfast; his plan called for a lunch stop in Bologna, a city noted for its excellent cuisine. Florence was closer, but he had no desire to relive that episode of his life.

Turning into the immense Piazza di Cinquecento, he made a last-second change of itinerary. Once more through the Via Veneto, where he and Lee had often shared a bottle of wine with Joe Green, sometimes at Doney's, sometimes at the Café de Paris. He consulted a street map of Rome and nodded as his memory came into focus.

The Excelsior and Ambasciatori were still there, with no visible signs of change. There were still the tables of the two celebrated cafes, now empty at this early hour. All that was missing—for the moment—were the prostitutes that had catered first to the Germans and then to the Allied army.

An impatient horn behind him rousted him from the daydream. The traffic was building up, and he had been warned about Italian driving habits. He waved a hand. "Okay, *paisan'*, I'm just about through."

From the Via Veneto, he turned right onto the Corso D'Italia, the Villa Borghese at his left and the Aurelian Wall at his right. Taking a left at the Via Salaria, he headed north for a connection to the Autostrada.

By European standards the Autostrada is an excellent highway, second only to the German Autobahn. Unlike American super highways, it consists of two lanes each way plus emergency shoulders. This posed a problem for the energetic European driver who, totally disregarding the speed limit, had to jump lanes constantly to pass the slower double trailers. Baron shook his head, smiled, and "hedge-hopped" with the rest. He neared Florence in less than two hours.

By this time he could feel the pangs of hunger and considered stopping at the Alemagna just ahead or continuing on to Bologna as planned. A stomach growl made up his mind.

Parking the car and noting the number of tour buses in the lot, he knew it would be a madhouse inside. The Alemagna was the Italian version of the fast food chains on American toll roads. Once inside, Baron viewed the clusters of tourists, hovering impatiently by the cashier's counter and at the sandwich bar. He decided to satisfy himself with a quick bite. He could hear at least four different languages as he squeezed toward the sandwich counter.

As he peered over the shoulders of the people crowding a glass case, Baron felt a tug at his elbow. A man showed him a cashier's slip. "Must have," he said with a heavy German accent, "then buy."

"Danke," Baron replied, nodding and grinning. Leave it to the Italians to turn a simple act into an ordeal. For the sake of expediency, he pointed to the nearest sandwich and shouted over the heads of the people in front of him, *"Quanto costa quello?" "Trecento lire,"* was the quick reply from the busy counterman.

Ten minutes later Baron was back, wondering what he was about to have. The bread was a thick pizza dough, sliced open and filled with ham and cheese. *"Caldo?"* the counterman asked. Perplexed, Baron nodded anyway and watched as the sandwich was sealed in a machine resembling a waffle press.

Baron found a table outside away from the crowd. The hot sandwich reminded him of the time when he had brought a whole ham to Lee's mother. With cooking gas rationed, they never had more than a couple of hours to complete all their cooking. Baron grinned suddenly, remembering what it had cost him. He had to develop and print a dozen rolls of pornographic film that the mess sergeant had shot.

Baron soon knew that he should have gotten something to drink with his sandwich, but he shook his head, unwilling to tackle that line again for a cashier's receipt. Instead he filled his Castillo pipe and lit up, then watched the smoke drift aimlessly in the bright sunlight. He was unaware of the stranger studying him.

"Very good aroma. American tobacco?"

Baron looked up. It was the German with the receipt. In his large hand, he held a stained meerschaum. Baron offered him his kid leather pouch. "My own mixture. Here, try some."

"Thanks," the man replied, with obvious pleasure, seating himself opposite Baron.

The true Aryan type, Baron assumed. Blond hair,

53

although graying, and deep blue eyes with all the authority of a German army officer. A moment later, he realized that he had made an egregious assumption. The tattooed numbers on the stranger's wrist were plainly visible as he filled his meerschaum.

"You still live in Germany?" Baron asked softly.

The man lifted his head sharply, his eyes narrowing. *"Nein*—why do you ask?"

Baron hoped his smile was reassuring. He pulled out the chain around his neck and displayed a gold "chai," the Hebrew symbol that means life.

The German's face lit up immediately, and he countered with his own chain that held a *mezuzah*.

Baron frowned. The stranger's abrupt movement provoked a long-forgotten memory—that afternoon in Florence when the chaplain . . .

"Why do you ask if I live in Germany?"

Baron waved a hand. "I apologize. Force of professional habit."

The German raised an eyebrow. The American didn't look like a policeman. He smiled suddenly. "A journalist?" Baron nodded, extended his hand, and introduced himself.

In five minutes, the German gave Baron an account of his life and was no longer a stranger. Ari Stefan was one of a few to escape from Auschwitz before the arrival of the Allied troops. Making his way into Italy, he had fled safely to Florence. He had been sheltered by an Italian family, and had later married their youngest daughter, Francesca.

"A *shiksa?*" Baron had interrupted.

Stefan didn't reply at once; he seemed to be having trouble articulating his thoughts.

"Mr. Baron, in the camp I heard religious Jews curse God for their predicament. Were we not the chosen people? Chosen for what? The gas ovens?"

Incensed at first, he calmed down quickly, rubbed his jaw reflectively, and forced a smile. "That is all finished now. I have been living in Israel since 1948 with my wife and two handsome sons."

"Are you a religious man, now?" asked Baron blandly.

Again Ari Stefan hesitated. "While I no longer curse God, neither do I praise him. Now, I believe only in Israel—and my sons. They will make the future, and maybe it will be better."

54

Baron nodded solemnly. The man's views were not original. He had heard the very same thoughts expressed by other survivors.

"And your wife? You have been happy with her?"

A distant look appeared in the man's eyes, a softness incongruent for a man of his size. "'After Auschwitz, I did not think life worth living. She changed my mind." Anticipating Baron's next question, he quickly added, "Yes, my wife is Catholic, but it has made no difference in our lives. We are a happy family." He paused once again and leaned forward on his elbows. "You find that difficult to believe?"

Baron studied his Castillo in silence. Before he could summon a reply, he heard Ari's name being called. Saved by the bell, Baron thought. He had no answers.

Ari Stefan got to his feet, extending his hand. "My wife, Francesca. The bus waits. We go to Florence for a few days to visit her brother and sisters before going back to Israel for the holidays." Baron took Stefan's hand. Oddly, he still thought of Stefan as a German rather than an Israeli. It was the lingering German accent.

"*Shalom*, Mr. Baron. If you come to Israel, you must see me. I grow oranges in Jaffa. Everybody knows me—you need just ask. My whole family will welcome you."

Stefan waved as he boarded the bus. Returning the farewell, Baron emptied his pipe and headed for the Lancia.

He sat in the car for a few seconds. A shadow crossed his features as he recalled "it has made no difference in our lives." He grimaced. His one consoling thought all these years was that it would never have worked out for them. Baron sighed audibly. He had perused the statistics on soldiers who had returned after the war to marry their sweethearts. He couldn't refute the facts, most ended in heartache and disillusionment. The situations created by the war no longer existed. The GI who did not return was more fortunate in that his memories remained untouched and indelible.

"Enough is enough," he said aloud. He started the engine and moved the Lancia out of the lot and back onto the Autostrada.

Like most of Italy, Bologna was a compound of sienna-colored buildings. Driving into the heart of the city, past endless arcades, Baron found his way to the Piazza Maggiore easily enough, but discovered parking to be a problem there. Turning into a narrow street, he was soon stymied by two tour buses that were themselves blocked by a poorly parked Fiat.

It took only a minute for Baron to become impatient. Leaving the Lancia, he strode past the buses toward the parked vehicle causing the trouble. He found that the two bus drivers there already pondering their dilemma. After a few seconds of deliberation and a lot of wild gesturing of hands, the larger of the two—a colossus of man— went to the rear bumper, directing the other to the front of the car. The smaller man flexed his muscles like a circus strong man for the benefit of the crowd. The other driver shouted impatiently, and the people lining the sidewalk answered him derisively. While they all offered suggestions, no one made a move to help. Grinning, Baron moved quickly to join the smaller man. *"Grazie, amico,"* the Italian grinned in return with some relief.

At a signal from the giant, they pressed down on the bumpers, bouncing them up and down in unison thereby inching the car closer to the curb. With a final effort, they lifted the side wheels onto the edge of the sidewalk. They had moved the car over at least a foot. Grinning triumphantly, the two Italians wiped their hands and pounded Baron on the back.

Aboard the buses, the chattering passengers began to laugh and applaud wildly. The sidewalk group joined in. Baron raised an arm and shouted, *"Viva Italia!"* The two drivers bowed majestically and shouted their *grazies* to an appreciative audience.

A few minutes later, after washing his hands in a nearby fountain, Baron selected a *trattoria* overlooking the Piazza Maggiore. The Church of Santo Petronio stared back at him from across the square. Twisting in his seat, he gazed about the restaurant, examined the faces of the diners, who were mostly tourists, and suddenly realized that he wouldn't mind seeing a familiar face. He frowned. Why should he suddenly feel lonely?

The feeling lingered briefly. Baron knew himself too well; no one had to explain his own idiosyncrasies to him. He had always remained an enigma to most of his friends and associates. Some thought him rude, others recognized him as a loner. He recalled Joe Green's cynical observation of more than a decade ago when he had fallen ill upon his return from an African assignment. Under protest, Baron was forced into a month's convalescence. When the doctors blamed overwork, Joe had blown his stack. "Overwork? Shit! It's his constant flight from a permanent relationship!"

Baron gave an almost imperceptible shrug, but his smile remained. He was in good humor and recognized the reasons for it. Picking up the menu, he glanced at it with unseeing eyes. It was the Italians—the drivers, the sidewalk brigade, and the incident with the car. He hadn't laughed so much in weeks, certainly not since Joe had talked him into visiting Italy again. The theatrical gestures of the two drivers revived old memories of wartime Rome. Never had he known a more outgoing, gregarious people, likeable and friendly despite the greedy black market and extremely trying times. What a fool he was to have put off an extended visit! How many trips to Europe had he made since the war? At least a dozen, he guessed offhand. And yet only two short visits to Rome. On both assignments, the coronations of Pope John XXIII in '58 and Pope Paul VI in '63, he had considered staying longer, but then decided not to open old wounds. He sighed audibly. Glancing at the menu indecisively, he realized that he was once again vacillating. Looking up, he caught the eye of the waiter.

He had noted *lasagna verde al forno*, another of Lee's favorite recipes, but decided against the pasta, ordering the house specialty instead—*filetti di tacchino*, turkey breasts baked with white wine, parmesan cheese and truffles.

"*Prego. Vino, signore?*"

"*Si, vino locale—bianco.*"

At the waiter's departure, Baron smiled wistfully. In the past decade Lee's image had become almost ephemeral. Yet since his return, everything he did brought her into sharp focus. He shifted his attention to the square where the sun, high overhead, brightened the pavement. He glanced to the building at his far right where a clock tower rose above its crenelated walls, bringing a vague memory of the Palazzo Vecchio in the Piazza Signoria. His one "visit" to Florence had consumed no more than a couple of hours—yet it had altered his entire life.

August 1944

Scuttlebutt had it that the Germans were putting up a vicious defense just north of the Arno. Rick and Joe were to be replacements in a cinematography unit just south of Florence.

Wearing a glum expression Rick shuffled uneasily to the center of three parked jeeps, which would lead a contingent of three troop carriers and a supply truck. Without speaking to Joe, who was already behind the wheel, he tossed his helmet into the rear of the jeep. Although the sun had come up only minutes ago, it was already uncomfortably warm. Joe glanced at him and saw the scared look that matched his own. After their two-month "Roman holiday," neither was prepared to return to war.

Rick climbed into the front seat, and after a minute of oppressive silence, asked hoarsely, "Gassed up?" Joe peered at him and nodded. Of course, he was gassed up.

"You gonna be all right, Rick?"

"Of course, I'm all right. Why shouldn't I be? Aren't we going to see the rest of Italy?"

Joe blew out air between his teeth. "Cripes, Rick, the war's not going to last forever. Lee'll be perfectly safe here in Rome."

"Forget it, Joe," came Rick's harsh reply. "Nothing you say is going to change anything."

Joe gestured helplessly, his mouth a grim line.

"What the hell we waiting for?" Rick suddenly exploded. "The war won't end without us!"

A moment later, the reason for Rick's mood became apparent. Unnoticed by either man, Chaplain Leveron had appeared at the side of their vehicle. "You've got an extra passenger, sergeant," he said. An orderly tossed the chaplain's gear into the rear of the jeep.

Joe could sense Rick bristling. He banged the side of his fist into Rick's thigh, telling him to keep his temper and praying he would.

As he squeezed into the rear seat, the chaplain signaled to the captain in the lead jeep who immediately acknowledged him with a wave of his hand. All engines started. They were about to leave Rome.

The Number One jeep turned into the Via Veneto,

heading north with Joe following ten feet behind. Halfway through the turn Joe slowed down on hearing shouts and cries.

Rick felt his heart miss a beat. It was Enzo Moscati and Lee beside him. She was running across the road, carrying a bouquet of flowers. Her face was tear-stained, and she was shouting for him to wait.

Reaching him, she dropped the flowers into his lap, grabbed him, and began kissing his face feverishly. In a moment, Rick's face was wet with her tears and kisses.

"God, Lee," he mustered through the lumps in his throat, "we said our good-byes last night. I've got to go."

Her words were incoherent at first, then, "Rick, my lovely Rick, you will not come back!"

From one of the troop carriers came a shout, "Take her along, Sarge!"

Joe leaped out from behind the wheel and ran up to the truck, waving a fist. "You don't shut that fat mouth of yours, I'm coming up and shut it for you!"

The chaplain got his feet, standing precariously he called out, "Corporal, get back in this jeep!" Joe returned reluctantly, muttering to himself.

By this time, the lead jeep had come to a halt. An irate captain left his vehicle and loped back to find the cause of the delay. "One thing after another," he muttered to himself, "we should have been out of the city an hour ago." Reaching the source of his latest problem, he glared at Lee. Hesitating briefly, he looked to the sky. Why me? he asked himself. Turning sharply to Chaplain Leveron, he spoke authoritatively. "Tell the sergeant he's got thirty seconds!" Before the chaplain could reply, the captain turned on his heel and strode away.

Torn between grief and a feeling of stultification, Rick pulled Lee from his neck and held her at arm's length. "Lee . . . you're making it too damned tough. I've got to go." He stared into the tear-stained face, struck by the quivering lips. "Wait for me, Lee. I'm coming back. Don't you ever forget it. I'm coming back." With that, he pulled her close and kissed her hard.

Releasing her abruptly, he shouted to Moscati, who was standing in the background looking on with sad eyes. "For God's sake, Enzo, take her!"

The chaplain, strangely silent, nudged Joe on the shoulder. Joe responded, shoving the jeep into gear. With head

59

bowed, Rick just stared at the yellow, white, and red flowers which had fallen to the floorboard. A heavy weight hung in his chest, and it took all his willpower to hold back the tears. He picked up the bouquet and held it to his face, sniffing the fragrance. It helped him hide his emotions.

After a half-hour of riding in unbroken silence, the Chaplain's pained expression reflected his self-condemning thoughts. What kind of rabbi am I? he asked himself. Have I nothing to say, nothing to comfort him? He had no words of wisdom for the sergeant; he was not as sagacious as the old rabbis. Just twelve years the sergeant's senior, he was no sage. A sadness appeared in his hazel eyes, and he shook his head. How could he go against all his religious principles and condone their marriage? As he remained deep in thought, a softness appeared in his eyes. He had witnessed something unique—true love. He touched a finger to his lips. Did true love have a character all its own that transcended all obstacles? His lips compressed, then he shook his head once again. No. Once the early passion wore off all minute obstacles would become glaringly apparent.

Rick, with a flat announcement, was the first to break the oppressive silence. "Joe, I'll take the wheel after the next relief stop."

Joe gave him a quick, searching glance. A pair of sunglasses hid Rick's eyes. Joe nodded without comment.

Chaplain Leveron took a deep breath; perhaps now would be the proper time to break the ice. With a deep sense of inadequacy lingering within him, he leaned forward.

"Sergeant, you must understand . . . there was nothing I could do." He waited for some response, but there was none. "I can assure you that I realize this was no fly-by-night affair, but the facts remain unaltered—you're both underage." Shame suddenly fell upon him for the use of such a lame excuse. The pained expression returned, written on his compressed lips. The sergeant's silence persisted and was cutting into him. No, he was no sage. Unable to cope, he leaned back in defeat.

Unexpectedly Rick twisted around and irreverently thrust the bouquet of flowers into the chaplain's lap. Rick's voice was hard. "Can you tell me, Captain, whether these flowers given with so much love came from a Christian or a Jew?"

Chaplain Leveron's face reddened and his manner changed abruptly. He leaned forward angrily. "Whether you like it or not, Sergeant, in a wartime army above all you are a soldier. If command would have given permission, I could have performed a civil ceremony for you. But—and you may as well know it now—I would *never* have condoned this alliance. With your religious background, that marriage would have eventually turned into a fiasco." He paused, looked up, and then wiped his face. Some way for a man of the cloth to behave. He gazed once more into the sergeant's face but could not see beyond the dark glasses.

"But Rabbi . . ." Rick's voice was tremulous.

The chaplain noted his jaw muscles working, battling to hold back the tears. So it's "Rabbi" again. A minor victory, but one gratefully acceptable. Placing a hand on Rick's shoulder, he spoke soothingly. "I sincerely regret this outburst very much, Baron. I know how you feel, but putting all religious reasons aside, war doesn't allow us to live our lives as we would wish."

Joe held a Zippo lighter to the Chesterfield dangling from his lip, then handed the cigarette over to Rick. Accepting it mechanically, Rick glanced at the olive grove as they glided past. The silvery leaves were still in the stagnant, August heat. Aimlessly, his eyes moved up a distant mountainside where an ancient, walled, hilltop town rested like a crown. On their grueling, almost fifty-mile, five-month "hike" from Anzio to Rome, they had passed many such towns and villages. Perched as they were, atop the crests of small mountains, Rick had dubbed them "fairy tale vistas."

Today, however, the ancient discolored walls held no interest for him. He stared at the grape vines traipsing across the hillside, hiding the entrance to the secluded village. He was in torment.

He released a heavy puff of smoke, his face tightening. How could the Rabbi be so wrong? Fiasco? Garbage! What kind of talk was that? A picture of Lee flashed in his mind and his features softened. Those bright blue eyes, sparkling with enjoyment whenever they were together. The way she loved, the way she taught him to love with all inhibitions thrown aside, his dark moods that she erased

61

with her mere presence, the way she held his arm as if she were afraid of losing him. This was Lee; there was no one like her. God, his tormented mind cried out, living with Lee was all that mattered. There would never be any problems they couldn't work out. He wiped his sweating face and then ran a hand through his tousled hair.

From the rear seat, Chaplain Leveron studied Rick's movements. Baron believes he can make it work, he thought to himself. But it's a lost cause, he argued to himself in emphatic terms. And yet, the heart-rending departure scene haunted him. Try as he might, he couldn't erase the picture of that girl, clinging as though for life itself.

Having switched at a relief stop, Rick now sat behind the wheel, Chaplain Leveron at his side and Joe in the rear seat. No one spoke. A few miles away dense clouds of battle were visible, stretching out far to the west and east all along the German Gothic Defense line above the Arno. In the lead jeep ten yards in front of Rick, a nervous GI voluntarily manned the .30 caliber machine gun mounted behind the front seats.

Rick expressionlessly twisted his head. "Light me, Joe."

His face pallid beneath the sweat and grime, Joe expelled a deep breath. Back to the old routine. Despite the relief stop a couple of hours back, nervous stomachs were reappearing. He offered the chaplain a cigarette, which was declined with a shake of the head.

The sounds of war encroached as they moved slowly along the bumpy road toward the Command Post just south of Florence. Broken and incinerated war machines hemmed both sides of the pockmarked roadway.

"Shit!" Rick exploded, flipping his cigarette into the dust. He turned sharply a moment later, chagrined.

"Sorry, Rabbi," he blustered, "I meant no . . ."

The chaplain waved his apology aside, seemingly preoccupied with other problems. At least Baron's mind is on the job ahead, he thought with some sadness. If God is willing, he'll return to that girl.

They pushed past mounds of supplies and a compound of tanks being repaired. There was great activity, and the GIs worked stripped to the waist in the stifling heat. In ten minutes, the short column came to a halt.

Immediately a sergeant ran down the line to announce a thirty-minute chow break.

Getting out of the jeep, Chaplain Leveron addressed Rick. "Take an hour. We're not leaving with the troops. They're heading toward Pisa."

Rick and Joe exchanged questioning glances, but didn't reply.

Chaplain Leveron unfolded a map of Florence as they neared the southern edge of the city of culture. A pall of choking dust and smoke hovered over the land ominously. In the fields surrounding them, there were a number of light tanks and half-tracks, all standing with their motors running and apparently awaiting further orders.

Joe, behind the wheel once more, stopped the jeep. The road in front of them had been demolished and was impassable. He looked at Rick, who turned to the chaplain. "Well, Chaplain, what now? We have to find our unit."

The chaplain, consulting his map, held up a hand and then looked around. His eyes caught a staff car about fifty yards away in the field to his right. He nodded in that direction. "Let's go."

When they reached the staff car, the chaplain got out to confer with a colonel. A few minutes later, they seemed to be having a disagreement. Rick watched in silence, wondering what the chaplain was up to.

The sun, suddenly breaking through the smoky haze, brought a suffocating and unbearable heat with it. "Holy cow," Joe exclaimed, starting to unbutton his shirt, "It's got to be murder in those 'iron maidens.'" Rick, biting his upper lip, merely nodded.

The colonel with a frown on his face accompanied the chaplain back to the jeep. Stocky and in his middle fifties, he walked erect despite the enveloping heat. His eyes showed an intelligence and a surety fitting to his rank, and yet, Rick conjectured, he had lost whatever argument he'd had with the chaplain. When Rick and Joe started to salute, he waved the formality aside. "Signal Corps," he said blandly, noting their insignia. To Rick he said, "What weapons have you?" Rick and Joe each had Colt semiautomatic pistols, .45 caliber. Satisfied, although still frowning, he addressed the chaplain. "The engineers won't have that bridge ready for another fifteen minutes.

These men can utilize their time getting pictures of the city from that hilltop." He waved to a hilltop a couple of hundred yards away. "Piazzale Michelangiolo—from there you get a panorama of most of Florence, including the synagogue."

At that moment, a lieutenant appeared and handed a message to the colonel. He read it quickly and named a tank unit to the lieutenant. "Get them ready, we're moving out in five minutes." He addressed the chaplain once again. "There's no German army in the city, but our patrols have warned of snipers. Stay behind the M-8, and you should have no trouble." Removing a wilted handkerchief from his back pocket, he mopped his face. "We've got our own problem with the Germans about ten miles west of here." He stuck out his hand. *"Buona fortuna,* Chaplain."

"Thank you, Colonel. And may God go with you and your men."

The colonel nodded, the hardness in his features easing imperceptively. "I'll take all the help I can get."

The Piazzale Michelangiolo was an open square that topped a rise overlooking the Arno from its southern side. A wide roadway circled a monument commemorating its namesake. Standing at the balustrade bordering the square, Rick took in the scene at a quick glance. Handing Joe the Paillard Bolex, he directed him to pan in from the east until he reached the Ponte Vecchio, the only bridge left standing over the Arno and into Florence proper. "Then switch to the telephoto and hold it there," he added.

At the sound of rumbling tanks, Rick quickly moved to the western side of the stone fencing and peered down at the scene before him. What little greenery there had been was now being ground into dust as the seventy-ton M-3 and M-4 tanks clanked and filed out to join up with the battle already taking place a few miles west of the city.

After a minute or so, his eyes moved away from the military activity, his attention drawn to what appeared to be thousands of people packed like sardines in the Gardens of Boboli, which adjoined the Pitti Palace. He was startled a moment later to hear the chaplain's voice.

"All displaced," he said with a sober expression.

"That's right," came from a sergeant who had joined them. The sergeant was one of six men attached to the two scout cars temporarily stationed there. Rick gave them a brief glance, noting the .30 caliber Browning machine guns mounted on each. The sergeant pointed down to the Ponte Vecchio. "You can see the wreckage and rubble of the apartment houses blocking the bridge entrance on both sides. Even though they left it intact, they made sure we couldn't get any heavy equipment across."

All eyes were on the renowned 600-year-old bridge with its shops appearing to hang precariously over the edges as the Arno beneath slipped by unobtrusively. Rick's eyes shifted further out to the burnt orange dome of the Cathedral in the Piazza Duomo and then to the Palazzo Vecchio. His eyes roamed the vista of Florence, noting that it was untouched by the war. The sergeant's voice intruded again.

"See that street down there—Via Dei Bardi—the one leading into the road running along the river? Notice the rubble at the intersection? Well, that used to be a palace."

It was the chaplain's turn to interrupt. "Thanks for the tour, Sergeant, but we have to be on our way."

Rick gave him a curious glance. "What's our destination, Chaplain?" He tried to follow the gaze of the chaplain, but couldn't pinpoint his objective.

"The synagogue. You can see the blue dome straight ahead in the distance."

Rick said nothing more until they got back into the jeep. "Why the synagogue?" he then asked.

As Joe pulled away, driving around the monument, the chaplain looked up at the huge stone figure on top of the marble base. "My father used to pray there every day. Many years ago, of course. Before the war."

Rick stared at him. "Your father was a rabbi in Florence?"

"No," an amused smile appearing, "he was studying art here in Florence."

"And he made his living in America as an artist?"

The chaplain seemed not to have heard the question. Then, he responded with a tinge of sadness. "No. He earned his living in America painting houses."

Rick nodded without answering as Joe slipped into a line starting to move across the demolished bridge that the Corps of Engineers had refurbished. The M-8 armored car with its six wheels, the car which they were supposed to follow, was more than a dozen vehicles in front of them. They drove slowly behind a troop carrier across the shaky make-shift bridge, and soon reached the Piazza Santa Croce. As the M-8 moved into the deserted square, its 37mm gun slowly revolved in its turret searchingly; the green and white marble facade on the Church of Santa Croce stared back placidly.

"Forget it, Joe," Rick said impatiently. "Keep going." He twisted around to face the chaplain. "After the synagogue, then what? We still have to report to our outfit."

"Just drop me off and go to the Piazza Signoria." He handed Rick the map of Florence. "If no one's there, you have the option of waiting for them to catch up or returning to the Pitti Palace, which is on the other side of the Ponte Vecchio. Use your own judgment." Rick nodded, not bothering to explain that the bridge they had just crossed was strictly a one-way street. He pushed back his helmet with a dour expression as the afternoon sun beat down upon them unmercifully. They continued north, driving in silence.

The chaplain leaned forward suddenly, his eyes bright with anticipation. "Turn here," he blurted out. "Then a left at the next corner." He pointed to the map in Rick's lap.

The street was narrow and deserted. Now they were on their own. Joe looked about warily. It was not characteristic of the Italians to remain in hiding after the Germans had departed. The celebration in Rome was not forgotten that easily. Slowing to five miles per hour, they turned into the street of the synagogue.

The street was littered with garbage, rotting and stinking in the hot sun. The rats who were feeding on the filth scurried away at the sound of their motor. Joe, his face tense, pulled up about thirty yards short of the wrought iron fence that led into the grounds of the temple.

Rick glared at him. "What's with you? Pull up to the gate."

Joe looked worried. Rick was getting careless—it was about time he forgot about Lee. "Not until I check it out," he said crisply.

After a few seconds of angry silence and self-admonishment, Rick rubbed his face. "Sorry, Joe, I'm just not thinking." Expelling a deep breath, he glanced up and down the street, studying the buildings. Most of them were apartment houses.

The chaplain, his face pale, spoke timidly. "You think the Germans . . ."

Rick held up a hand for silence, continuing his inspection of the buildings on the opposite side. Although he could see no one, he felt a thousand eyes upon him. A deep frown appeared, and he whispered to Joe while pointing to an entrance that led into a courtyard across the way. Joe nodded, shifted into reverse, backed the jeep into the opening, and shut off the motor.

Rick turned to Chaplain Leveron. "Do you drive?" he asked unexpectedly. At his nod, Rick spoke quickly and authoritatively. "Good. You stay behind the wheel until we get back. If you hear shooting, start the jeep and get ready to take off without us. Understand?"

The chaplain scowled. "Nothing doing! I'm going along."

"You're a Rabbi," Rick said flatly. "A noncombatant. You'll be in our way."

Chaplain Leveron showed a determined jaw. "Nevertheless, I'm going with you. I'll follow your instructions, but I'm still going along."

Rick fought to control his temper. "Sometimes I could be right, and you wrong. What about the rules now, Chaplain?"

The chaplain climbed out of the rear seat and spoke sharply.

"Enough of this audacity, Sergeant! From now on, address me as Captain. Now let's get on with it."

Joe rolled his eyes and nudged Rick. "As the Captain said, let's get on with it."

They moved along the wall stealthily, their Colts drawn, Rick leading. Reaching the iron fence, Rick dropped to the ground and peered through the bars, his heart beating like a trip-hammer.

A grassy lawn, now burned brown from the heat and lack of water, was bisected by a paved stone walk leading to the pinkish-white marble temple. Rick allowed a perfunctory glance toward the Moorish building with its minaret towers flanking a huge, arched roof over which a great dome loomed. His prime interest was in the dense foliage at the left side of the paved walk. Though the grounds were empty, the stillness filled him with foreboding.

Rick wiped his face, the sweat dripping off him. He signaled to Joe. "One-minute intervals, understand?" The question was directed to the chaplain.

The gate was wide open. In a half-crouch, Rick moved onto the grass, raced across the walkway, and dove into the dense shrubbery. The area remained quiet. On schedule, the others followed. Rick signaled for them to follow as he crept through the underbrush. After a minute, terror struck him—he was staring into a pair of rifles.

The faces behind the rifles were grinning. "What the hell took you so long?"

Rick stared in amazement at the unshaven faces, the sparkling eyes, and the unkempt hair. Although he wasn't in uniform, he was undoubtedly an American, and that was a Garand rifle in his hands. The other man simply grinned with delight.

"Shit!" Joe exclaimed. "You damned near scared the pants off us."

"Crap!" the American retorted. "You're damn lucky we were the only ones who heard your jeep. The Germans are busy in the Temple, taking out the last of the stolen paintings they were storing there. We were waiting for them to come out before making our move. Their truck is at the side door."

"Who the hell are you?" Rick asked, his relief apparent.

He gave his name as Mancini. He had been working with the partisans for more than three months, relaying information by secret radio to the Allied command.

Rick nodded. "Don't the Germans know we have a full column coming in just a few blocks east of here?"

The American shrugged. "Apparently not. Or else they're just following orders right to the end." He jerked his head toward his companion. "By the way, this is Aldo."

As they acknowledged his introduction, Aldo's eyebrows arched. The dark eyes, set deep in a thin face, spied the chaplain's insignia, the Ten Commandments patch. "Rabino?" he inquired timidly. From around his neck, he pulled out a *mezuzah*.

With grim face, the chaplain merely nodded.

"Holy Christ!" the American exclaimed. "What the hell are you doing here?"

"Don't ask," Rick answered dryly.

The American shrugged. "Well, at least he can pray for us." A second later, he held up a hand. An engine was idling.

It was an open, armored half-track with two Germans sitting in the front seat. A canvas was thrown over the looted treasures in the rear. The truck came around to the front of the temple, moved slowly down the paved walk, and then halted. The two German soldiers looked back and waited, unaware of the hidden watchers no more than a dozen feet away.

Overeager, Aldo catapulted into the open and trained his light machine gun on the Germans. "*Raus, Nazis!*" he shouted. Startled at first, the Germans stared, then quickly grabbed for their rifles. Aldo didn't hesitate. He let go a burst, and watched the enemy slump forward.

"Damn you, Aldo!" the American cried out from the shrubbery. "Get the hell back here!" To Rick he said, "Now he's warned the others still in the temple."

It was too late. Two soldiers appeared beneath the arched entrance of the synagogue. They fired at Aldo before he could move. Aldo was dead before he hit the ground. As his knees buckled, his hands flew up, throwing his gun back into the hedge. It landed at the chaplain's feet. The chaplain stared at it in disbelief, his face ashen.

"Don't anybody move," the American directed in a whisper. "I don't know how many there are, but keep your guns ready. The shit's gonna fly any minute now."

The two German soldiers waited a full minute before advancing to the truck. While one kept a watchful eye on the shrubbery, the other kneeled over the body of Aldo. He reached down and pulled out the chain from around the neck. "Juden!" he cried out, cursing. He lifted his rifle and peppered the dead body of Aldo.

An overwhelming rage possessed Chaplain Leveron. Before the others could move, he reached down for Aldo's weapon and stepped out from his cover. His finger on the trigger, he fired blindly.

"Damn!" Rick exploded, leaping out and firing three quick shots at the remaining German soldier.

Joe and the American trained their guns on the temple

69

entrance, waiting, but apparently there weren't any more. The entire action had taken no more than a few seconds but it was definitely over. Rick stood beside the chaplain, noting the horror in his face.

The chaplain started to sob. He dropped the gun and held his hands to his face. "My God! What have I done!"

Rick placed a compassionate hand on his shoulder. "Rabbi, it can't be helped."

The chaplain shook off Rick's hand and straightened his shoulders. "You're wrong, Baron," he said sharply. "Under no circumstances should I have done this!" He waved to the dead figures. "I am here to console the living and the dying. What I have done today is beyond the realm of my vocation." He turned toward the synagogue. "I must say a Kaddish for them. I will ask for their forgiveness—and pray that they hear me." He started walking away.

Rick made a move to follow, but the American partisan fighter stopped him. "I'll keep an eye on him. I have to hang around anyway because of that truck."

The sweat beaded on Rick's forehead as he waited for the chaplain to enter the synagogue. For no obvious reason, he felt they would never meet again. Abruptly, he turned to Joe. "C'mon, let's go."

Back in the jeep, Rick studied the map and directed Joe to the Piazza della Signoria. On the way, they passed through more streets littered and piled with garbage, streets so narrow that the late afternoon sun's slanting rays couldn't penetrate. On two occasions they passed men pulling two-wheeled carts laden with bodies. The Germans, they learned, had confiscated all motorized wheels for their departure.

The Palazzo Vecchio was on their right, the Uffizi Gallery at their left. Joe pulled up in the square at the statue of David. They both gazed in awe at the famous works of art surrounding them: The huge statue of Neptune and Cellini's Perseus holding up the head of Medusa in the Loggia dei Lanzi. Rick pointed out Giambologna's *Rape of the Sabines*.

"I guess it was too heavy for the Germans to lift," Joe offered. At Rick's smile, Joe felt a sense of relief.

At that moment, a breath of wind blew in from the west, bringing with it the disconcerting smell of smoke, demolition, the odor of death. The rumbling of big guns could be heard, vanishing when the wind shifted.

A wave of apprehension beset Rick suddenly without warning. Cold beads of sweat formed on his brow. He gave Joe a cautious sidelong glance. About to speak, Rick changed his mind as two M-3 tanks rumbled past to station themselves in the center of the square. Attempting to make his movements appear casual, he rubbed his arms gently to rid himself of the strange prickling sensation. The gesture, nevertheless, invited a questioning glance from his friend.

Astutely, Joe always seemed to recognize the causes of Rick's changing moods, but this time he knew something was wrong. Was it fear? He rubbed his cheek, ruminating. They had always been scared; they were not heroes. Like most GIs, they were simply performing a dirty task foisted upon them. Shouting then interrupted his ruminations.

Some Florentines had come out to surround the tanks, bitterly complaining about the loss of electricity and water. The Germans had not only knocked out their utilities, but also their flour and pasta mills. A lieutenant vainly tried to placate them.

Joe brought his attention back to Rick, gazing at him for a few seconds. "We gonna wait?" he asked.

Rick delivered a sullen glance. "Joe, do me a favor—don't patronize me."

Damn, how we read each other's thoughts, he said to himself. He gestured helplessly. "Okay. What then?"

Rick already had the Bolex in his hand. "Pull around the far side. I'll start the pan on the Loggia, then I'll hold it on the David statue before swinging to the tanks. The lens is wide open. Close it three stops when we hit the sun on the Palazzo."

Joe smiled; they were back to business.

Ten minutes later, Rick pulled out the maps again. "Let's see how close we can get to the Ponte Vecchio. Maybe we can walk across."

On the Via Porta Santa Maria, they got within a block of the bridge. The buildings on both sides of the street had been demolished, and the rubble piles dammed the entrance to the bridge. At Rick's signal, Joe made a right turn, then a left. They came out by the Arno with the ruins of Ponte Santa Trinita confronting them. Because of its statuary and graceful architecture, the bridge was more loved by the Florentines than the Ponte Vecchio. The street to their left was covered with debris from collapsed buildings. All fires were out, but a smoky haze permeated the area, and the odor of cordite was still very strong.

After removing the distributor, Joe put it in the gadget bag with their equipment. With extreme care, they made it across the hot rubble to the picturesque Ponte Vecchio. At an easy pace, they strolled along the partially blocked walkway. The shops on both sides were shuttered and locked. A line of rubber-necking GIs filed past them.

Coming off the bridge, the Via Dei Bardi to their left was in complete ruin. Rick decided he had to shoot the German Consulate, a short distance nearby. He could see the building, its windows shattered and its roof caved in.

"It's off limits," an MP shouted. "Some of the buildings are still shaky."

There was another street running along the river that led off from the Via Bardi. Rick pointed. "How about there? Almost everything's down already. I just want a shot of the Consulate."

After mulling it over, the MP finally agreed, warning him to stay in the center of the street. Rick nodded and threaded his way into Lungarno Torrigiani.

It was immediately apparent that he was too close to his subject to get it in the proper perspective. Not even his wide-angle lens could get both the destroyed Palazzo Bardi and the Consulate together. He had to move back. The MP had departed, but Joe was watching him, shaking his head disapprovingly.

He made his way safely to a thirty-foot-high wall, all that remained of an apartment building. With his back against the wall, he brought the camera to his eye, unaware of the crackling sounds behind him. The motor of the Bolex was already purring when he thought he heard shouts. He looked up and saw Joe waving frantically.

Then he heard it—the sounds of the wall breaking up. Lifting his head, he could see the top of the wall bending over. He looked about. There was nowhere to go without getting in its path. In a split second he made his decision. He sprawled on the ground against the base of the wall, praying that it would topple beyond him. The rumbling

72

turned into a roar, and the dust swirled all about him. Then he heard nothing.

He thought he heard voices. That was Joe, wasn't it? He tried turning his head, but the pain. . . .

More than a dozen men worked at the removal of the debris. Two medics waited patiently.

Joe pulled at the sleeve of one of them. "I tell you he's alive. I'm telling you I saw his foot move." He ran a hand through his hair, then tried to light a cigarette, throwing it away in disgust. "Dear God!" he muttered to himself. "We've got so many plans. Don't let it happen."

The medic was at Rick's side with a stethoscope before the final piece of debris was taken off him. He saw the crumpled helmet and studied it carefully before removing it. There was a bloody gash at the hairline above Rick's left eye. He checked his eyes, then Rick's entire limp figure.

"Well?" Joe cried out, near hysteria.

The medic looked up. "No broken bones as far as I can see. But he's got a concussion for sure. Just guessing, but I'd say the war is over for him."

Rick's eyes flickered. "Is that you, Joe?"

Joe leaned over him. "Yeah, it's me, Buddy. You're gonna be okay. The Doc said so." He rubbed his eyes.

Rick grabbed at Joe's shirt. "Tell Lee to wait for me. Joe. Tell her to wait."

Joe could just about speak. "Yeah, sure. You can bet on it. I'll be waiting, too. We've got a business to start."

CHAPTER 4

Venice—September 1973

The woman in black pushed aside the curtain, leaned out over the window sill, and debated about whether she needed a sweater or not. Dusk had settled early on the narrow canal, the water dark and unseen from her second-story apartment. A light from another apartment caused an eerie glow to play on the small crests of the lapping water. Fascinated, she watched it for a while before turning away. At least the smells were gone, she thought with some satisfaction, although it didn't really matter. In a few days, she would be back in Israel.

She allowed her glance to linger briefly on Tovah's suitcase, which although filled, rested unlocked on the vanity bench. In two days, Tovah would rejoin her brother Riv and his family.

The woman in black found the lounge chair in the twilight and settled into it gratefully. A sigh escaped, giving her some measure of relief. The call from Riv earlier in the day had unnerved her, as any unexpected call from Israel always did.

Riv's voice came through at once, rich and powerful, allaying the fears tugging at her breast. "Everything's all right, Mama. Nothing's wrong. I'm fine, Debbi's fine, and the children are okay."

Although somewhat relieved, her trepidations didn't

altogether fade. "Something is wrong! Why are you calling now? I'll be home in another week."

"Stop worrying, Mama. Everything's all right. It's just that the Reservists are being called up. I have to report in three days to serve my time. Can you spare Tovah to give Debbi a hand?" He laughed suddenly. "Meanwhile I'm breaking in Dov Laslo." Again he laughed. "Even a best-selling author shouldn't have trouble selling a few *chachkas*."

An icy chill ran down the woman's spine. "Riv, you're not telling me everything. Something is happening again. You weren't due to report until after the holidays."

Riv answered placatingly. "Nothing is happening, Mama. They're allowing the regulars to go home for the holidays. If trouble was brewing, would they do that?"

When a silence followed, Riv spoke quickly. "Mama, are you there?"

"Yes, I'm here."

His mother's thickened voice caused him alarm. "Mama, I'm sorry. I wasn't thinking. Are you and Tovah well?"

"Yes, we're both well," she replied, regaining her composure. "I'll make arrangements with Angelina—and if necessary, her brother Antonio. Tovah can leave tomorrow or the day after, at the latest." She paused for a moment and then said: "Thank Dov for me. I hope he's well."

Again Riv's laughter reached her, so rich and cheerful. "He's a good man, Mama, and we all like him. You know you have my permission."

Vexed, she rolled her eyes. "Riv, I don't need your permission. And besides, I might have other plans."

"Other plans, Mama?" Riv's bewilderment came through over the phone. "What other plans?"

The words had no meaning. They had just slipped from her lips. "Never mind," she retorted hastily. "This call is becoming expensive. Take care of yourself, and give my love to all. We'll be seeing each other soon." She hung up without further explanations but with a sense of guilt.

In the lounge chair, the woman opened her eyes and for a moment felt lost. Had she fallen asleep? The room was in darkness except for a dim light entering from one of the curtained windows. She got up, walked to the wall, and switched on the lights. When she picked up her watch from the vanity, she made a face. It was after eight. After giving her shoulder-length hair a few strokes with the brush, she examined herself in the mirror. A slender woman with luminous blue eyes studied her in return. Any resemblance to a forty-six-year-old was purely coincidental. Pleased with herself, she glanced at the two necklaces on top of the vanity. A heart-shaped locket was attached to one, the Star of David to the other.

She looked from one to the other, trying to make up her mind, finally choosing the Star of David. She put it on, straightened it, then stared at the locket. Picking it up, she undid the clasp of the heart and gazed at the picture of her deceased husband. She had selected the Star of David, feeling that it would be more protective with Riv on duty in the troubled land. Her lips pursed, she closed the locket and returned it to the vanity.

Before switching off the lights, she gave another glance toward the locket left behind. Then she nodded, satisfied with herself. She was sure Enzo would understand.

A strange sense of building exhilaration had puzzled Baron since he passed through the toll gate. With just another mile to go on the Ponte Della Libertà before the ferry entrance, he was surrounded by a steady stream of cars and tour buses from all over the continent. A quick glance at the faces of the passengers, and he saw the looks of anticipation and excitement within. At his far left, paralleling the wide boulevard, the Ferrovia was darting toward the *stazione* where Venice was waiting. For Baron, the past was already a forgotten memory.

As soon as the Lancia was parked aboard the ferry, Baron got out and with the eagerness of a schoolboy, took the steps two at a time to get to the upper deck lounge. While a number of people crowded the snack bar, others were laughing and chattering with an eager expectancy, gazing out of the windows. Baron smiled. As the engines throbbed, he decided to step out onto the open deck. The Lido Di Venezia would be the next stop.

The twilight was darkening, and as the ferry plied its way through the more or less commercial Canale Della Giudecca to blend with the Canale di San Marco, the lights of Venice were slowly coming to life. Less than a half-mile to the port across the lagoon, the Piazza San Marco was now discernible.

Oblivious to the cool breeze, Baron stuck his hands into his jacket pockets and stared at the lights bordering the Riva Degli Schiavoni, a promenade fronting the Grande Canal where it merged with the lagoon. Even from this distance, he could see the docked, black gondolas, bobbing in the water as the *vaporetti* churned up the surface.

The ferry shifted to starboard into the lagoon and away from the *piazza*, but Baron continued to stare across the water, unable to take his eyes away. He had been all over the world, yet here he was strangely moved. There was no logical explanation, unless—he turned to note the expressions of other passengers—a visit to Venice affects everyone in a similar way. Fascinated, he tried to crystallize his thoughts. What was it that this sinking island imparted to her endless parade of guests? A sense of history, a special setting? Or simply the hint of romantic interludes? Did all these visitors assume that Venezia, for centuries Europe's most famous courtesan now turned gracious dowager, was still waiting to greet them as she had the famous and powerful? Baron shook his head, the sentimental ruminations bringing a smile. Bemused, he noted an elderly, gray-haired couple holding hands at the railing. Were they recalling memories of a previous visit or simply romanticizing? His smile broadening, he wondered at what age anticipation faded.

The Grand Hotel des Bains exuded dignity. Strolling aimlessly through one of the lounges, Baron glanced at the huge chandeliers. Except for the electricity, he could have stepped into the nineteenth century. Checking his watch on impulse, he decided to postpone further examination.

His room had high ceilings and was large enough to accommodate a good-sized studio apartment. An immense armoire partially covered one wall, and the appointments included a vanity, a bureau, and an elegant desk. Pleased that the room in no way resembled the sterility of most hotel rooms, Baron emptied his luggage immediately. The bathroom was all marble, and he wasted no time in using the huge bathtub.

Refreshed and dressed, he checked himself once more in the mirror. A satisfied smile played on his lips. He admired his full, soon to be salt and pepper hair. He grinned and patted his stomach—no middle-age spread there. Traipsing around the world for two decades had prevented that. The lines around his eyes crinkled as he grinned. He went to the desk where he had left his pipe with his tobacco.

Discounting his relationship with the Greens, Baron lived within himself—responsible to no one for his manners or his attire. Owning only two pairs of jeans, he rarely wore them outside the studio. Ever since the war, he disliked anything that even resembled fatigues. Yet, he preferred casual sportswear. Wearing dark blue slacks, a beige corduroy sport jacket, and a rust turtleneck, he was ready to invade Venice.

He stood on the wide portico of the hotel, debating about whether to take a cab or walk the half-mile to the *vaporetto* station. There was no point in taking the Lancia, then having to look for a parking spot. Not one to be indecisive for long, he called for a cab.

In five minutes, he had his ticket and was standing on a floating platform, waiting for the waterbus. At its appearance, a dozen or so people surged forward, carrying Baron along with them. The *vaporetto* was already jammed with passengers as they pushed onto the deck. Below in the cabin, all seats were taken and those standing were packed like sardines. Next to Baron, clinging to the wall and each other, a young couple grinned. "My God!" the boy exclaimed, "it's the New York subway on water!" Baron grinned in return, enjoying himself.

When the *vaporetto* pulled into the platform, the crowd on deck started forward before the boat was docked. Baron aided the young couple through the jostling crowd and across the unsteady platform. *"Grazie,"* the girl murmured timidly. "You're perfectly welcome," Baron replied.

The boy's eyes widened. "Hey, you're an American! Man, oh, man! What a way to travel!"

On the Riva degli Schiavoni, Baron watched them depart, their arms around each other. Honeymooners, he guessed. "Good luck," he said quietly.

Standing on the stone pavement, Baron took in the scene with a practiced eye. The famed Danielli was at his right where Joe and Mindy had spent part of their honeymoon. The promenade was before him with two hump-backed bridges leading to the Piazzetta. The bobbing gondolas were to his left tied to striped poles. It was the middle of September, and a number of tourists strolled about, all in good humor, most heading for the Piazza. From force of habit, he reached for his pipe, then suddenly changed his mind. Later, he thought.

He followed the crowd across the first bridge and paused with some of them at the entrance of a narrow lane to his right. The alley—it couldn't be called anything else—was dark and somewhat forbidding. The attraction was a blaze of light farther in, inviting and encouraging some to enter. On impulse, he turned in.

There were restaurants, brightly illuminated, with showcases displaying the varied menus of the establishments. The alley was jammed with people, many taking advantage of the extreme light to shoot movies of the savory fare displayed. Seafood *Adriatico,* meats, and pasta confronted all on both sides. With difficulty, Baron squeezed through while peering into the open fronts, seeking an empty table.

He was fortunate in that it took him only five minutes to find an empty table—one positioned so that he could watch the swarms of people passing by. With a particular dish in mind, he scanned the menu. Smiling, he gave his order to the waiter. *Zuppa di pesce,* a stew consisting of many varieties of fish.

Baron checked his watch: 8:30. Deciding not to chance getting lost in the maze of alleyways in Venice, he retraced his steps back to the promenade. Sated and with a lit Savinelli, he crossed another bridge, noting the Bridge of Sighs further down the canal. He continued into the Piazzetta when he studied the Doge's Palace with its pinkish-red, lace pattern, then in a state of exhilaration impatiently moved toward the Piazza. Tomorrow in daylight, he could give more attention to the Palace.

A spirit of gaiety pervaded the Piazza San Marco as its visitors strolled about, in awe of the gold mosaics of St. Mark's Basilica. Baron's eyes strayed from the Basilica to the Moors atop the clock tower, waiting to strike the hour. The square was surrounded on three sides by columned loggias, with the famed restaurants, Florian's and Quadri's, facing each other from opposite sides.

Many stores were still open beneath the arcade, encouraging window-shoppers.

Drawn by Florian's musicians, Baron selected a table where he could listen as well as watch the emotions of the people—a habit he never lost. He snapped his fingers for the waiter, ordering a cup of cappuccino. He was beginning to miss American coffee, but he did enjoy cappuccino, preferring it over espresso.

Totally relaxed and amused, he watched the drama of the sexes take place in the square—the young Italian men trying to appear suave as they ogled and measured the possibilities of unescorted female tourists.

As the waiter set the cup before him, it suddenly occurred to Baron that Venice wasn't a place to be enjoyed solo, and as if on cue, a stately brunette seated two tables from him directed an inviting smile his way. He shook his head, offering no encouragement. She gave a slight shrug and a wistful smile, then got up and left. He watched her weave through the tables and disappear into the shadows of the square. No, he simply wasn't in the mood to share Venice with an ordinary pickup. He was not that lonely yet. He returned his attention to the musicians.

Shades of Hepburn and Brazzi, he thought, damned if they weren't playing the theme from *Summertime*—a movie he had always favored. As if listening to a dream, he took the music in and at the finish, applauded with the rest of the appreciative audience. Feeling a bit foolish he realized they probably played it a dozen times every evening—but it still was enjoyable. He lifted the cup of cappuccino to his lips and gazed along the arcade.

Not more than twenty feet from his table, in front of a brightly illuminated window display, a woman was conversing with a man. Baron concentrated on the woman, dressed in black—widow's black, he assumed. In Italy, it is not uncommon to wear black in mourning for years after a loved one's death. Her back was toward him, and he could see her hair, silver-frosted black, reaching down to her shoulders. For no apparent reason, he strained to study her as people strolled by, blocking his vision. After a minute or so, the conversation obviously coming to an end, the man took her hand, kissed it, and moved around her. When the woman turned, Baron was able to see her face.

Baron tried to get to his feet, but his legs suddenly turned to rubber. His mouth was dry, and he thought his heart was about to leave his chest.

My God! If Lee had had an older sister I could be looking at her right now, he thought. His hands became clammy, and a peculiar prickly sensation ran along his arms. Without the strength to move, he continued to sit there, staring and straining his eyes in disbelief. He couldn't make out the details of her face, but her smile —that smile—hadn't altered with the years. The somber black of her attire highlighted a gold chain hanging from her neck. He wasn't sure, but could that be a Star of David attached to it? He didn't bother to dwell on that speculation, his mind racing in turmoil. She was about to leave. What should he do?

She was walking away, and Baron felt the urgency within him growing. He held a hand to his chest. Man, if I don't calm down, there's going to be a cardiac victim in the middle of this *piazza*, he said to himself. Placing his hands upon the table, he pushed himself to his feet. Groping into his pocket for some *lire*, he dropped some money onto the table.

He started slowly, then took long strides through the square, never taking his eyes off the woman. She turned from the arcade into the street beneath the clock tower, and a second later, she was lost in the swarm moving through the Mercerie. He cursed himself. Move, move! You can't lose her now!

The Mercerie led to the Rialto bridge. Perhaps that was her goal. People grumbled as he pushed through the crowd. Then he saw her again, just several feet ahead. She had stopped in front of a gift shop and was studying the display. A moment later, she entered.

Baron stood at the window, peering in. There were two young women behind the counters, one in conversation with a customer, the other walking toward the rear to talk with the woman in black.

It was Lee. There were no doubts in Baron's mind that he was finally looking at the "girl" who had deserted—yes, it was apparent now—deserted him almost thirty years ago, leaving him with nothing but anguish and anger for most of that time. Curiously, none of those feelings were present, only a growing impatience with himself as he pondered his next move. He could catch no more than a glimpse of her as the younger woman—in her early twenties, he guessed—blocked his view. There was a vague resemblance—her daughter, perhaps?

Distracted momentarily by a tourist bumping into him, he happened to notice the sign on the window pane. "E. Moscati."

Enzo—Enzo Moscati! So after all these years, she was still working with him. He rubbed his cheek. The name provided him with an opening. But as he entered the shop, the woman in black went through a curtained doorway at the rear.

The young woman, dark-haired and dark-eyed, came toward him, smiling pleasantly as she glanced at her watch. "We're closing in ten minutes, *signore*. Can I help you?"

Her English was perfect, but Baron detected an Israeli accent. Pulling himself together, Baron replied, "Good evening. Is the proprietor in? Enzo—Signor Moscati?"

She looked at him peculiarly. "No, he is not. Can I ask why you wish to see him?"

Baron answered without hesitation. "We're very old friends. We knew each other during the war."

A bewildered expression appeared on her attractive face. "*Signore*, this may sound foolish, but which war are you talking about?"

"World War Two, of course." Baron was aware of her studying him.

Before she could reply, the woman in black returned, seating herself at a desk.

"Your mother?" Baron asked of the girl. Not waiting for an answer, he placed a finger to his lips. "Ssshh—we're also old friends."

Perplexed, the girl watched him move away quietly. A strange thought rambled through her head. "I do not know this man, yet somewhere, I have seen him before." As her eyes followed him, that thought persisted, although she knew that in her twenty-one years she had never met anyone from her parents' wartime past.

Baron stood in front of a showcase that displayed Murano glass. The tension was building up within him. Again, her back was toward him. He wet his lips and took a deep breath.

"*Ciao*—Lee," he mustered.

Eleanora's back stiffened. It was as though her spine had turned to ice. A flurry of thoughts overwhelmed her, the first of which was that she was losing her mind. She couldn't have heard it. Lee . . . Lee . . . who existed that would call her by that name?

"Ciao, Lee. I'm a bit late, but I'm back."

This was not a figment of a lost mind: she had definitely heard it. She shivered, feeling cold suddenly, fearful of turning and viewing a specter. Her face ashen, her lips trembling, she forced herself to turn and confront the voice from the past.

Baron gazed at her with drawn breath. It was incredible—she didn't look more than thirty-five. Time had been gentle with her. It had transformed the freshness of youth into a mature beauty that defied age. Her cheekbones were high with small hollows beneath, a perfect face for molding the play of light and shadow. Only barely discernible were the lines at the corners of her eyes—the eyes that were still bright blue, peering over half-glasses, searching his face.

That face did not reflect the youthful Rick Baron. It was more rugged, deeply tanned, with lines of character. The hair was full and wavy, unlike the tousled head her memory dredged up.

Baron forced a smile. "Have I changed that much?"

Her mouth fell open and her hands went to her cheeks, the tears forming. "No . . . no . . ." she whimpered, "it is not possible."

When Baron saw the color drain from her face, he wheeled around the showcase to confront her. Kneeling, he replaced her hands with his own, tilting her head to face him. "Yes, it is possible. It's Rick, many years older and without a uniform." He wiped at a tear lingering on her cheek. He had an overwhelming urge to take her in his arms. Despite the passing years, she was no stranger to him.

Dumbfounded, Eleanora's daughter rushed to her side, while the other saleswoman was busily engaged in locking the shop. "Mother! What is it? What's wrong? Who is this man?"

Eleanora took a deep breath. "It's all right, Tovah. I am only surprised." Baron removed his hands and stood up. "We're very old friends. Very old friends."

Extremely agitated, Tovah eyed Baron with suspicion.

If they were old friends, why was her mother so upset by their meeting? Why did her eyes reflect so much sadness?

Tovah? An odd name for an Italian girl, Baron thought. Looking up, he noted the uncertainty in her expression as she stared at him. An explanation was in order, even if lame. "I knew Lee—your mother—during the war. I was in Rome with the American Army of Occupation."

Lee? Tovah seemed more bewildered than ever. She had never heard her mother addressed by that name. And this man Rick, who was he? Mother had always evaded discussion of the war with the Nazis. And yet, Tovah pondered, a memory chord was struck. The photo album. The photo album she had inadvertently discovered while searching through her mother's bureau for some jewelry. It had been many years ago, and she tried to recall the contents. There were many pictures of Rome. There were pictures of mother and father . . . and yes, the soldiers . . . two of them. She struggled to bring the pictures into focus. Her eyes widened suddenly. Yes, now she remembered—she had thought one of the soldiers was Riv, her brother. When she questioned her mother about the strange uniform, she had become very angry and had warned her to never mention it again. She never had, and she also never saw the album again. Composed, she returned Baron's gaze and wondered, finding it difficult to cope with the recognition.

Baron, anticipating unasked questions in Tovah's dark eyes, turned from her to face Lee. "Are you all right now, Lee? Is there someplace we can go . . . and talk? We've got an awful lot to discuss."

Almost in a daze, she nodded in silence. How odd to be called "Lee" once again after so many years.

Tovah was not one to give up easily. "Are you married, Signor Rick?"

Indignant, Lee got to her feet hurriedly. "Tovah, I said we were old friends. Where are your manners?"

Tovah bit her lips, searching her mother's eyes. "Yes, mother, I know. But . . ."

Lee studied her daughter intently. "Tovah, you know nothing, nothing. Do you understand?" But as she said it, she realized that her daughter did know. Was it resemblance to Rick? She dismissed the idea immediately, turning to the young saleswoman who had been staring at them with uncomprehending eyes. "Angelina, when Antonio comes, would you both please accompany Tovah home?" At the girl's bewildered nod, she reached for her purse and withdrew a handkerchief. "Allow me a moment to freshen up," she said to Rick.

After unlocking the front door of the shop, Lee waited for Baron to follow her. Baron halted halfway through the doorway. Smiling, he looked back at Tovah, who had been watching their every movement. "Tovah, my full name is Rick Baron, and I'm not married. *ArrivederLa.*"

As Tovah watched them melt into the crowds of people, a furrow blemished her smooth forehead. Rick? Riv? Could it be possible? The names and the likeness were too astounding, the more she thought of it.

Although Baron took Lee's arm, she more or less led him through the congested Mercerie. No words were spoken between them as they crossed over a small canal and turned into a narrow lane. Baron could feel the tenseness in her arm as they traversed the dimly lit alley. They were like strangers, and yet they were not strangers. They were walking too fast, he suddenly realized.

His arm wrapped in hers, he reached for her hand. "Slow down, Lee. There's no need to rush."

Slowing down, he noted her forced smile as they passed beneath a lamp hanging from a stained wall. She's frightened, he thought. Or was it his imagination? Nervous or even upset, he could understand. But frightened? It was time for small talk, he decided. At least, it would be a beginning.

Lee prayed that her face didn't mirror her frenzied thoughts. Although Tovah has apparently guessed, she thought, he does not know. This is a trick of fate, a chance meeting—how could he know? Guilty thoughts harassed her, plaguing her conscience. No, she argued with herself, her mouth a grim line, it will not be necessary. In another week I will be back in Israel, and it will all be forgotten. None of us will ever see him again. A frown creased the soft skin of her brow, her anxieties stubbornly reluctant to depart. She felt his warm hand in hers, imparting sensations she thought she was no longer capable of. For a fleeting moment, she was a young girl once again—a girl madly in love with an American soldier.

"Still working with Moscati?"

She halted abruptly just as they emerged from the shadows, a surprised look on her face.

"Enzo was my husband. You did not know?"

Baron was startled. "No . . . how would I know? I didn't even . . ." He was about to say something about a Dear John letter, but instead, almost phlegmatically said: "I didn't even know you were alive until a few minutes ago."

He pulled her aside to permit another couple to pass, grateful for the respite. Married! And to Enzo! It was no longer a fantasy; the one girl he had truly loved had been the only one to reject him. He absorbed her disclosure, becoming aware of the black dress and the past tense of her statement. There were a number of questions on his lips, but he suppressed them with a strong will. It was all water over the dam, and it would be pointless to dredge up what might have been if. . . .

He shrugged. His voice was a soft murmur, "I suppose I can't blame you for not waiting for me. It was a difficult time for a girl to be alone."

Lee caught his eyes. "Rick, tell me what happened after you left Rome that morning."

He gave her an oblique glance. So she did remember something, he thought. "Well, without going into details, I was injured in Florence that very afternoon." She looked shocked. He made a gesture. "Forget it. It's unimportant now. It was a long time ago, another time in another world."

Lee bit into her lip, knowing that her eyes were moistening. "Rick, I must know the rest. Why didn't you write to me?"

He took a deep breath; she was making it difficult for his injured pride. "I did write you, you know. But all I got back was 'Address Unknown.'" He gestured impatiently. "Forget yesterday, Lee. There's only today and that's more important."

Lee held a hand to her bosom, hoping it would slow the pounding of her heart. Dear God! He thinks I left him for another! she thought. His unstated recollections were so vivid, it was almost as if it had happened yesterday. Fighting the tears, she swallowed hard and forced

87

herself to respond. "And this accidental meeting tonight has brought all this back?"

Baron sighed deeply, his eyes never leaving hers.

"You think I am only remembering the past now? Lee, I have *never* forgotten you."

Lee averted her glance and fumbled in her purse for a handkerchief. There was an importuning ache in her chest that was slowly devouring her. It was all too incredible, and glaringly apparent that he had lived all these years with only bitter thoughts of her. And all because of . . .

He could not know that she hadn't shared Enzo's bed until three years after their marriage. With understanding and patience, Enzo had been her strength, helping her put the thoughts of Rick in the background while accepting Riv as his own son. The erasure had been almost complete with the birth of Tovah, and they had never been happier. Both Riv and Tovah had been born in Israel, and while the early years were hard for Lee and Enzo, it was promising. However, as the years passed, the diminished memories of Rick began to reappear. The children had converted to Judaism and when it was time for Riv's Bar Mitzvah, Enzo had studied the boy closely and said to Lee, "The American sergeant will always be with you." She had said nothing but understood only too well. Riv was growing up an almost exact duplicate of Rick.

Baron eyed her with compassion, wondering whether it was guilt that was upsetting her so. Reaching for her arm, he wrapped it in his own. "Come on, this is no way for old friends to behave. Where is this place you're taking me to?"

"Just ahead," she replied, a bit nonplussed. It was almost as if the young Rick had returned with his ever changing moods.

The *trattoria* was half-full despite the hour. Baron selected a corner table, outdoors and overlooking a rippling canal. A striped awning and potted greenery protected them from the cool breeze sweeping along the dark water.

The waiter took their orders for *espresso*. Baron also ordered an Italian pastry. An embarrassing silence followed with the waiter's departure. Baron glanced at Lee, then toyed with his napkin, folding it over and over.

Damn, all the years I've lost! he thought. What did I ever do to suffer losing her? At least she had a daughter to raise. Why couldn't I have shared that privilege with her, instead of roaming about the globe like a pedantic itinerant?

Lee, sensing his mood, forestalled his questions by taking the initiative. "You were never married, Rick?" A strange feeling came with saying his name.

Baron's eyes were riveted to the napkin. "Yes, I was. Once. For three months. The girl was merely a reasonable facsimile of someone who did not exist anymore. She was not to blame for my mistake." He answered matter-of-factly without a trace of bitterness.

There was a heaviness in Lee's chest which refused to subside. Unconsciously, she reached across the table to take his hand. "Oh, Rick, I am sorry. . . ." She could say nothing more.

Baron lifted his head, searched deep into her eyes, and spoke softly. "Lee, I'm going to be quite candid with you. I've been very successful in business, and it has permitted me to lead a life of my own choosing. And with the exception of one period after the war . . ." He pursed his lips. "Well, it would serve no purpose going into that now."

Lee could feel his eyes probing into her depths, beseeching her for answers that—even when disclosed—only fate could explain. After three decades, fate had brought them together again. Why now? she asked herself. For what purpose? She gripped his hand, fighting the helpless feeling that pursued her.

The waiter's appearance lessened the strain momentarily. He asked Baron to make a selection from the cart of pastry he wheeled in. Baron glanced at Lee, then pointed to a cream puff dripping with chocolate. *"Per signora?"* he said. Seeing her expression, he spoke quickly. "I haven't forgotten how you used to like sweets." For himself, he chose a rum-dipped cheese cake.

A smile came easily to Lee's face, gently softening the anxieties. If only for a few seconds, the scene had brought back memories of how they had relished each other's company.

Baron watched her silently until the waiter had served the *espresso* and departed. "Do you remember the jelly doughnuts?" he asked her. He used to sneak them out of the mess hall, and they would eat them, sitting on the Spanish steps one day, at the Trevi Fountain on the next. They would wash them down with a bottle of wine that cost a dime.

The memories were alive for them both. Lee nodded, a mist forming in her eyes. "We were so young, then," she said hoarsely.

"And so much in love," added Baron laconically.

She said nothing but took a quick sip of the hot liquid. It was coming, the time for confession and the truth. Would he understand? Would he believe? She tried to think of anything that had occurred that day that portended this evening.

Baron waited for her to set down the cup, then leaned forward on his elbows.

"Lee, I'm going to be blunt. It's not my intention to make you feel miserable, but boiling all the questions down to one . . ." He paused deliberately, peered into her eyes, and saw her nod nervously. "It is a question that deserves an answer. Whatever happened, happened a long time ago, but I still must know why." He took a deep breath. "Whatever your reasons, why couldn't you have written to me?"

He watched her bring her hands to her face, her lips trembling. Deeply moved, his heart went out to her.

"Just tell me, Lee. It'll be all right. I promise . . . no remonstrations. I will ask nothing else from you."

Again, Lee asked herself why this was happening after so many years. She swallowed, took a deep breath, and found her voice.

"Rick . . . everything that has happened to us since that time happened because I believed you were dead." She noted his expression, but quickly continued, unable to stop once started. "I waited for more than a week to hear from you after that dreadful morning. Yes, I remember that morning very well . . . and the morning when I finally decided to inquire at the American headquarters. Enzo accompanied me, and we were told you had been killed in Firenze. It is obvious now that it had all been a cruel mistake.

"For me, the world had ended that day. If it were not for Enzo . . ." She left it unsaid. "At first, he tried to console me, then failing, he offered to marry me."

Baron's chin rested in the palm of his hand, his

manner somewhat subdued. He spoke without malice. "And you were married almost immediately? Is that the remedy recommended to forget lost loves?"

Her eyes bored into his. Although Rick spoke calmly, the resentment was apparent to her.

"Rick . . . if Enzo hadn't offered to marry me, I would not have lived past that day. He not only saved my life, but your son's too!"

Baron was being crushed. He could feel the crumbling wall crashing down upon him. It was Florence all over again. Unconsciously, he held a hand to his head, feeling the scar above his ear. In a state of helplessness, he tried to speak, but his mouth had gone dry. My God! his tormented brain cried out. A son! All those lost years, I've had a son!

Baron put his hands on the edge of the table as if to push away. He stared at her, struggling to control a rising anger. He found his voice finally, "Lee, you never meant for me to know. . . ."

Lee, shaken and torn between what she had revealed and its effect upon Baron, reached for his hand in a contrite gesture. She spoke haltingly, "I . . . I'm sorry, Rick. It would serve no purpose . . . now. . . ."

"No purpose!" Baron's eyes flashed. He pushed away from the table and got to his feet. He needed to move to control his emotions. He blew out a stream of air and with an effort said: "Give me a minute, Lee. I've got to think." He stood there, undecided for a moment, suddenly aware of her moist eyes, pleading forbearance. He then pushed through the potted plants and leaned on the wrought iron railing overlooking the canal. He rubbed his face, trying to coordinate his thoughts. Why was he angry? Under the circumstances, should he have expected her to react in any other way? He shook his head. *No purpose?* Wasn't he the one responsible for her pregnancy? Surely, he had a right to see him! A son he had never known!

Lee rested her elbow on the table, her chin in the palm of her hand. There was an urgent need to compensate for her hasty confession. With mixed feelings, she lifted her eyes and surreptitiously regarded the stranger who had unknowingly fathered her son. Standing there, his face in shadow, he seemed to be a tourist studying the canal. She resisted the urge to go to his side and comfort him. Although realizing that she had upset his world, she also knew that Baron and Riv could not meet. She was sure that Tovah had guessed. She must have associated the "old friend" with the old snapshot. Lee lowered her eyes, wondering why she had this penchant of late to speak without thinking. She compressed her eyes determinedly. Riv must never know!

Baron peered into the dark water. To probe its murky depths, he thought, one had to break the surface. He took a deep breath, turned, and returned to the table. He leaned forward and studied her solemnly.

"And my—our son—where is he now?"

Lee appeared terrified. "Rick . . . he must never know. Enzo died in the Six Day War and went to his grave without revealing our secret. Do not . . ." When he nodded deferentially, she leaned forward insistently. "Rick, you must promise!"

With a change in manner, Baron compassionately reached for her hands. "Lee, I'm not trying to disrupt your life, I'm sincerely sorry about Enzo, but surely you must recognize my desire to see the son I never knew existed." He squeezed her hands tenderly. "Just tell me where he is. Don't you think you at least owe me that much?"

Lee's heavy breathing slowed, a sense of relief flooding her. This stranger's hands were warm—and yet he was no longer a stranger. As her anxieties lessened, she felt her face crimsoning. She replied cautiously as she gently eased her hands from his. "Yes, of course, but Riv is in Israel."

Baron's pinched face altered abruptly, a quixotic smile following his wide-eyed gaze. Life had suddenly become one big surprise. Her daughter's name, Tovah, and now his son, Riv, and in Israel. It was extraordinary the way things were developing, almost as if they were all pawns in a master game.

Her eyebrows arched as she said, "It's all coincidence. Why extraordinary?"

Baron shook his head. "No way, I don't believe it. Venice is merely a short stopover for me. I have to be in *Israel* next week." He continued to smile, watching her stunned expression and thinking her more beautiful than he ever could have imagined. Even though disturbed, there was an unconscious grace about her that was totally unlike the young Eleanora he had known. His nostalgic memories had always focused on a young, vivacious, bright-eyed girl who had clung to him tenaciously and had loved him with such ardor.

When she remained silent, Baron decided on a new tack.

"Can I interest you in some chicken livers?"

She laughed suddenly for the first time, and he could almost picture the young Lee whom he had loved. "I see you haven't forgotten," he said.

"No, I haven't forgotten. One doesn't forget the follies of one's youth so readily." She paused and then added lightly, "But it was such a long time ago, Rick. We are much older now—and wiser."

Baron repressed a sigh of disappointment. He had hoped for something more from her. "Yes, I suppose you're right. You've lived a full life since then."

Hiding his feelings, he stuck his fork into the untouched cheese cake, tasted it, and said, "But tell me— Riv, what does he look like? What kind of a boy is he?"

Her eyes sparkled with amusement. "Boy? Riv was twenty-eight on his last birthday. He is married and has two sons of his own."

Baron was flabbergasted. "You mean," he stammered, "that I'm a grandfather?"

Lee realized that she had shocked him. She placed her hand on his compassionately. "I'm sorry, Rick. I shouldn't have been so blunt. I should have realized . . ."

Baron laughed suddenly. To her surprise, he lifted her hand to his lips and kissed it. "Blunt!" he exclaimed with extraordinary exuberance. "Do you realize what you've done? In the course of a few minutes, you've transformed a confirmed bachelor into a grandfather? Shouldn't I be shocked?"

Lee gazed at him with confused feelings. As he held her hand, there was an exhilaration within her that she could not suppress. This is foolish, she said to herself, we're both middle-aged people—the clock cannot be turned back. She averted her eyes, feeling an ache within her, a yearning to be the young Lee once again. Unconsciously, she gripped his hand tighter.

Baron's smile faded. He looked at her hand, felt the warmth imparted, then lifted it to his lips again. He knew at that moment that he was in love with her—

not with the young Lee he had known, but the lovely woman she had matured into. There was an ache in his groin and a growing urgency. Lifting his head, he was about to speak before he saw her blushing. He released her hand.

Following a long moment of awkward silence, Baron signaled for the waiter.

"Will that be all, *signore?*" the man inquired politely.

Nodding, Baron caught Lee glancing at her watch. Involuntarily, he checked his own and frowned. After eleven already and there was still so much to discuss.

He held her elbow close to him, savoring her nearness as they strolled through the almost deserted alley. Neither spoke until they reached the Grande Canal, where the Rialto Bridge straddled the dark water a short distance to their right. The lone reflections dancing upon the choppy surface emanated from the street lamps and a single canalside *trattoria* that remained open to accommodate late-nighters.

"Where next?" Baron asked. He saw her shoulders tremble from the early autumn breeze drifting in from the Adriatic. Quickly removing his jacket, he draped it over her shoulders, dismissing her mild protest.

Lee appeared flustered as Baron pulled the lapels closer together across her bosom. Strange sensations coursed through her veins with his nearness. It was obvious that he had not allowed himself to deteriorate with the passing years. His arms were muscular and his waist flat, the physique of an athlete.

"How's that?" he asked, smiling. "Comfy?"

His familiarities warmed her with old memories, bringing a flush to her face. She nodded and turned her head, grateful for the dark shadows disguising her thoughts.

Clearing her throat, she found her voice. "Let's go across the Rialto, then a short distance."

Deep in their thoughts, they moved past covered, black gondolas swaying to the tune of the slapping water. Reaching the *vaporetto* station, Lee suddenly halted. "Where are you staying in Venice?" she asked.

Baron gave her an oblique glance. "At the Grande on the Lido. Why do you ask?"

"The *vaporetto* is here. It does not run all night."

Baron studied her for a moment, then smiled. "It'll still be here after I take you home. Come, show me the way." With that, unable to take her elbow from beneath his jacket, he slipped his arm around her waist.

Lee said nothing, mystified by her own behavior in allowing such permissiveness. And yet, the gesture was familiar—except that it used to be the reverse. She was always the one clinging to him.

Confused and filled with consternation, Lee twisted out of his arm. They were just short of the apogee of the deserted Rialto Bridge. Her action was one of exigency, and her voice broke as she tried to speak.

"Rick . . . I'm not the young girl you remember. What's happened . . . can't be helped. I cannot turn back the clock." She paused, catching her breath. "I've lived a full life without you."

Baron exhaled slowly, a pained expression on his face. "Yes, I know you have," he replied sullenly, failing to comprehend her sudden emotional outburst. It was as if she was dismissing him from her life. Why? What had he done to disturb her so? The initial shock of their first meeting had already dissipated, and hadn't he promised to keep her revelation secret? He had been so sure that there was a spark of the young Lee when she had taken his hand. With all the women he had handled in his lifetime, he was at a loss as to how to cope with this one.

Defeated, he said, "Come, Lee, I'll take you home . . . and then say goodbye." He stuck his hands into his pockets and started to move away.

The next five minutes passed in silence as they crossed the Rialto and walked along the canal. Turning into a narrow lane, they reached another bridge in a few moments where, instead of crossing, Lee turned and stepped onto a marble patio fronting a small canal. A single lamppost cast an eerie light over the area. At the door of the building, she turned to face Baron, her thoughts in utter turmoil.

His "goodbye" was so final. Did she really want it? If only someone would help her! After Enzo's death, her mind had been made up—no more relationships other than her own family. She had endured too many wars, and had thanked God that Riv was now only a reservist. Riv was the crux of her present situation. If he should ever discover that Enzo wasn't his father . . .

Her eyes were moist as she handed Baron his jacket.

95

"I'm sorry," she said, her voice trembling, "I can't give you back the years."

Baron saw the tears, and they bewildered him. Why was she doing this? He was positive she didn't want him to leave. Instead of voicing his suspicions, he said, "Well, Lee, if fate has decreed this one night to be the total compensation for all the lost years, so be it." He eyed her soberly and then added, "You realize, of course, that I must see my son, sooner or later." The little fears tugging at her showed in her eyes. Baron took her hand. "I promise, Lee. He will never know. But I must see him, even if only from a distance. Don't you think I have that right?"

He saw the tears come in earnest. Dare he take her in his arms? Would she reject him as before? He thought his heart would burst. He pulled her to him, holding her head to his chest. "Give me tomorrow, Lee. I ask for nothing more. You can decide on the other tomorrows after that. I will hold you to nothing."

She lifted her head but remained in his arms, her tears blurring her vision. Then unable to speak, she nodded.

Fishing into his jacket, Baron pulled out a handkerchief and dabbed the tears on her cheeks. Lee took it from him to clear her eyes, Baron's face just inches from hers. When she finished, she caught his eyes gazing into hers. Transfixed for a second, she leaned closer expectantly.

Her lips trembling beneath his, he kissed them tenderly without passion, again and again. Breathless, his lips caressed her cheek. Then abruptly, he pulled back from her arms encircling him. "My God! Lee!" he blurted out. "For a second, I thought I was back in the jeep on that . . ."

She understood perfectly, only now there was no Enzo waiting to pick her up should anything happen. Refusing to dwell on the thought, she spoke quickly. "Tomorrow morning at eleven, I'll be in the shop. You'll find it?"

Baron nodded, "You can guide me through Venice just as you did in Rome. We'll talk and have lunch—and talk some more. We'll have dinner. And after that, another tomorrow will be your decision."

He tried the knob of the door behind her. It opened at his touch. "Go, Lee! Go now before I drag you off in a gondola." With that, he kissed her lips, moved away, and disappeared into the dark alley.

Somewhat dazed she shut the door behind her, hearing another close at the same time on the floor above. A stillness followed, and she was afraid the pounding of her heart would echo around the circular, stone foyer. Her footsteps made clicking sounds as she ascended the marble stairway.

As soon as she entered the apartment, Tovah greeted her with a hug, her voice plaintive. "Oh, mama, I am sorry."

Mystified, Lee inquired, "Sorry? For what?"

"Mama, I was in the foyer. I overheard. I didn't mean to listen, but I was worried." She stepped back, bit her lip for a second, then said, "This man . . . he is Riv's papa?"

Lee allowed a heavy sigh escape. She was weary, and it was late, but she could not have Tovah guessing at the truth with all the wrong reasons. Could a secret be shared by three people? She wondered apprehensively, then made her decision. "Come inside, Tovah."

An hour later, except for the extremely intimate details, Tovah knew the whole truth.

Tovah's eyes glistened with a moistness. "Oh, mama, to have two men love you so much in one lifetime!"

"Yes . . . and now I have none."

Tovah cocked her head. Her hair, much like her mother's, fell across one eye. She brushed it back impatiently. "Mother, do you still love this American?"

Lee, sitting in an easy chair, straightened. "Don't be foolish! How could I? This man is a stranger." She became aware of Tovah's shift from "mama" to "mother" with each question.

"Mother—the truth. You must have some feeling for him. You must have shared much more than you've told me."

Lee appeared flustered. "I don't know, I really don't know. When I'm with him, I'm a young girl again—in love with an American sergeant. But that's all in the past. I know nothing of this man today." Unconsciously, she touched her lips, his kisses still lingering there in a fleeting memory.

Tovah leaned forward on the ottoman she was sitting

on. "Mama, aren't you even going to find out? You're not going to see him again?"

Lee explained their plans for the day.

Tovah leaped to her mother's side and kissed her on the cheek. "Don't be afraid of relighting old fires, mama. You're much too beautiful to sit around and watch me grow up."

Lee hugged her warmly and said, "You're an incurable romantic. Come, let's get some sleep. This 'much too beautiful' woman needs her beauty nap."

At the doorway of her bedroom, Tovah hesitated. "Mother, please don't wear black when you meet tomorrow." She moved into the room before her mother could reply.

Lee said nothing. She picked up her purse from the floor, opened it, and withdrew a handkerchief with the initials "RB" embroidered in one corner. She stared at it for a moment, then brought it to her lips. Yes, she had to meet with him, she thought, and had to find out. Fate was decreeing it. If nothing else, she was sure of that.

Baron eased himself into bed. His movements were involuntary, his thoughts only of Lee. His eyes were tired from the drive from Rome, the evening's excitement and exhilaration, and the double scotch he had had at the hotel bar to help him sleep.

It was curious that in all those years, he had never imagined her growing into a beautiful woman. He tossed his head suddenly. The past be damned! There was only the future. He wasn't in love with a teen-ager now. She was a beautiful woman, desirable and . . . He sat up in bed, filled with both anxiety and anticipation. He switched off the night table lamp, and lay back down, looking into the darkness. "I don't know what You're planning for me, but You better include her in it."

CHAPTER 5

Although autumn had officially arrived, the early morning sun failed to take notice of it. Along the wide veranda of the Grande Hotel, a number of tables were already occupied with guests taking advantage of the weather, enjoying their *cappuccino*, and chattering about trying the beach later in the day.

Baron, standing at the top of the steps, glanced at his watch, his eyes showing signs of restless sleep. Having already had a full American breakfast, his impatience was growing. Only eight-thirty, he thought. He stood there undecided, having been forewarned about attempting the *vaporetti* during the Venetian rush hour. Earlier, he had tried to contact Joe Green at the King David in Israel. Having failed to find him in, Baron left a message that he would call again later.

Shifting uneasily, he unzipped one of the six pockets of his tan safari jacket and pulled out his pipe and tobacco. He tapped his breast pocket, checking for his passport, then foraged in another for his lighter. The old Leica hung halfway down his chest, dangling from a strap around his neck. With all his equipment in Israel, it was on sentiment alone that he decided to bring it to Italy. Old as it was, it had been kept in top condition and could still produce negatives of excellent quality.

His first puff eased the schoolboy nervousness infecting him. Descending the wide stairway, he crossed the driveway, went through the hotel gates, and stood on the sidewalk of the Lungomare Narconi. Across the road on a white beach, the thatched roofs of the hotel cabanas stirred in a mild breeze. He lingered only a moment, his expression impassive, then moved unhurriedly toward the corner of the Gran Viale Santa Maria Elisabetta, a wide street bisecting the Lido.

The slanting morning sunlight washed one side of the boulevard, creating a warmth as it splashed off buildings of yellow ochre, russet, and bleached terra cotta. Deep in thought, Baron mechanically reached for a pair of sunglasses. There was little time to kill, but now, in the light of day, it was time for self-analysis—or at least, self-examination.

What was he seeking? What should he expect of Lee now that she had divulged the secret of having borne his son? *A son!* He was enthralled with the thought of it. The word had never before held any meaning for him. A tinge of guilt crept into his eyes, imagining what she must have gone through—pregnant and believing him dead. Still, he couldn't dismiss the disturbing thought that, even without him, fate hadn't been that unkind to her.

He stopped suddenly as his right eyelid developed a nervous twitch. He rubbed it, annoyed that he was allowing himself to become possessed by self-pity. What was the point of reliving the past? he asked himself. He did that many years ago, and it had led nowhere. It was senseless to seek nonexistent answers. For whatever the reasons, it had happened. He should be concerned with just one thing—would it change anything in the present or the future?

A frown appeared as he puffed heavily on the Castillo, a disquieting urgency growing within him. Perhaps she had a lover? She was too beautiful a woman not to. The frown deepened. Lee? He shook his head. Not if she was wearing widow's black. The debate with himself continued. It could have simply been a black dress. Nothing was impossible, he admitted grudgingly. But despite his veneer of sophistication, he found the idea of Lee having a lover depressing.

Confused by his own thoughts, he removed the briar from his mouth and examined it. Was he really falling in love with her once again, or was it merely an infatuation with the memory of his first love? In those two short months, they had poured a love into a mold that he had thought was unbreakable. He halted in the middle of his thought. Mold? Even if she wanted to forget, there was always Riv to remind her.

He smiled, despite the persistent sense of foreboding. For a brief moment, he had the strangest feeling that someone was laughing over his shoulder. He looked about, almost as if searching. With each passing minute, the avenue became more immersed in sunlight. You're a damn fool! he berated himself, afraid of an old flame!

A wince hardened his smile. Old flame? Hardly! She was definitely more than that. She was the mother of his son—she did owe him something more! And yet, thinking of Riv only made the situation more ironic, bringing guilt along with it. How does one pursue a woman, no matter how desirable, when she is the mother of your son? He emptied the pipe abruptly, talking to himself all the while. Hell! Why am I dawdling? If there is a purpose to our meeting, let's find out. He had been in limbo long enough, and Lee—even if not available—was at least waiting for him now.

He moved quickly with long strides, without giving a passing glance to the variety of shops along the way. He had no jeep, and there was no Bernini fountain, but—as it had been when they were both so young—she was waiting.

"Mama, you're behaving like a schoolgirl going on her first date. Don't be so nervous. It isn't as if you were strangers. You're old friends."

Lee gave her daughter a reprimanding glance, but made no response.

"Mama, waiting at the door will not make the time pass faster."

Lee made a face. "Stop being childish, Tovah! I'm worried about Angelina. It's almost ten o'clock. She should have been here already."

Tovah smiled prudently, busying herself with wiping a Llardro figurine. "Yes, of course, Mama," she replied.

A middle-aged couple entered the store. Lee, grateful for the interruption, waved Tovah to tend to the couple. Seeking a temporary haven, she moved to the rear of the shop where she could at least make an attempt to discipline her thoughts. She was both excited and frightened by Rick's reincarnation, she decided, trying to find the correct word. Had she made the right decision in telling him of Riv? Vacillating, she finally decided she had. The anguish she had unknowingly caused him had been only too apparent. It would have been a mortal sin not to let him know that he had fathered a child.

Hearing Angelina's voice, a feeling of relief temporarily shunted aside her disturbing thoughts. Turning around, she saw Baron following behind Angelina.

So worldly, so sure of himself, she thought. This was not the shy, lovable . . . She bit her lip and waited. She was to be a guide for a day, she told herself, nothing more.

Allowing the prospective customers to browse, Tovah glanced at her mother, her expression curious but not overly concerned. Baron's effervescent *"Shalom"* caught her unaware. Involuntarily returning his smile, odd sensations coursed through her as she realized the role he had played in her mother's life. Seeking his eyes which were invisible behind the dark glasses, she could read nothing. His face was not unattractive, she decided grudgingly. His carriage was that of a much younger man. It was not too difficult to envisage her mother young and innocent getting involved with him.

Baron was conscious of the change in her demeanor since the previous evening. He had read enough faces in his life to conjecture that she somehow shared their secret and was now sizing him up. For a brief moment, he wondered whether her seeming approval of him was predicated on his past or the present.

Seeing Lee emerge from behind the rear curtain, Baron took her unresisting arm and held it to his side. He was like a kid again, grinning with pure pleasure. Lee was a sophisticated, mature woman, yet happily she was responsive to his boyish gesture.

Lee couldn't resist his effusive smile, although she did realize that her own would encourage him to take minor liberties. While she felt it somewhat presumptuous of him, it was also harmless, she decided. Consoling herself, an amorphous enjoyment accompanied her acquiescence. There was little enough she could do for him, and it was so long since she had felt so young.

Countless pigeons scattered and fluttered about them as they strolled through the square toward the Ducal Palace. Once there, however, they found it necessary to bypass clusters of late-season tourists being led by gesturing guides. Entering from the Piazzetta past the four porphyry Moors, they found themselves in the middle of a magnificent Renaissance courtyard. On one side, leading to an upper *loggia*, was the Giants' Stairway, so named because of the Sasovino statues. Without hesitation, Baron unsnapped the camera case.

"It's time for your first picture, Lee," he said.

For the first time, Lee became aware of the old camera. Squinting, she spoke hesitantly. "The camera. It's not the . . ."

"Yes, the very same," he replied quickly. "Not everyone can discard a first love so easily."

She pouted. "Rick, I was hoping you would let the past rest."

"Sorry, Lee. Perhaps it was a bit facetious. The reference was meant to be pure sentiment."

Thinking it over, searching his face, she decided to reserve further comment. "Very well," she said, "but I find it extraordinary that you've used only this camera after all these years."

Baron couldn't suppress his grin. "Lee, we've so much to learn about each other. This may surprise you, but photography is my profession." He didn't know if modesty or shyness kept him from elaborating. "I've already told you I have to be in Israel next week. My partner is there now, checking out our equipment." He paused momentarily and then quickly added, "By the way, I've another surprise for you. Let me test your memory. Do you remember Joe?"

Her reaction was immediate. "Verdi!" she exclaimed excitedly. "Your partner is Verdi?"

Speechless, Baron merely nodded as he gazed at her in awe. The elation displayed in those luminous, blue eyes momentarily threw him off balance. Attainable or not, he knew at the moment that he wanted her. The past be damned! She was really something, he thought.

He regarded her candidly. "Lee, I could easily fall in love with you again."

Lee, avoiding his eyes, glanced blankly at the Stairway of Gold, her heart fluttering nervously. She had slept very little the previous evening, recalling the most minute details of their love affair. With it had come an exhilaration she no longer thought herself capable of. "Well, nothing to say?" she heard him ask. She faced him once again, the determination in her voice forced.

"Rick, this is not the proper place nor the time for us to behave like old fools."

Imperturbable, Baron smiled. Her manner was forced, belying her response. A vestige of the young Lee he had known was still there. She felt something, he was sure of it. "All right," he countered, "you name the place and give me the time."

Beset with consternation, she bit her lip. He was moving too fast for her. This was not the shy, young Rick. She was not prepared for such foolishness. What motivated him? Had she given him reason to believe?

Regaining her composure, she cocked her head as if studying his smile. Two can play the game, she decided and said, "Later, perhaps when we have lunch, we can sit and talk intelligently." Bewildered by her own acquiescence, she allowed him to take her arm.

After an hour of strolling from salon to salon, they eventually made their way to the grand Maggior Consiglio. Veronese's *Triumph of Venice* covered the ceiling, but Tintoretto's *Paradise* sprawled over the Grand Council chamber.

Lee, pointing out details of the massive work, noticed Baron staring at her. She eyed him obliquely.

"Rick, you're embarrassing me."

He seemed to be examining the ruffled, vee-neck collar of her white blouse, the one departure from her somewhat conservative light gray suit. He smiled.

"Sorry, Lee, but you're an addiction from which I've never fully recovered."

Lee answered cautiously. "I am not the young girl you once loved."

Baron arched an eyebrow. "If I loved a rosebud, shouldn't I love the rose?"

She smiled in spite of herself. "Very prettily stated. Like most Americans, you have a quick answer. But, Rick, it alters nothing. You don't even know me."

"True enough. But, if you remembered anything at all about me, you would know that I was always an eager learner."

Amusement appeared in her bright eyes. "You were a paradox, Rick, both eager and shy at the same time."

Baron studied her in silence for a few seconds before replying. "Then you do remember everything?"

Lee averted her eyes. "You shouldn't make too much of it. Every woman has her memories."

From a distance, the sound of the Moors striking the noon hour reached them. Baron checked his watch. "I have to call Joe at one o'clock, Lee. To go back to the Lido would take too long. Where do you suggest I make the call?"

"To Israel?"

"Yes, it's a matter of business. I've already mentioned that before."

She seemed hesitant, then said, "Why not the shop? It would be more private."

There was only slight protest from Lee when Baron insisted on taking care of the charges. But, in fact, she appeared relieved, he was quick to note. "Come," he said, taking her hand, "let's get into the sunlight again."

Reentering the Piazzetta, her hand linked with his, her permissiveness filled Lee's mind with confusing thoughts. It was just one of the slight liberties she allowed him since their reunion. But with his obvious persistence, would he misunderstand? She frowned suddenly. Did *she* understand? Was it a reawakening of an old love for her, or was it simply that he made her feel so young again? Or was it compassion for Riv's father?

"A penny for your thoughts," abruptly interrupted her mental probings. She looked up at him, releasing her hand, not quite sure of herself.

"Why so serious?" Baron asked.

As was her habit whenever troubled, she bit her lip, "I'm sorry, Rick. . . ." Her voice faltered as a feeling of warmth engulfed her. Unnerved, she simply could not discard the memories of the years of happiness spent with tender, gentle, loving Enzo—not even for a meaningful first love.

Baron, observing her intently, said, "You seem troubled, Lee. What have I done to upset you?"

"You've reappeared, Rick."

Her reply was totally unexpected. Bewildered, he sought an answer. Had she suddenly decided the "homecoming" was too much to cope with? If so, did she expect

105

him to vanish by the day's end? The thought was disturbing. He felt as if he were being dismissed.

Somewhat annoyed, he found his voice. "I realize our discovering each other has brought on complications. But, Lee, you can't expect me to simply disappear. Not now, after learning of our son."

Torn between two desires, Lee struggled with her conscience. Her first fear concerned Riv—could he ever possibly discover her secret? Would he note any resemblance? Would her friends? No, she decided, not unless they knew Rick when he was much younger. Sighing deeply, her fears turned inward toward herself. There was a need within her, consciously growing stronger with each hour she spent with Rick—a need she was afraid to acknowledge.

Baron saw the torment in her eyes. Unable to comprehend her behavior, an air of dismay surrounded him. She was actually turning away from any kind of relationship with him. It was a new experience for his ego; never before had it been necessary to sell himself. It was incomprehensible to his way of thinking because he had been so sure of her.

He gave her a steadfast look, disguising his thoughts. "Well, Lee, do I just walk away in silence?"

She turned to him quickly, a hurt expression on her face. "Oh, Rick, why must you be so aggressive! You're overwhelming me! No, I don't want you to leave. Not this way. Why can't we simply be old friends?"

Baron's heart beat like trip-hammer. "Aggressive!" Was that it? Was he being too callous in his pursuit? Had his intentions been so easily read? It had never entered his mind. He searched her face—a face that seemed to be growing more beautiful with each passing hour. His eyes narrowed. What was she afraid of? Him? Herself? Sensing a reprieve, he pursued his train of thought openly.

"I don't understand, Lee. I'm not an ogre. Why are you afraid of me? Has my reappearance disturbed a commitment to someone else?"

Lee struggled to keep her emotions in check, but a trace of impatience persisted. "Reappearance!" she exclaimed. "Don't you mean resurrection? Haven't you realized yet that I believed you were dead all those years?" She glared at him, her temper rising. "Why can't you understand that I'm not the young girl who ran after you? I am committed to no one but my family!"

Baron stared at her, too stunned to reply.

She stared back at him for a long moment, unwinding. Then, as quickly as her anger had erupted, it now vanished. With an abrupt turnabout, she brought her hands to her face. An embarrassed laugh followed, then a helpless gesture with her hands. "This is ridiculous," she said, addressing herself. "Why should I be angry?"

Baron eyed her obliquely but, noting her amused smile, said nothing.

"Rick, it isn't really me, is it? Your overtures are the very same you use for all your intended conquests."

Baron pursed his lips. She was really something. He said finally, "How could it be? As far as I know, you're the only one who has given me a son."

"So that's how you see me—the mother of your son."

Baron rolled his eyes. "Lee, you're twisting my words. That's not the way I meant it." But within him, he suddenly wondered.

Lee's evasive smile offered only slight encouragement as she said, "All right, truce then? Between old friends?"

Subdued, Baron nodded. "You win, Lee. Perhaps I was coming on too strong, but not for the reasons you expressed." With that, he looked toward the clock tower. "It's almost one, Lee. That call has to be made. Is your phone offer still open?"

"Of course. Did you think I was dismissing you?" The amused smile reappeared. "Rick, if you would just forget about trying to seduce me, our reunion could be much more enjoyable." She laughed suddenly. "Besides, I did want to speak with Tovah before she left the shop."

Baron gaped at her. With her ever changing attitudes, he was becoming unsure of himself. One second, provoked; the next, friendly. When she slipped her arm into his, he shook his head. "Lee, you're just too much."

They eased through the square without difficulty, the crowds having dispersed for lunch. Most of the tables at Quadri's and Florian's were already taken. Beneath the clock tower, Baron was the first to break the silence that had settled between them. "Have you selected a place for lunch yet?"

She flashed a smile at him, her eyes radiant. For Baron,

the world brightened again. "Yes," she said, obviously in good spirits, "I think you will enjoy their menu."

Baron nodded without comment. Whatever the reason for her mood, he had decided once and for all to let her take the initiative.

At the shop, Tovah, after first registering surprise, cast an inquisitive look toward her mother without speaking.

"So glad I caught you, Tovah," Lee said promptly. "I wish to speak for you while Rick, uh, Signor Baron is making a phone call to Israel."

"Israel?" Frowning, Tovah glanced at Baron, catching his amused wink as he moved toward the rear of the shop. She was befuddled. Turning back to her mother, she repeated, "Israel?"

"Yes, it's a business call," she said, then added quickly, "He's taking care of the charges."

Lee had forgotten to mention Riv's call from Israel to her. Now, it would be the time, she thought carefully. Angelina had already departed, and Baron was out of earshot.

It took thirty minutes to get the person-to-person, collect call through to Israel. Joe Green's voice came over the wire excitedly.

"Rick, is that you? What the hell are you doing in Venice? You're suppose to be in Rome! Is everything okay?"

"Hold it, Joe!" Baron replied quickly, fending off the questions, a smile softening his features. Joe Green would never cease playing big brother. "Everything's fine, relax. First things first. Did all the equipment arrive in one piece?"

"Equipment? Yeah, sure." Baron could sense Joe's impatience. "Including Mindy—and *Paul*," Joe added, his tone mellowing somewhat. "You know how Paul's been pressuring us to allow him out in the field. Well, the timing is perfect. There's nothing special at home that the studio can't handle by itself until our return."

Baron nodded to himself. Paul Green, twenty-four years old and the elder of Joe and Mindy's two sons, was a good kid. Good in everything: photography, journalism —and unlike most of his contemporaries—devotion to his parents. Paul and his brother, Michael, who still had another year of college to go, were like sons to Baron. The entire Green clan, as a matter of fact, was Baron's adopted family.

Joe Green's impatience returned. "Okay, Rick, let's stop the horsing around. What's up? I assume you must have a reason for leaving Rome in such a hurry."

"That's unimportant right now, Joe." Baron noticed that Tovah had departed. "Hold on, Joe, I want you to speak to an old friend of ours." He could hear Joe mumbling something indistinguishable as he motioned Lee to the phone.

Eyeing Baron timorously, Lee couldn't deny the excitement growing within her. At first, she shook her head but then at his insistence, finally took the phone.

"Hello? Verdi? Joe?"

Silence greeted her.

"Hello? Joe? Are you there?"

Joe's voice came through, slow and hesitant. "Who is this?" Verdi? he thought, who would call him Verdi? A moment later, it struck him, before she could reply. "Oh, my God!" he almost shouted. "Lee, LEE! Is it really you!"

Lee couldn't control the tears. "Yes . . . it's Lee," she mumbled through trembling lips.

"Lee, Lee! I can't believe it! Rick's actually found you."

His exuberance forced Lee to laugh through the tears.

"My God, Lee! There are so many questions I want to ask you, I don't know where to begin. If it was only possible for us to meet, it would be great seeing you again. I hope Rick hasn't been giving you a hard time."

Her laughter came easily, her heart filled with warmth. She glanced at Rick, her eyes glistening. "No, he's been very understanding so far."

Smiling, Baron returned the gaze, knowing he had won another inning.

"Lee, I can't get over it," Joe's voice continued effusively. "How are you? Have you changed? Are you married? A family?"

Her girlish laughter pervaded the room. "Joe, you must wait. I will be in Israel in a few days. My family is there. We will meet, and I will introduce you. We have a shop in Jerusalem." Only a moment later did she grasp the full meaning of what she had confided. Her vocal chords froze, and beseechingly she stared at Baron.

Recognizing her dilemma, he took the phone from her. "Okay, Joe, what is this? Twenty questions? I'll be there in another week."

If Joe felt any concern over the abrupt change of parties, he didn't let it creep over the phone. "All right, Rick, I'll let the personal stuff hang, but fill me in on the rest. This shop of hers—give me the name and location."

Baron stole a glance at Lee, who had moved to the front of the store. Gazing through the glass door, her concentration appeared to be elsewhere. Baron knew better. Putting his mouth closer to the phone, he spoke in a half-whisper, "Enzo—Enzo Moscati. Remember him?"

"Moscati?" Joe echoed, not sure that he had heard correctly. "Holy Christ! You mean the wheeler-dealer?"

Baron could almost visualize Joe's raised eyebrows. "Ironic, isn't it? That after all . . ." He stopped himself, then spoke hastily. "But that's neither here nor there, Joe. Enzo died in the Six Day War—and now she's available."

Joe Green's concern was instant. "Available? What is that suppose to mean? This is Lee you're talking about. Christ! Have you forgotten what she meant to you? Available? What the hell are you thinking of?"

"Joe, I'm not a bastard."

After a slight pause, "All right, as long as we understand each other, I'll take your word for it. Now tell me, what does she look like?"

"A total knockout, Joe. You won't believe it."

"I can believe it." He laughed, then sounded hesitant. "Rick . . . any complications with your meeting?"

"Some, but you'll have to wait for the details."

Joe sighed. "All right. When are you arriving?"

Lee absently watched the play of light filtering into the alley. Here and there, it softened the shadowed areas of the Mercerie, where some stragglers still lingered at the windows of shops which had closed for the afternoon. Her composure had recovered miraculously, remembering that in two more days Riv would be on temporary duty. The chances were very slim indeed that he would be accosted by anyone from her past, accidental or otherwise. Her breathing was normal when Baron approached.

"You all right?" asked Baron solicitously.

She nodded, her eyes sparkling with anticipation. "Permit me to change my bag, and we will go to lunch."

Curious but pleasantly surprised by her transformation, Baron said, "Would you mind very much if I left the camera here? I don't need a range-finder to keep you in focus."

They both laughed, decidedly comfortable in each other's company.

They cut across the square of San Marco, passed beneath a *loggia*, and went through an arcade, coming out onto the Calle Larga. Lee, clutching a shoulder bag with one arm, intertwined her free arm with Baron's. Although continually bewildered by her behavior, Baron kept silent, determined not to break the spell. Reveling in her nearness and the fragrance of her perfume, he felt a mild stimulation and wondered whether she was similarly affected. He gave her an overt glance, but could read nothing in her attractive features that coincided with his feelings. However, although she was preoccupied with her own thoughts, she did seem self-satisfied, he noticed.

The square was bright with sunshine but not overly warm. A cooling breeze swept across the pavement and stirred the awning flaps of the *trattorie* bordering the *piazza*.

When Baron asked "Which one?" she surprised him once again. Giving him a warm smile, she took him by the hand and led him across the square.

Seated in the center of the bustling restaurant, Baron glanced around. Even though it was late in the season, most of the patrons were tourists, he guessed, because of the number of cameras present. He returned his attention to Lee. "Why this one?"

She answered, almost shyly. "The pasta here is exceptional . . . especially their *tortellini*. Unlike many restaurants, they make it with a thick cream sauce here."

Baron nodded. "The way you used to make it."

"Then you do remember?"

Baron smiled. "Why shouldn't I remember? It was a most pleasant time in my life."

"And what of your life since?" she asked, somewhat subdued.

"It's been full—rewarding. I can't complain."

Lee eyed him studiously. "How you must have hated me when I didn't write."

"Not really," he lied. "I soon got over it. I had my

111

career to start." He spread his hands helplessly. "It was a long time ago, Lee. As a matter of fact, it was only two days ago, in Rome—in the Piazza Navona by the Bernini Fountain—that all the details came into focus."

Lee gave him a look of disbelief, but knew better than to make any comment.

Following a heavy silence, Baron made a complete turnabout. He reached across the table for her hands. "Enough of the past. Let's just have a light lunch now, and tonight we'll take in the best restaurant in Venice. We can even go for a gondola ride before dinner."

All went smoothly for the better part of an hour until they were finishing the last of the Bardolino. Baron stiffened abruptly, a chill sweeping through his body. Damn! he muttered under his breath. It was as if someone had walked across his grave! He drained his glass in a gulp.

Lee was watchful and appeared concerned. "Rick, what is it?"

Baron tried to brush it aside. "Nothing. Just a chilling breeze. The weather must be changing." He saw that she wasn't appeased. He forced a laugh. "Look, I don't feel like going back to the Lido to change. Suppose you help me shop for a shirt and jacket."

Her eyes widened. "Rick, I can't. It wouldn't be proper."

Baron leaned forward. "Oh, c'mon, don't go prudish on me now. It might even be fun."

"Well," she hesitated, "all right, I believe I know an inexpensive place." It was a shop she rarely visited, but there was always a chance of meeting an acquaintance.

Relieved, Baron smiled easily. "I can well afford the best, Lee."

"Really?" She regarded him suspiciously, not knowing whether to take him seriously. "You are a rich American?"

He nodded. "Money-wise, I'm considered a good catch."

"Hmm . . . then why have you not been caught?"

He laughed. "I've never stood still long enough to be caught." Struck by another thought, he added slyly, "But I am standing still right now."

At first she just stared, then she laughed. It was a soft, amused laugh, "You are joking, surely!"

It was a stupid ploy, he realized immediately. Christ!

I must be getting old. I'm losing my touch! He toyed with a napkin. "Yes, of course," he said with forced laughter. "But you can't blame a guy for trying. You're a beautiful woman, Lee."

She laughed in return, no longer afraid of Rick. He had become obvious to her and she understood him now. The game he was playing with her had been played with others—many times. She was attracted to him, she admitted grudgingly, but this was not the Rick that she had known. The youthful Rick had been less worldly, more loving. . . . She caught herself, feeling disappointed, not quite sure why she should. She sipped her wine. He couldn't have been serious. It had to be a nostalgic yearning for the woman who gave birth to his son. She glanced at him over the lip of the glass, unbidden thoughts coloring her face.

Baron hadn't noticed, he was checking his watch. "It's almost four. The stores should be opening shortly."

Lee nodded, a mischievous smile playing on her lips. You fight fire with fire, she decided defiantly. It was an old role for her—one which she had almost forgotten.

Once again, she perplexed Baron by intertwining her arm with his, causing a mixture of confusion and elation. He said nothing as they started across the square. Pondering his own behavior, he tried to justify the hidden proposition he had put to her. It was idiotic; it was thoughtless. This is *Lee,* the mother of Riv. Surely, he didn't expect. . . . Her hip rubbing against his side halted his train of thought. He couldn't understand it. What was she doing? Why the turnabout? He could feel an urge growing stronger within himself. A frown creased his forehead.

Lee glanced at him questioningly.

"It's just a chill," he said hoarsely.

She patted his hand playfully. "Yes. Of course. That's why we're buying you a jacket."

Baron merely stared. She was amazing. This was the playful Lee that he remembered. Dumbfounded, he couldn't think of a reply.

Midway across the square, the sky darkened, casting a gray pall over the immediate area. Baron looked up to see a dark cloud ominously blotting out the sun. He shivered slightly as a cool breeze seemed to brush over them resentfully.

"I think you're right," he said. "I need that jacket."

Baron frowned, his expression uncommonly grim. He was never one to be superstitious, but crossing the *piazza*, an uncomfortable feeling pursued him relentlessly. For a fleeting moment, he thought he saw a wall toppling in his mind's eye. He glanced at Lee, then looked upward, muttering to himself, "Not another Florence. Don't you dare."

CHAPTER 6

Israel—September 1973

Charter buses and cabs lined the curb along the entrance of Lod Airport, gathering the influx of tourists visiting the Holy Land. Joe Green, a safe distance away from the milling Israelis who were awaiting friends and relatives, watched them, seemingly uninterested. He tossed a casual glance toward the Fiat a hundred yards away on the opposite side of the road, where Mindy was behind the wheel patiently waiting for his signal.

Joe Green was in a quandary. He took a final drag on his cigarette and tossed it beyond the curb impatiently. He was wondering whether Rick knew about Riv, and if he didn't, what would he do when he found out. He ran a nervous hand through his thinning hair. Good God! All you had to do was look at the kid to recognize the truth, he thought.

After another few seconds passed, he reached into his jacket for a cigar. Although well-cut, the sport jacket failed to hide a growing paunch. About to light up the Macanudo, Joe saw Baron come out onto the sidewalk. He called to him and signaled to Mindy at the same time.

Joe grabbed Baron's forearm. "Cripes, it's good to see you, Rick." He looked around, seeking another familiar face. "Where's Lee? I thought she'd be with you."

115

Baron made a face, suddenly shy. "No, she'll be here in a couple of days."

"Anything wrong?"

"C'mon, Joe!" Baron laughed. "This place is too open for a confession. Where's the car? We can talk later."

The screech of braking wheels was heard. Mindy had pulled up, double-parking beside a tour bus. "Oh, man," Joe moaned, "that woman is going to give me heart failure."

Scampering around the bus, Baron found the rear door of the Fiat and tossed in his bag. Scrambling in beside the bag, he leaned forward to kiss the green-eyed blond behind the wheel. "Hi'ya, gorgeous. You here to keep tabs on Joe?" It was the first foreign assignment in over five years for Joe.

Mindy didn't reply immediately. She was eying Joe in the seat beside her and the unlit cigar stuck in his mouth. "If you're going to light that, Yussel, keep that window open." Joe grimaced but didn't light up.

Baron laughed. "Yussel? Since when?"

The willowy blond twisted toward Rick. "You know the old saying, 'When in Rome . . .'?" She made an impatient gesture. "So much for the small talk, Rick. I've been dying to meet Lee. Where is she?"

Baron sighed audibly. "She'll be here in a couple of days. She's closing the shop in Venice for good. The new owner takes over on the first of the month."

Mindy pursed her lips. "Is that good or bad?"

Baron shook his head, a smile appearing nevertheless. "Man, you're a nosy broad. How the hell would I know?"

Persistent horns hounded them. Joe groaned and gestured helplessly. "Min, I'm starving. Let's get into Tel Aviv and get something to eat."

Baron leaned forward quickly. "If you can hold off, Joe, I'd prefer going straight to Jerusalem."

Mindy and Joe eyed each other without speaking.

Baron studied them for a moment. "What's going on between you two?"

Joe told Mindy to head east. As she eased the Fiat out of the airport traffic, Joe turned to Baron.

"We stopped in Moscati's shop the day after you called."

Baron's heartbeat quickened. "Yes, so?"

"Did she tell you about her children?"

"Of course. Riv and Tovah. What about them?" Baron began to sweat.

"Well, I introduced myself to Riv as an old friend of his parents. We spoke to him for only a few minutes before he had to leave to pick up Tovah coming in from Venice." Joe paused and glanced at Mindy who was breathing heavily. "Pull over, Min. I'll take the wheel."

Baron wiped his forehead with the back of his hand, his suspicions aroused. Damn! They knew! Somehow they knew! How? He kept silent as she parked on a sandy shoulder.

When Joe got out to take the driver's seat, Mindy slid over to take his vacated seat. Aware that Mindy was purposely avoiding his eyes, Baron abruptly decided to end the games. Just as Joe slid in behind the wheel, Baron spoke crisply. "Let's cut the horseplay, Joe. You know about Riv."

Joe and Mindy exchanged startled glances. Then Mindy exclaimed, "You mean it's no secret to you?"

"Some secret," Baron muttered to himself. Aloud he said, "Lee told me everything, but how the hell did you find out?"

"Oh brother!" Joe groaned. "Holy Christ, Rick, all you have to do is take one look at him. I thought Mindy was going to keel over when she laid eyes upon him. Except for being a bit taller and maybe a little thinner, he could be an exact double of you twenty years ago."

In a cold sweat, Baron leaned back, his arms prickling annoyingly, staring blankly at the rocky landscape.

Mindy showed genuine concern. "You all right, Rick?" she ventured guardedly.

Baron nodded, took a deep breath, then exhaled heavily. It was time for full explanations. Mindy and Joe Green had shared too important a part of his life.

Baron's father had passed away within a year after his son's return from the war. Leading an almost monastic existence since the loss of his mate and greatly disillusioned with his son's turning away from the Orthodoxy, he died a lonely and bitter man. "What good are prayers?" Baron had rebuked his father. "Millions had prayed as they died to sate the whims of a power-mad, satanic lunatic."

Nevertheless, pushing aside the lingering guilt, he made a promise to himself. Lee was gone and he would not easily forget her, but unlike his father, he would not die of loneliness. He forced himself to end his state of vegetation and, together with Joe Green, his only close friend, registered in the Columbia School of Journalism under the GI bill.

In those early years after the war, Joe Green and Rick Baron were practically inseparable. Even with Joe's marriage to Mindy, a vivacious, green-eyed blond, there was hardly an interruption in their friendship. For Joe, Mindy was the greatest prize of his life and, as it turned out, for Baron also. Joe and Mindy Green became his brother and sister, his father and mother—his family.

Joe Green maneuvered a dogleg curve in the road and then gunned the engine past a hillside grove of gnarled olive trees. Baron sniffed. The familiarity of the pungent odor emanating from the hillside terrain made him unsure of himself. He couldn't decide whether it was pleasant or otherwise. Dismissing it from his mind, other guilty thoughts crept in, an ache forming in his chest. If only his parents were alive to see this land, he thought. Sighing deeply, he became aware of Mindy studying him intently. Altering his thoughts, he smiled and winked good-naturedly.

"All right, lover boy," she smiled back, "Isn't it about time we got the lowdown on Lee? What did you two do in romantic Venice for a whole week?"

Joe rolled his eyes. "Holy cripes, Min! Don't you think the man deserves some privacy?"

"Privacy, Yussel!" She laughed, her palpable good nature self-evident. "What privacy? For over twenty years, we've shared everything with him but our bed." Withdrawing from Joe in mock disdain, she twisted in her seat to confront Baron. "Really, Rick, that girl must have guts to disclose such a secret. But to tell the truth, as incredible as the facts are, I find it remarkable that you two met again." She paused and pushed back a wisp of hair fluttering in the warm breeze. "So tell us. What does Lee look like now? How much has she changed over the years? And what's more, how has she taken to you? Your own feelings are only too obvious."

Baron gave her an oblique glance. Mindy could be tenacious at times, and there was no stopping her once she started. Gazing at her, he was forced into making a comparison between the two women. In appearance, they were like night and day; one fair with wide, clear, deep green eyes, surmounted by a dazzling display of glistening blond tresses (although now aided with an occasional touchup); the other with luminous blue eyes in a deeply tanned face that was framed by an abundance of black hair with gray frostings. While Mindy's character was more revealing, Lee's was peculiarly esoteric. Lee had endured too many wars, had seen too much of death, and had lived too long in an air of uncertainty. If there was any similarity between the two women, it was in their eyes—the bright, clear look, each one's distinctive in their own way, defying their age.

Mindy pouted coquettishly. "Cat got your tongue, Rick?"

Baron forced a smile. There was no denying her.

"Well," he said, measuring his words, "she's much more reserved than I remembered her. But I must admit that she did seem to loosen up after the initial shock wore off."

"To what extent?" Mindy asked. Joe shook his head and eyed Baron surreptitiously in the rearview mirror, but said nothing.

Self-conscious for a few moments under the scrutiny of his dearest friends, Rick suddenly burst into laughter.

"What a nosy broad!" he exclaimed. Joe and Mindy joined in the laughter spontaneously.

When the laughter subsided, Mindy gave him an impatient stare. "Rick," she demanded.

"What can I tell you? Once we got over our stage fright, things went smoothly. We had a damn good time for a few days." Baron leaned forward, suddenly eager to talk. "I don't know how good your memory is, but there's a square loaded with *trattorie* just beyond the Fenice Theatre. There, we would have lunch every day, then go for walks afterward. We must have hiked about fifty miles that week. Lee was terrific—tireless and never complaining. Man, the endless corridors and bridges, she showed me everything. For dinner, we took in a different restaurant each evening—Harry's Bar, Columbo's, and even the rooftop of the Danieli." He paused, noting the expression on Mindy's face, and smiled tolerantly. "I guess I opened up a memory bank there."

Mindy bit her lip, nodded, and smiled wistfully with

119

the memories he evoked. She blew Joe a kiss and received a wink in return.

She savored the mood temporarily and then eyed Baron
warily. "Stop putting me off, Rick," she continued un-
relenting, "that's all you did for a week? Just eat and
walk! Really, Rick, what did you discuss? What are her
feelings toward you? And will this end up being just a
pleasant reunion of sorts?"

Baron settled back into the seat, once again subdued.
"You're posing a question that has no answer. I don't
even know what I should expect. Occasionally, that free
and easy spirit that I remember would crop up and, while
we did have a marvelous time together, in reality neither
of us is the same person we once were. And she's certainly not the type to get involved in an affair."

About to explode, Joe pre-empted Mindy's ready response.

"Good Lord, Rick! After all those early years that she
preyed on your mind, is this what you want? An affair?
What is this? Some new kind of masochism?"

Baron sighed. "No, it's nothing like that, Joe. I don't
even know what I want. I've been a bachelor too long.
Admittedly, Lee is a challenge, but I don't think she's
prepared to accept me as anything but an old friend."

Joe, following a Mercedes tour bus, reached the crest of
a hill. Descending the road devoid of traffic, he gunned the
Fiat past the surprised bus driver. Mindy, frowning,
reached for a cigarette.

"Joe, remember the fine for speeding here. If you get
caught, it comes out of *your* shopping money—not mine."

Their antics summoned a smile from Baron. Grateful
for the respite from importuning questions, he sank
deeper into his seat. Turning his head, he watched the
landscape glide by.

Even before reaching the cities, it became obvious to
Rick that Israel was a mosaic of the past and the present,
each segment a separate entity. Only from a distance
where the two appeared to merge, did they seem to blend
together formlessly. The road to Jerusalem ascended,
dipped, then wound through bare patches of moonlike
terrain. Occasionally, one would pass a stone hovel sporting a Coca-Cola sign, spelled out both in English and
phonetically in Hebrew. At one point, a short distance
away from the road that allowed modern contraptions,

120

an Arab encampment depicted an ageless Biblical scene with its herd of goats grazing alongside an exceptionally long tent whose roof undulated in the warm breeze. A television aerial incongruously protruded from the center of the tent.

They were a few minutes away from the Holy City when Baron, in a semi-lethargic state, smiled superficially. He just realized they had not discussed any business at all. It was the first time in memory that he had allowed anything to sidetrack an assignment. It was a totally new experience for him. Not in years had he permitted anything to take preference over his work. He shook his head, feeling defenseless. He hadn't even asked Joe who he had already interviewed. Rick scratched at his cheek, Lee obsessively interrupting any thoughts of the job at hand. Reflecting on the days in Venice, he knew they both had recognized the amative mood growing between them. He had spent only one evening in her apartment and then only long enough to share a pot of *espresso*, Lee offering no encouragement for a deeper relationship. Her change in manner after the first day had bewildered him. Was she biding her time, or was she merely accommodating him for another week or so until he would again be out of her life? His lips compressed in a thin line, the thought was depressing. His mind refused to dwell on such a possibility. His mouth displayed determination. Just finding each other could not be the final chapter.

He thought of Riv—his son and a perfect stranger. Are close blood ties sensed? he wondered. A twenty-eight-year-old son! A new thought brought a flow of apprehension. How does one greet a son one has never known? And without revealing the true facts?

"How about the American Colony Hotel for lunch?" he heard Mindy ask Joe.

Joe nodded, glanced into the rearview mirror, and addressed Baron. "How about it, Rick? They've got a nice courtyard restaurant. You know, tomorrow is the holiday. We won't be using the car."

Baron shrugged. "Okay with me. But aside from eating, what else have you accomplished?" He asked the question almost mechanically, knowing that sooner or later he would have to get down to detailed business.

Joe grunted. "Are you kidding? While you were ca-

121

vorting around in Venice, Ralph and I finished three interviews."

"Any more trouble with the Eyemo?"

"No. Ralph repaired the shutter, but I used the Mitchell anyway."

Baron sat up. They were on the outskirts of Jerusalem. "'How about the front lines? Did you get security clearance for Yom Kippur?'

Joe lifted his left hand to the back of his neck as if to scratch it, making a hand motion for Baron to back off. Baron understood; Joe didn't wish to discuss it in Mindy's presence.

"We've got the green light for the Golan Heights," Joe said. "But the Bar-Lev Line, forget it. Security is too tight. No outsiders."

Baron's face clouded. Those three interviews—had Joe inadvertently hit upon something? Or was he simply being overly cautious? He wondered. The airport security didn't seem any tighter than usual except for Joe having to wait outside the entrance for him. A frown creased his forehead. If there was trouble brewing, why hadn't Joe warned him earlier? Pondering, he watched Mindy search her bag for a fresh pack of cigarettes. When she turned, he shrugged disarmingly for her benefit.

"Okay," Rick addressed Joe, "so we forget about it." He sensed Joe's relief.

"Jaffa Road, Rick," Mindy said, her eyes aglow beneath the moon-shaped sunglasses she had just put on.

"Yes, I know. I remember it. How far down is the shop?"

Joe lifted his head sharply. "I'll point it out if you don't insist on stopping." He glanced at his watch. "Besides, they're already closed for the afternoon."

Restraining his gnawing impatience, Baron watched Joe maneuver Nordau Square and follow a steadily growing stream of traffic. As they progressed deeper into the city, the scene became a convolution of modern and ancient architecture with condominiums and contemporary high-rise hotels encroaching upon myriad curio shops and archaic coffee houses. Baron allowed a desultory glance to linger briefly on the tourists and *kaffiyeh*-garbed Arabs ambling along the walks.

"Well, Joe!" he demanded, his stomach beginning to churn. "How much farther?"

"Relax, Rick. It's just ahead. There! You can see it from your side."

Baron leaned forward and rolled down the window with eager anticipation, his blood racing. He realized his behavior was unconventional, knowing that Riv was with his unit—wherever it was. But just being this close . . .

Mindy watched him, emotionally affected, but said nothing.

Except for the name painted across the window pane, the shop looked like all the others—inconspicuous in its similarity, its ochre stone facade a common sight in Israel.

As the car continued to move, Baron reluctantly turned away. Settling back, he took a deep breath, then gave vent to a heavy sigh. "Relax," Joe said. Good Lord! How? Rick thought. He hadn't been so moved since. . . . Since when? He left the question unanswered, noting Mindy watching him with misty eyes.

"What's with you, gorgeous?" he asked huskily.

Her voice sputtered. "Oh, you dumb dodo! I'm just as anxious to meet Lee as you are to see your son."

My son, he thought. My son—the boy he would never know. What would they have to say to one another once they met? Grim thoughts pressed upon him, recalling the final days with his own father. No, Riv must never know.

He reached suddenly for his pipe and tobacco, attempting to dismiss all father-son relationships. "What about the shop, Joe? Do they make a living from it?"

Joe laughed. "I'd say they were doing very well, considering the taxes here. But leave it to Enzo. From the black market, he graduated into high finance. He owns— or rather Lee now owns—an apartment house in Rome. In the Trastevere section, not far from where she used to live."

"You're kidding!" Baron exclaimed.

"No, I'm not. The shop in Venice is another story. It's a money-maker, but only if she stays there to handle it. And she has no desire to do that."

Baron leaned forward. "Where the hell did you get all this information?"

"From Tovah."

Baron was astonished. "She confided all this to you in one visit?"

From Mindy came an unexpected burst of laughter.

"We were in the shop more than once, but we learned this from Paul. He's dated her twice in the past week."

"Well, I'll be damned!" Baron exclaimed, at the same time experiencing some anxiety. "I hope they haven't discussed Riv in any way. It has to remain our secret."

"C'mon, Rick," Joe protested. "Would Paul say anything to hurt you! Besides, he doesn't even know about the relationship."

"Yeah. Sorry, Joe. Forget I said it." His misgivings began to subside. It was true; Paul would never open his mouth, even if he did know the whole truth.

"I'll tell you something else," Joe interjected. "Tovah offered to drive us to the Golan Heights on Yom Kippur. She says she's never seen an American film crew in action."

Baron arched his eyebrows. "You think it's wise to take her along? She might be in the way." He kept his voice even, hoping the uneasiness he felt wouldn't be detected.

"On Yom Kippur! What could possibly happen? Besides, we're leaving on the day after. It would give the kids a last day together."

Baron winced, and his misgivings persisted. A last day together, he reflected. He wished Joe had selected different words. It was obvious, to Baron at least, that Joe wanted Mindy and Paul out of Israel as soon as possible. Their original plans had called for their leaving the following weekend.

Mindy, unaware of the unspoken information being passed between the two men, glowed with anticipation.

"Rick, you'll just love this restaurant at the Colony. It's situated in a weathered courtyard so peaceful and serene that you can't help but be at ease."

Baron returned her smile unfeelingly. The circumstances of this semi-atavistic land refused to permit a permanent peace. As far as he was concerned, the history of mankind never altered. Man, although indulging in a progressive sophistication, always remained uncivilized. The causes of war didn't matter; if there weren't any, they would be manufactured. The struggle between good and evil would continue unabated. Mulling it over somberly, Baron recalled a passage from Dov Laslo's *The Struggle for Tomorrow*. "In this age of curious enlightenment, it is with dreaded wonder that we view the will of

124

man injected with ignorance and hate . . . no matter how virulent the evil thoughts and deeds of Israel's enemies, it is the destiny of Jews, here and elsewhere, to survive. . . ."

"Yeah, sure," Baron cynically muttered to himself. "As long as their armaments hold out."

Mindy's voice crisply cut into his thoughts.

"What's with you, Rick? Why so grim? Look around you, you're in the 'Promised Land' where you have more waiting for you than you ever anticipated."

He forced a smile. "I was just thinking. Perhaps with Lee's help, we could persuade Dov Laslo to sit and talk before the camera." He hesitated briefly, then, "I'm assuming you met him."

Joe shook his head. "I'm way ahead of you. I've already been turned down. He's a loner, talks only to his typewriter. As a matter of fact, I was shocked to find him in Lee's shop." He looked into the rearview mirror. "I also got the feeling that they're pretty close friends."

Baron smiled, self-satisfied. "You're wrong, Joe. You're misinterpreting. Laslo's intentions are honorable, but Lee has turned him down. They are good friends—but that's all, just *good friends*."

Mindy straightened in her seat. "You needn't be so smug, Rick. What are *your* intentions?"

Baron rolled his eyes. "Oh, man, still a nosy broad."

"Rick, you're impossible," she protested. Smiling, nevertheless, she turned on Joe. "Yussel, are you going to get this toy moving? I thought you were hungry."

Grinning, Joe shook his head and, unmindful of his two passengers, engineered a sharp left into an alley. The ochre and sienna-stained structures walling them in were not unlike those in Italy. "Shortcut," he stated simply, disregarding Mindy's "Oh, brother!" After easing past a young Arab boy astride a small donkey, Joe gunned the car through the otherwise deserted alley.

Baron leaned forward. "Did Ralph retape the sound tracks before shipping them home?"

Joe nodded. "Of course. If you want to, we can go over them right after lunch. But what's the rush? We'll have all day tomorrow."

"That's right," Mindy interjected. "No business today. I still have to hear about your week in Venice." She peered through the windshield. They were on St. George

Road. "We're almost there, Rick. Now it's time to relax and enjoy. I promise I'll leave you two alone all day tomorrow."

Baron decided not to press it for the present. Somehow he would get Joe alone later. His cryptic signaling earlier still left Rick with some apprehensions.

CHAPTER 7

Israel—October 3, 1973

Dov Laslo was tall, at least four inches over six feet, with a mane of white hair drooping toward rounded shoulders. In his middle fifties, he appeared much older. His skin was textured like aging leather, and the lines beneath his wire-rimmed glasses were deeply etched. His one youthful feature was the gleam of elation in his intelligent gray eyes as he beheld Lee at arm's length.

"You look absolutely wonderful, Eleanora."

And she truly did, he thought, eying her studiously. Something extraordinary had to have occurred. She was positively radiant, her eyes alive with hidden pleasures. Controlling an inexplicable feeling that he had somehow lost her, his face creased into a warm smile once again.

"You don't know how happy we are now that you've finished with Venice." His eyes teased her. "How could you stay away from your family for five months?"

Lee kissed him on the cheek. "Perhaps one more visit —to settle with the government. Then no more, Dov. I'm home to stay. It was good of you to help with Riv away."

Laslo shrugged. "For me, it was a pleasure to work with such a family. Besides," he laughed abruptly, "in return for my services, I requisitioned Tovah to type up my manuscript on her free evenings." A sly expression appeared. "That is, when she is not too busy with her young American."

Lee turned and peered at Tovah questioningly.

Until now, Tovah had been listening and watching unobtrusively from behind a glass showcase. A warm smile played on her lips. There was no one else in the shop. It was 9:30 in the morning, and Debbi was upstairs, preparing the children for the nursery.

"Paul Green, Mama. You know, the son of Joe and Mindy Green."

Lee frowned. "You said nothing to me."

"You were too tired last night, Mama. I didn't think it worth mentioning at the time."

Lee nodded understandingly, but made no reply. There was no reason to be upset, she told herself. After all, it was Verdi's son. She forced a smile, despite a thought that fate was weaving an intricate pattern around her.

"He's a nice boy, Mama," Tovah quickly offered. "A little too much money, but a nice boy." A soft laugh followed as she glanced at her watch. "Soon you will see. They will all be here—the Greens and Mr. Baron."

Tovah watched closely to see the effects of her words. Like Dov Laslo, she was acutely aware of the change in her mother. If nothing else, the green and white flower-print dress she wore this morning was enough to arouse suspicions. Was her mother no longer Eleanora? Was she now Lee?

Her mother ignored her scrutiny but found it hard to contain the excitement growing within her. She would not only see Rick again but the Green family, too.

"Yes, I know," she murmured softly. "I promised to take Rick—Mr. Baron—through the old quarter this afternoon." She looked up at Laslo. "Dov, you'll be a dear and stay for one more day? I promise you dinner before and after Yom Kippur."

Laslo was no fool and by no means blind, but judiciously, he kept his thoughts to himself. His sense of loss was pronounced, but he shrugged it off and took her hands in his own. "For you, Eleanora, and your friends, how can I refuse? Besides, the Greens have been very good customers." He laughed at the change in her expression. "They purchased three of the most expensive, handmade, linen prayer shawls, not to mention a dozen of the stone *mezuzahs*."

"Really!" Lee exclaimed. "I hope you gave them a bargain."

"Bargain? They didn't even question price."

Lee appeared disturbed. "Dov, you didn't." Then she saw his teasing look. "Oh, Dov. . ."

"Of course, I gave them a discount. Especially after they told me of your relationship. Knowing you, I wouldn't dare do otherwise."

Reassured, Lee led him to the back of the store. "Come, Dov. Have you had breakfast?" At his nod, she said, "At least have another cup of coffee?"

Tovah watched them disappear behind the curtained doorway at the rear, her face a picture of dampened spirits. She felt sorry for Dov Laslo. His feelings were only too apparent as far as she was concerned, and she wished her mother wouldn't take advantage of him, unintentionally or not. Disconsolately she pondered, And what about you, mother? What happens after your Rick Baron leaves in a few days? Tovah bit her lip. "What then, Mama?"

Lee timidly stole a glance when Baron seemed to pause to study the vaulted Jaffa Gate. It was their first opportunity to be alone after the Greens had dropped them off near the entrance. Ever since he came to the shop she had been aware that this was not the Rick of the final days in Venice. Even now, scanning the stones of the Gate that led into the Old Quarter, he seemed preoccupied.

It was wonderful meeting the Greens. With more weight and less hair, Joe was still the same Verdi she remembered. And Mindy was an absolute delight. When Mindy greeted her with a hug and a kiss and tears in her eyes, she had been stunned to realize that Mindy knew all about her former relationship with Rick. And Paul Green, with his short beard and long hair, dressed in a sport shirt and blue jeans, was just as Tovah related—truly, a nice American boy.

Lee, shrewdly keeping silent, took Baron's arm and led him through the shadowed alcove entrance.

Emerging into bright sunlight on Omar Ibn El-Khattab Square, a cacophony of foreign dialects confronted them. The conglomeration of humanity moved about in groups of all sizes, wandering to and from David Street, exploring the narrow alleys. A short distance to their right, the Citadel and David's Tower stretched skyward with the strong afternoon sun beaming off the Jerusalem stone in a melange of golden shades.

Lee's sigh of relief went undetected as she watched Baron's obduracy vanish. She could bide her time; soon she would be able to question him.

Baron, viewing the many diverse faces and the pulsating vitality of the square, had his problems temporarily shunted aside. Two Arabs, one adjusting the *agal* on his headdress, walked by hastily. Baron glanced at Lee and, for the first time in a long while, was able to smile without effort.

"Come," she said, her arm hooked in his. "There is much to see." With that, she steered him into a side street to the right towards the Armenian Quarter.

They strolled along the macadam street without speaking, stopping at an Arab curio shop. The shop was bursting with ancient artifacts, some authentic, others obviously modern replicas. Smiling, Lee pointed out the Jewish restaurant alongside.

"See," she said. "It is possible to get along peaceably."

Baron merely nodded and urged her forward. He was not about to reveal his as yet unfounded suspicions. He had learned much in the past two days, but could get no definitive answers from the higher-ups. Not even from Mrs. Meir, who had taken time from a busy schedule to converse privately with him on the previous evening.

"Mr. Baron," the venerable Prime Minister had queried, "does it seem to you that we are preparing for an imminent war?"

"No," he was forced to admit. Other than the usual precautions, which were always necessary, there was nothing out of the ordinary to support his suspicions. Yet like Joe, his gut feelings persisted. Could both of them be wrong?

Proceeding past the Citadel, the street assumed a tunnel-like appearance, as the high walls on both sides seemed to close them in. After a minute or two, he glanced at Lee.

"Where are we going?"

Lee continued to be cheerful despite the misgivings beginning to gather within her. "To the Zion Gate, and then the Jewish Quarter."

When he nodded without replying, she studied him

momentarily. He wore a pale gray safari jacket with charcoal slacks. It was a casual but costly outfit, she recognized at a glance. She didn't like the troubled look he couldn't seem to shake. Timidly she said, "You did not bring your camera." It was more of a statement than a question.

"No," he sighed, seemingly disinterested. "Paul and Joe already shot all we'll need of the old quarter." He didn't even realize that she meant his old Leica.

Disturbed, Lee glanced at the Zion Gate, where there was still evidence of the Israeli breakthrough during the Six Day War, the macadam surface beneath their feet corrugated from the tanks.

Stopping momentarily, they idly watched two young Israelis wearing bright-colored *yarmulkes,* aid an ancient, black-garbed, white-bearded Armenian priest through the Gate.

"See," she offered timorously, hoping he would somehow break out of his doldrums. "There *are* changes taking place."

Baron's face hardened. "So, in one little corner of the world, God appears to have renewed his interest in humanity. What does it prove? It changes nothing."

Lee turned away, her fingers clutching her shoulder bag nervously. She didn't understand his cynicism or his aloofness.

On that final evening in Venice, she had been on the threshold of giving in to his desires. For the first time in her six years of widowhood, she had felt the awakening need for a man. Fully realizing that Baron was the catalyst for her emotional fantasies, she nevertheless used all of her willpower to divert all desires. The impetuosity of youth had faded, and she was not about to chance a path that might lead to a disenchanting finish.

And yet, as she looked at him once more, she knew that she had missed him terribly, waiting to see him in Israel. Is he angry? she asked herself. Or is he simply—to use an American idiom—"turned off" by her refusal of his permissiveness. No, she decided, he was not angered, but he was definitely troubled. Did it have to do with Riv? She knew he hadn't been able to see him yet.

She watched him pull out the tobacco pouch from a zippered pocket and waited for him to fill his briar. A

131

sigh of relief followed the first puff, and she decided it was time to speak openly.

"Rick, why so much sadness? Is it because of me?"

Baron, startled by her blunt questioning, broke out of his lethargy. Regaining his composure, his features softened.

"Good Lord! What a boor I must seem to you!" He scratched his head boyishly. "Because of you? Nonsense! You could never cause me unhappiness."

"Well, then . . ."

"It's Riv," he blurted out. "It seems that there are insurmountable obstacles preventing me from seeing him."

Lee's eyes widened, trepidations coursing through her. She caught his free arm. "Riv . . . Riv is all right? You are not hiding something from me?"

Baron smiled reassuringly. "Of course, he's all right. It's just that he's stationed on the Bar-Lev Line. As long as he remains in that zone, I can't get permission to see him. It was just last night that I got the information of his whereabouts from the Prime Minister herself."

A surprised stare displaced the apprehensions that Lee had been feeling. She looked at Baron in disbelief. "You spoke with Golda Meir last night?"

Baron found Lee's sudden admiration disconcerting. It was never his intention to flaunt his reputation. He spoke hurriedly.

"All right, so I have access to certain people. It's unimportant, Lee."

She placed her hands on her hips in dismay.

"Unimportant, you say! Then Dov wasn't joking when you were being introduced. He said you were a well-known photojournalist."

"Coming from Dov Laslo, that's a compliment. But what's more important is that I must leave for America right after the holiday. Would you come back with me?"

The question caught Lee off guard. She pursed her lips and eyed him with forced amusement.

"Is that a proposal or a proposition?"

"Would you consider it either way?" he tossed back unexpectedly.

Astonished rather than indignant, Lee's pulse quickened. She eyed him obliquely; surely he's playing games.

"Really, Rick. In all seriousness, you don't expect me to answer that."

Baron searched her face briefly and then laughed lightly. "No, of course not. Excuse me. It's just my sordid sense of humor."

With that, they both laughed, forgetting Riv for the moment. She took his hand voluntarily, and leading him past the Zion Gate, turned left into the Jewish Quarter.

With the amount of reconstruction taking place, it was the Old Quarter in name only. Walkways, new condominiums, and small plazas were made of the same pinkish-ochre Jerusalem stone, and it was hard to tell the newly quarried stone from the ancient recycled rubble.

They watched two young Israelis working stripped to the waist, their skins as dark as Arabs'. One glanced up from his task of measuring the level of a wall. He grinned broadly and waved. "*Shalom.* Soon will be ready. Be patient."

Baron and Lee returned the grin and wave, Baron remarking to Lee, "It's nice to see a man happy with his work."

Lee looked up at him. "You are not happy with your work?"

He laughed. "I was merely generalizing. My work has always been satisfying."

They moved on and meandered through twisting passageways until they came upon an old synagogue under restoration. They gazed at it in silence for a few minutes before continuing.

By this time, they caught up with an American tour group that had halted before a huge arch. It was all that remained of an ancient synagogue. The tour group was a mixture of ages, all listening intently to their guide.

The guide was a young man in his early twenties, sporting a large mustache and long hair. He looked almost American in his blue jeans. He removed his dark glasses, to stare at Baron and Lee, who lingered just beyond the edge of his group. Smiling suddenly, he motioned them closer.

Puzzled, Lee complied. Baron guessed that he had been recognized. He said nothing to Lee.

The guide scanned the assembly of a dozen or more, then addressed them.

"Unlike the other synagogue which was desecrated by the Arabs using it to stable their animals, this one was destroyed by them. The reason? For them, it was

133

simple. The dome of this synagogue was too high—to the Arabs sacrilege."

At this point, a portly middle-aged American stepped forward, his dark eyes flashing angrily. "And to destroy a synagogue was not sacrilegious!"

The guide frowned. "You must ask that of an Arab. They have their own values, but I can assure you that it will never happen again."

Somewhat placated, the gentleman stepped back, his face flushed.

Finishing his discourse, the guide excitedly rushed to Baron's side. "You are Rick Baron, no?" He spoke hurriedly without waiting for an acknowledgment, keeping an eye on the group ready to move on. "I have a collection of old *Life* magazines, many with your pictures in Korea. I have also your book, *Faces in Combat*." He threw another quick glance at his group. "I must hurry. Please, you must sign your name for me."

Baron pulled out a felt-tipped pen, signed the travel folder handed to him, and then, after a vigorous handshake and a *"shalom,"* watched the elated guide rejoin his chattering sightseers.

Baron turned and noted Lee's expression of awe. "Please, Lee, don't say anything. You'll only embarrass me."

"But, but," she sputtered, "he's only a young boy, and he knew who you are."

Baron gazed at her with loving eyes. Every so often, she would revert to the exuberant, exciting young Lee of long ago. He lifted her hand to his lips and kissed it. "I love you, Lee."

She reacted by rolling her eyes. "Don't change the subject. And you also wrote a book?"

"Two, as a matter of fact." He shrugged. "Big deal—it's unimportant. Are we going to the Western Wall now?"

She nodded, suddenly becoming silent. There was so much she didn't know, and so little time left to learn. Her own thoughts began to bewilder her as she accepted his arm.

Wherever they went in the old Jewish Quarter, reconstruction was in progress. Of the almost fifty synagogues destroyed or desecrated after the 1948 war, some were being restored while others were being replaced. With determination, the Israelis were creating a new quarter with new apartments and a new way of life—one which would not tolerate the poverty, oppression, and degradation forced upon them for nineteen years. The new genesis in the old quarter was the culmination of the Six Day War.

Lee was still clinging to his arm when they reached a widened walkway. A restaurant to their right displayed a sign advertising their *kasha varnishkas*. The outdoor tables were almost filled with customers.

"Care to try it?" Baron asked.

Lee shook her head. "No, I'm not really hungry. But if you wish, I'll share a plate with you."

When Baron laughed, she peered at him inquisitively.

"Sorry, Lee. I couldn't help it. I never cared for *kasha*. I haven't eaten it in years."

She studied him for a moment with an awkward feeling.

"Rick, you really haven't changed that much over the years."

Baron laughed again. "I was thinking the very same of you."

She responded by playfully digging her elbow into his side.

Baron's eyes were teasing. "See, even that habit hasn't disappeared. It makes me wonder what else has stayed with you."

Lee's face flushed. "Rick, you're impossible. We're middle-aged people."

"Baloney! It may be trite to say you're only as old as you feel, but right now I feel twenty again."

Her heart beating faster, she prodded him forward. "Come, there is more for you to see." She bit her lip, annoyed with herself because she was unable to cope with her own feelings. He was right, she admitted disconcertedly. She hadn't felt so young in years.

An awe-inspiring panorama greeted them at the end of the stone walk, which overlooked a sea of people massed in the plaza below. Baron's studious gaze swept past the congregations waiting to pray at the Western Wall, the holiest of all Jewish sites. Throngs of humanity all eager to say a prayer or merely touch the ancient blocks of stone just to let God know of their presence.

A shade of pale orange, the ninety-by-sixty-foot wall displayed only moss and wild grass protruding from

135

timeworn cracks and crevices. There were no intricate or ornate designs for archaeologists to study. None was necessary. For the Jews standing there with their hands caressing the stone in silent prayer, they were in God's presence.

Baron's gaze was riveted to the men in prayer shawls who he could see even from this distance, weeping openly as they prayed at the Wall. The realization followed a moment later that he was viewing the Mecca of all Judaism.

Lee could see his face harden but said nothing, fearful of intruding into his thoughts.

Baron's lips were compressed. "Vespasian, Titus, you bastards! Who's praying at your triumphal arches!" he thought.

A crowd had gathered about them, their chattering bringing him out of his thoughts. A weak smile appeared as he saw Lee's expression. "Quite a sight," he said, almost apologetically. "It's enough to turn you to religion."

Lee's puzzled expression didn't alter. "Shall we go down? For a closer look?"

He held her glance for a second, then nodded and took her arm, heading for the stone staircase which twisted down to the plaza.

Until the Six Day War, the Hakotel Hama'aravi had stood for centuries, towering over a narrow alley no more than twelve feet wide. With the liberation of the "Old City," alterations began almost immediately. Bulldozing the Moors Quarter, the Israelis created an immense plaza, which made the Wall accessible to thousands at a time. A fence formed a courtyard, preventing the populace from storming the Wall en masse. Another fence running to the Wall separated the men from the women to preserve Orthodox ritual.

"Come," Lee said, pulling him through the multitude.

With a curious sense of guilt, Baron allowed her to lead him across the square. Why did it seem like she was pressing him? He said nothing until they got into the line that was waiting for entrance into the courtyard.

"Lee, why are we here?"

She hesitated before answering. "I thought it would do you some good. Sometimes when you're troubled . . ." She left it unfinished.

Baron was getting more uncomfortable by the second.

136

"What purpose would it serve? Lee, I'm not that re-lig . . ." He stopped, reading her expression. Rick wiped a bead of perspiration forming on his brow. "My God, Lee, what do I do when I get there?" Without waiting for a reply, he tried another tack. "Besides, it could take an-other hour of waiting."

The bright blue eyes sparkled. "I'm a very patient woman. I can wait." Baron stared at her. What kind of game was she playing?

"I don't have a hat," he said, still protesting.

She smiled suddenly. "They'll give you a *yarmulke* at the gate. Anything else?"

My God! he thought. She was just like the way he re-membered mother. He was going to *shul* once again, being led like a child. His heart beat faster with the memory.

He spoke, resigned. "Okay, mama. What do you really expect me to do when I reach the Wall?"

When she turned her head, he followed her eyes. They watched a young soldier stuff a piece of paper into a crack in the Wall. The young Israeli, with his rifle slung over a shoulder, caressed the stone with the palm of his hand before walking away.

Lee turned back to Baron. "It's very simple. All you have to do is write a prayer—or a wish, if you prefer—then stuff it between the blocks of stone. I'm sure you can think of something." Her eyes twinkled humorously. "After all, you wrote two books. You shouldn't have any trouble filling a small piece of paper."

Beads of perspiration were forming on Baron's fore-head, but unaccountably, his heart was swelling as he continued to stare at her. It was all he could do to resist taking her in his arms, kissing that delightful face. He saw her flush and turn her head away, sensing that some-how she had read his thoughts. Flustered, Lee reached into her bag.

Before she could find a scrap of paper, she felt a tap at her shoulder. A man behind her spoke softly.

"I'm sorry, madam, but this is not the line for women."

She looked up, glanced from the stranger to Baron, and then addressed the man. "I know. I'm merely accom-panying my—uh—friend to the gate."

To the stranger's bewilderment, Baron burst into laugh-ter. "Man, oh man! Nothing beats a stubborn Italian broad!" He extended a hand to the befuddled Good

Samaritan. "Sorry. Please excuse the laughter. Just a private joke." To Lee, he said, "If you're looking for paper, forget it." He patted a pocket of his jacket. "I always come supplied."

Once inside the courtyard reserved for prayer and worship, he adjusted the skullcap that was given to him. He took a couple of steps and turned to look at Lee. She was standing just a few feet behind the barrier. He saw her lips move.

"Don't ask for anything impossible," reached him in a muffled tone. Holding her gaze for a few seconds, he nodded and then moved toward the Wall.

Nervous as a child attending his first day of school, Baron entertained an odd thought. "I wonder if Mom and Dad know I'm here." He nodded to himself as if satisfied, the thought lending encouragement.

Ten feet away from his goal, he hesitated. From a distance, the stones hadn't appeared so large or so imposing. He stood still, frozen. Finally, reaching into a pocket, he pulled out a small scratch pad and a pen. His fingers trembling, he started to scribble. Men, old and young alike, moved about him unaware of his presence. It didn't lessen his self-consciousness.

He reread the note for the third time, feeling like a fool standing there. Was it guilt, he asked himself? He hadn't been to synagogue in years. Did he have a right to be standing there, asking a favor of God? He remained there, undecided, unable to move, berating himself. The scrap of paper was still unfolded in his hand.

Then a voice reached him, startling him out of his recriminations. It was an old Orthodox Jew, who had been leaning on the Wall, now beckoning to him. The ancient Rabbi was like something out of the past. Dressed entirely in black—the caftan, the suit, and the fur hat despite the warmth of the day—only his face, beard, and prayer shawl projected any color. A prayer book in one hand, he continued to beckon impatiently with the other. Baron went to his side hesitantly.

The Rabbi's eyes glittered with amused tolerance as he took the paper from Baron's hands. Tucking his book under his arm, he folded the small scrap and handed it back. "Put, put," he said in a thin voice, taking Baron's elbow.

Tongue-tied, Baron gaped at the crack in the Wall

created by the erosion of time and added his note to those already there. His little scrap wouldn't be lonely.

The Rabbi straightened his stooped shoulders and peered up at the strange American Jew who appeared so disturbed. He smiled gently. "Do not worry," he said in his thin cracking voice. Although heavily accented, his English was perfect. "No matter the language, He will read them all."

Baron looked at the deeply lined face and finally found his voice. "Thanks . . . thanks, Rabbi. Sometimes the simplest act becomes very difficult." He took the Rabbi's bony hand and shook it briefly, an evanescent sense of elation coming over him.

A rueful expression increased the lines in the old man's face. He released his hand from Baron's and shrugged resignedly. "If a simple act should not be difficult, we would have everlasting peace." Sighing, he gestured that he had to get back to his prayer book.

"Thanks again, Rabbi. And *shalom*," Baron said before moving away.

He went only a few feet when he stopped to look back. The old man licked a thumb to flip the pages of his Bible. Some things never alter with time, Baron thought. That ancient Jew could have been standing there centuries ago. He swept a glance along the Wall, which was now in deep shade. The late afternoon sun had crept behind the Wall, creating a sharply etched line of light and shadow across the center of the courtyard.

He smiled suddenly, an effusive feeling of accomplishment—or relief?—coursing through him. Slightly confused, he shook it off. He was feeling too good. Lee was waiting.

A coquettish smile played on her lips. "May I ask the contents of your note?"

Baron scratched his cheek. "Well," he said haltingly. "I can tell you this much. First, I requested a favor. Then on another matter, I asked for guidance."

"That's all you're going to tell me?"

"For now," he answered quickly, enjoying himself. Reaching for her hand, he said, "So now what? Should we be heading back?"

She nodded, pursing her lips.

"Yes, it will be cool once the sun goes down."

To Lee, the change in Baron was apparent. Reluctant

as a child before he went to the Wall, he had returned with an effulgent spirit. Her brows knit with questioning thoughts. What could he have written that would cause him to be so evasive? Yet as she pondered, she realized he had a right to his privacy. Although disappointed, she decided to say nothing more about it.

They made it halfway through the crowded plaza when Baron halted abruptly. He slid an arm around her waist, a grin on his face. Confused, Lee stared at him.

"Remember, Lee," said Baron. "Whatever happens, don't blame me because it was you who literally backed me to the Wall."

Their laughter erupted spontaneously. Disregarding surreptitious glances from onlookers, he held her tighter.

Oh, it was so good to be alive again—truly alive, she thought, looking up into his face.

Boisterous sounds possessed the Arab bazaar—the gibberish of the merchants like 2,000-year-old echoes pervading the twisting alley. Baron and Lee descended crumbling stone steps, squeezed through a milling mob, then held their noses as they maneuvered by a malodorous abattoir. A fly-covered donkey head hanging on a wall was the object of vociferous bargaining between two Arabs. Across the way, a baker was piling up tiers of pita. Some resembling huge bagels were ringed on a tall wooden peg. In other establishments, tourist junk hung over doorways that unexpectedly led into bedroom workshops.

The scent of exotic spices blending with the aromatic fragrance from Arab hookahs permeated the Street of the Chain. Beneath vaulted ceilings darkening the street, Baron, with his arm protectively around Lee, pushed through the ever growing horde of people. Reaching a corner, they stopped to catch their breath and watch a procession of Armenian priests heading north toward the Via Dolorosa. From another direction, they saw a group of young Hassidic Rabbis turn into the old Jewish Quarter. Baron glanced at the *aba*-garbed merchants and then eyed the weary tourists. The men, some clad in shorts, and the women in their oversized Dior sunglasses suddenly, for no accountable reason, struck him as funny.

It was a never ending sideshow, a carnival, a costume party, everybody and everything in motion. Depending on the direction one looked, only time stood still. Keyed up with a curious excitement, Baron started to laugh.

A moment later, it was stifled by an angry shout from the narrow alley at their right. Baron and Lee peered in anxiously as did others crowding the corner.

An Arab merchant was screaming at a small donkey that had decided to urinate in front of his shop. Despite the man's angry epithets, the obtuse animal continued to empty his bladder near the antique brassware displayed on the ground.

Baron erupted into uncontrollable laughter.

"This is too much, Lee," he said, trying to contain himself. "C'mon, let's get out of here."

Lee's grin was genuine, but controlled. Baron's hand had slipped to her hip, resting there. His hand was warm, and she could feel the pressure as he moved her away from the mob. She said nothing, knowing it would cause her embarrassment if she made him aware of it. She denied the growing titillation of his close presence.

Minutes later on David Street once again, Baron said, "How about going back to the King David with me? We can have dinner on the terrace—just like Paul Newman and Eve-Marie Saint in the movie *Exodus*."

She eyed him cautiously and shook her head. "Rick, it's been a lovely day. Don't spoil it."

He returned her gaze innocently. "I'm only asking you to dinner."

"Are you?"

A soft laugh escaped from Baron. "Still don't trust me?"

"Frankly, no." She eyed him candidly. "You know very well that I'm not dressed for dinner."

Baron hid his disappointment with a forced smile. He nodded amiably, taking her elbow to guide her through the crowd. How could I have been so wrong? he wondered. The matter of her attire is merely an excuse. But why? He had been so certain of the stirrings within her. Her eyes, her breathing. . . .

He held her arm close to him. After walking only a few yards, he said, "Are you sure you won't change your mind?"

Lee pulled her arm from his. "Rick, why do you persist? I thought we came to an agreement in Venice."

"Agreement? What has that got to do with having dinner at the David? The hotel is only minutes from the

Gate. I need another jacket, but there's nothing wrong with your dress. If you have to, you can freshen up in my room."

If it weren't for the jostling mob, Lee might have made a scene. Controlling her temper, she peered at him out of the corner of an eye. Was Rick too casual, too innocent, or was she being overcautious? She doubted very much that Rick was too innocent. She eyed him cynically.

"Rick, you're behaving childishly."

He returned her look, unsmiling. "Am I?"

She shook her head. "This is nonsense. I'm sure you don't expect me . . ."

"Why not?" he interrupted. When she didn't reply, he said hastily, "What are you afraid of, Lee? Me? Or yourself?"

She turned away, pondering. *Was* she afraid of herself? She who had always remained faithful to Enzo and to his memory? Her heart beat like a trip hammer.

"Lee, I have no wish to embarrass you," she heard him saying. "I'll wait in the lounge while you use my room."

She rolled her eyes, grateful that he couldn't see her face. "I don't know, Rick. . . ." he said, turning to face him. "I'm not the impetu—"

Lee stopped speaking; Baron was no longer listening to her. His eyes were on two men who had entered David Street from Murisan Road. "What is it?" she asked, bewildered.

Baron put his memory to work. The large, stocky man —where did he know him from? It always bothered him when he couldn't place a familiar face.

Then he snapped his fingers. The Alemagne on the Autostrada outside of Florence. "Ari Stefan," he said aloud.

The two men turned at the sound of Baron's voice. No more than ten feet away, the larger of the two stared at Baron quizzically. A moment later, his face lit up in a wide grin. He came forward eagerly, his hand outstretched.

"Mr. Baron, the American journalist with the tobacco," he said, obviously pleased with the unexpected meeeting.

Introductions followed. Stefan's companion was a major in the Israeli army. Both men wore tan, short-sleeved shirts, open at the neck, but devoid of insignias.

142

"And what is your rank, Ari?" asked Baron unexpectedly.

Stefan smiled. "Ever the astute journalist," he remarked in good humor. *"Colonel* Ari Stefan—which only proves how desperate our little country has become."

Baron returned the smile. "You are much too modest. You don't become a colonel without the capability."

"Speaking of modesty," the major interjected. "You're quite famous in your own right. We know you had a private audience with the Prime Minister yesterday evening. You must be quite privileged."

Grateful for the intervention, Lee allowed the men to do all the speaking, but as she watched Baron, a vague sense of elation flowed through her. She remained silent, unable to define her own feelings.

Listening to the clipped British accent of the major, Baron wondered just how privileged he was. He was grasping for straws, he realized, but . . .

"Colonel, Major, I wonder whether either of you could grant me a favor." He noted their questioning looks and quickly added, "A much needed favor."

"If it's possible," Stefan said simply.

"I need to interview Mrs. Moscati's son who is on reserve duty at the present time."

"So," Stefan shrugged, smiling, "that should be no problem."

"He's on the Bar-Lev Line," Baron added softly.

Stefan's smile faded. He pursed his lips and looked at the major. The major's hazel eyes scanned Baron for a few seconds before turning to Stefan. He didn't speak to the colonel, but his eyes implied "impossible."

Stefan turned a kindly eye to Baron. "You know, of course, that's a military zone and off limits to civilians."

Baron pulled out what he hoped was his ace. "Ari, do you have any idea how much of an inducement it would be for Americans to purchase Israeli bonds if they could see an Israeli soldier guarding the front line on Yom Kippur?"

Stefan hesitated, then said, "You spoke with the Prime Minister. You did not ask her?"

Baron sighed. "The Prime Minister said she doesn't interfere with the military. I didn't think it politic to press her further."

Stefan scratched his cheek, then rubbed his chin. "I'll

see what can be done, Baron, but I can promise you nothing." He smiled suddenly. Before Baron could offer his thanks, Stephan glanced at his watch. "Where will you be at ten o'clock this evening?"

Baron looked at Lee and then said, "The King David. I'll be there all evening, waiting for your answer."

"I'll call you, Baron, but you must understand, I can promise you nothing."

Baron nodded. A victory of sorts, he thought.

Stefan grinned, and they shook hands all around. "Until ten o'clock then," he said.

"It's very important, Ari. I'll be waiting."

Stefan regarded Baron, then Lee. "Yes, I can see that." He glanced at his watch again. "Well, I'll do my best."

Baron turned to Lee and saw her blue eyes, lustrous and shining, gazing at him curiously. "Well," he said, "do we go back to the King David or . . ."

"Do I go alone to your room?"

He smiled and gave a helpless shrug. "If that's what you want."

She hesitated only a second, then nodded without speaking.

Two doors, inches apart, opened into Rick Baron's room. With daylight fading, the room was in semi-darkness. Lee reached for the wall switch. The artificial light dispelled the shadows. She turned and removed the key from the outer door. She closed the door behind her and, without thinking, dropped the key into her bag.

She stood there for a few moments, hardly breathing, looking about the room—his room. A red print wallpaper that somewhat matched the predominantly red Turkish carpeting covered three walls. Two chairs, a round coffee table, and a bureau comprised the furnishings. And a bed.

Lee stared at the double bed. It seemed to be mocking her with its dominance of the room. Out of curiosity—or escape—she walked to the window and peered through the metal slats of the blind. The Christ Tower across the street stretched over the domes of the YMCA building.

"My room is in the old section of the hotel," she recalled Baron saying. "The Greens are in the new wing."

She spun around, half-expecting him to be there. Self-doubts crept in as she viewed the empty room. Why have I come to his room? she asked herself. Am I *hoping* he'll walk in? She brought a finger to her lip and bit the nail nervously. Realizing that her hand was trembling, she grew annoyed. Tossing her head defiantly, she sought the bathroom.

In all her life, she had shared her bed with only two men. With one it was an ecstatic two months; the other, twenty years of a satisfying marriage. Since Enzo's death, she had never felt the desire or the need to share it again. Even for Dov Laslo, she felt no desire. It was much simpler to accept him as a vicarious brother.

She bit her lip as she walked past the bed, reproaching herself for indulging in peculiar fantasies. "Foolish old woman," she murmured.

In an alcove beyond the front door, a huge armoire faced the bathroom door. Uncomfortable, Lee pushed the door and switched on the light. Moving to the sink, she looked at her image in the mirror.

For a brief moment, a stubborn conscience refused to acknowledge the truth facing her. It's yourself you're afraid of, not Rick. Her eyes moist, she could barely focus on the strange woman filled with desire. A feeling of weakness settling upon her, she leaned on the sink for support. Tormenting thoughts rambled through her mind. Why now? Why did he return to upset my life? What would I gain by accepting his advances? He had no intention of marr . . .

She straightened abruptly, the irrational thought bringing her back to some semblance of reality. She twisted the tap and quickly splashed water on her face.

Downstairs, Baron sat in a soft chair in a corner of the lounge, tapping his fingers nervously on the arm. Growing impatient, he glanced at his watch again. Twenty minutes had passed since Lee left for his room. Having already reserved a table in the smaller dining room—bowing to her desire for a less formal atmosphere—there was nothing for him to do but wait and think.

He didn't dwell on his image of Lee in her youth. He was no longer concerned with the past. It was Lee in the present, desirable and. . . . He thought of the week in Venice and then this very afternoon. He had been so sure of her. She had seemed so responsive, up to a point. He smiled ruefully. A tinge of guilt followed his ruminations, a sense of shame overtaking him. To think of Lee in such terms—the mother of Riv. He frowned suddenly. When had he last passed judgment on his morals?

He got up from his chair, unable to sit any longer, a discordant thought entering his mind. Had she walked out on him? Was it possible that he had pressured her to that point? He shook his head. The new Lee was a woman of complex emotions, but it was highly unlikely that she would leave before knowing Colonel Stefan's reply.

He walked into the lobby toward the elevator, debating whether he should go up and check. He glimpsed at the time on a wall clock—almost a half-hour now. Could something have happened? His pulse quickened. Could she be waiting for him? He played with the thought, realizing there wasn't sufficient reason for him to suspect. She had given no indication. Pondering the situation, his impatience took command.

He glanced at the staircase beyond the elevator. His room was only on the second floor. He turned back to get another room key.

Lee, totally composed once again, picked up her bag from the chair and started for the door. With her hand on the knob, she froze. She could hear a key turning in the lock from outside. She stepped back, clutching her bag for moral support.

Lee, although relieved that it was Baron and not a housemaid, was also aware of his appraising look.

"You were supposed to wait for me downstairs. Remember?"

Baron found it difficult to keep from gaping at her. She was wearing the barest touch of lipstick, her hair was brushed back. He found his voice finally, mustering hoarsely, "Lee, I was getting worried."

She gave him a knowing smile. "I'll just bet you were."

Saying that, she avoided his eyes and stepped past him into the corridor. Baron reached for her elbow, but she moved away from contact.

"You don't really want to leave, do you, Lee?" Baron persisted.

In the corridor, totally in command of herself, she eyed him coyly. "You did promise me dinner." She smiled, then walked away before he could summon a reply.

He closed the door behind him, muttering, "Damn!

What a stubborn woman!" He moved into the room and glanced at the bed. "Christ!" he said aloud. I must be slipping, trying to read my own cravings in another's face! A heavy sigh escaped, but it didn't alleviate his desire for her.

He headed for the bureau to get a fresh shirt. "Get dressed," he said churlishly, "before your thoughts alone require asking for atonement on Yom Kippur." The churning in his stomach refused to let up, no matter what argument he gave himself. Damn! How he wanted her! The women in his life had been mere means to assuage his physical needs. It had been different with Lee; remorse never followed passion.

He leaned on the bureau as if a great weight was on his shoulders. Young Lee, middle-aged Lee, it made no difference. He was in love with her. Grimacing, he bowed his head.

It is curious that no one can stand at a bathroom sink without examining oneself in the mirror. Although disgruntled, Baron was no exception. He blinked at his mirror image. It was a face wearing the mask of an animal in heat. This was a new experience, seeing himself as a lustful being. An involuntary laugh erupted. Christ! Like a hot teen-ager!

He grabbed for the bar of soap and, grimacing, wondered whether Lee had ever seen him in this light.

"Enough!" he muttered, splashing water upon his face. Lee was waiting for him.

Joe and Mindy Green strolled through the lobby of the King David Hotel, footsore and weary after a full day of sightseeing. Mindy eyed the cigar stuck in Joe's mouth.

"Joe, I hope you intend to finish that before we go back to our room."

He smiled coyly. "I'll stop smoking cigars the day you cut out cigarettes." He continued to smile, knowing that he'd ended the discussion. "Let's get a cup of coffee in the cafe."

"Mother of God!" Mindy exclaimed. "You're not going to eat again after the dinner we just had?"

"Just coffee, just coffee—so I can finish the cigar."

Just inside the cafe on the first floor, Mindy halted, spying the familiar couple seated at the far end beside a

147

window. "Oh, oh!" she said to Joe. "Do you see what I see? Like lovers tucked away in a corner."

Joe shook his head in reproach. "Stop romanticizing. You should know Rick by now. He always picks a spot where he can observe rather than be observed. C'mon. It's a table for four. Let's join them."

She held back. "I feel like we're interrupting."

Joe's lifted his eyebrows. "Interrupting? Since when did that stop you?" He took her elbow.

Baron chewed on a morsel of his cheese omelet thoughtfully, staring at Lee who was watching him intently. "Lee, if you keep looking at me like that, I'll have to insist we go back upstairs."

She looked askance, smiling nevertheless. "Do you always forget a promise so easily?"

He grinned. Ignoring her question, he asked, "You wouldn't consider coming back to America with me? We could have some great times."

She smiled indulgently. "You've mentioned that idea before. I hope you're not expecting me to take you seriously."

His smile faded. What the hell was he thinking of?

"No, of course not. But it's a thought to ponder."

She laughed softly. "Rick, I thank you for a wonderful day and for reminding me that I'm a woman, but . . ." A blush appeared in her cheeks. This was a confession new to her.

Lee lowered her eyes. It was a peculiar situation. Neither had openly declared a love—yet. They were dwelling in the past, mixing it with the present, and with no destination. In Rome, as a young girl, she never considered the final outcome. The stolen minutes of efficacious indulgence had been shared in sheer enjoyment. Their present circumstances didn't warrant a replay of the follies of their youth. Nonetheless, recognizing her vulnerability, Lee realized that if Rick had returned to his room earlier, he could have taken her to bed without the slightest protest. For his late arrival, she was at least grateful. Thinking of Enzo, feelings of guilt returned. In her own mind, she tried rationalizing her behavior for the benefit of her late husband. "Enzo, you know what he had meant to me," she thought. "Surely you can understand. It isn't as if I am offering myself to him. Never in our marriage have I . . ."

From the corner of her eye, she saw Joe and Mindy Green approaching.

"What is this? A late breakfast?" Joe asked, glancing at the half-finished omelets. Noticing the potato *latkes* with sour cream, he leaned over and grabbed one with his hand. "Sorry, Rick, can't resist."

Mindy, after seating herself, addressed Lee. "Would you believe we just had a big dinner?"

Lee's early trepidations and self-consciousness diminished with Mindy's ingenuous friendliness. "Where did you eat?" she inquired, smiling warmly.

"The Shemesh Restaurant," Joe interjected. "You know it, Lee?" He rolled his eyes. "The baked lamb—just terrific! You've got to try it, Rick."

When Baron merely nodded, Mindy looked at him searchingly. "How come you two didn't go out for a real dinner?"

Baron lifted his head, but Lee, feeling it exigent to explain, interceded. "Mindy, it was at my suggestion that we came back to the hotel. We had just come from the Old Quarter, and I didn't think it necessary to go home, then go out again. Besides, they make a delicious omelet here."

Mindy observed her candidly. "You really live dangerously, Lee. I should have warned you that Rick can seduce an orange into an apple tree."

"Your broad is at it again, Joe!" retorted Baron, mildly exasperated.

Joe twisted in his chair, seeking their waiter. The cafe was filling fast with late noshers, and it took him a few seconds to grab the waiter's attention. He finally nodded understandingly at Joe's gesture of pouring coffee.

Grinning, Joe faced Baron. "Yeah, so she is. Isn't she always? Just because we're in Israel, did you think she was going to get religion?"

Mindy raised her head, her eyes glistening with excitement. "Talking about religion, Rick, we were at the Masada this afternoon. I've never experienced anything like it."

Baron smiled for the first time since their arrival.

"You walked up to the top?" he asked Joe.

"Are you kidding?" Mindy interjected. "It was the cable car for us old folks. We did walk down, though." Remembering, she added, "We had to. I was too embarrassed because of your junior partner. You'll never believe what he pulled off. When we reached the top, he gets up on a wall overlooking this vast valley. Then what does he do! He stands there shouting like an idiot, 'Flavius Silva, you'll never get me!' Needless to say, I could have brained him."

Lee was delighted, her eyes glassy with memories. "You're the same Verdi—the very same. The years have not changed you."

By this time, they were all grinning. "Like hell they haven't, Lee. I thought that hike down would kill me."

"You can say that again, Bubi!" Mindy interjected. "I have no more illusions. I don't know about you boys, but my gung-ho days are over."

Before anyone could respond, the waiter came with extra cups and a carafe of coffee.

Joe took a sip of the hot coffee, then addressed Baron. "I'm going to need help tomorrow, Rick. We've got two cabinet ministers, and I'd rather have you handling the questioning."

Baron glanced briefly at Lee, and nodded. He hadn't been much help to Joe on their present assignment. "Of course, Joe. And thanks for everything."

Lee judiciously understood their meaning. She spoke quickly. "Yes, this will give me an opportunity to do some necessary shopping. I want all of you to come for dinner on Yom Kippur Eve. And, of course, that includes Paul."

"We would be delighted," Mindy said, "but you must let me go shopping with you. I've never been in an Israeli supermarket."

"By the way," Baron said, glancing at his watch. "Where is Paul tonight?"

Joe laughed. "He picked up a pizza and took it back to Tovah and Debbi." He laughed again. "A kosher pizza, no less." Although they all laughed, he was aware that Baron was checking his watch again.

"You expecting someone, Rick?"

"What time have you got?" Baron asked.

Joe glanced at his own watch. "Ten of ten. Why?" Something was in the works. He could read the signs.

"I'm expecting an important call, Joe. Keep your fingers crossed. It could turn out to be the most important assignment of my life."

150

In the silence that followed, Joe refilled all their cups. It didn't take a great deal of intelligence to guess what Rick's "assignment" was.

Joe shifted uneasily in his seat, thinking of the disappointment to come. He had tried to make the connection himself, but had failed utterly in the attempt. There was no way Rick could be successful. It was a forlorn endeavor.

Joe broke the silence. "Rick, what makes you think you have a chance?"

Baron mulled over a reply and then said, "I've asked a favor of a higher-up."

A higher-up? Joe thought. Not even the Prime Minister could do anything for him. He said nothing but looked to Lee, who had paled visibly.

Lee's pulse had picked up a few beats. Higher-up! She understood immediately. This was the favor Rich had placed within the ageless cracks in the wall.

Mindy took her hand unexpectedly. "Are you all right, Lee? You don't look well."

"Yes, of course," she answered, her voice quivering. "I'm sorry if I seem upset, but . . ."

The waiter reappeared. "Mr. Baron, the phone call you were expecting—you can take it in the lounge."

Baron shoved back his chair, looked at Lee biting her lip and winked at her.

In the lounge, Baron picked up the phone.

"Ari? Yes, this is Rick Baron." He paused. "Yes, go ahead. I'll listen."

He listened for five full minutes without speaking, then, "I agree to everything." His face contorted with emotion. "And, Ari? Thanks."

After hanging up, he stood there a few seconds, rubbing his face in an attempt to restrain his feelings.

Lee was the first to see him return. She held a nervous hand to her cheek. There was no ready answer in his face, except, perhaps, in his compressed lips. What did they imply? Would he be able to see Riv? As quickly as the question entered her head, she realized that more than anything in the world she wanted them to meet. For Rick to discover what a wonderful son he had, it would not only be an emotional triumph for him, but also for her. Paradoxically, the good feeling matched her overwhelming anxiety as he took his seat.

All eyes were on Baron, who was accepting their stares with an impassive face. Knowing full well that in another second they would erupt, he eased into a grin. He made a circle with the thumb and forefinger of his right hand. In truth, his action masked his inability to speak.

Joe's reaction was immediate and uninhibited enthusiasm.

"Son of a bitch!" he exploded. "You did it! You really pulled it off!" Oblivious of the shocked stares directed their way from nearby tables, Joe continued. "Holy Christ, Rick! Out with it! How did you work it?"

"Joe, you idiot!" Mindy blubbered. "Give me a handkerchief." She glanced at Lee. "And, Rick, you better find one for Lee."

Baron looked hard at Lee, seeking answers for his unasked questions. There were tears in Lee's eyes, but her smile came through. An overwhelming desire to reach across the table and wipe away the tears had to be fought back. But the answer he sought was there in her loving eyes. She was happy for him. She wanted him to meet their son. He knew there were no longer any doubts in her mind.

Joe's manner sharply contrasted with the others. He addressed Baron impatiently. "All right, Rick. How did you manage to pull this off?"

Baron first cleared his throat, then spoke huskily.

"The higher-up has granted my favor." He noted Lee's understanding smile, but continued speaking to Joe. "But with certain restrictions from others."

Joe peered at him, the gut feeling returning. "Can we talk?" he said softly.

Baron gave a shrug. "Why not?"

Joe deliberately put his hands in his lap, realizing that he was beginning to tap his fingers on the table. He knew damn well that Rick was putting on an act for the benefit of the women. "All right," he said flatly. "Let's hear the catch."

Baron leaned on his elbows.

"I'm to be picked up before eight on Yom Kippur morning. A jeep and driver will be waiting for me on Jaffa Road, where I'll be searched. I will be allowed only a recorder and four cassettes. That's it, Joe. No cameras and no one else. At our destination, I get two hours to do whatever I have to do. Then it's back to Jaffa Road, and they take the recorder and tapes. After the censor gets through with them, they'll be returned. The extra cassettes are in case there's a bad one." He made a helpless gesture. "That's it."

Joe nodded. There was a feeling in the pit of his stomach, and it had nothing to do with his meal. What's more, he was certain that Rick was experiencing the same sensation. No cameras he could understand, but why shove him out after only two hours? He turned to the women, forcing a smile. "Well, do we celebrate or something?"

"Why not?" Mindy said, blowing her nose. "We've already knocked off a bottle of wine at dinner, but what the heck—this occasion calls for something special."

"What about the hotel bar right here?" Baron suggested. "They must have champagne."

Joe got to his feet, a grin spreading across his face. "Good idea. It'll be a lot easier getting Min to our room afterward."

Mindy rolled her eyes. "Just enjoy yourself now, Joe, because when we get home, you're going on a diet."

The good-natured exchange wasn't lost to Lee. Moving from the table, she said to Baron, "You've been very fortunate to have such fine friends."

"Yes. Until now, they've been my only family."

She said nothing then, but going through the lobby, her arm linked in his, she looked at him. "Your favor was granted. But the other, the guidance you asked for . . ."

He returned her look, then kissed her on the cheek. "We'll see . . . we'll see."

CHAPTER 8

October 5, 1973

Baron leaned on the stone railing of the second-story balcony, looking out upon the street, seemingly studying the new pink, white, and ecru apartment houses springing up about the neighborhood. The quiet street was almost empty, most of its inhabitants involved in the preparation or enjoyment of their final meal before the feast. The *yeshivahs* and synagogues in the area would soon be filled.

Baron fixed his gaze upon the Imca Tower, the one recognizable landmark far to the south. As his mind was preoccupied with troubled thoughts, it proved to be an abstract study. He closed his eyes to rub them, as if that action would dissipate the tension building up within him. Everything was happening at once—Lee, Riv, and trouble in Israel. He was sure of it. The murmuring and the bickering among the members of the Knesset always stopped whenever he approached them. He thought of the people inside getting ready for the holiday meal, his apprehensions growing. For the first time in years, he was more concerned about others than himself. And to heighten his worries, little three-year-old Uri Moscati ran to him with outstretched arms, calling "Papa." He had picked him up and hugged him, feeling the little arms clinging to his neck. Debbi had laughed. "He has no grandpa," she said. "I think he's decided to adopt you."

155

Baron had nodded, thinking to himself. Perhaps there's a sixth sense within this little body.

"A penny for your thoughts, lover boy."

Baron spun around sharply to confront Mindy.

"Perhaps I should make it a dollar," she said, regarding Baron studiously. He cocked his head, his eyes daring her to get too smart. "Getting edgy about meeting Riv?" she asked simply.

"What do you think?"

A smile brightened her face. "Since you ask, I'll tell you. I think you're missing the boat if you let this ready-made family get away from you."

Baron took a deep breath, then exhaled slowly, "It's entered my mind, but you know, old dog and new tricks. . . ."

"Rick, is there any chance at all of you and Lee . . ."

Baron interrupted tersely. "Min, don't pry! Not this time."

Her green eyes glinted. "This time you're mistaken! I have good reason to pry."

He turned away from her. There were times when Mindy was just impossible.

"Rick, you know Joe and I both love you, but if you hurt that woman in any way . . ."

Baron shook his head, a weak smile appearing. "I have no intentions of hurting Lee. You should know better than that."

"Do I?" Refusing to be put off, she continued, "Then why don't you answer my question?"

He gestured helplessly. "How can I when there is no answer." Seeing the dejected look on her face, he laughed unaccountably. He took her cheeks in his hands and kissed her loudly. "Mindy, I love you, but you're simply too much."

Joe stood in the doorway of the small terrace. "Please, Rick, don't tire her out. The evening's still young."

Baron stepped toward him. "She's all yours, Joe. Take her—please!"

At Baron's departure, Joe turned to Mindy.

"You know, Rick's always been right."

"About what?" she asked.

"You ARE a nosy broad!"

To accommodate the eight adults and two children the

console table had to be opened and extended; it took up most of the living room in the small apartment. Two arm chairs, one at each end, were reserved for Laslo and Baron. "Privilege of the elders," Laslo remarked to Baron.

The table was elegantly set with candlesticks, linen, and a lace tablecloth. A serving of gefilte fish awaited each diner. Mindy, wide-eyed, examined the lace cloth.

"Lee, this is exquisite. Where on earth did you get it?"

A flush appeared in Lee's cheeks. She glanced at Baron covertly. "Burano. Rick insisted that I accept it as a gift. I can assure you I would never have purchased anything so expensive. He bought it before I could stop him."

"Well, I'll tell you," Mindy exclaimed, "he wouldn't have to break my arm to accept it."

"That's good," Baron interjected, "because I got a similar one for you."

Mindy's back straightened. "Rick, you dog! You never said a word."

Baron shrugged. "It was to be a surprise when we got home." He looked toward Lee. "Some people can't keep a secret." A grin followed, softening her embarrassment.

Lee and Tovah were the only ones not seated yet, and when little Uri and Aryeh Moscati started to eat, Tovah cried out, stopping them. "Boys, not yet. First the *yarmulkes*." She handed them out one by one until she came to Paul. Placing it on top of his head, she pressed it into his scalp and said, "That goes for you, too." He grinned sheepishly.

Baron's glance to Joe was returned with an understanding nod. A definite love-pat if they ever saw one.

Lee, busy checking the table, wasn't aware of the action. Celery, lettuce, tomatoes, olives. She pinched her cheek. Horseradish! She had forgotten the horseradish. She asked Tovah to bring it from the kitchen, and then addressed Laslo.

"Dov, the *motzie?* The blessing for the bread."

"I would be honored," he said, getting to his feet.

"Blessed art thou, O Eternal! Our God, King of the universe, who bringest forth bread from the earth."

All chorused "Amen" as he cut into the *challah*.

Lee and Debbi, seated with the two boys between

157

them, cut the fish for the young eager mouths. Lee, accepting a slice of bread, unaccountably found her thoughts drifting to Riv and Baron.

Riv was the only common ground with Rick, she was trying to convince herself. Her emotional instability at Rick's hotel had been provoked by the intimacy of his room. A similar situation would not again occur; she would not allow it. And yet, vividly recalling her craving, she felt no revulsion, but rather, paradoxically, both relief and disappointment. Inexorably, she had to ask herself, Am I that vulnerable? She couldn't deny the pleasures that enveloped her when they were together, but as for his "proposal" . . . Proposal! Ridiculous! It was a proposition! He could not, even in his wildest dreams, ever expect her to consider seriously such an insane idea! It was nostalgic daydreaming. She was not the Lee he had known. Just as she had made a new life for herself, so had he for himself. Rick was not about to alter his lifestyle for her. He would forever be chasing around the world. And how could she leave Israel and her family? No, she reasoned, indulging herself, it is too much to give up at this late stage in life. In another four days, he would be gone, and it would be merely another short episode in their lives.

With Baron's help, a huge tureen of soup was brought to the table. The women ladled it out, Tovah personally attending to Paul.

"Holy cow!" he exclaimed, examining the minestrone soup rich with vegetables. Tovah cocked her head toward her mother.

"You can take the girl from Italy, but you can't take the Italian from the girl." An instant later, she pinched his cheek. "Eat hearty, my American friend, for tomorrow we go to the Heights." Smiling, she took her seat beside him, apparently enjoying her own cryptic humor.

Paul shook his head, his eyes narrowed, giving her a sidelong glance that said, Wanna bet? Befuddled, he scratched at his beard. He simply couldn't make her out. How am I supposed to handle this twenty-one-year-old Sabra virgin? he wondered. She's been giving me nothing but the hots, and I don't dare touch her. He winced inwardly. Touch her! That's as far as she ever allowed him to go. "No one but my husband will ever get more," she had stated flatly, although without further recriminations. The room was warm and the soup was hot, but he knew there were other reasons for the beads of perspiration forming on his brow. Man, what a way to get your kicks! he thought somberly, wiping his forehead. This Tovah—she was something else! Grudgingly, he was forced to admit that he was at a loss as to how to cope with her. He'd have to talk to Rick about her. Rick had to be the world's greatest authority on women, and besides, he knew he could discuss it with him.

He felt a sudden pinch on his thigh and knew she would be smiling at his discomfort. He took a deep breath and shook his head once again. She simply was too much!

Tovah sipped the hot soup. I really like him a lot, she thought, but why should he expect further privileges from me? He would be leaving soon and what would I have? A memory of my first lover? Such involvements she didn't need. It was not to be "like mother, like daughter." And unlike her mother—who had been so young and innocent at the time—she realized that she was skirting the edge of a precipice from which, if she slipped, there would be no climbing back. Once that thin veneer of personal privacy was destroyed, self-respect would be lost. She sighed wistfully, debating with her own reasoning, knowing how close she had come to being conquered, and wondering how far he would have gone if she let him.

She lifted her eyes from her plate and caught Paul studying her. "Isn't it delicious?" she whispered, nodding toward his plate.

Smiling, he looked her straight in the eyes, and said, "Yes, it has all the perfect ingredients to be enjoyed."

She felt her face crimsoning. Looking away, she suddenly discovered that she really did like him!

Baron, watching with some amusement, kept silent, determined to speak to Paul at the first opportunity.

Finishing the minestrone, Tovah decided that an explanation of the menu was in order. Smiling with pride, she addressed the table.

"In honor of our American friends," she looked from Joe Green to Baron, "and the memories they treasure of Italy, mother decided to deviate from the traditional fare. She—we—were sure that you would enjoy it."

Baron's eyes narrowed slightly. She's a real cutie! he

thought. This one could hurt a fella. He gave her a smile, but made no comment. While the others displayed delighted interest, Baron withdrew. He lifted a glass of white wine and sipped it thoughtfully.

Soon, platters of *braciola de madera* were brought to the table with a variety of vegetables. With her mother and Debbi in the kitchen, Tovah waited expectantly for Mindy's response, which she was certain would be forthcoming with her first taste. She smiled triumphantly a moment later; Mindy's face displayed pure ecstasy.

"Hmm! Joe, did you ever taste anything like this?"

He looked at her, grinning. "Not in our kitchen, I haven't."

In another world, Baron was toying with his dish. Breaching his thoughts, a seemingly disembodied voice reached him. Startled, he looked for the source—It was Debbi.

"Rick Baron, you are not eating?"

He stared at her. She had pronounced his name "Reek." Somewhere in his head, a bell was ringing. Lee used to say it that way years ago. His hand trembled slightly, forcing him to release his fork. The truth was coming back to him. He looked up at Debbi. "Yes . . . of course. You just reminded me of something that I should have remembered."

Joe shot him a questioning look.

"Remember Enrico Barnes?" Rick said slowly.

All eyes looked up at Baron's ponderous tone. Puzzled, Joe scratched his nose. "Rico . . . Rico . . ." he repeated to himself. Snapping his fingers, he suddenly lit up with recognition. "You mean *Reeeco* Barnes?" He stretched out the first name as Lee would have done it then. "My God!" he muttered to himself. He held a hand to his forehead and gaped at Lee.

A pale Lee watched him. She turned to Baron. "This Rico Barnes . . . he was killed in Firenze when you were there?"

Baron nodded. No explanations were necessary. There was no longer any need for recrimination or blind guessing. He lifted his wineglass and waved it to Joe who followed suit. "Here's to Rico—wherever he is."

Mindy jammed her elbow into Joe's side. "Will you please tell me what's going on?"

Joe gave her a hard look. "Later," he replied tersely.

Dov Laslo, having observed each one with a studious eye, finally entered the conversation. "This," he addressed Joe, "I gather, is not one of your treasured memories."

"You can say that again," Joe remarked dryly without further explanation.

Dov Laslo nodded affably, trying to stem the sinking feeling that he had lost yet another battle in his life. Outwardly impassive, he turned back to his plate.

Always an introvert, his few friends had learned to accept him for what he appeared to be—a sensitive man with deep convictions. Even he recognized the change in his personality that had taken place over the past two decades. Officially, if one could readily define it in those terms, it had begun with the abandonment of his terminally ill wife in Hungary during the '56 uprising. "Go!" she had demanded. "God is showing you the way out. Accept it without guilt!"

Enzo Moscati, whose previous partisan training had consisted of sifting through Nazi lines to steal food and supplies, had been instrumental in Laslo's escape through the "freedom fence" to Austria and eventually to Israel where his dispirited soul found solace in its attachment to the Moscati family. There he was also able to work without fear of dire consequences, a freedom he had not known since his early twenties. Although his writings brought him world-wide attention he disdainfully shunned publicity. Even the unconscious gesture of hiding behind sunglasses had become mechanical. In due time, with a nagging sense of owing something to Israel for offering him a haven, he agreed to conduct an occasional seminar at the university.

After Enzo Moscati's death in the bombing of a coffee shop during the Six Day War, Laslo waited two years before approaching Eleanora on the subject of marriage. At the time, he believed he was prompted by a sense of duty. It was only after her gentle refusal, however, that he realized he was truly in love with her. The proposals continued over the next few years, as did her refusals. Maintaining their close friendship, he never questioned her reasons. He continued to be a man of honor, never being any more demonstrative than to give her a kiss on the cheek.

"Dov!" Lee exclaimed ruefully, standing beside his chair. "You're not enjoying my dinner?"

He looked up, startled for a moment. A smile came slowly, softening the cynical lines. "My dear Eleanora, I would enjoy your meal if you served nothing more than plain boiled beef."

I bet you would! Baron reflected solemnly. It was not too difficult to read the look of endearment expressed on Laslo's face. Perhaps, Baron mused with some misgiving, Laslo was the cause of Lee's hesitation, if one could call it hesitation. A dour expression followed his further thoughts. Laslo couldn't be ignored. Perhaps he was better for her. Together, at least, they would know what the future held for them. Already having a family, they would have financial security, peace, and . . .

Baron backtracked, scratching his cheek. Peace? What peace? In Israel? Fighting with himself, he became exceedingly edgy and impatient. He was never one to sit and ponder. As far as he was concerned, events always reached fruition when he was on the move. He rubbed the nervous tic in his eye. If tomorrow would only come, then maybe—just maybe—a lot of problems would be solved. How? he asked himself. How the hell do I know? he answered.

At that moment, disrupting Baron's discomforting ruminations, Uri and Aryeh Moscati started to argue over a single apple that topped a water-filled bowl of fresh fruit.

Baron reached for the apple, cut it in half, and gave each boy a section. "What kind of world would this be," he offered, "if one person wanted it all? We must learn to share and share alike." Uri accepted his half elatedly, but when the older boy continued to whine, Baron threw up his hands in defeat. "You can take it from here, Debbi. I'm afraid this is out of my department." His resignation was greeted with laughter from all, save Dov Laslo who merely smiled.

Shared? Laslo repeated to himself. The lines in his face deepened. What he suspected was too difficult for him to accept. And yet, what else could they have shared so many years ago that they could be so easily reminded of it? He rubbed his cheek. And what will be the outcome of it a few days from now when this stranger departs? Then it occurred to him that if nothing untoward

162

happened in those few remaining days, then perhaps Eleanora would be more responsive to another one of his proposals of marriage.

No, he decided resignedly, steeling himself against further rejection. Eleanora had never been receptive to his previous proposals. Why should she change her mind now? He had no attributes to entice her, except his reputation as a writer. He smiled dolefully. Save for his writing, he was a born loser. Immersed in his new book, his first novel, he would be safe in his own world where his characters were mere pawns in the hands of fate. Reflecting for a moment, a thin smile appeared. Pawn of Fate? The thin smile endured. An appropriate title for his new book, he thought. Seemingly reconciled, he lifted a hot cup of tea to his lips.

Baron lit his pipe and settled into an easy chair. The women had cleared the table, leaving only the fruit and a pot of coffee. He opened his jacket and locked his hands across his stomach. Sighing, he caught Lee smiling at him. He patted his stomach and said, "Can't do this too often, Lee." A rankling thought crossed his mind. "Will I ever get the chance again?"

"Just one more time, Rick. Tomorrow, when we celebrate your return."

Baron removed the pipe from his lips and stared at her. She was the most beautiful thing he had ever seen. The lamp-light played on her dress, leaving her face in soft shadows. Her hair was pulled back, exposing her cheeks and ear lobes. As she moved, faint lights in her eyes sparkled teasingly.

Deeply moved, Baron spoke sotto voce. "I love you, Lee." Her lips parted in a joyous smile, but she gestured with her hand signifying that he was impossible. He returned her gesture with both hands, his stating, "Can't blame a man for trying."

Lee was rolling her eyes in a parody of desperation when Tovah spoke. "Mother, it will soon be dark. Paul and I are going to the temple now."

Baron glanced toward the opened French doors leading to the terrace. The sky was turning magenta, and the gathering darkness was heralding Yom Kippur.

"Wait," Mindy cried out, "we'll go with you."

Laslo lifted himself from an armchair. "I will also join

163

you. I am not a religious man, but each year at this time, I relinquish myself to God's hands."

As all eyes turned to Baron, Lee spoke hesitantly. "I have Riv's *talleth*, Rick."

Baron shook his head decisively. "No, what have I to atone for?"

"Oh, brother!" Mindy remarked coyly. Baron directed a hard look in her direction, but made no comment.

Baron had never forgotten Chaplain Leveron's refusal to marry them. If the ceremony had been performed then, the misunderstanding in names would have been temporary and meaningless.

"Will you all be coming back after services?" Lee asked the group.

"No," Joe replied. He tossed Baron a glance. "We're not using the car tonight, and it's a long walk to the hotel. And besides, some of us have an early start in the morning."

"Where's Debbi?" Lee inquired of Tovah. "Isn't she going with you?"

"Yes, she's writing a note for . . . Here she is now."

Debbi, holding a small envelope in her hand, approached Baron timidly, her dark eyes imploring. "If you would grant me a small favor . . ." She held out the envelope to Baron. "It's just a little message for Riv. I was hoping . . ."

Baron frowned, knowing she was about to be disappointed. "I'm sorry, Debbi. It's not possible. I'm not permitted to bring anything but a tape recorder." Seeing the pinched look on her small face, he set down his pipe and got to his feet hurriedly. Tilting her chin, he leveled his eyes with her own. "Look," he murmured softly. "They didn't say anything about delivering a verbal message."

She failed to comprehend at first. Then, a rosy flush slowly bloomed on her cheeks.

"Oh, no! It's much too personal!"

Disregarding her protestations, Baron took her hand and led her into the kitchen. "Now!" he said determinedly. "For my ears only."

Bewildered by his definitive action, she deliberated briefly, and then shrugged. Turning his head, she whispered into his ear.

"Tell him that I love him very much and"—Baron could almost feel the palpitations of her heart as she

164

breathed each word—"when he returns, it will be a good time to try for a daughter."

The message engendered a grin from Baron. He spun around and caught her off guard with a quick kiss. "I'll relay it word for word. Cross my heart."

Smiling shyly, Debbi awarded him a peck on the cheek.

When Baron and Debbi reentered the room, they found the group waiting with obvious impatience. He addressed them with mock indifference. "Okay, the merry mailman has returned. You can all leave now." He winked at Mindy. "Say a prayer for me, Min."

"That, I'll do," Joe interjected. "For all of us."

Laslo took Baron's hand. "Give my best to Riv, and I'll see you tomorrow night." Baron nodded silently.

Standing on the terrace, Baron watched the familiar entourage move down the darkening street. Before they were out of sight, he saw Debbi turn and throw him a kiss. Emitting a deep sigh, he waved to his "daughter-in-law."

The street became empty and silent. No cars would be moving until the next sunset.

Although it wasn't in his original plans, he had intended to go to at least the Yiskor service on the next day, but even that had been precluded by fate. The service would be long over before his return from the desert. Being a somewhat reluctant agnostic, he wondered whether God would accept his excuse. Distressed momentarily by an encroaching sense of inadequacy, he shook off the enigmatic sensation as quickly as it appeared. "Enough," he muttered to himself. Turning quickly, he caught Lee in the threshold of the doorway, watching him.

A smile softened his features, and he held out his arms for her. She came to him willingly, kissed him lightly on the lips, and then rested her cheek on his shoulder. Baron held her close, savoring the feel of her, then said, "You can't deny it, Lee, you do feel something for me."

Lee lifted her head and backed away from him. She moved to the balustrade where she gazed beyond the rooftops, noting the last remnants of daylight fleeing Jerusalem. When she answered, her voice was tinged with sadness.

"I know it only too well, Rick, but it's much too late for drastic changes." The look she gave him was one of finality.

"But, Lee, it's obvious . . . we need each other."

She shook her head. "It's not true. We don't need . . . we merely want." She paused, stemming a rising anger, then added, "And that's not reason enough for me to desert my family."

Baron sighed, a vast emptiness consuming him. It took so many years to rediscover this lovely creature—and now to lose her again. He took a deep breath, trying to dismantle this defeat. In a seemingly disembodied voice, he managed to speak. "You grab happiness when you can."

She eyed him unhappily. "At any cost?"

Baron felt his temper rising with his disappointment. "What cost? I'm very well off. You can go back and forth from America to Israel as often as you wish!"

Her eyes flared. "Rick, you're not used to refusal, are you?"

Taken aback, Baron glared at her without speaking.

Lee recognized the hurt, her heart welling up in her throat. But she persisted. "You've seen what a close-knit family we are."

"But you stayed in Venice for five months without this close-knit family!"

"Yes. That's why I sold the shop. So it will never happen again." She hesitated, fearful of breaking down. "Tomorrow you will meet Riv. Perhaps you will understand better then."

Baron couldn't reply. The memory of the years of wondering and longing oppressed him. Was this to be the end of it all? What was the point of another brief episode? Why did it have to happen?

Lee could feel her heart pounding. She wanted to hold him, comfort him—but she didn't dare. She fought the trembling in her lips. "It's cold, Rick. Let's go inside."

He looked at her, failing to comprehend her seeming indifference. "All right," he said, regaining his composure. "I have to leave anyway. I have an early start in the morning."

Neither spoke until they reached the front door of the apartment. Then Lee said, "Rick, promise you'll say nothing to hurt Riv."

His brows knit. "You don't have to ask me that. You know I wouldn't cause you any unhappiness."

She nodded without speaking.

"You won't change your mind?" Baron ventured once more.

"I can't," she said simply.

He let a tender gaze roam over her features. "Whether you fully realize it or not, Lee, I love you." He kissed her quickly and was gone.

Lee waited a full minute after his departure, then allowed her tears to flow.

CHAPTER 9

October 6, 1973—The Day of Atonement

The lobby was deserted except for a couple of porters and a young man behind the front desk. Hearing footsteps, he quickly removed the container of coffee from his lips and hid it beneath the desk. Adjusting his owlish glasses, he peered cautiously at the American correspondent striding across the lobby. He checked the time on the wall clock behind him—6:30 A.M. Only the Orthodox attended services at this hour, but certainly not in that outfit—combat boots, fatigue slacks, and a belted, short-sleeved jacket with a number of zippered pockets, one of which was jammed with what appeared to be a small radio.

Baron turned just before reaching the exit. "A good *Yom Tov*," he said smiling. "Sorry I can't share that cup with you." The clerk, his face crimsoning, prudently remained silent. *"Shalom,"* Baron added and, with a wave of the hand, went through the door into the street.

Once outside, he stopped just long enough to don a pair of sunglasses. He strode north along David Hamelech Street, where the slanting, early morning light failed to warm the shaded areas. Without breaking stride, he crossed into Shlomzion Hamalka which eventually led him to Jaffa Road. Obsessed with distressing thoughts, he didn't give a second glance to the number of foreign embassies he passed along the way. Lee, whose shop he had to pass en route, absorbed all his thoughts at the moment.

Derech Yafo was devoid of cars, buses, tourists, even Arabs. He was alone on the silent thoroughfare, and he felt both lonely and conspicuous. He continued walking, vexed, knowing that nothing short of a miracle would change Lee's attitude. Although she had intimated a love for him, he was only too aware that she had never once said "I love you." It was obvious that she put her feeling for her family above anything she felt for him.

He was a fool, he told himself bitterly. Until his return from the dead, he had been practically nonexistent to her. In all probability, he wouldn't even be a memory, if it weren't for Riv. What right did he have to presume that her true feelings would be anything other than a remembrance of a first love? He shook his head. No, it wasn't true. Her feelings for him were evident; she had admitted as much. What did she expect of him? Marriage? He knit his brows. It was out of the question. He had been single too long. He touched his forehead as if caressing an invisible scar. Why couldn't he accept the fact that in a few days she would be out of his life forever?

A grim expression reflected his turmoil. Would she expect him to stay in Israel? He shook his head imperceptibly, arguing. What would he do there? Retire? Just to be with her? Sadness replaced the hard lines in his face. No —she hadn't even asked that of him and probably never would. He took a deep breath. It was finished. He could do nothing, it was out of his hands. To believe otherwise would be to perpetuate an illusion. He had to be satisfied that he was going to meet a son he had never known. That, at least, was no illusion.

As if reminded, he cast aside all burdening thoughts with some resolve. Cutting across the street he walked faster toward his destination, Herut Square.

Sergeant Michael Radaver yawned and idly scratched at his tousled hair. He was twenty minutes early. If the American was on time, he had time to relax. Leaning back, he stretched his long legs, wondering why the strict briefing. If something was up, why bring him out there at all? Two hours they said, no more. They had to be out by 2:30. He yawned once again and scratched the stubble on his chin, lazily dreaming of last night's dinner cooked by his new bride, Rachel, and their lovemaking afterward.

Footsteps, echoing in the otherwise deserted street, rudely brought him to attention. Straightening, he jumped from the jeep and waited for the American correspondent. Must be in good shape, he thought, smiling. Moves pretty well for a middle-aged guy. He continued smiling. It would be good to hear the latest news from home, he thought.

Baron saw the tall young man leap from the vehicle. The jeep was parked and waiting just off Herut Square on Hanevi'im, facing east.

"I'm Rick Baron," he stated, holding out his hand. "Waiting long?"

"No, sir. I was a bit early. A habit of mine." He accepted Baron's hand with a strong grip. "I'm Sergeant Michael Radaver. If you're ready, hop in and we'll be on our way."

Baron's face displayed surprise. "You're American!"

"Yes, sir. But we better get moving. We're on a time schedule."

"Right," Baron said, climbing into the front seat. "Okay if I call you Mike? We don't need formalities."

"May as well—everyone else does."

As the jeep swung east on Hanevi'im, Baron asked, "Aren't you supposed to check me out, Mike?"

"Yes, sir, but not until we get out of the city limits. It could be too conspicuous here."

Baron nodded. "All right, but forget the 'sir.' It's just plain 'Rick,' just another American. And one who's dying for a cup of coffee."

Radaver eyed him, smiling. "If you can wait, I've got a thermos bottle under the seat."

"Terrific!" Baron exclaimed, studying him for a brief moment. About Riv's age, he surmised. Would Riv be as dark? he wondered.

"Tell me something, if you don't mind a prying reporter, what made an American boy become an Israeli?"

Radaver was adjusting his sunglasses. "Came here about five years ago. Got my master's at the Hebrew University, then married the cutest little Sabra and stayed."

Baron raised an eyebrow, but was disinclined to question the whys and wherefores of Radaver's rank. Many of the "boys" in his old outfit had turned down OCS despite their qualifications. He decided on another approach.

"With a master's degree, why should you find it necessary to join the army?"

Radaver tossed an unstudied glance toward the minaret of the Italian Hospital to his left, then turned to Baron. "This is a country fighting for its survival. Wouldn't you say it's a greater cause than Vietnam?"

"No argument," Baron answered reflectively. "Any children yet?"

"No, we haven't been married that long. Perhaps after the next war, God willing."

An enigmatic uneasiness prickled Baron's arms. "You expecting another war?"

Sergeant Radaver chuckled despite his pessimistic outlook. "It's become a way of life. Right now, we're enjoying the 'timeout' between halves."

Baron steered away from the subject, realizing that the sergeant would have to clam up if he persisted. Their relationship had to continue on a friendly basis. Conversation remained in a quiescent stage until they reached the Damascus Gate in the wall of Old Jerusalem on the far side.

Baron broke the silence as they approached the huge square. "Damascus Gate?" He knew it was, but was simply attempting conversation again.

Radaver nodded without speaking, wended his way around some vehicles, and turned left onto Paratroopers Road. Paralleling the wall, he then spun right and headed south on Derech Jericho. Here, a Moslem cemetery separated them from the wall.

Although annoyed with his own impatience, Baron asked abruptly, "Sergeant, have I said something to disturb you?"

The sergeant smiled sheepishly. "No, sir. It's not you. Yom Kippur or not, I wish I'd had breakfast with my wife before leaving."

Baron looked at him searchingly. It was time for the play acting to end. "Something in the wind you're not telling me, Sergeant?"

"No, of course not!" he answered quickly. "I always have this feeling when I go out to the Bar-Lev. If there was any suspicion of trouble would I be taking you out there?"

Baron wondered, recalling the grudgingly offered, somewhat evasive statements of certain diplomats he had questioned. He also thought Radaver's explanation, although plausible, was too quick. But why would they permit him to enter a border outpost if there was the slightest hint of trouble brewing? His trepidations lingering, he scanned the panorama of the Mount of Olives. Both men became silent again.

To Baron's left, nestled in the hillside, the onion-shaped domes of the Russian church protruded among numerous surrounding poplars. The rolling hills were suffused with old vegetation and ancient stone. Radaver slowed the jeep when passing the Church of All Nations, allowing Baron to study it momentarily. A bright, colorful religious mural covered the stone facade above the arched entrances.

"Fascinating, isn't it?" Radaver offered. "Nowhere in the world is there more contrast. Here, the past and the present are one and the same." Turning onto Silwan Road, the jeep picked up speed and shot past a donkey cart. He jerked his head toward an ancient Muslim holding the halter. "See what I mean?" he said, smiling. When Baron nodded without comment, he added, "We'll be stopping in another minute. A little coffee should do us both some good." Baron smiled in spite of himself, feeling that the sergeant was a very likable young man.

Pulling over onto a narrow dirt shoulder, Radaver said, "Sorry, sir, but it's time for that check."

"Don't apologize, sergeant. It's worth a cup of coffee."

Baron emptied his pockets onto the front seat of the jeep: the tape recorder, four cassettes, a pad, two pens, his pipe and tobacco pouch. Routinely but with expert hands, the expatriate American went over Baron's figure. Satisfied, he moved to the objects left on the seat. "The square structure over there with the pyramid roof is the rock-hewn tomb of Zacharias, the father of John the Baptist." He paused as he poked a finger through the tobacco pouch. "Beyond that, you can see the Jewish cemetery." Straightening, he grinned. "If you check back far enough, you might find an ancestor there. Some of the graves date back to Before Christ."

Baron nodded, his eyes agleam. It was a strange sight, the stone coffins lying side by side above ground on the sloping hillside. It was possible, he thought, wondering how they had lived and died. Ancient graves lying there for centuries, their moldering bones untouched while countless wars were waged around them. If they came back to life, would they find any worthwhile changes in the philosophies of mankind?

"Sir!" Radaver called out. Baron turned to see him pouring black coffee from the thermos. Baron reached for the aluminum cup gratefully. "We've got a minute, then no more stops," the sergeant said. "We have to be back by six."

Baron eyed him over the hot cup. Why did that sensation in the pit of his stomach persist? he wondered. "Why six?" he asked blandly.

A grin creased the young man's face. "I've got leave to go home for dinner tonight. I can't think of a better reason."

They continued south toward Bethlehem, descending hilly curves into Hebron Valley. The hillsides along the way were dotted with inhabited caves. Just before entering the city, a sign directing the way to Rachel's Tomb became visible, but the two men had no time to spare for sightseeing.

Bethlehem, the birthplace of Christ and King David, is known to the Israelis as Beit Lechem, the house of bread. Curiously, to Arabs, Beit Lahm is the house of meat. For sixteen centuries, visitors have come from all over the globe to view the Savior's cave and manger. It was from here that David ventured forth to fight Goliath, and later was summoned by Samuel to be King of Judah.

The jeep passed through the city in minutes. Hebron and then Negev had yet to be traversed. Passing Hebron, Baron released an imperceptible sigh of relief. Alertly he had been watching for anything that would indicate any military activity. With each passing mile, his misgivings dissipated. His thoughts returned to Riv and how he would direct his conversation with him. He began to sweat, and his hands became clammy.

Feeling a nudge at his elbow, he saw Radaver holding out a baseball cap for him. "The sun gets to be murderous out here," he said as he slapped one on himself. "And we've still got the Sinai after the Negev. There's a tank of water and some salt pills if you feel the need." Baron waved a refusal. Not very talkative for a foreign correspondent, Radaver speculated. He's sweating too much also, the sergeant thought, have to keep an eye on him. As an afterthought, he added, "Watch out for the metal, it gets hot in this sun." Baron again nodded noncommittally, his eyes studying the terrain.

The Negev was unlike anyone's conception of what a desert should look like: a wilderness with countless boulders and wind-carved mountains, a landscape that seemed to belong on the moon. The only signs of humanity were the road and an occasional Bedouin encampment. Baron looked to the west toward Beersheva, where the Israelis had conquered part of the Negev, greening it when no one thought it possible.

Sergeant Radaver decided to reopen the conversation. "Masada is to our left. Have you ever seen it?"

"No, didn't have time," Baron replied blandly. "But made Beersheva and all points west."

Radaver gave him a quick glance. "You were here during the Six Day War?"

"From the third day on and a couple of days afterward. There wasn't time for sightseeing."

The sergeant grinned. "At least, you don't chase wars on army pay."

Baron gave him a sidelong glance. The phrase struck a reluctant memory chord. Something Lee had said? Dismissing it a moment later, he asked, "Tell me something, Mike. How were you able to identify me as Rick Baron?"

Grinning boyishly, Radaver reached into an upper pocket, pulled out a photograph and extended it to Baron. In the picture, Baron was talking to a well-known cabinet member. Baron's face eased into a smile. Taken in the Knesset, the photo was immediately recognized. He returned it to Radaver, shaking his head. He never knew it had been taken.

"We going down all the way to Eilat?" he asked.

"No, we'll be turning into the Sinai before that. Won't be too long now." With that, he pushed down on the gas pedal.

Hot air rushed over the windshield as the jeep maneuvered through deep wadis, the harsh, barren cliffs seeming to envelop them as they roared through each canyon. A drink of water with a salt pill became a necessity as the shirts of the two men streaked with sweat. Baron kept his hands in his lap, the metal of the jeep too hot to touch. The road became a ribbon in a wasteland of sand.

Baron caught Radaver occasionally glancing at his

watch, but remained silent. The heat was too oppressive for conversation. After another long hour, Radaver suddenly slowed the jeep and downshifted, leaving the road to cross the sands of the Sinai. Startled, Baron gave him a questioning look, finally asking, "Kind of chancy, isn't it?"

Radaver, tilting back his cap, wiped the sweat from his forehead with the back of his hand. "No, it should save us a half-hour. I could always radio the tanks on our checkpoint. They'd be here in minutes if we got stuck."

After another half-hour of bouncing over the undulating sandscape, a road shimmering like a mirage became visible on the horizon. The sergeant turned on the radio, making contact with an unseen Israeli tank.

"Yes, we can see you," a voice crackled. "We're about a mile southwest of you. Are you in trouble?"

"No," the sergeant answered into his handmike. "Give us a couple of minutes." He returned the mike to its clip.

When they bounced onto the smooth surface of the road, Baron shifted uneasily in his seat, his clothing clinging to him uncomfortably. Glancing at his watch, he noted the time. It was almost noon.

The approaching tank looked like a modified Sherman to him. It ground to a halt as Radaver pulled alongside. A tanned lieutenant dropped down from the tank to confront Radaver, who immediately pulled his papers from his shirt pocket. The officer examined them briefly, then flashed a warm smile. Extending a hand to both men, he addressed Baron, "*Shalom*, Mr. Baron. Welcome to no-man's-land. I'm Lieutenant Moses. Like my namesake, I have also spent much time wandering in the desert."

Despite the tightness in his chest, Baron couldn't help smiling. In what other army could there be so much informality? The two soldiers, neither one yet thirty years old, hadn't even bothered with a military salute. It was almost like meeting a family, and if it weren't for the circumstances, Baron might have enjoyed it more. The sun beat down on the road relentlessly, the heat so intense the men's tan uniforms stained to a deep brown.

Although acutely aware that the men seemed to be more concerned with their own loneliness than any impending trouble, Baron contained his growing impatience. "Then it's all quiet on the western front," he stated blandly.

The lieutenant's eyes flashed for a fraction of a second.

"Look about you! We are mere specks in a sea of nothing. Could anywhere be more quiet?" He smiled genuinely, then addressed the sergeant. "You're cleared. But remember— you have only until 2:30 at the latest." Radaver nodded and saluted for the first time.

Baron checked his watch again: 11:55. Always a question answering a question, he thought wryly. His stomach groaned in complaint. "How much farther?" he asked heavily.

The sergeant gave him a searching look. "Another five minutes. If you're hungry, you can get something to eat there. We'll both have to replace the water we've lost to prevent dehydration on the return trip."

Baron nodded, his eyes squinting behind his sunglasses. Five minutes? he thought. He could see nothing but sand in every direction. They had left the road after parting with the patrol tank. Baron kept his silence until the jeep, with much grinding of gears, reached the crest of a sand dune.

There it was—the small fort and the Canal less than a hundred yards beyond it. Involuntarily, Baron checked his watch: twelve noon exactly.

"Holy Christ!" he exclaimed. "This is it!"

In reality, his excitement was more for his meeting Riv than the unexpected sighting of the fort.

While some forts were more complex than others, this one resembled a piled-up sand hill about thirty feet above the surrounding dunes. A watchtower was at the peak, facing the canal, surrounded by sandbagged firing positions. From the bunker, a trench led to other firing positions which guarded the rear of the fort. The command bunker itself, a corrugated iron structure, was buried beneath the huge mound of sand.

Radaver was already on the radio, identifying himself and Baron to two men in khaki fatigues at the lone break in the coiled barbed-wire fence encircling the fort. They were waved into the compound and directed to a parking space alongside two other jeeps, dug in beside the rolled wire fence. The two soldiers were young, lean, dark, and seemingly interested in meeting Baron, the first American correspondent, to their knowledge, to visit the post.

The two visitors were greeted with excited *"Shaloms"* and were hurriedly escorted into the trench. When

177

Radaver protested, explaining that he had to gas up the jeep, his protestations were waved aside.

"It will be taken care of," one said. "You've been in the sun long enough!"

Captain Avram waited just inside the door with hand outstretched. "*Shalom*, Baron," he smiled warmly. "I don't know how you managed this, but it must be for good reason."

"Everything we do nowadays is for good reason," Baron replied amiably, removing his sunglasses and sliding them into an upper pocket. "Quite an establishment you've got here," he remarked, his eyes getting accustomed to the new light.

Three men, all in short-sleeved shirts, poked their heads in from other doorways. Having come out of the glare from the sun, Baron couldn't distinguish one face from another yet.

"Would you like something to eat?" the captain offered, smiling broadly. "God will forgive you. After all, you've crossed the Sinai to pay us an important visit. You must be dry as a bone." He addressed Radaver, "How about you, Sergeant? Are you fasting?"

Radaver smiled awkwardly. "A nosh would be forgiven, I guess," he answered.

"Captain," Baron interjected, "I don't have much time. If it's not an inconvenience, I'd like to get started immediately."

"Of course, of course," the captain replied fretfully. "Forgive us. We don't have guests very often. I'll show you around, and you can speak with anyone you please. The sandwiches and drinks will find us."

He led Baron into another room, which apparently doubled as the captain's office and a radio room. A wooden desk stood in one corner, the walls lined with metal filing cabinets. At the opposite end of the room, a man was peering through a narrow slot in the wall facing the canal. He reached for his binoculars, shaking his head while he adjusted the lenses.

"I don't like it," he said to his companion who sat at a shortwave radio. "I don't like it, Riv. Too much dust. Something's going on there. What does Dov say from the tower?"

"Nothing to add to what you're seeing," the radioman

offered. "Just dust and lots of it, going far back from the high banks."

"Leib, what's going on?" the captain shouted, leaping across the room. Startled by the captain's unexpected appearance, the two men spun around.

"I can't tell," Leib said, handing the binoculars to the captain. "Could be a cover-up for some activity."

Baron stood there, frozen, unable to move or speak. The radioman was Riv, all right, Riv Moscati. There was no doubt in his mind. He was looking at himself, twenty-five years ago. His hands were suddenly clammy, and his stomach was churning. He noted Riv's friendly nod and returned it irresolutely, allowing heavy seconds to pass without speaking.

It was only when Captain Avram barked instructions at Riv that Baron awakened from his daze. A sixth sense chastised him for not doing his job properly. He was asleep and had been all morning. He had learned nothing of any consequence from Radaver, despite the long hours spent with him. He looked toward the captain hovering over Riv and, until now, couldn't have even described him.

"Shit!" he muttered to himself, pulling the tape recorder from his pocket and moving within a few feet of the two men. He pushed the record button, made sure the tape was running, then aimed the built-in condenser-mike at the Israelis.

Captain Avram gave him a quick glance, but returned to his task sedulously. His dark eyes and angular face appeared to be more than a little concerned. "Ask Dov if he can hear anything! Motors! Tank treads! Anything!" Riv clicked a switch and, in a few seconds, the reply came.

"Nothing! The wind's changed direction." A pause, then, "Could be a smoke screen. Can't make out a damn thing! Unless the wind gets stronger, that screen is going to hang there."

Avram ran a hand through his closely cropped, prematurely graying hair. Baron guessed him to be about thirty-five. The captain spoke hurriedly. "Contact Bunker Yehuda to see whether they know anything. And if not, find out whether they have contacted Air Command."

Another three minutes dragged by, with voices on the two-way radio confirming similar situations all along the Bar-Lev Line. Air Command had no planes up and

179

wouldn't have, unless there was an immediate urgency.

The Captain exhaled deeply, then clapped a hand on Riv's shoulder. "All right, Riv, it might not mean a thing, but keep me posted on the slightest change. I will be checking the boys." Turning to Baron, he saw him stop the recorder and said, "Could simply be maneuvers. Sometimes they even lob a few shells in our direction just for practice."

Baron nodded, thinking the explanation a bit too specious, but said nothing. "Mind if I start here? With your radio engineer?" he asked.

Avram shrugged. "Not at all, but you do realize that much of what you just recorded will probably be censored?"

Baron nodded with a brief smile, wondering what was considered an "immediate urgency." Aware of his son watching him—his blue eyes just like his mother's—he set the button to record.

"This is Rick Baron reporting to you on the Day of Atonement from a bunker on the Bar-Lev Line overlooking the Suez Canal. The voices heard previously were those of the Fort Commander, Captain Avram, and Riv Moscati, his radio engineer"—he saw Riv raise his eyes in astonishment—"who was contacting other bunkers to check out suspicious activity taking place on the Egyptian side."

He stopped the recorder, realizing that Riv had been caught off guard with the mention of his name. Riv stared at Baron, an odd expression crossing his face. "Should I know you?" he asked in a deep voice.

Baron prayed that his voice remain steady.

"No, not really. But I have seen your picture. I'm an old friend of your parents. I bring regards from your mother, your sister, and Debbi and the children." He forced a smile. "I had dinner with them last night, and they're all well."

"Baron, Rick Baron," Riv muttered to himself in confusion. Not the slightest bit familiar, but the face—had he seen it somewhere?

"You needn't be so perplexed," Baron offered amiably. "I knew your mother and father many years ago. In Italy, before you were born."

"I see," Riv murmured, not really understanding at all.

Baron stretched out his hand. "It's a pleasure to meet Lee's son, even under these circumstances."

Riv got to his feet, all six-foot-two of him, and accepted Baron's handshake, looking more bewildered than ever.

"Lee?" he repeated.

Baron immediately attempted to rectify his faux pas.

"That's what she was called . . . as a girl."

Scratching his head and about to reply, Riv halted abruptly. An alien sound was increasing rapidly. A soft whine rose with a howling screech and passed overhead, exploding beyond the fort.

Spurred into action, Riv didn't wait for the second shell, which followed a second later. Plopping into his seat, he removed a cover and hit the alert button, although knowing it was unnecessary by now. He faced the radio, twisting dials, trying to reach the tanks on the outer perimeter.

Baron, watching Riv with mixed emotions, said, "They're lousy shots! Scare tactics, Riv?"

Riv shook his head without looking up. A steady stream of shells were now passing overhead. "They're aiming for our tanks and possibly our mobile artillery unit."

As if in answer, they could hear returning shells. Baron glanced at Leib, who was swearing while unlatching the frames around the narrow slots that he had been peering through. There were now wide openings in the wall facing the canal.

The captain came running in with three men carrying machine guns. The three men joined Leib at the openings.

"Did you get Moishe?" he shouted to Riv.

"I'm trying, captain, but not so far!"

Moishe, Baron thought, must be Lieutenant Moses, the tank commander. Little fears tugged at him. He had met his son, and now this! His heart filled with misgivings, he started the tape recorder, but didn't speak into it. It wasn't necessary; the actors were all around him.

The sound of machine guns reached them, coming from the positions atop the bunker. The men at the slots peered through the openings, seeing nothing as yet.

"Get Dov!" the captain cried out.

Dov's voice came through the loud clatter.

181

"Egyptian infantry are crossing the canal. The peace is over!"

The captain leaned into the mike. "Dov, is it a full-scale assault?"

"You can bet on . . ." His voice was drowned out as mortar shells started dropping all around the fort. The machine guns came alive in the hands of the four men facing the canal. The sound was deafening as it clattered off the metal walls.

A neutral unable to help, Baron watched in awe, feeling his age as he studied these young men in battle. But he knew, reassuring himself, that it was the standing around as a fifth wheel that caused his brooding, not his age. If only he had a camera, he wished.

Radaver came bursting in, a *talleth* around his neck. Excited, at first, he breathed easier, spying Baron.

"I'm responsible for you," he said, approaching Baron.

Baron pointed to the recorder, alerting him that he was being taped. He nodded, rubbing his chest to calm down.

Captain Avram switched on the intercom. "Start the oil drums!" he ordered.

"It's not working," a reply came back. "Something with the pumps."

The captain made a face, then noticed Radaver. "Sergeant, you're suppose to be a good mechanic. Give them a hand." Radaver darted off, anxious to join in.

Baron stopped the recorder to conserve tape. He had to cup his hands for the captain to hear him. "Why the oil drums?" he shouted.

The captain's dark eyes looked tired, worried. Avram put his lips to Baron's ear. "We have a series of fifty-five gallon drums buried in the sand. They're attached to pipes leading into the canal. We release the oil, toss in a Thermite bomb, and the Suez is a blazing inferno."

As Baron nodded understandingly, Radaver returned.

"There's nothing wrong with the pumps," he said, breathless. "The Egyptians must have plugged up the openings!"

The mortar shells kept dropping; one landed atop the bunker, causing a shower of dust. The guns positioned around the watchtower stopped abruptly.

Riv tried contacting Dov before the captain asked. Getting no response, Riv became grim. He looked to his captain helplessly.

The captain glared, his jaw set like stone. "Where is God today?" he muttered. He turned to Radaver. "Get two men from the rear and check on Dov and the others. It's possible they're only wounded."

"Yes, sir!" the sergeant cried out, sliding the *talleth* from his shoulders. "Thank you, sir!" he added, dropping the prayer shawl on the captain's desk as he ran from the room.

Baron gaped at the disappearing figure. This was the first note of formality between enlisted man and officer Baron had seen.

Captain Avram spun toward Riv. "Get Captain Olan!"

Riv twisted dials, first listening through the earphones, then switching on the loudspeakers for all to hear. The men at the slots whirled around when they heard the almost hysterical voice spilling into the room. Baron grabbed the tape recorder.

". . . resemble suitcases on their backs"—a loud explosion came through the speakers—"opened, it fires a missile. Something new from the Russians! With three shots, it's knocked out three of our ta . . ." Another explosion mixed with machine gun fire and drowned out the voice.

Avram grabbed the mike from Riv. "Where's Captain Olan?" he shouted.

A new voice came on, shouting over the background noise.

"This is Lieutenant Braun, sir. The captain is dead!"

Avram paled visibly. "What are your circumstances? Will you be able to hold out?"

"Not for long without the tanks!" He paused, then spoke frantically, "Where are our planes? What's happened to them?"

Avram clenched his fist in frustration, but his voice remained stolidly calm. "Hang on. They'll come. Be patient and trust in God. We'll keep in touch!"

As soon as he handed the mike back to Riv, there was a tremendous blast just outside the slots. Shells then hit the fort. Billowing, yellow smoke filled the room; choking men were forced to stop firing.

Riv didn't wait for instructions, getting the fort doctor on the intercom. Seconds later, they were informed that it was a smoke screen and not poison gas.

The machine gun fire began again. Leib shouting,

"They're ashore—all around us!" He ripped the grenades attached to his belt.

With a growing feeling of dread Baron looked away from Riv, who was again trying to contact the mobile artillery unit. Baron grabbed Avram's arm, staring at him determinedly.

"Enough of this nonsense!" he shouted. "If they're about to come through your front door, I want a gun!"

"You?" The officer stared, greatly astonished.

"Don't act so surprised, captain! I handled a fifty-caliber Browning when you were in your diapers!"

"So what!" he retorted angrily. "You're a neutral and an observer. You're here to verify that we didn't start *this* war!"

Baron was speechless for a moment.

"Verify! Is that why I was given permission to come here?"

The captain ran a nervous hand through his graying hair, realizing that his anger made him phrase his reply indiscreetly. He took Baron's sleeve, leading him to another corner beside his dust-covered desk. With his free arm, he shielded his eyes from the smoke as a new shower of dust descended upon them.

"Look," he said to Baron. "So there is no misunderstanding, I'll explain quickly. In truth, we were expecting an attack, but not before six o'clock. You would have been out of here hours before . . ."

"Bullshit, captain!" Baron interrupted. "You've got mostly reservists here, and I didn't see anything remotely resembling troop movements anywhere along the way here."

The captain's impatience was growing by the second. He had no time for this macho American, regardless of his good intentions. He measured his words carefully, speaking into Baron's ear. "If we had shown the slightest bit of military activity, the Egyptians would have screamed that we were starting another war. We couldn't have the world believing them."

A soldier came running into the room. He was no more than twenty years old, the youngest Baron had yet seen. He carried an armful of hard hats and immediately started handing them out. When he thrust one toward Baron, the captain nodded. "Put it on!"

Baron complied without comment, then watched the

captain stride across the small room to answer Leib's outcry. Besides the captain, Leib was the only man there who wasn't a reservist. Baron moved to join them, bringing the tape recorder.

Taking position behind Leib and the captain amidst the ear-shattering din of small arms fire and the lingering, choking dust, Baron noticed Riv half-turned in his chair, observing him with more than a little curiosity. Or was it uncertainty? Baron thought, wincing. He was convinced the boy was wondering about the bravado displayed by this middle-aged American correspondent who claimed to be an old friend of his parents.

Bravado! Hell! The journalist's pen is not always mightier than the sword, he thought. With a growing sense of frustration, he crammed the tape recorder into a lower pocket of his jacket and pulled out his pen and notebook from another. Possessed as he was by concern for his son's safety, he would at least keep himself busy with the notebook.

He wrote hurriedly in shorthand as was his custom, mindful of the fact that, until now, he had been derelict in his duties as a reporter. He glanced up occasionally, noting the grim, dedicated faces. Leib and the captain had moved away to one side in earnest conversation. Baron could not hear what they were saying.

Baron moved beside one of the gunners who didn't bother to give him a glance. From the slot, Baron could see the Egyptian infantry moving through the dense smoke, bypassing the fort, stopping only briefly to fire machine gun blasts. Baron knew exactly what was happening: the shelling had halted to allow the first wave of Egyptians to pass. The second wave would follow with heavy armor.

Baron started to point out the "suitcases" to the gunner when a grenade rolled up to their slot in the wall. "Grenade!" he screamed, pulling at the gunner's arm. Everyone dropped to the floor. The blast sent a shower of sand and smoke into the room. They could hear pieces of metal hitting the wall.

The Israeli nodded, smiling and shaking Baron's hand. Getting up, he pulled Baron to his feet and immediately went back to his job. Baron went to the captain who was checking the men for injuries. Miraculously, no one had been hurt.

The captain started to express his thanks, but Baron stopped him. "Well, captain! What now? The heavy armor will soon follow. Do we become expendable?" Leib looked at Avram and left him to deal with his own dilemma.

Avram pulled him aside away from the others.

"Baron, we're grateful, but you're a problem. You know too much; you've been chasing too many wars."

Baron smiled cynically. The phrase "chasing too many wars" did not sit well with him. "Correction, captain," he objected, "I was practically invited to this one."

"True," Avram conceded. "But it doesn't alter my opinion of you." He wiped sweaty dust from his cheek. "For whatever reason, someone in the government apparently thought your presence here could serve some purpose." He noted Baron's impatience but continued, forestalling his attempts to interrupt. "In reality, though, I don't believe they intended for you to be caught up in an Arab-Israeli con . . ."

"Captain, cut the stalling! What's your backup plan?" Baron stared at him, saw the look of indecision, and for the first time, began to have doubts. "Holy Christ!" he exclaimed loudly, his exasperation apparent, "You do have one!"

Avram sighed. What could he possibly tell this American that he did not already guess? Baron was probably as knowledgeable in the tactics of war as he was. It amazed him that Baron seemed more annoyed than worried over their plight. Again he sighed, feeling the lines beneath his lower eyelid and thinking that he was aging much too quckly.

"The Egyptians are clever," Avram said solemnly. "The sun is already at their backs, blinding our tanks." He gestured helplessly. "If they are unable to reach us, our only hope will be the air force." A frown appeared on the tired face. "I can't understand . . ." He left it unfinished.

Baron's heart pounded as he watched Riv trying to make contact with outside forces.

"How long can we hold out?" Baron asked.

"We're pretty well dug in. They won't find us easy."

"Yeah, sure," Baron grimaced. "That's what they said at the Alamo."

Avram's look of puzzlement disappeared as the radio

came on with a blast. Riv had reached command. Avram leaped to the set to take the microphone.

The men in the besieged bunker learned from command that there would be no immediate reinforcements for them. The Syrians were attacking the Golan Heights with hundreds of tanks, and what little of the air force that was prepared was being sent to that sector.

The colonel who addressed Avram was calm and hopeful.

"Captain, how grave is your situation?"

Avram relayed the information in as composed a voice as he could muster.

"Can you hold out until after dark?" the colonel interjected.

"If we have to, we will!" Avram replied stoically, his hopes rising.

"Good! Abandon your position at twenty-four-hundred. Check your map and find Sector X. God willing, we'll pick you up at about two-thirty."

The captain rubbed his face. "Colonel, will we be getting any support? The Egyptians are already crossing with heavy armor."

When a long pause followed, anxious eyes watched Riv at the radio. Baron regarded his son with a heaviness in his chest, fighting to control his emotions. More than ever, he yearned to speak with Riv, to learn more about him, his hopes, his dreams, his likes and dislikes. Try as he might, he couldn't avert the dismal thoughts creeping into his head. It was possible that all they would share would be a grave.

Lips compressed, he returned his attention to the tape recorder and saw the cassette running out. Grateful for something to do, he flipped it over and let an inaudible sigh escape. Baron was becoming well-aware of his new role with a feeling of responsibility for the well-being and safety of someone other than himself. He tilted his helmet back, wiped his sweating forehead, and wrinkled his nose as the fetid odors grew stronger. An overbearing heat mixed with the dust, smoke and the sweat of men fighting for their lives. He glanced at Riv, saw the young Rick, and sighed.

Suddenly, the ebullience of the colonel's voice penetrated the machine gun chatter.

"Avram, servicemen are still being pulled from the

synagogues. Radio silence throughout the country will be broken at fourteen-forty and all will know we're at war. In two hours, our planes will be giving you support. We're also shifting all available tanks to your sector. They'll open up a path for you before twenty-four hundred. When you leave your position, go straight back to the perimeter road. Do you understand? No deviation! or else you will be swallowed up in our own line of fire!"

Avram nodded eagerly, his eyes blazing with a new light. "Yes, Colonel! Understood!"

The tired faces behind the guns appeared less strained as they let out cheers. Leib was the only one to hold a look of constraint. Leaving the butcher, the clothing salesman, the confectioner to their posts, Leib moved quickly to join the captain.

"Avram, the Golan. The colonel said nothing of how it goes there! Hundreds of tanks!"

Baron straightened suddenly, then quickly checked his watch. Two-thirty! He brought a hand to his cheek. "Oh, my God!" he muttered. Joe, Paul, Ralph—and Tovah! "Oh, my God!" he repeated. If their trip was on schedule, they could be caught right in the middle.

For the moment, at least, they were safe in the twenty-foot deep concrete bunker. Paul Green stood at the porthole with the Eyemo resting on his shoulder, filming the Syrian T-54 tanks as they lumbered through the wadi at the base of the bunker.

"Holy Christ, Ralph! It's like watching a war movie!"

Ralph Corelli's olive complexion had turned ashen. He had to swallow before speaking. "Just make sure you're in focus—there's no time for retakes."

Paul laughed. "Who has time for focusing? I've got it set on infinity!"

"Jesus Christ!" Ralph cried out. "You act like you're enjoying this!"

"C'mon, Ralph! What the hell you worrying about? Just think of the bonus we'll get. Cripes, man! We're right in the middle of the scene!"

Ralph groaned, holding a hand to his stomach as if wounded. "Bonus? Crap! I just hope we can stay alive to collect our pay."

The Eyemo was running out of film, and Paul was obviously reluctant to relinquish his position. Then, he noticed his companion's face. "Hey, buddy boy, relax. We're all neutral here. Our only ammunition is film."

"You been asleep, *buddy boy*," Ralph retorted facetiously. "Take a look over there at your girlfriend."

Paul gaped at Tovah, dumbfounded and blanching. She had positioned herself at a higher level, holding an Uzi machine gun through a narrow slot of the pillbox. Terrified, Paul finally found his voice.

"Tovah! What the hell are you doing?" he cried out shrilly.

Garbed in a tan jump suit, Tovah, spun around, terrified. She glared at Paul acidly. "Don't do that to me!" she reprimanded sharply. "This isn't the time for games."

"Games!" Paul exploded. "You're accusing me of playing games? What's that thing in your hands?"

At this point, Joe Green came running in with an Israeli lieutenant. Peering at the two of them, he shouted, "What's going on?"

Tovah looked the lieutenant in the eye. "Will you please tell this American that I've served two years in the army."

The Israeli, in his middle twenties, glared at Paul from beneath a crop of unruly red hair. "This is not America. Here, man or woman, it makes no difference. All have a duty to perform." He paused as a salvo harmlessly struck the top of the bunker. "We do whatever is necessary to survive." He nodded to Tovah, terminating the discussion.

They could hear tank treads grinding about them between each salvo. Ralph nudged Paul, whispering, "God! What a way to exist." Abashed and suddenly fearful, Paul made no reply.

Tovah gave him a lingering look as if in apology, then turned away. Joe Green watched her as she peered at the land sloping away from the bunker, then addressed his son gently. "Paul, you two got something going?"

Paul stared off into space, perplexed at first, then slowly beginning to understand himself. A nebulous anxiety was working at his stomach. He looked into his father's eyes, his expression becoming grim. "I don't know, Dad, but it's possible."

Joe nodded. Smiling, he ruffled Paul's hair.

With Ralph watching and listening, Paul felt a moment of embarrassment. Joe apparently hadn't done that to his son in years. "All right, Dad, what about us?" he said hastily. "What can we do?"

"Do!" Joe exclaimed abruptly. "We stay here until help arrives." He addressed Ralph. "How many reels have you got?"

"Eight, not counting what's in the Land Rover."

Joe made a face. "You'll have to make do with what we've got here. The Rover's been on fire for the past half-hour."

"Holy Christ!" Ralph cried out. "How do we get out of this?"

"Stop worrying," Joe said, pulling a cigar from his jacket. "If you listen, you can hear the Israeli tanks returning fire." He unwrapped the cigar and held a flame to the tip before bringing it to his lips. His actions were slow and methodical in an attempt to placate their fears. "Give them time—the'll pick us up. They haven't forgotten. . . ."

The sudden outburst of Tovah's machine gun stifled him.

Joe, pulling his stomach in, leaped up onto the platform to join her, the cigar still in his mouth. His shoulder pressed against the wall, he peered out from the opposite corner of the concrete abutment. The smell of cordite was overpowering.

Less than fifty meters away, on the sloping rocky terrain, an Israeli Patton tank had been caught and set afire by a group of four T–54s. The men inside, if still alive, were trapped and unable to escape because of the Syrian guns. Two machine guns from another section of the bunker had joined Tovah in trying to draw fire away from the dying Patton. Ignoring the machine gun fire, three Syrian tanks lumbered away, moving into position with others apparently on a predetermined course. Their actions were accomplished with a peculiar complacency since they didn't even bother to return the fire from the bunker. The remaining T–54 swiveled its turret from the disabled Patton to confront the concrete abutment, its 100mm cannon now aimed directly at Tovah's window.

Joe Green pulled back and stared at Tovah. She had run out of ammunition and was gaping hypnotically at the Syrian tank. Horrified, Joe slipped beneath the transom and grabbed her around the waist, pulling her down and against the wall. He shouted to Paul and Ralph to do likewise and crawl toward them. Terrified, they complied and not a second too soon.

They heard the *whoosh,* and chips of concrete splattered like buckshot against the opposite wall. Choking dust filled the narrow room.

Paul felt a hand seize his shoulder. Jerking his head around, he caught Ralph's ashen face in a grimace of pain. "What is it? Are you hit?"

"Jesus! No!" Ralph cried out, hysteria creeping into his voice. "Is there a john in this place? I gotta go real bad!"

Paul expelled a deep breath and, despite the situation, almost laughed. "Holy cripes, Ralph! You almost made me wet my pants."

Tovah, who had fallen into a state of lassitude, snapped out of it abruptly. Leaning forward, she caught Ralph's attention and pointed to the lieutenant's station beyond the partition bisecting the bunker.

"There's an emergency toilet on the other side," she shouted above the spasmodic cannon fire. Ralph saluted gratefully. "Don't stand up," she cautioned as an afterthought.

"Don't worry." Ralph groaned. "If I did, I wouldn't need that chamber pot." He started crawling on all fours, then looked back at Paul. "If we get out of this, buddy boy, I'm never leaving the studio again."

Paul nodded, half-listening. On his stomach, leaning on his elbows, he looked up at Tovah sitting on the raised platform. Joe Green's interest was centered ruefully on the empty Uzi.

"Not exactly like home, is it?" Tovah said to Paul.

"You can say that again. Like the man said, if we get out of this, I'm taking you home with me."

Joe perked up, but before he could speak, thundering jets passed overhead. Scrambling to his feet, he held back Tovah who was following him. Cautiously, he peered out from the transom.

Within seconds, the roaring diminished as the planes ranged far into Syrian territory. "Israeli Skyhawks," he said to Tovah, who was tugging at his sleeve impatiently. In the distance, he could see the trails of the 30mm Defa cannon over Syrian targets. Smiling, he said, "They're after the supply convoy."

Paul and Tovah joined him on either side, and together

they watched clouds of black smoke erupt skyward from a wadi beyond a range of hills. Their smiles, although somewhat grim, were short-lived. A tremendous explosion nearby almost threw them off the platform. Paul caught Tovah, preventing her from falling off.

"Oh, no!" she cried out. "It must be our tank!"

When they heard cheering from the other side of the bunker's partition they stared at each other in bewilderment. Joe was the first to get to his feet.

The Syrian T–54 was ablaze. The disabled Patton had risen like a phoenix and made a direct hit at twenty yards with its 105mm cannon. Two men climbed out of the Patton, one wearing a shirt blackened and smoking.

The Israeli lieutenant suddenly emerged from behind the partition, carrying a submachine gun and running across the room to the exit. He threw a glance to Tovah without stopping. "Why are you standing there?" he shouted angrily.

Tovah stared at him dumbly.

"No ammunition!" Joe cried out.

Murmuring epithets in Hebrew, he stopped for a second and shouted over his shoulder. "Yacov!"

Yacov was short, thin-faced, and looked like a bar mitzvah boy. Scurrying after the lieutenant, he leaped up the few stairs to help opening the heavy metal door. Finding an open trench, they started firing on the single T–54 halted at the rim of the slope. A number of T–54s at the base of the bunker continued by without stopping as if bent on another mission. The lieutenant called out to the two Israelis crawling up the slope.

Joe grabbed Paul's shoulder as Ralph came running in. "What are you waiting for? Is the Eyemo reloaded?" Paul stared at his father. Pictures! Who gives a damn about pictures now! he thought. Joe read his expression; he had seen it before, many years ago.

Overhearing, Ralph brought the camera to Joe. "It's loaded, Mr. Green."

Joe took it without further comment. Hurriedly checking the lens, he lifted the heavy camera to his shoulder and, leaning against the concrete sill, focused on the two Israelis scrambling up the rocky slope.

Paul stared at Tovah helplessly. When she touched his cheek without speaking, he leaned forward to kiss her lightly upon the lips, then scrambled to his feet. At his father's side, he said, "Here, Dad! Let me have it before your shoulder gives way!"

"You'll have to wait," was the terse reply.

The two Israelis were pinned behind a boulder, twenty yards short of the metal door to the bunker. The guns of the lieutenant and Yacov were useless, pinging off the tank like angry bees. The lieutenant's angry cursing could be heard rising above the chattering fire.

"Dad! Quick! Let me have it!" Paul cried out, pointing. Two tanks had crested a hill above the burning Syrian tank and already had their guns trained upon the lone T–54 imprisoning the hapless men. "They've gotta be ours, Dad! C'mon, quick! Lean over, I'll take it!"

Joe relinquished the heavy load with relief, a trace of a smile on his lips. "Ours," Paul had said. How right he was. "Israeli British Centurions," he said to Paul.

Fitting the collar of the camera base onto his shoulder, Paul spoke softly. "Sorry, Dad. I didn't mean for you to take over my job." He paused briefly to position his elbows on the concrete sill as his father had, then murmured, "I think you're terrific."

Joe squelched his fatherly pride; their circumstances demanded a complete lack of parental emotions. "Bull!" he said brusquely. "Just keep your eyes peeled. If that Syrian tank swings around on us, drop down fast!" He peered at Ralph, who appeared more bewildered than ever. "How's the power-pak holding out? Are you keeping a check?"

"Shit! I'm trying, Mr. Green. I'm doing my best."

"I know you are," Joe said compassionately. "Stop worrying. Just keep busy and things'll work out. You can bet your life on it."

The bunker was hot and steamy, the smell of cordite overwhelming in its small confinement. Joe sidled past Tovah, who stood rooted to Paul's shoulder, her dark eyes narrowed and fixed with dread as she watched the tank battle taking place. Good kids, he thought somberly, reaching the end of the platform.

Settling down on the dirty wooden surface, he leaned back against the stone wall and languidly stretched his legs out before him. Placing a hand over his chest, he could feel his racing heartbeat. "Shit!" he muttered under his breath, "I'm getting too old for this crap!" Away from prying eyes, he allowed the fret lines to deepen. He was scared and had known it from the beginning, but steadfastly he refused to reveal his emotions to the others. They had enough to worry about on their own. Listening to the booming cannons, each one 100mm or more, he was reminded of the fearful German 88s. He shook his head, wondering how Mindy, Lee, and Debbi were taking the news of the fighting. And Rick who was safe in a military zone.

He closed his eyes and rubbed his face as if to rouse himself. Damn! he sputtered. Mindy and Lee must be going out of their minds by now! Instinctively, he opened his eyes and got to his feet, acutely aware of the splashes of reddish light intermittently invading the darkening cavern. An inner reserve taking effect, he resolutely stalked the length of the room, passing his young cohorts without as much as a glance. His misgivings, however, were reconstituted upon reaching the bottom step of the landing where the lieutenant and Yacov were sprawled before the open door. Their guns were strangely silent. Either they were cooling the Uzis, Joe conjectured, or they were running low on ammunition. Hesitating with a strong awareness of their dilemma, he looked beyond the two Israelis who didn't notice him.

From his position, Joe could see the Syrian tank silhouette against the slanting, setting sun, the lengthening shadow of the T–54 blotting out the pink terrain all the way to the edge of a small hill.

Joe winced, the blast of the 100mm cannon roaring in his ears. "God!" he moaned. Only four hours ago, he had arrived in peace.

As planned beforehand, they had picked up the lieutenant and Yacov in Deganya, where Russian pioneers had founded Israel's first *kibbutz* in 1909. Rich farmland having displaced the malarial swamps, the settlement was now enhanced with the beauty of subtropical plants and towering palms.

After proper introductions, the party of six continued north without delay. Joe drove the British Land Rover, the lieutenant acting as guide with Ralph and Yacov settled behind them, Paul and Tovah occupying the rear seats. From the start, they got along well together, the amiable conversation constant. While young Yacov—a mere eighteen and only six months in service—seemed greatly interested in their camera equipment, Ralph's

194

attentions were drawn to the submachine gun which Yacov never released.

"Do you have to hold that all the time?" he asked.

"It is my third hand," Yacov replied tersely, unsmiling.

"Is it necessary?"

The young Israeli snorted. "In the Golan, one never knows."

Listening, Joe addressed the lieutenant softly. "Isn't he kind of young?"

The lieutenant scratched his crop of red hair. "To subsist in this land, one has to mature in a hurry." He smiled suddenly. "Enough of such talk. Look over there. You can see where the Jordan meets the Sea of Galilee —the very spot where, for centuries, pilgrims have been baptized in the holy water of the river."

Highly knowledgeable in the Biblical and contemporary histories of the territory, the lieutenant caught and held the attention of his American audience with his running commentary. The land all around them, coveted by Moslems, Christians, and Jews alike, was nurtured by hate. The soil, moist with their blood, harvested only remnants of ancient and contemporary relics. A tank at the gate of the Deganya settlement was a constant reminder of the 1948 battle with the Syrians. Yet, just a few miles northward, headless Roman statues bordered the landscape. It was believed, the lieutenant explained, that the heads were intentionally removed simply for economical reasons—when a new emperor came into power, only the heads had to be replaced.

They reached the ancient town of Tiberias, one of Israel's leading winter resorts today. Although its waterfront consists of modern bathing beaches and beautiful hotels, it is an incongruous sight when one is reminded of the many battles fought here over the centuries by the Arabs, Crusaders, and Turks. The past remained in evidence as they sighted archaeological excavations on the outskirts of the town. Rife with ancient history—at one time the seat of Jewish scholarship after the fall of Jerusalem—Tiberias is now frequented by tourists partaking of its curative hot springs. Famed for over 3000 years, it has been surmised by some Biblical scholars that Christ cured the sick and the maimed here.

"You're kidding!" Ralph blurted out, awe-struck with

195

the knowledge. "You mean this is actually the place where the Saviour performed miracles?"

"It's possible," Yacov answered for the lieutenant, adding as an afterthought, "Did you visit the Via Dolorosa in the Old Quarter?"

"You bet. And I still can't believe I was actually there. My parents will flip when they see the shots I took."

Smiling, Joe drove with moderate speed through the almost deserted street. "Sorry, Ralph," he then offered. "If it weren't for Yom Kippur, and the fact that we've got a job to do . . . Well, you understand."

"It's okay, Mr. Green. I'm still getting a kick from it."

Tovah pushed Paul's persistent hand from her knee and leaned forward. "Are you very religious, Ralph?" She twisted around at Paul's sudden burst of laughter.

"Hah! Ralph does all his praying in the singles bars at home." Then, realizing he was embarrassing his friend, he said loud enough for his father to hear, "Jew and Christian alike could learn a lot more if the firm would allow us a few extra days."

Joe's eyes widened, then he smiled. "All right—three extra days at the company's expense. But I expect you to earn it."

Paul winked at Ralph, who stared back at him in astonishment.

The three Israelis glanced at each other. Tovah merely shrugged and said in sotto voce, *"Americans!"*

It took just minutes to reach and pass through the ancient, Biblical villages such as Migdal, the birthplace of Mary Magdalene, where the land abounded with thick vegetation and tall eucalyptus trees. The air, redolent from the indigenous growth, pervaded the slowly moving Land Rover and brought a mild sense of elation to the riders.

Once beyond Tabgha, the lieutenant drew their attention to a high hill and the famous Mount of the Beatitudes, explaining that it was where Christ preached the Sermon on the Mount. Now, it was the site of an Italian convent and hospice.

Ralph's eyes glistened with a euphoric light. Twisting suddenly, he faced Paul. "We gotta come back. We can use the fast slide film in the Nikon. My parents just gotta see this!"

"Why didn't you bring them to Israel?" Yacov inquired casually. He had unobtrusively examined Ralph's slacks and expensive safari jacket that they wore while working. After all, he thought innocently, if these Americans were so wealthy . . .

Ralph made a face. "Are you kidding? They're too old to travel. I'm twenty-four, the youngest of *ten* children— the pictures will have to do."

Fragments of dark, volcanic rock in the garden of an excavated synagogue led down to the sea. Although the synagogue was on the supposed site of Christ's preachings, archaeologists dated its construction around the second century A.D. While tall columns and marble steps displayed Roman-like architecture, numerous carvings revealed its true religious background. Rams horns, Stars of David, and seven-branched candelabras were decidedly not Roman.

About to leave Capernaum, Joe unexpectedly pulled the Rover off the macadam road and parked on the slanting, grassy shoulder. The lieutenant peered at him questioningly. Joe smiled. "Five minutes only. We've got work to do." Then turning around, "Get out the Eyemo, Ralph. Paul, go back about twenty yards and start shooting from your left. Pan down the slope to the water and then to the Franciscan monastery. Hold it there and then bring it to the synagogue. Hold it again and then zoom in for a closeup. Got it?"

"Perfect, Dad."

"No audio on this, Ralph. Commentary will be dubbed in later," Joe added.

Ralph looked up. "Mr. Green, can I do the shooting as long as there's no sound? I rarely get the opportunity."

Joe looked at Paul and saw him nod. "Okay, it's all yours. Get going."

Tovah got out of the Rover. "Mind if I join you?" she asked Paul.

"Course not," he smiled, regarding her with approval. She was devastating, he thought, even in the long-sleeved olive drab jumpsuit. Her eyes twinkled with amusement as she took his offered hand.

The lieutenant indicated that Yacov should accompany the others. Yacov complied willingly. He had never before seen such a camera.

Joe stood outside the Rover, sniffing the unusual, clean, crisp air, the Israeli officer at his side. He glanced down at the Galilee, then scanned the distant hills of the Golan.

"Is it always this quiet?" Joe asked.

About to reply, the lieutenant saw the American's shoulders stiffen suddenly. "What is it?" he asked warily, his eyes alive, searching the landscape.

"I could have sworn . . ." Joe began hesitantly. "You heard nothing, Lieutenant?"

The lieutenant was puzzled. Other than the voices of the young people a few yards away, there was no sound or movement. "What should I have heard?" he asked simply.

Joe pulled out a cigar case and removed a cigar. "Don't laugh," he said, unwrapping a Macanudo. "I heard a *shofar.*"

"A *shofar!*" At first astonished, the Israeli then smiled. "In these ancient hills, one's imagination is easily stirred."

"Yes . . . I suppose you're right," Joe answered, trying to hold the lighter steady to his cigar, vague premonitions gnawing at him. Suddenly wondering how Rick was faring, he glanced at his watch. It was a few minutes past noon.

Undulating winds followed them on the narrow road through the Golan hills, the air crisp despite the warm sun. Deserted trenches surrounded some of the overgrown hillsides; abandoned bunkers crested each hilltop.

"All built by the Syrians after the '48 War," the lieutenant remarked. "We took it back in '67."

"You have no use for it now?" Joe asked.

The Israeli shook his head, pointing to the warning markers in the fields. "It would take years for us to dig out the thousands of mines left by the Syrians. It would serve no purpose. We have new bunkers overlooking Syrian territory. That is where we are going now."

They crossed a flat plain strewn with the rubble of basalt stone. Off to one side, small cone-shaped pinnacles jutted out from the ground as reminders of extinct volcanic activity.

The lieutenant touched Joe's arm. "Once beyond that pass ahead"—he gestured toward two hills a mile away—"slow down. At the fork, turn right onto the dirt road. There is a farming *kibbutz* to the left of the fork, which you can visit later, if you wish. You would all be most welcome to share the after–Yom Kippur supper."

"Thanks, Lieutenant. The invitation is mighty interesting, but we have a previous commitment in Jerusalem.

But the visit—that I would appreciate." Joe glanced at him. "By the way, Lieutenant, would you mind being filmed? I'd like the camera to catch us being met at the bunker. Then afterward in the bunker, I'd like to get your background on both film and tape."

The Israeli laughed. "Why not! If you can find it interesting . . ."

Joe looked into the rearview mirror. "Ralph, Paul, I guess you've heard!"

"We're ready," was Ralph's instant reply.

Triangular, yellow and red signs in Hebrew atop barbed wire fences lining the dusty road designated mine fields. Joe followed a sharp curve, then downshifted for a steep incline. Cresting the rise, they found themselves on a small, barren plain, pinkish in color. Ominous concrete bunkers topped the range of hills to the right.

The lieutenant gestured for him to pull over. "We're here," he said simply.

Two men and a woman in civilian clothes watched them cautiously from a promontory overlooking the plain. When the lieutenant waved, the woman and one of the men came down to greet them. The woman was a young, slim, blue-eyed blond. A scarf protected her hair from the wind. With a start, Joe noticed she held a machine gun in her small hands.

Suddenly recognizing Yacov, she waved her free hand excitedly. *"Shabat Shalom,* Yacov. Do you know your father is on the next hill?"

"Holy Christ!" Ralph muttered, staring at the smiling face. "Christ, Paul! She'd need that gun back home in the city just for protection."

Grinning, Paul shook his head. "Ralph, you watching that meter? I'm about ready."

"Protect that mike, Ralph," Joe cautioned. "There's a lot of wind flutter here."

The microphone was already on an extension. "It's okay, Mr. Green. We're all set." He sneaked another look at the young Israeli girl and, shaking his head, gave an approving whistle.

Yacov introduced Tovah to Hannah, and together they watched the Americans at work. Just a few minutes ago, they seemed to be young boys at play, but now . . .

Tovah heard her name called, as did Hannah and Yacov. Turning from Paul, who had the camera resting on his shoulder, she noted Ralph wearing a set of headphones. He already had the mike on its extension hovering above the heads of Joe Green, the lieutenant and the Israeli from the bunker.

"Raise it a bit, Ralph," Paul cried out. "Okay, that's it."

Joe conducted the interview.

They were from the *kibbutz*, at present acting as a vigilante group to spell the regulars on the religious holiday. Mostly, they attended the vineyards, whose grapes were used solely for wine making. The vines, now brown, were withering in the autumn sun. Soon it would be time to build a *sukkah*. Their small bunker, recently completed, as yet had no armaments and was being used merely as a lookout at present.

Paul carried the camera, and Yacov lent Ralph a hand with the sound equipment and the case of film. The incline was steep, and they ascended with difficulty to the bunker.

The lone guard, in his twenties, tall and lanky, saluted the lieutenant and surveyed the strangers curiously, greeting them merely with *"shalom."*

"Quiet?" asked the lieutenant.

"Quiet."

"Nothing unusual?"

"They start their motors occasionally. That is all."

The lieutenant nodded, studying the tall Israeli. "When is your relief?"

"About a half-hour."

The lieutenant decided to release them from further duty since he and his group would remain there until the relief arrived. Getting their rifles from inside the bunker, the vigilantes saw that the lieutenant was unarmed and left two Uzi machine guns.

Hannah, about to depart down the slope, was stopped by Ralph.

"Hannah," he started hesitantly, "if I come back to the *kibbutz* in a couple of days . . . would I be able to see you?"

She tossed her head impishly, her blue eyes shining. "I'll be there."

Fascinated, he watched her and, when she was halfway down the slope, returned her promising wave.

Paul nudged Tovah. "He never could resist a blond. Now me—I'm different. I'm partial to brunettes."

"Paul, aren't you ever serious?"

He grinned. "I am serious. Didn't you know?"

She shook her head, unable to suppress a smile. About to retort, she noticed Joe Green emerging from the bunker. He seemed disturbed.

"Paul, you're not on vacation. Did you forget you have a job to do!"

"Sorry, Dad." Paul's manner changed abruptly. "What's the next step?"

The bunker commanded a view over a range of hills that stretched far into Syria. Vineyards and olive groves were in evidence throughout the hillls. A bleached village, curiously without any signs of life, nestled against the base of a mountain a mile away. Green followed the contour of the land, settling on a plain a half-mile west of the village. In orderly rows of deep trenches, a great number of Syrian tanks were dug in behind mounds of sand. Reaching fifty, Joe stopped counting. God! he thought with a sense of dread. Like cats waiting to pounce!

The lieutenant appeared at his side, suddenly extremely vexed. He spoke curtly.

"You are my responsibility! Into the bunker! All filming will be from inside!" He glanced disapprovingly at Yacov, then turned and entered the bunker. The young Israeli, newly humbled, followed him.

Once inside, the lieutenant sent Yacov behind the dividing partition to stand watch at a slotted opening overlooking Syrian territory. The lieutenant accompanied him, Joe following.

"I'm sorry, Yacov," the officer murmured, referring to the incident outside.

Yacov looked him in the eye. "It was necessary. I should have known better." The lieutenant appeared relieved.

Joe, waiting for the proper moment, offered his own apology. "I'm the one that should have known better."

The officer shrugged indifferently. "If you wish, I will accept your apology. But it does not excuse Ya . . ."

The sound of motors drifted in on a flurry of wind.

Yacov, now standing above them on a high platform, turned, his eyes showing disbelief. "Lieutenant, the tanks are heading for Israel." His voice had suddenly become hoarse. "I don't think it's a scare tactic."

In an instant, the officer leaped up the steps of the platform to join Yacov. Stunned for a few seconds, Joe ran after him, his heart pounding.

Fifty yards from the bunker, a high wire fence followed the contour of the border. Beyond the fence, a steep slope tapered gradually into the Syrian plain.

The Syrian tanks were on the move. Five abreast, they drove forward as if on parade. The lead T–62 tanks crossed the plain unimpeded, descended into a deep wadi, then climbed up and over a saddle between two ranges. In a lesser wadi, about a mile from the Israeli bunker, they crashed through the barriers onto Israeli territory. An instant later, Israeli tanks from the far ridge opened fire upon the invaders.

A loud explosion brought Joe Green to the nightmarish reality. Leaning forward on the steps, he peered over the heads of two Israelis crouched in an open trench just outside the doorway. A Syrian tank, its turret torn off, was ablaze. Through the dust and smoky haze, he saw what appeared to be part of a human torso lying on the ground ten yards from the inferno. Joe turned away, sickened, his throat constricting. He was no longer disciplined—if he ever had been—to the ravages of war.

Starting a retreat from the steps, he was alerted by an unexpected shout. Instinctively spinning about, he saw the lieutenant and Yacov leaping down the steps into the bunker. Hard on their heels came the two previously trapped Israeli tankmen. As one stumbled, Joe made a grab and prevented him from falling. The young soldier, glancing at him wth bloodshot eyes, panted his thanks, then sank down to the dirt floor. Leaning back against the wall, he rubbed his face and tried to catch his breath. The other man, a tank commander, was older and stockier, with iron-gray hair. To Joe's surprise, he embraced Yacov with a bear hug.

Yacov, grinning and holding back tears, said chokingly, "What took you so long, poppa?"

The commander held Yacov at arm's length, squeezing his shoulders in appreciative appraisal, then laughed aloud. His voice boomed, "You hear that, Lieutenant? My son has a sense of humor!"

"Enough of the family reunion, Major Aron. What's happening outside?"

Lines creased the major's ruddy face. "They do not worry about us. They are moving on a prearranged course." At that moment, a group of Skyhawks zoomed past overhead. The major jerked a thumb upward. "For the moment, that is our salvation. They must blow up the gasoline trucks. A few of the lead Syrian tanks have already run out of fuel."

"But what about us, here? How do we get out before they use flame throwers?"

The major gestured reassuringly. "So far, they have not. It will be dark soon, and our own tanks will pick us up." He looked around and, for the first time, seemed to notice the Americans. He noted Paul with the camera on the platform. His voice carried across the room despite the booming cannon fire. "You photographed the invasion?"

"Sure did!" Paul cried out. "It's all documented on film —including your escape!"

Major Aron nodded, then frowned while regarding Joe. "Mr. Green?" Joe extended a hand, apprehension pulling at him as he tried to read the major's expression.

"Yes, Major, something on your mind?"

The officer studied him for a moment, his frown deepening. "You do not know?" He appeared bewildered and addressed the lieutenant. "You have no radio?"

"What radio? It's in the Rover! What are you trying to tell us?"

The major rubbed a bushy eyebrow, then gestured helplessly. "The Egyptians have made a full-scale assault on the Sinai."

Joe, paling visibly, asked, "When?"

"It started right after noon."

Joe glanced at his watch. "Oh, my God! It's after . . ."

CHAPTER 10

October 6, 1973

". . . six already," Baron said.

Captain Avram nodded, preoccupied with the stillness that surrounded the fort. They could not leave as yet, but later, despite HQ's instructions, might be too late.

After the initial shelling, the first wave of Egyptian infantry and medium tanks had bypassed their bunker, mortar shells and smoke screens protecting the invaders as they ranged far into the Sinai. The bunker was now caught in the middle.

"It will be dark soon," Baron said, not waiting for Avram to offer information. "Heavy tanks and supply trucks won't be long in coming. That first spearhead will regroup with other units that have crossed the canal, but they can't go very far without supplies."

The captain eyed him with undisguised curiosity. "Baron, since you know that much, if you were in command, what would be your orders as of this minute?"

Baron wiped his forehead, a trace of a smile showing in the growing darkness. "I would suggest, captain, that since the Egyptians are giving us a slight respite, we terminate our fast."

The fret lines in the captain's face eased, but he remained unsmiling. "Of course, Baron. An empty stomach only fogs the mind." He turned to Riv who sat at the

205

radio, his chin in his hands; he had not received a message in hours. "Riv, get the mess sergeant on the intercom and find out whether anything is prepared."

Two things bothered Riv. The last message received, just before their aerial was blasted away, had come from an Israeli tank in the desert: Egyptian paratroopers had landed ten miles inside the Sinai. The second thing was Baron. Who was this man who knew his parents and referred to his mother as "Lee"? Why had his parents never mentioned him? But there was something so familiar about him. Plagued by these thoughts, he heard the captain speaking.

When Baron requested of the captain that Riv be relieved to join him, Riv's bewilderment increased. Turning the radio over to Leib, Riv cautioned him to leave the incoming switch on—"just in case." Then standing, he asked Baron to follow him.

Leaving the room, the bunker became a long, narrow tube. Double-decker bunks lined one wall. They had to walk single file through the remaining space, Baron at Riv's heels. A dim bulb lit posters of movie stars on the wall. Baron's eyes never left the back of the tall figure before him. *My son!* he kept thinking. That's my son in front of me!

Compressing his lips to contain his emotions, he almost ran into Riv. A voice coming from the other end of the narrow corridor said: "Okay, Riv. I've eaten." Peering past Riv, Baron saw the soldier slide into a bunk so they could pass.

"Thanks, Ehud," Riv said. "Anything good?"

He made a face. "Ehh, if you like fried vegetables. He has no time for anything else." Becoming aware of Baron, his eyes lit up. He stuck his head out from the lower bunk. "The American! How you like our Holiday Inn?" he queried, grinning.

Baron grinned in return. "I've seen better—and I've seen worse."

A whooshing sound grew louder and then exploded over their heads. A shower of dust draped their shoulders. Riv turned and motioned Baron into a bunk.

No one spoke during the five minutes of shelling. Then, satisfied that it had stopped, Riv slid out of the bunk. Baron followed, asking, "Mortars?"

"They're using 82mm." Ehud shook his head. "They

never give up." He glanced at Riv and Baron dusting themselves off. "Go eat, gentlemen. I must relieve Leib."

Sliding from the bulk after they passed, Ehud suddenly called back, "We have Coca-Cola. It is warm, but just like in America."

Baron grinned. "What! No apple pie?"

Ehud appeared perplexed.

Riv shook his head, smiling. "It's an American joke, Ehud. Go already."

Almost at the end of the hall, Baron touched Riv's shoulder. "Listen," he said softly.

Riv lifted his head, alert to the strange scratching sounds. A moment later, he smiled. "Desert rats. They're growing fat on our garbage."

Baron shrugged. "Okay, let's go get some fried vegetables—and a warm Coke."

Twenty-three-hundred hours and the darkened fort was charged with impatient anticipation. In the flashing bursts of constant mortar and artillery shelling, the strained faces of the men appeared garish. With the hour of evacuation approaching, all recognized that it had become a race with the clock. An hour ago, GHQ had relayed information on shortwave that the bunker directly north of them had been engaged in savage, hand-to-hand fighting. News from the Golan was equally perilous. The Syrians were attacking with planes, missiles, tanks, and heavy artillery.

Surprisingly, Egyptian infantry, having crossed the canal on amphibious carriers, continued to bypass the bunker. Watching the infantry follow the tanks that fanned out into the desert, Captain Avram knew that once the Egyptians regrouped, their fort would be assaulted. A question kept repeating itself: Was the evacuation worth the attempt? Was it better to die fighting in the bunker than to be annihilated in the desert sands?

Grim-faced, he went through the bunker, checking his men and their equipment, readying them for the deadly race. He could not conceive of sitting and waiting for inevitable capture or death. His decision made, he ordered canteens of water for the men.

In the dark, Baron felt the machine pistol in his pocket. Unbeknownst to the others, he had stashed the gun and an extra clip in his jacket during one of the shellings. Reassured, but with an urgent sense of helplessness, he leaned against the steel wall and glanced in Riv's direction.

He had learned much while sharing a meager repast with Riv. It was only after four years of discussion that Riv had convinced his mother to give up the shop in Venice. At the moment, she was considering the sale of the apartment house in Rome because the money could be put to better use expanding their shop at home. Riv's own interest was in radio, and until his father's unexpected death, he had dreamed of owning his own business. Since that time, he satisfied himself doing radio repair in the shop's back room. Baron had seen his eyes light up when he expounded on plans for a new and larger shop, should his mother decide to sell out in Rome.

Baron had watched him, listened without interruption, and continued to be amazed that he was sitting opposite his own son. Containing his emotions obdurately, he rubbed his cheek and measured his words carefully. "How much would you need to start this business you're interested in?"

Riv sipped from his coffee mug, then shrugged his shoulders. "Right now, that's difficult to say. It could be anywhere from . . ." He had halted suddenly, his confusion evident. "Why do you ask?"

Baron prayed his face didn't betray his emotions. He answered casually, "I owed your father some money during the war—which I never got the chance to repay. I was wounded and sent back to the States, and was never able to get in touch with him again."

Riv leaned forward, intrigued in spite of himself. "How much money is involved?"

Baron chose carefully. Too little money was inconsequential, too much would be unbelievable. "About five hundred dollars."

Riv leaned back, his mouth pursed for a soft whistle, his eyes displaying disbelief. "My father gave *you*, an American, five hundred dollars? During the war?"

"Not in cash," Baron replied hastily. "In goods. We did a lot of business together—mostly cameras." Baron felt the stickiness creeping under his arms. "I figure the five hundred with accrued interest should run around twenty-five hundred by now."

At this point, Riv was summoned back through the

intercom. He stood up uncertainly, then said, "My mother knew about this?"

"About the dealings at the time—yes. Regarding the amount—no."

Riv tarried a moment longer. "Finish your coffee, Baron. We'll talk again."

Baron watched him rush off. Picking up his coffee mug, he became aware of the slight tremble in his hand.

The bombardment started on schedule. In minutes, a swath of craters was created behind the fort. The nightmarish scene of three burning Egyptian tanks could easily have been mistaken for comets exploding on a lunar landscape. The enemy infantry had been dispersed, scattering north and south.

Captain Avram crouched in the trench beside the open doorway of the darkened fort. Peering through the smoke, he watched the Egyptian tanks return the fire of Israeli artillery. The night sky was alive with flashing bursts of colored light. Straining to read his watch in the glare, he signaled one minute to go.

Baron patted the reassuring muzzle of the machine pistol in his pocket. At the last moment, he had stuffed the *talleth* in another pocket, though he wasn't sure why.

The Israeli artillery barrage halted, and the men began to surge forward at the captain's signal. Leib spoke quickly to Sergeant Radaver at his side. "Don't you lose the American!"

Baron's instructions were explicit. He was to stick with Leib, Riv, and the sergeant. If, by some small miracle, one of the jeeps should still be intact, it would be their means of escape.

The silent men advanced all in a half-crouch, moving along the trench skirting the bunker. Flashes that resembled heat lightning lit up the horizon, but no firing was directed their way. Captain Avram stood at the end of the trench, urging the men into the desert. Ten men had passed when Leib reached him. "Go! Check the jeeps, I will wait." He peered at Riv, the sergeant, and Baron. "You all right, Baron?"

Baron felt the muzzle of the gun in his pocket again and straightened the canteen of water dangling on his chest. "I've had better moments, Captain, but I'm okay.

209

Stop worrying about me. You've got enough to take care of."

The captain didn't reply. Strange man, he thought, good officer material. Dismissing Baron, he turned his head impatiently for Leib's return, knowing the lull would not last.

Leib, breathless, was back in less than three minutes.

"A small miracle," he said. "One is ready. No guns, but a half-tank of petrol." He paused. "Captain, come with us."

Captain Avram was already moving away. "No, I will catch up with the others. Go, Leib. We will meet again." He waved, moving stealthily across the sands. *"Shalom, shalom."*

An embankment of sand covered the jeep on three sides. Sergeant Radaver got behind the wheel as Leib ordered Baron and Riv to lie prone on the ground. If the engine started, the noise would carry to the Egyptian infantry.

Radaver cursed as the motor coughed twice without catching. A moment later, when it sprang to life with a roar, Riv and Baron leaped to their feet, Riv taking the seat beside Radaver, Baron behind him. Leib jumped in behind Radaver.

The jeep's four-wheel drive pulled them out of the pocket. Gunning the engine, Radaver raced through an opening in the crumpled barbed wire. The whoosh of a mortar followed them a second later. Radaver drove the jeep into a drop between two sand dunes just as the shell exploded on the crest. Leib tapped him on the shoulder, directing him to follow four o'clock as best he could.

Radaver drove expertly, cresting the dunes only when necessary to keep his direction. The mortars followed them persistently, occasionally spraying them with sand. The three passengers gritted their teeth, powerless to do anything but hold on to the bouncing vehicle.

Baron laughed suddenly, and when Leib stared at him wide-eyed with suspicion, he said sporadically, "Haven't had a ride like this . . . since I rode the Cyclone in Coney Island when I was a kid." Seeing Leib's bewilderment, he added hastily, "Sorry, Leib, it . . ."

An explosion roared in Baron's ears, and he felt himself being lifted into the air.

He found himself lying on the sand about ten feet

away from the overturned jeep. Stunned, he rubbed his forehead and tried to focus his eyes. The smashed radiator hissed, and black smoke swirled upward. He sat up and could see no other movement. He rubbed his face again, trying to clear his thoughts. How long had he been out? And where were the others? And Riv! Where was Riv!

A whining shell passed overhead and exploded harmlessly fifty yards away. Coming out of his disorientation, Baron guessed that the missile was heavier than a mortar. An Egyptian tank? It had to be! He felt for his machine pistol, though he knew it would be of little use if he was spotted. His mouth had gone dry, and the canteen was no longer around his neck.

"Damn!" he spit out in mental anguish. "Dammit, Riv! Where the hell are you?" Realizing that he was on the verge of losing control, he slapped himself, muttering, "Stop it, stop it! This is no time to panic!"

He stared angrily at the rear of the jeep, then decided a closer inspection was necessary.

The disabled vehicle rested precariously atop a small dune, its underside facing a downward slope in total darkness. Baron crept to the jeep. Alert to any sign of movement, he peered into the void.

Nothing! It was impossible, he thought. All three of them couldn't have just vanished. He slid over the edge and down into the trough.

He knew instantly that the body he saw was lifeless. God! he thought. But who? He lifted the head, holding it inches from his own. Dear God! It was Leib! He felt for a pulse in the neck, though he knew it was useless. Cursing to himself angrily, he crept along the bottom of the trough, fearful of what he might find.

He came upon another figure. He felt a chest, caved in and bloody. "God! Don't do this to me!" he muttered, more in anger than prayer. Dipping his hand into the sand, he tried to rid himself of the blood. He leaned closer to identify the figure, his own heart pounding as though it could offer life to the still form.

Radaver! The sergeant! At first, relief, than grief beset Baron. He was going to be sick. Taking deep swallows, he became irate. "You stupid bastard, what can you offer your *sabra* bride now? You don't die for a cause, you live for it!" He fought the aggression and the tears, then touched the sergeant's cheek. "I'm sorry, Mike. You knew what you were doing. Sleep well."

Fearful of his next discovery, he stiffened. His hand accidentally found the sergeant's canteen. Easy does it, he cautioned himself, unlocking the cap. He took a slow swallow, savoring it, then recapped it before his willpower gave out.

Ten yards in either direction, there was no sign of Riv. Bewildered, he struggled up the incline of soft sand and found himself bathed in bright moonlight. Settling in the shadow of the smoking jeep, he tried to reason out Riv's whereabouts. The sergeant and Leib were on the left side of the . . . "Stupid!" he admonished himself.

On all fours, he started around the front of the wreck, searching the skies in all directions. The sounds of cannons rolled across the desert like thunder, the northern horizon flashing over a critical tank battle. To the south, the fighting was more sporadic. No shells had landed near the jeep in the last few minutes, and for the moment, Baron felt a sort of safety.

Baron thought his heart had stopped as he saw Riv, lying on his back, alongside the jeep. Moving quickly, he checked for Riv's pulse, almost laughing when he felt the beat. Riv mumbled incoherently as Baron wiped sand from his face.

"Can't drive, papa. It's too dark . . . and my leg hurts."

Baron opened the canteen and spilled a few drops onto Riv's lips before allowing him a swallow. Riv coughed, and then caught his breath, his lips twisted in pain.

"Poppa, it's my leg. How can I walk?"

Puzzled, Baron glanced down Riv's form, his face blanching at the sight of the left leg buried beneath the jeep. "God!" he muttered as he leapt to his feet, intending to right the vehicle if possible. He realized an instant later that the idea was unthinkable. Visions of the jeep toppling down upon the lifeless bodies of Radaver and Leib appalled him. Baron knelt down and studied the trapped limb, which was covered to the thigh. Sweat poured from him as he contemplated the possibilities. Broken? Smashed? No, he wouldn't accept the worst. The sand was soft. It was possible that the leg had merely been pushed into the fine surface. He began digging furiously, making a trough six inches wide down the length of Riv's leg. Then he started on the sand beneath the injured limb. Riv moaned as his leg slipped into the makeshift trough.

Baron glanced at him worriedly, heaved a deep sigh, and stretched his arm until he found Riv's ankle. Feeling it gingerly, he ran his hand slowly along the skin. Nothing broken. Nearing the knee, he felt the stickiness of blood on torn trousers. Hesitating, he looked at Riv, who seemed to be unconscious, then he continued his examination. His hand felt like it had been dipped in oil; he couldn't find the bulge of Riv's kneecap. Sweat trickled down Baron's face, and he withdrew his hand as Riv groaned.

Baron stared at his blood-soaked hand in horror, then jammed it into the sand to rid himself of the sight. It was years since he had to contend with the injury of someone close to him. He set aside his horror as he realized Riv was trying to speak.

Riv's voice, a raspy whisper, quavered in the air. "Poppa, how will I walk?"

Baron's eyes filled with pity, anger, and pain. Leaning forward, he touched Riv's cheek gently. "You needn't worry, son. Poppa will take care of it." Riv's eyes closed, and he seemed to rest. Deliberating for only a moment, Baron grubbed at the sand beneath the injured leg.

Five minutes later, having freed Riv from the jeep, Baron examined the damaged knee. The flesh covering the knee joint had been torn away, but as near as he could make out without disturbing the coagulating blood, the kneecap had remained unbroken. Fighting off a wave of nausea, he tore the trouser leg further up the thigh. Dampening a handkerchief, he tried to clean the surrounding flesh. His mind raced. Riv needed immediate attention; he had already lost too much blood. Despairingly, he looked down at the still form. "Why you!" he cried. "Why you and not me!"

Riv would have to be carried; Baron didn't question it for a moment. But how? Any undue movement and Riv would bleed to dea . . . He stopped, refusing to form the word.

In desperation, he looked to the southeast, as if seeking an answer from the only area where there were no bursting missiles. In the distance, the mountains of Sinai were a shadowy outline against the moonlit sky, offering nothing more than a bleak haven. Infuriated with his own helplessness, he punched his thigh.

The frayed strands of the linen *talleth* fell from his pocket.

He yanked the prayer shawl from his pocket and quickly got out his pen. Working without hesitation, using the pen to twist the linen around Riv's thigh, he made a perfect tourniquet. The prayer shawl was long enough to cover the injury and darkened instantly when he applied it to the area. Somewhat apprehensive, Baron placed his palm across Riv's forehead. The boy's head was cool beneath the perspiration. He took a deep breath and looked away, trying to formulate a plan. If he could reach the mountains, then turn north, he *might* come upon an Israeli unit.

He reached under Riv's armpit and said, "Time to go, son."

Riv's eyes fluttered open. "I can't drive, poppa."

"I know, son. You won't have to."

A sense of elation filled Baron each time he addressed Riv as "Son," knowing full well he would never have another opportunity. Overcome, he fought his desire to hug this tall young man. Then, deliberately suppressing all traces of emotion, he lifted the limp body. Riv mumbled incoherently, sounding panicky.

"Don't worry," Baron said. "I won't let anything happen to you." He felt the sting of tears in his own eyes. He pulled the body onto his shoulders and began what he hoped would be the journey to safety.

Befuddled by the crazy angle of the world, Riv tried to lift his head. Suddenly realizing that he was slung across someone's shoulders, he cried out in a strangled voice, "What the hell's going on?"

Baron took a deep breath as he plodded through the sand. "Just relax—uh—Riv, and enjoy the ride."

"Baron? What am I doing up here? Where are the others?"

Baron's speech came haltingly between breaths. "Dead —all dead."

Riv, totally bewildered, tried to think clearly. Was this a dream? He thought of his leg. There was no pain, only a strange numbness. He closed his eyes. His brain

214

whirled as he tried to focus his thoughts. In an anguished voice, he gasped, "Who *are* you?"

Baron, intent on each step, his footing precarious in the soft sand, was too distracted for conversation. The moon had slipped behind a cloud, and the darkness was foreboding. The raging tank battle to the north was at least a mile away, but acrid smoke drifted across the landscape. Finally Baron said, "I'm an old friend doing a favor for your family." Misreading Riv's tortured "God!" he added quickly. "Hang on, we just have to make those foothills."

"Put me down!" Riv exploded unexpectedly.

Baron held on to the squirming figure firmly. "No dice. You could have a ruptured blood vessel."

"You're out of your mind, Baron. Those foothills are at least three kilometers away. You'll only kill yours . . ." Baron's abrupt halt forced him to twist his head. "What is it?" he mumbled as dizziness overtook him.

"Quiet!" Baron said sharply. "Just listen!"

The ground quaked underfoot, and they could hear the rumbling of an unseen tank. By the sound, it was not too far off and heading their way. Shifting his weight, Baron scraped his shoe and realized they had reached the perimeter road. Spurred into action, he scurried across the hard surface. Riv groaned with each jounce.

"God, Baron! My head's coming off!"

"Just don't lose it!" Baron gasped. "Not much further." He prayed the moon would remain hidden and almost ran into a smoking, burned-out, abandoned Patton tank. Circling around, he ran a few feet, then lost his footing as the ground dropped out from under him. As he fell forward, he felt Riv tumble away from his grasp.

As he came to rest at the bottom of the sand dune, Baron brushed the coarse material of a soldier's uniform. Wiping sand from his mouth, he called out softly, "Riv?"

There was no answer from the still form.

Unable to distinguish anything in the blackness, he felt for the hand of the unconscious figure, his heart pumping wildly. "Dammit, Riv, not now!"

A moment later, his hand froze. The face was cold and lifeless—but it wasn't Riv. Crawling on all fours, he moved around the body and found another one—also dead for hours. Israeli tankmen. Distracted for a mo-

.ment, a wolf's howl in the distance sent him scurrying for Riv.

He found him, hardly a yard from the second inert figure. Baron cleaned the sand from Riv's face, alarmed by his overly warm forehead.

Riv groaned. "Baron? Go . . . leave me . . . you can make it alone."

"Yeah, sure. And what about the baby girl Debbi wants when you get back?"

Riv lifted a hand to his head, trying to erase the painful cobwebs. "What the hell you talking about?"

Baron placed a hand across Riv's mouth. "Listen . . ." he whispered, " . . . and be quiet!"

Crawling up the slope of sand, he peered over the edge at the once again moonlit landscape. A T-62 tank had halted on the perimeter road apparently to observe the burned-out Patton. Seemingly satisfied, it started to move on when the stillness was suddenly shattered by three Phantom jets thundering past. "About time," Baron muttered. They were the first Israeli planes he had seen since the initial assault.

The Egyptian tank moved off the road hurriedly, apparently in search of shadow. Baron saw one of the Phantoms break from the group, bank rapidly, and return for a pass at the tank. The machine gun atop the tank came alive as the Phantom swooped in.

In the blink of an eye, the Phantom was on top of and beyond its target. The T-62 burst into flame from a direct hit.

Baron stared at the metal inferno, displaying no emotion. Even though they were the enemy, these senseless deaths appalled him. Then his passivity left him. "You stupid bastards!" he muttered in the direction of the flaming tank. "Couldn't you have stayed on your side of the Suez?" He thought of Radaver and Leib, and wondered, "Are they happier now?" Perhaps they were, having left a disturbed world for a peaceful one. They had donated their lives for the preservation of Israel. Would it be for nothing? he asked in silence. How many wars had been fought? And how many more must be endured before peace would come to the Holy Land? Baron flicked an insect from his grimy cheek and shook his head. Having lost the one great love of his life, he had devoted all his energies to depicting the horrors of war.

It was a futile gesture, though, his pictures and writings having no effect upon the gods of war.

He pushed aside his philosophizing as a sixth sense alerted him to danger. He lifted his head.

As the jet disappeared into the night, two men climbed out of the blazing tank and ran for the cover of the smoking Patton. Baron, aware of the guns they were carrying, spun out of his lethargy and slid down to Riv's side. Pulling out a handkerchief from his pocket, he stuffed it into Riv's mouth. "We're going to have company, Riv. Understand? If you have pain, just bite this." With his entire body aching, Riv was beyond caring, his diffused thoughts on Debbi and a baby girl. His eyes closed. Sorry, Debbi, I'm too tired to think.

Baron, working furiously yet methodically, slid one of the lifeless bodies across Riv, carefully keeping its weight off the injured leg. A moment later, he pulled the other corpse across himself. The machine pistol out and in readiness.

Baron waited, trying to control his heavy breathing, his nose pinched by the odor of death. He was suddenly struck by the irony of his situation. In the unfolding drama the cameraman had become the actor. In a few moments, he could be murdered—or become a murderer.

He watched the two figures silhouetted against the brightened night sky. One leaned forward, murmuring something unintelligible in Arabic. The only word Baron could make out was "Zionist," which was spat out. The other instantly lifted his gun.

Baron pressed the trigger; the pistol jerked in his hand as it raked both men. One man fell forward, the other fell back and out of sight. Baron waited in a timeless void, his temples pulsing furiously, wondering whether he had emptied the clip.

Although there was no sign of movement, Baron waited out another minute, then pushed out from under the corpse lying on top of him. At Riv's side, he pulled out the gag and forced him to take a swallow from the half-full canteen. Riv opened his heavy eyelids.

"Baron? You still here?"

"You can bet on it."

"I want to go home," Riv said, sounding incredibly childlike.

Baron, unable to reply, wet his handkerchief and wiped the feverish face. There was an ache in his chest as he looked at the helpless figure. The recurring urge to comfort and console him was overwhelming, but time was unyielding and didn't allow for sentiment. Suppressing his emotions, he simply said, "Time to go, son."

His legs on the verge of giving out, Baron staggered through the scraggly outcrop following the rock formations. Reaching a sheer cliff and finding the sand hard underfoot, he moved in a northerly direction without stopping. Although his mouth had gone dry and sweat was running into his eyes, he refused to concede that he was attempting the impossible. He peered along the wall, eyes stinging, searching for a place of concealment. The rock formation, ascending fifty feet from the desert floor, offered no haven from an unexpected visitation. He plodded on, his breath coming in short gasps.

Directly north about two miles from his position, the night sky was constantly brightened by bursts of blue, red, and yellow flashings. It was as if he were watching a Fourth of July celebration. Becoming light-headed, he stared hypnotically at the desert. It was gray in the moonlight and wind-sculptured into uniform, ridged patterns.

Dazed for a moment, he came to a standstill and shook his head. A bead of sweat stung his eye. As if awakening from a dream, he called out huskily, "Who's there?"

There was no answer except for the rumbling of cannon fire rolling across the desert, its echoes resounding in the wadis behind the rock formations.

Wavering beneath Riv's unconscious weight, Baron stared to his right at the spines of rock flanking an entrance into a small cul-de-sac. Overjoyed, he reeled into the opening, falling to his knees beneath a rock overhang. As gently as he could manage, he let Riv slide from his shoulders and heard the expected moan.

Too tired to respond, Baron just blinked his eyes for a few seconds, then ran a sleeve across his burning eyelids. He turned to face Riv and caught his son watching him.

Baron wiped Riv's face, aware of the feverish eyes studying him unflinchingly. Lowering his gaze, Baron

218

reached for the canteen. "Swish it around in your mouth before swallowing," he said, hoping the tremor in his voice would pass unnoticed. Riv took a sip and coughed, turning his head away when offered another swallow.

"Save it for yourself, Baron. You're doing all the work."

Baron nodded, then smiled indulgently, keeping to the pretense that their situation wasn't entirely hopeless. He forced a laugh. "Of course. After all, the old man's going to need it. Right?"

Riv lifted a hand to his forehead. "Baron, let's cut out the bull! No matter how well you knew my parents, it doesn't require this ultimate sacrifice on your part."

About to wet his lips on the canteen, Baron stopped and raised an eyebrow. "Ultimate sacrifice? Hell! You're out of your mind if you don't think we're going to make it!" He took a quick sip, savored it, and fought off an overwhelming desire to finish the canteen. Capping it hastily, he stared at Riv with admiration. What guts he must have, in his condition, to throw aside self-preservation—a character of extraordinary strength. And for whom? Baron asked himself. Truly a perfect stranger was his easy reply. He grimaced suddenly, knowing they would always be strangers of a sort—no matter what the outcome.

Suppressing morose thoughts, he got to his feet and said, "Nature calls, Riv. Give me a few seconds." Then added, "Don't go away."

"I'll be here," came back at him with a soft laugh.

Riv lay under the rock overhang, sweating but feeling chilled. He stretched a hand to his thigh and fingered the *talleth* wrapped around the numbed flesh. Rambling thoughts ran through his throbbing brain; images of his mother, father, Debbi, and the children intertwined. Distressed, he brought his hand back to his head, fighting the sinking feeling in his chest. No tears, he commanded to himself, this American must not see tears. Baron—he thought, willfully focusing his thoughts—*who was he?* Why had his parents never mentioned Baron? He must have been an important part of their lives at one time. Riv could feel the weight lifted from his chest as he thought of the man. There was an aura of strength that emanated from this man, offering a ray of hope that he could accomplish anything he set out to do. It wasn't a physical strength but a strength derived from a sense of purpose. He lapsed into dizziness again. As he struggled to calm himself, he heard Baron.

"Take it easy. We'll be on our way in five minutes." The moon, hidden again, left them in darkness. Baron felt for the *talleth* and, finding it stiff with dried blood, released a sigh of relief. "How about another sip before we start?" Riv shook his head.

Frowning, Baron stood up and studied the intermittently lighted northern horizon. They would have to travel northeast; an Israeli combat unit was their only hope. He wondered briefly whether Captain Avram and his men had been picked up, then turned back to Riv. "How about it, Riv. You ready to go home?"

Riv chuckled. As hurt as he was, he had to admire Baron's spirit. "I'm ready, my friend, but first tell me something. What about your own family? Do they know where you are?"

"I have no family—only old friends."

Old friends. Instinctively Baron thought of Joe and the others, and the last reports of the Golan fighting. Although filled with misgivings, he tossed his head defiantly, refusing to dwell upon unwanted and possibly needless anxieties. Unaccountably, despite his best effort to dismiss her from his mind, an image of Lee persistently emerged. "You will see Riv tomorrow, and then you will understand." He could see her saying it, the scene etched in his brain. Her eyes so sad . . . Lee! I do understand! I understand now, more than you can imagine! He's a part of me, too!

Automatically, he went into his pocket for his pipe without thinking, but then heard Riv coughing.

He turned, bent over Riv, and with a look of determination, muttered hoarsely, "You ready, Riv? We're going to take off."

Riv made a disconsolate gesture. "Hold it, Baron. It's useless. I'm no help—you'll kill yourself."

"Let's cut the crap. We've got some important people waiting for us at home. Don't make it any more difficult for me. Now lift your arm."

Riv raised his arm mechanically and, a moment later, grit his teeth fiercely as he felt himself being hauled onto Baron's shoulders. His leg was a heavy weight trying to separate from his body. He took deep breaths, tears

220

coming to his eyes. Baron's voice reached through his pain. "You all right, son?"

Nodding, he said, "You're a fool, Baron—but thanks."

Baron blew out a deep breath of air. "Yeah, sure. That's the story of my life."

Baron plodded around the spine of rock. All he had to do was watch the northern horizon, which now resembled the aurora borealis. Viewing the gray landscape, he offered a silent prayer. God, give me strength. Don't let me down now. Not now, after I've found . . . Riv's voice interrupted his prayer.

"Thank God mother's home. She's more level-headed than Debbi." When Baron made no response, he added, "Perhaps your friends are with them—the Greens."

For the women, Baron thought, it would be a trying vigil, but at least they were safe. As for the rest of his "family," he refused to consider the worst. To his right, a slanting rock reached into the night sky, seemingly aimed at a translucent cloud veiling a bright, obstinate moon. Wetting his dry lips, a protesting growl escaped from the caverns of an empty stomach. He turned away, his eyes narrowing, yet with no sense of panic. Far from being heroic, he was simply performing a duty that had to be accomplished before he could reach an unfulfilled destiny. He scanned the horizon, searching beyond the borders of the tank battle to the unseen territory of the Golan. His lips compressed, his inner voice said, "I'll take care of my end, Joe. You take care of yours."

The concrete shelter in the *kibbutz* was at least twenty feet deep with its roof safely hidden under a mound of solid earth. Standing at the head of a trench nearby, Joe Green surveyed the far horizon where a fierce tank battle was taking place among the hills. Absently chewing on an unlit cigar, he turned to observe the newly arrived flatbed trucks unloading Patton tanks. He was unaware of Tovah's presence until she spoke.

"Paul's all right, Mr. Green. The temporary strapping will hold the wrist until we're able to get it into a cast."

He looked at her, noting the slim figure, but couldn't read her features in the dark. "I know," he replied, expelling a deep breath, "but it was stupid of him to try saving a case of film. I can always replace a case of film—but a son . . ."

Tovah regarded him for a moment, debating whether she should voice her thoughts. "It's not Paul on your mind—it's your friend, isn't it?"

Joe dropped the cigar from his mouth and ground it into the earth. "Yes. But not just Rick—Riv, too."

Neither spoke as the Pattons roared into life. But as the ponderous machines rumbled away toward the hills, she spoke in a voice thick with emotion. "I'm a fatalist, Mr. Green. I have a strong feeling that Mr. Baron was meant to be with Riv." Acutely aware of his staring at her, she continued undaunted, as if goaded by a need to express the formless dread enveloping her openly. "I sincerely believe that's why your friend and my mother met again."

Dumbstruck, Joe pursed his lips in silent contemplation. Was she implying . . . ? No—he told himself, frowning—there was no way she could guess the truth. Realizing he had to respond, he tried another tack. "I never argue with a woman's intuition, Tovah, but about your mother—I don't know how Lee can take this. First, it was your grandfather, then your father, and now . . ."

"And now her former lover?" she interjected.

"How long have you known?"

Oblivious to the scurried movements about them, she told him of their meeting in Venice and her remembrances of the photo album.

Before he could say anything more than "Some secret," the sky lit up with a salvo of phosphorus shelling. Three men ran toward them, shouting for them to return to the shelter. Pushing Tovah ahead of him, Joe asked the nearest Israeli, "What's the latest news? What's happening in the hills?"

Breathless, the man waved Joe forward and replied in short gasps. "The shelling . . . is from artillery. We've knocked out . . . about a hundred Syrian tanks. Some have run out of gas . . . and are being abandoned." He took a deep breath as they entered the shelter. "We've slowed them down already . . . now it's our turn to take the offensive."

Joe stayed him just inside the doorway. "What about the Sinai? The Bar-Lev line?"

The man scratched his cheek, eying the American who seemed to have more than a mere reportorial interest in the Bar-Lev. "Relatives there?" Without waiting for confirmation, he added, "The same thing there. We've stopped the Egyptians about ten kilometers inside the Sinai, thanks to the Air Force. As for the outposts, one has been recaptured, according to latest reports. The others"—he shrugged—"we'll have to wait and see."

Joe nodded, feeling an emptiness within him, but with Tovah at his side, he didn't press for additional informaton. Tall and lanky with a rifle slung over his shoulder, the young Israeli already had said enough.

Another man, older and stocky, carrying an Uzi machine gun, came running. "What are you doing, Saul?" he yelled angrily. "Get them ready for evacuation." The younger Israeli moved quickly into the candle-lit interior.

"Sorry," Joe offered lamely. "It's my fault."

The man gave him a cursory glance and then peered inside. Turning back, he said, "You're the American?" His look softening, he added, "Your boy is all right?"

Joe nodded. "How do we get out and where are we going?"

"By truck to Tiberias. The badly wounded will continue on to Jerusalem."

"Thanks," Joe said. "And would it be all right if I questioned the injured for possible publication?"

The man smiled for the first time. "There will be three trucks outside. Ask for Mordechai, a tank radio operator, he has both hands burned. He will tell you enough for all world Jewry to listen."

They waited fifteen tense minutes before they were allowed to leave the shelter. The noise was incredible as Israeli jets thundered past aiming for artillery positions beyond the Golan. The three trucks, ordinarily used for fruit and produce, were waiting at the end of the trench with motors running. Joe helped Paul over the tailgate, then Tovah.

"What about the equipment?" Ralph asked.

"Shove it on board next to Paul, then come with me."

Paul, his arm in a sling, struggled to his feet indignantly. "Dad! Where are you going?"

Joe was in no mood for arguments. "You almost got yourself killed saving this stuff. The least you can do is to keep an eye on it." He turned to Ralph. "You got that recorder?" Ralph felt his pocket and nodded. "Okay then." To Paul and Tovah, he said, "We'll be in one of the other trucks."

Moving aside to allow others to scramble aboard, Joe noted Tovah's look of hesitancy, as if she needed assurance from him. Instinctively, he knew it had nothing to do with the evacuation. He waited for the truck to fill up with the workers from the kibbutz—all men, the women and children having been evacuated earlier—and then shouted above the chattering and noise.

"Tovah, there's no one more resourceful than Rick. If there's a way out, he'll find it."

Waving acknowledgment that she had heard, she watched him disappear into the darkness.

"What was that all about?" Paul asked as she settled down onto the floor. She leaned back against the rear of the cab and sighed wearily. "You worrying about Riv?" he persisted. The tarpaulin-roofed wooden slats allowed only vague lights from burning debris to enter the interior of the truck.

She nodded finally, saying, "Aren't you concerned about your friend Rick?"

"Rick! Cripes! Rick's been involved in so many situations, I can't even imagine him getting harmed." He felt her back stiffen. "Of course, I'm concerned, but I don't want to think about it. Will it help him if I sit here worrying?"

Tovah reached for his good hand. "This Rick Baron —he means an awful lot to you."

He was silent for a moment, then said, "You can't possibly know. It's as if I had two fathers all my life."

Tovah squeezed his hand warmly. "Your father was very angry with you."

"Not really," he answered, giving vent to a small laugh. "It was just concern disguised in anger—a fatherly prerogative." Then, as if anxious to change the subject, he said, "I wonder why he didn't join us."

"He's looking for a soldier named Mordechai."

Mordechai's hands were heavily bandaged, but he was in good humor, his eyes brightening at the prospect of being interviewed by an American newsman. Though he was only nineteen, he seemed even younger.

With the exception of two men on stretchers, all the others in the truck were ambulatory wounded. Mordechai was seated on a fruit crate, braced against the side of the bouncing truck. Joe, holding a hand-mike, squatted uncomfortably by the tailgate, facing the grinning Israeli. Ralph sat on the floor, holding the small tape recorder in his lap, his eyes going from the machine to the bandaged hands of Mordechai.

"Your hands bother you?" Joe asked.

"Only when I try to scratch my head." Mordechai grinned, enjoying his own humor. There were retorts from others, which made him grin more broadly.

"Mordechai," Joe began, "can you start with Saturday morning."

Mordechai's unit had been warned that there might be an attack by nightfall. By noon, their tanks were already loaded with fuel and ammunition. It was two o'clock when two Sukhois flew overhead. The tanks fired at them, then spread out as Syrian artillery bombarded their position. A dozen of their tanks moved out, passing their own forward positions. In minutes, they found themselves facing more than twenty Syrian tanks.

The duel began instantly. In a half-hour, the Israelis had lost two of their own, but had knocked out ten of the enemy tanks. The others dispersed in the hills. The Israelis continued forward and soon looked down upon thirty Syrian tanks and troop carriers. The duel began again at 1500 meters.

The firing never let up. With darkness coming, the Syrian tanks resembled huge torches blighting the landscape. They were forced to withdraw. Because of their advantageous position, it cost the Israelis a lone tank.

Picking up their survivors, the nine remaining Israeli Pattons pressed forward but with strict orders not to go beyond the old cease-fire lines.

Their respite was brief, however, as new orders came over the wireless to aid another company in trouble.

Phosphorus shelling had turned the night into day, and the noise was earsplitting.

"We had about twenty of our own against sixty of theirs," Mordechai stated, his eyes bright with excitement as he relived the battle. "Many of the Syrian tanks had run out of gas and were standing targets. There was a whole row of T-54s burning, and we could see the enemy running away on foot." He paused to catch his breath, then said, "That's when we got hit."

"Holy shit!" Ralph exclaimed. "What happened then!"

Joe gave him a reprimanding glance, pointing to the tape recorder, then addressed Mordechai. "Go on," he said simply.

"A shell had landed on the lid of our tank, wounding our gunner. The flames started to spread, and we had to get out in a hurry. Getting out, I burned my hands on the hot metal." He gestured helplessly. "Another tank picked us up and brought us here to a first-aid station."

Joe switched off the mike. "I guess you'll be glad to go home now." He saw the smile vanish.

"Of course, I'll be glad to go home, but the job is not finished."

"You've done your job," Joe said. "No one can ask any more of you." Mordechai didn't reply.

Finished, Joe thought, when will it finish? This was the fourth Arab-Israeli war in twenty-five years. He looked about him, saw two cigarettes glowing in the dark, but heard no voices. He handed the mike back to Ralph and stared at the night sky.

The smell of cordite was still with them. In the distance the sky was lit up, haloing the far hills. The road was black-topped and smooth, but the truck moved slowly as no headlights were permitted. The opposite lane had a steady stream of traffic, all military heading for the Heights. He turned to Ralph.

"You okay, Ralph?"

"Yes. Thanks, Mr. Green—but I'd be lying if I told you I'd not had enough already. I could never be a war correspondent. To watch strangers killing each other and to just stand there taking pictures of it . . ." He fell silent for a moment, then, "Christ! I'll bet my parents are in church right now, lighting a candle for me."

Joe winced. Lighting a candle, he thought wryly. Mindy must be going out of her mind by now, not to mention Debbi and Lee. He wondered whether they were all together, sharing the tortuous waiting. Disconsolately, he strained his eyes, trying to see the time on his watch. 2:30 A.M.

Mindy pushed a cup of tea across the kitchen table. "Do you have lemon?" she asked Lee.

Lee shook her head without speaking. She accepted the cup, thinking Verdi has a good wife, much stronger

226

than me. She directed a perfunctory glance toward the lone window of the dark room, where the vague light of a bright moon slanted through the taped panes. The oblong light reached the floor with the tape forming a shadow that resembled prison bars. Appropriate, she thought morosely, for someone who was forever a prisoner of war.

"Debbi is finally sleeping," said Mindy. "I don't know what she'd do without you."

Do without you, Lee repeated to herself. It was ironic, she thought, that in reality it was a two-way street. She bit her lip, holding back the tears. That was the only reason she had stayed on after Enzo's death. She had had no other choice with the children refusing to leave Israel. Where would she go without them? The shop in Venice had been a lesson for her. She learned that she couldn't leave them, no matter the circumstances.

In the dark, Mindy refilled the teapot and placed it with the other water-filled pots and containers, then reseated herself at the table. Her lips quivered, but she spoke almost casually. "Why don't you lie down for a while, Lee. There's no point in both of us staying up."

Poor Mindy, thought Lee, her expression solemn. This was a new and unexpected experience for her. And taking it so bravely. "No," she said finally. "But thanks. It was wonderful of you to come over."

Mindy straightened. "Wonderful? What's wonderful about it? I'd have been tearing my hair out if I were alone."

Lee had known early in the morning that something unusual was happening. With the sound of Phantom jets swooping low over Jerusalem, she had run out to the terrace. At the apartment house across the street, a military jeep was picking up a uniformed man. Not overly concerned, she watched the jeep move away. But when it stopped at a house down the street and she saw the driver run in and come out a minute later with another uniformed man, her apprehension started to build. She shivered, glancing toward the streets beyond. The sound of building traffic reached her. A worried frown deepened. Considering it was Yom Kippur, it was more than unusual.

At two o'clock, air raid sirens wailed all over Jerusalem. Immediately thereafter, the radio broke the traditional Yom Kippur silence with the announcement of the Arab attacks. The Civil Defense Command ordered all windows taped and the observation of a strict blackout through the night.

Lee, Debbi, and the boys returned to the apartment from the shelter an hour later after the all-clear siren. Lee tried calling Dov Laslo on the phone, but the lines were tied up. She tried getting Mindy at the King David, also without success.

When Mindy walked in unexpectedly an hour later, they greeted each other with relief and tearful hugs.

The two women sat at the table, sipping their tea and suffering their vigil in the dark. They were silent now, since everything to be said had already been discussed repeatedly. A small radio set at low volume was playing classical music. They waited anxiously for the news bulletins that interrupted every fifteen minutes.

Both women jumped when the telephone broke the silence.

Lee picked her way through the dark and lifted the receiver with a trembling hand. It was the first call to come through all day.

An excited Dov Laslo came on.

"Eleanora? I knew you would be waiting. Wonderful news! I've just learned that an American film crew that had been trapped in the Golan has been rescued. It has to be Tovah and your friends."

"Oh, Dov . . ." was all Lee could muster tearfully.

Laslo responded sternly. "Hold yourself together, Eleanora. They'll be home for breakfast." Then more gently, "Do you have enough food in the house? The people have already emptied the markets."

Lee found her voice. "Yes, yes! But Dov . . . what about Riv? You heard nothing?"

"No, nothing. The news from the outposts is sparse. So far, we know of only one garrison rescued, and we have no names as yet." He paused momentarily. "Have courage, Eleanora. It is after two in the morning—get some sleep. If I hear anything further, I will call."

Mindy, comprehending the gist of the conversation, hugged Lee as soon as the phone was cradled, her feelings a mixture of relief tinged with sadness. "They're safe, Lee," she uttered hoarsely. "Joe, Paul, Tovah—they're safe. The battle is half-won."

"Mama!" Debbi cried out unexpectedly from the doorway to the living room. Her voice rose hysterically. "Riv's not coming back!"

Lee released herself from Mindy and moved quickly to confront her daughter-in-law. She grabbed Debbi's shoulders and shook her roughly. "Don't you dare believe the worst! I did that once and . . . and . . ." She stopped herself abruptly as she realized that her need for Baron had reached a pinnacle, matching that of another time. Indeed, her concern for Baron had become as deep-rooted as that for her son. Confused, she turned to Mindy, her voice breaking. "Oh, Mindy, what's happening to them?"

Baron plodded wearily along the base of a small ridge, not quite knowing his position except that it was somewhere between Ismailiya to the north and Tawafik in the south. He could guess that much, seeing Israeli planes range past the tank battles to blast Egyptian bridgeheads along the canal.

He had reached an opening into a dark wadi when he heard a pebble fall from the ridge behind him. Emitting a sharp gasp, he dropped to his knees and let Riv slide from him, instantly cupping one hand over Riv's mouth while pulling out the machine pistol with the other.

From the crag overlooking the wadi, a voice cracked out in a sharp whisper. Baron could see no one, but the language was unmistakably Arabic.

In the next instant, Riv shoved Baron's hand from his mouth and shouted angrily in Arabic.

Baron stared in amazement as he heard the unseen Arab reply with a snicker.

"A Bedouin lookout," Riv whispered. "His tribe is camped on the other side of the ridge. I told him I preferred privacy when emptying a weak bladder."

"Friendly or dangerous?"

"They're a nomadic people and usually keep to themselves, but right now I wouldn't trust them."

Unsettled for a moment, Baron eyed the moon slipping behind a cloud, then spoke quickly. "This means we can't linger, Riv. You know that. Put the handkerchief back in your mouth. Make it easy on yourself." He saw the head nod, the face grim. "Good boy," Baron muttered encouragingly.

A mile into the desert, Baron pondered the improbability of his undertaking. His head throbbed, and his parched throat ached with each swallow he attempted. He scanned the sand, gray in the shadowed moonlight, searching for some evidence of the men from the garrison.

Nothing. All the fighting was to the north and south of them. They were alone in a vast, sandy wasteland. He tucked his head in and continued to plod eastward.

Riv twisted suddenly, and Baron almost stumbled. He felt Riv wiping the sweat from his face.

"Thanks," Baron muttered hoarsely.

"Give it up, Baron," said Riv, grunting with each step Baron took. "You've already repaid whatever debt you think you owed."

"Shit! Riv, you talk too much."

The sky thundered with waves of sound as three Phantoms encountered four Egyptian MIGs. The dogfight was taking place about a mile above Baron's head, but he trudged on without looking up. His legs felt like two wooden sticks; he didn't dare stop.

Seconds later a tremendous explosion reddened the night sky. Baron lurched to a halt, his heart pounding furiously, his legs almost giving way.

Horror stricken, he watched a plane descend in a screeching dive, its fuselage wrapped in a ball of fire. As if hypnotized, Baron remained frozen in his tracks. Somewhere in the recesses of his mind, he thought he heard Riv crying out.

"Baron! Are you crazy? We're too close!"

Baron nodded, his legs refusing to respond.

The plane, its identity unrecognizable, crashed in a massive incendiary, not a hundred yards from them. Another explosion followed instantly, rocketing flaming debris across the landscape. An eerie orange light bathed the sand before them.

Baron lowered his head, shifting his gaze from the unreal scene. He began to sway unsteadily.

Riv shouted at him. "Baron, look down! Look down!"

As if awakening from a bad dream, he followed Riv's pointing finger.

His eyes popped with a resurgence of energy. They were standing in tank tracks. Half-tracks were also in evidence. They were fresh, he thought, as the uncanny, wavering light defined the sharp edges. The timeless desert winds hadn't softened the crispness yet. "Can you tell whether they're ours?" he asked Riv.

Riv shuddered, then spoke chokingly. "What the hell's the difference? If . . . it was a rescue team . . . they were here already."

His neck, arms, and shoulders stiffening, Baron answered harshly. "Shut up, Riv! As long as I'm on two feet, you just hang on!"

He moved his left leg forward, planted it in the sand, then moved his right, then his left, then his right, following the tracks.

He lost all sense of time, only knowing that if they weren't picked up soon, the rising desert sun would accomplish what the enemy couldn't. He looked up from his relentless scrutiny of the tank tracks, his imagination playing tricks. He thought he heard voices. He licked the salt on his lips and tried to shake the sweat from his eyes.

"How about that, Riv?" he said, his throat burning with each breath. "Ever hear of a sound mirage?"

Riv didn't answer. The only reply came from booming cannons in the distance. An amorphous thought crossed his befogged mind—they had been deserted, not merely by the Egyptians and Israelis, but by God, too. His lips twisted in an ironic smile. "Some joke," he began. Stumbling, his legs suddenly buckled on the crest of a sand dune.

Riv fell from his shoulders, and uncontrollably both men rolled down the small grade, the sand clinging to their damp clothing making a doughy paste. Baron made a frantic grab for the shadowy figure, the machine pistol cutting into his ribs painfully.

Coming to rest at the bottom of the slope, Baron fought a wave of despair as he groped in the encompassing darkness for Riv's silent form.

Anger joined his despair when he found Riv's feverish face beneath his finger tips. Muttering an epithet, he again swore as he felt for Riv's thigh above the tourniquet. It was hard as stone. Other than a single moan, Riv remained silent. Beset by an overwhelming sense of helplessness, Baron wept as he wiped the grit from his son's face.

He reached for the canteen, but it was no longer

around his neck. He cursed himself for not tying it to his belt. Bitter anger assailed him.

"Damn you, Riv! Is this why God put us together? To have wild jackals feed on us, leaving dry bones for a wandering Bedouin tribe to find?" Riv's only response was heavy breathing.

Baron sat there, hunched on his knees, trying to think clearly. "It can't just end here," he muttered, straightening his thoughts somewhat. "Pull yourself together, man. Get your bearings." He moved away from Riv and crept up the slope on all fours.

At first, he thought it was an optical illusion. A light seemed to have flashed from a hilltop—he couldn't judge the distance—but the whining shell that followed was no illusion. Baron was alert. It had to be Israeli artillery, coming from the east. A barrage followed the initial salvo.

Baron gasped as they exploded 500 yards north of him. What the hell are they shooting at? he wondered, his eyes narrowing.

The answer came immediately. The bursting shells lit up an area suffused with Egyptian tanks and infantry. "Christ!" he muttered, coming alive. It must be a whole brigade out there.

From another ridge less than a mile away to the northeast, cannon fire was directed at the Egyptians. Stunned, Baron could do nothing but watch as the battle ensued. Pandemonium broke out when, from behind the cover of a sand dune a hundred yards from Baron, small arms fire raked the Egyptian infantry. The sound was incredible —machine guns chattering away and cannons thundering across the desert. Automatically, he pulled out his machine pistol and then just stared at it. He was about to adjust the lens. Realizing his absent-mindedness, he removed the used clip and replaced it with the remaining full one.

Baron's movements were performed mechanically, almost listlessly, his reflexes having slowed down considerably. His shoulders and arms, although now feeling weightless after the hours of carrying Riv, were stiff with fatigue. Pursing his lips, then licking them, he felt only slight relief with the discovery of the Israelis a short distance away. Why had they been so foolhardy as to give away their position? What had they hoped to accomplish except sign their own death warrants? Pondering, he tried to figure out their strategy logically.

This area of the desert had been peculiarly quiet until the Israeli artillery had begun the barrage. Israeli tanks from a closer ridge then joined in. Baron wondered why the Egyptian force had been waiting there in total silence. Were they short of gas? Supplies? Or were they simply waiting for air support to precede them as they readied for the drive toward . . . toward where? Pondering deeper, he guessed with little enthusiasm, that it was the Mitla Pass southeast of them. He shook his head. It still didn't explain why the Israeli foot soldiers opened fire when they did. Filled with unanswered questions, he idly watched tracer bullets line the night sky in strange patterns and waited with the pistol ready in his hand.

As he heard tanks flanking their sand "forts," it struck him suddenly. How did the Israeli artillery know the Egyptians' position? He slapped his forehead. Of course! The trapped Israelis had a radio. There was no other explanation.

As if to verify his conclusion, a green flare shot up into the night sky. Baron's heart pounded. The purpose of the flare was to point the way for a rescue force. His elation was short-lived as shells whined overhead. He ducked beneath the crest of the dune, sprayed by a shower of sand. Above the bombardment, he could hear the wild shouting of the Arab infantry as they readied an assault on the trapped men.

Sprawled on the slope, Baron peered over the edge. Through the smoke and haze, he could see men falling. It was a slaughter. He saw one figure flip up into the air as a grenade went off, then winced as another grenade exploded behind the Israelis' dune. The cries of the wounded on both sides carried across the hundred yards. It was only a matter of time, he thought grimly.

He was an unseen spectator, mechanically viewing the grisly, violent scene between his thumb and forefinger as if framing it for the proper lens. A tank blew up just below the tip of his forefinger sighting. The crescendo of battle stifled the broken screams of the surrounding infantry. Unaccountably—perhaps because of the dissimilarity of the terrain—another battle was remembered.

In a driving rain, the mud reaching almost to their knees, they had pushed forward to the base of a rock-strewn hill. There was a road to their left, but German artillery had already knocked out a dozen Shermans like picking off ducks in a shooting gallery. The foot soldiers clambered up the incline, picking their way around huge boulders, keeping out of range of the Germans returning fire. In comparison, Baron's job had been easy—capturing the men's struggle to take the hill with the Bolex. Eventually and at extreme cost, the rise was crested. Their target, a village with less than two thousand inhabitants, was nestled between two placid hills. The innocuous setting had been deceiving; the village had to be reduced to rubble before the Americans could take possession from the Germans.

Hearing the whoosh of a shell overhead, he dug his face into the sand. An explosion followed, and angry shouting reached his ears. Lifting his head, he spit out sand from his mouth. An Israeli Patton, about to pick up the survivors from the other dune, was spinning on one tread. Another tank was blasted to pieces. His heart leaped as another Patton appeared through the smoky haze with an armored carrier right behind it. The wounded tank stopped spinning and turned its cannon in Baron's direction.

He felt the rush of air and could almost smell the missile as it shrieked toward its target behind him. The explosion blasted his ear drums. A fiery glow lit up the area less than fifty yards behind him. Pushing himself to his knees, he waved frantically to capture the attention of the rescue team.

Getting no recognition, he started to get to his feet, the fires behind him silhouetting his figure. Then, terror stricken, he saw the tank's machine gun train upon him. He fell back over the edge of the dune just as the gun started spitting. He felt as if a hot poker had been run across his cheek. Touching his face, his fingers became sticky with blood.

"You crazy idiots!" he shouted. "We're on the same side!" Continuing to curse, he looked toward Riv's still form as if seeking an answer from him. Fighting off the hysteria, he realized that he had no more than a minute to come up with something.

Suddenly a tight smile appeared. Riv *was* the answer.

Stumbling back to Riv, he started to untie the tourniquet, thankful that he was unconscious. He'd never be able to stand the pain once the blood started to circulate.

Breathing heavily, he labored up the slope on rubber legs, stopping just short of the crown. He thrust his hand up into the air, waving the bloodied prayer shawl.

Interminable seconds seemed like minutes until shouts and cries of encouragement reached his ears. Dropping his arm, he flopped over onto his back. Emotionally drained, he brought the *talleth* to his lips.

Four young men raced across the ridge of sand and dropped down beside Baron. Straightening, Baron pointed toward Riv. "Careful. He's got a bad leg. He needs a medic fast."

One man nodded, and the other three moved energetically to Riv's aid. The first soldier pulled a canteen from his belt. "Slow," he said, holding it to Baron's lips and checking the gash on his cheek. Then, eying Baron's face, the young Israeli became awed. "You're the American correspondent that was with Captain Avram's garrison!"

Baron nodded, his eyebrows arching. "You found the captain!" He twisted around. "Those are his men over there?"

A slow whistle escaped from the Israeli. "No, they were rescued hours ago." He shook his head in disbelief. "Those are from the garrison further north."

The three soldiers reappeared, carrying Riv between them. One spoke worriedly, "It'll be first light soon, Lieutenant, and this man is in a bad way." The lieutenant nodded and whispered a few words to them. All three stared at Baron incredulously but remained silent as he struggled to his feet.

The lieutenant cast a cautious eye over the dune. "Get ready," he said to his men, "they both go into the half-track." He turned to look at Baron. "I still can't see how you did it. You're at least fifteen kilometers from the outpost. That man couldn't have walked it even if he had been conscious."

Baron smiled wearily. "It's a long story, Lieutenant. Someday you might read it." He looked at Riv with concern as he began to moan incoherently.

"There's a doctor on board," said the lieutenant.

The armored carrier waited not ten feet from their position. Eager hands reached for Riv, then Baron. A machine gun atop the carrier chattered incessantly.

"*Shalom*, American!" the lieutenant shouted, starting a run to the rear with his men following. Baron gave a half-salute, noting their objective.

Out of the hell of burning tanks, a Patton emerged with at least a dozen survivors aboard. Watching them climb onto the tank, he could hear a radio crackling unintelligibly. In the next moment, he was almost jerked from his feet as the half-track moved out.

"Get down!" an unseen voice yelled from the floor. "You're not even armed!"

Baron involuntarily reached for his pistol, realizing that he had left it behind. He dropped to the flooring listlessly, beside the angry voice, too weary to reply. Leaning back against a bench, he stretched his legs out and brought balled fists to rub his itching eyes. Waves of heat from hot metal and the acrid stench of burning oil permeated the vehicle.

Uneasy, he permitted himself only a few seconds of a dubious relaxation before seeking Riv. Glimpsing someone attending a prone figure, he guessed him to be the doctor. Crawling on all fours, he squeezed past two still forms.

The doctor was encasing a hypodermic when Baron accosted him. "Well, Doc," Baron began impatiently. "How is he? How bad is the knee?"

The doctor rubbed his cheek, sighed, then ran a hand over his high forehead. He scratched what remained of an unruly crop of hair on top of his head. "I can do no more here." Baron noted the covered knee. "I've given him a strong sedative. It'll hold him till Beersheva."

"Then what?" Baron persisted. "Can't you tell me more than that?"

The doctor looked at him for the first time. "He's not going to lose his leg if that's your worry. But he has lost cartilage and some bone—the leg will be stiff."

Baron could feel an angry heat rising within himself; he had won the battle, but lost the war. "Are you sure? You can tell me all that on such short diagnosis?"

The doctor weighed his reply, then spoke compassionately. "Perhaps I am hasty. The hospital will tell us more."

"In Beersheva?"

"No." The doctor hesitated. "This fellow he lives where?"

"Jerusalem. Why do you ask?"

"Then he'll be sent to the Hadassah Hospital in Jerusalem." Seeing Baron's astonishment, he added quickly, "By helicopter."

Baron sat back on his heels, a tentative relief settling upon him.

"Relative?" asked the doctor.

"Yes," he answered simply.

The doctor reached into his bag. "I can offer you a mild sedative . . . if it'll help."

Baron waved the suggestion aside. "Not unless it's a double Scotch."

A smile appeared. "Sorry I can't help you. If you'll excuse me, I have other patients." He crept to the figure beside Riv, his thoughts lingering on Baron. Peculiar— a middle-aged American here in combat. He shook his head, leaning toward his new task, dismissing Baron from his mind.

Baron pulled out his tape recorder. There was still a half-hour of tape left. A bandaged soldier was only too eager to be heard by an American audience. Baron blew loose sand from the machine, his eyes darting from the boyish Israeli to the unconscious figure a few feet from him. His grimy forehead was furrowed, thinking that although he had been the instrument of Riv's rescue, he didn't dare harbor any illusions that this had solved a damn thing. He tossed a question at the soldier, his mind sweeping to the Golan. Envisioning broken bodies, he rubbed his misty eyes. He dismissed those thoughts. Joe was always able to take care of himself, and anyone else with him.

CHAPTER 11

October 7, 1973—Evening

Mindy knew something was wrong the instant she saw Joe returning to their table. His expression solemn, the cigar was clasped in tightly between his lips. The teacup trembled as she replaced it in the saucer. She brought a hand to her lips. Oh, God! Don't let it be bad news! she thought.

Joe slid into a chair and, removing the cigar, said, "Are you up to baby-sitting, Mindy?" At her perplexity, he continued quickly. "I finally got through to Lee. She's been alone with the grandchildren since noon." When he paused, Mindy gave an exasperated "Well?" Sighing heavily, he said, "Debbi's been at the Hadassah Hospital all day with Riv. Riv needed surgery on his knee. But stop torturing yourself, it's not critical."

Mindy's fine eyebrows knit agonizingly. "Oh, those poor women. Of course, I'll go." She hesitated, fearful of inquiring. "You heard nothing of Rick?"

Joe shook his head. "I can't get Colonel Stefan, and no one else seems to know anything."

Mindy got to her feet, her hands trembling as she straightened her collar. "I'm ready as soon as you are," she said. A thought was annoying her. "Where are Paul and Tovah?" she asked.

"The army has requisitioned Tovah for clerical work,

and I've got Paul and Ralph scrounging for film among the news people. Our new supply won't get here until late tomorrow."

Mindy bristled. "You're letting Paul roam around with a cast on his hand?"

Joe smiled in spite of himself. "Are you kidding, Min? Paul and Ralph are having a ball! They're heroes to the reporters. They won't dare refuse them a favor."

She nodded, her thoughts turning in another direction. She placed a hand on Joe's arm. "Joe, you don't think . . . Rick . . ."

Joe relit his cigar, averting his eyes. "Stop worrying. Rick can take care of himself." He blew out a cloud of bluish smoke. "Perhaps Riv will have some information." He took her arm. "Let's go. I'll get a cab, drop you off, and then take Lee to the hospital."

Rick Baron pushed through the doors of the King David a half-hour after the departure of Joe and Mindy. His clothes, although dried out, were sweat-stained and wrinkled. The loss of sleep was evident in his blood-shot eyes. Crossing the lobby, impervious to the stares from the knotted groups congregating to discuss the war, he confronted the clerk behind the front desk.

"Are any of the Greens in?"

The clerk wrinkled his nose, then blinked his eyes in sudden recognition. "My Lord! Mr. Baron! Yes—ah—no, they're not. They left a few minutes ago—after dinner." Recollecting, the clerk offered, "I got them a cab. I believe they mentioned north Jerusalem . . . and the Hadassah Hospital."

It wasn't difficult to figure out. They had to be seeing Riv. He scratched his stubbly chin in deep concentration, taking for granted their safe return from the Golan. He blinked his tired eyes, knowing he had no right to assume anything. Nevertheless, he could feel a great weight falling from his shoulders. Wrung out, he said lethargically, "Please get me the Hadassah Hospital." The clerk obligingly turned to the switchboard operator.

Baron spoke into the phone, inquiring of Riv's condition. The patient was in excellent condition after surgery on his knee, he was told. Baron said, "Can you relay a message to one of his visitors? A Mr. Joe Green?"

"I'm sorry, sir, but we simply don't have the time for . . ."

Baron interrupted. "Listen. I've just returned from the Sinai, and it's *urgent* that I get a message through."

Baron waited out a pause, then heard, "Very well, but please make it short."

Baron spoke slowly, "I'm still in one piece, but beat. Give me a dozen hours sleep, and I'll give you the entire story. Sign it, Rick." He hung up and found the clerk waiting for him with mail. He gave each letter a perfunctory glance, knowing they could be read later, but stopped at a note from Colonel Stefan. It was brief, giving a telephone number to be called immediately upon his arrival. He sighed wearily and shook his head. He didn't need another long conversation, laden with questions and answers. No, it would wait till morning. "Do you have a safe here?" he addressed the clerk.

"Of course."

Baron pulled out the tape recorder. "Put this away and then call this number." He tore the phone number from the note and handed it to him. "Ask for Colonel Stefan or any one of his aides. Tell him I'm indisposed, and they'll have to pick it up."

When the clerk returned from the safe, Baron reached for his wallet. The clerk sheepishly interrupted the movement. "That won't be necessary, Mr. Baron. You've already paid for the privilege."

Once inside his room, Baron peeled off his clothing, letting it fall wherever he stood. He walked into the bathroom, stripped. The face in the mirror revealed old eyes —eyes that had seen too much, too often. His shoulders were red with a rash, but he focused on his stomach, hard and flat. He'd lost at least a dozen pounds in the past twenty-four hours.

In Beersheva at the Soroka Medical Center, Riv had already received emergency treatment and been shipped out by copter with other wounded by the time Baron had his cheek treated. With no other recourse, Baron waited for a supply truck to return him to Jerusalem. He had washed, been fed, and to pass the time, gotten accounts of the battles from Israeli soldiers. The ride back had been long and tiresome.

After a shower, he examined the tape on his cheek.

Another memento, he thought disconsolately, moving back into the darkened bedroom. He trod across the carpet, tripped over his jacket haphazardly left there, cursed, and then flopped onto the bed. He released a heavy sigh. A vague picture of Lee's farewell in Rome unaccountably flashed through his befogged mind. A premonition? The nebulous thought was erased a moment later as vengeful sleep overtook him.

Debbi was just coming into the corridor outside Riv's room when she spied Lee and Joe Green walking toward her. Her eyes, red but now dry, looked up at them. "Mama," she exclaimed, "the boys . . ."

Lee gestured reassuringly. "It's all right. Min—Mrs. Green is with them. Riv—how is Riv?"

Debbi's eyes began to tear. "He's all right now, mama. He's been asleep for more than an hour."

Lee pursed her lips. Her eyes intent on Joe, she said, "Joe, would you please keep Debbi company while I go in alone to see Riv?"

"Of course." He comprehended her look. "She could probably use a cup of coffee or something." He took Debbi's arm. "We'll be back in a few minutes." Although not quite understanding, Debbi made no protest as she was led away.

Lee stood at the foot of the bed in the small room, gazing at her son's pallid complexion, making an effort to contain her emotions. She started for the lone chair at his bedside, faltered, and then saw Riv open his eyes.

A weak smile greeted her. "*Shalom*, mama." Moving quickly to his side, she kissed him on the lips, an impatient tear dropping on his chin.

Riv brought his hand up to tilt her face. "Please, mama, sit. No more tears." With a broader smile, he said, "If nothing else comes from this, at least I'm out of the army for good."

She seated herself, dabbing her eyes with a tissue. She nodded ever so slightly, unable to return his smile. "Yes, at least we have that much."

Watching her with an odd curiosity, he waited another moment, then bluntly asked, "Mama, who is Rick Baron?"

The query caught her unprepared. Visibly blanching, she managed, "Why . . . why do you ask?"

He regarded her, the words forming in his mind, only too eager to be expressed. Finally he said, "I owe my life to him." He focused his blurry eyes upon his mother and thought he saw her bring her hands to her face, but continued unrestrained. "Mama, that man was a total stranger to me, yet he reached beyond the limits of human endurance to carry me for miles through the desert." He paused to swallow. "Why? Why should he have done this?"

Sobbing, Lee tried to find her voice. "Riv . . . where is he?" She hid her face, fearful of the answer.

His head aching, Riv closed his eyes. "I don't know. I don't even know if he's alive." Growing sleepier, he fought the sedatives. He took his mother's hand. "Who was he, mama?"

"Was?" Did he say "was"? Not again, she thought, the torment crushing her. She squeezed his hand, released it, and got to her feet.

Riv tried to keep his tired eyes open. "Mama, was he more than a friend when you lived in Italy?"

Lee was in turmoil. Something had to be said, but what could she admit? She saw the fatigued, puzzled eyes searching for an answer. She took a deep breath. "Yes, Riv. He was more than just a friend. A long time ago . . . before I married your father."

He rubbed an eye, but did not seem surprised. "But you did not marry him?"

"No. He was reported killed in the war."

Riv shaded his eyes as if the light bothered him. "I see. Then I'm the son he might have had . . . if . . ."

Lee's concern was torn between his loss of speech and its content. She leaned over him. Listening to his even breathing, she realized that he'd fallen asleep. She kissed him on the cheek, resettled herself into the chair, and waited.

Debbi pushed the door open silently with Joe Green behind her. She took in the scene at a glance: her husband asleep, her mother-in-law in utter silence gazing at him with a distant look in her eyes. "He still sleeps?" Debbi said, mildly surprised, a peculiar gleam in her eyes. "Mama, Mr. Baron . . ."

Joe interrupted brusquely. "Not now, Debbi." He crooked a finger for Lee to leave the room. Perplexed by their behavior, she got to her feet unsteadily and moved around the bed.

In the corridor, Joe pulled her to one side. "Did you speak with Riv at all?"

"Yes, he told me of . . ." She stopped abruptly and studied him. "You already heard what happened to Riv?" When he nodded, the tears began again.

"That's enough, Lee," he said, barely able to keep a firm voice himself. Reaching into his pocket, he pulled out a scrap of paper. It was a note containing the dictation from Baron.

She read it, her eyes blurring. "Oh, Joe!" she exclaimed, pressing against his chest and sobbing.

He held her for a moment, then pushed her back. A joyous smile broke out. "The ordeal's over, Lee." He tilted her chin. "It's not as if we were leaving Rome."

She laughed softly, remembering. Then with her eyes strangely fixed on his, she seemed to be mulling over a difficult decision. She said finally, "I must go to him."

Joe's countenance altered. His expression was sober. "Wouldn't you be better off waiting until morning?"

She smiled coyly. "You're still Verdi—the corporal looking after his sergeant."

"No, Lee. This time it's you who needs looking after." Noting the arched eyebrows, he continued doggedly. "I don't want you to be the girl left behind—for the second time."

Her eyes took on a luster, her entire appearance brightening. She touched his cheek. "Joe, you're sweet, but, you of all people should know what I owe him. Don't you see that I have to go to the man who risked his life to bring back his son to me?"

"And you offer yourself in payment! What can you possibly gain from it?"

Despite Joe's protestations, Lee gently smiled. "You've nothing to fret about. I know exactly what I'm doing— what I must do . . . for a lasting remembrance."

He peered at her strangely, but prudently made no immediate reply. What was left to be said? She was reaching into the past probably for the last time, to once again become the impetuous girl of her youth. He turned away from her, from the eyes unashamedly seeking his blessing, and looked down the dreary corridor. Turning back resignedly, he took her hands in his own. "All right, Lee,

244

I can only hope that you really do know what you're doing." He felt her lips quiver as she kissed his cheek. God forgive me, he thought, for allowing this tragicomedy to continue.

He waited for the cab to depart, then slowly moved back up the stone steps of the hospital, his shoulders weighted down with a heavy sadness. "For a lasting remembrance." What irony! he thought. So this is how it all ends—a class reunion after thirty years, then they all return, each to his own oblivion.

Her compact was of little use to her in the darkened taxi. Hoping to at least look a bit more respectable, she dabbed her face with a small handkerchief. Respectable? she thought suddenly, qualms of guilt besetting her. She had never been this brazen with Enzo. Joe's mistaken impression of her attitude as being a reward for Rick was ironic. In truth, what was uppermost in her mind was her own overwhelming need for Rick—even if only for a few treasured moments.

Lee pushed through the doors of the King David, relieved to find herself an unobtrusive figure in an already overcrowded lobby. She pulled her jacket around her, the chilly Jerusalem night staying with her despite the swarm of people. She tucked in her chin and made her way to the staircase, pausing only to remove a key from her change purse. She had inadvertently forgotten to return it.

Almost at his door, she suddenly spotted an unexpected, gray-haired housemaid entering the corridor. Aware of the elderly woman's inquisitive look, Lee hesitated only briefly. "I'm a relative of Mr. Baron's. He's just returned from the Sinai, and I'm making certain that he's all right."

The woman eyed her speculatively. Appraising her, she noted Lee's red eyes. How many tears had she witnessed this day? Sighing deeply, she gave a discreet shrug and, without comment, withdrew a set of keys to enter another room.

Closing the door behind her, Lee was left in total darkness. Breathing deeply, she tried to gather her thoughts and recall the layout of his room. The bed should be opposite and to the left, she thought. Her heart pounding, she leaned forward. Straining her ears, she was not quite sure whether it was Baron's or her own heavy breathing she heard. Standing still until her eyes adjusted to the darkness, she made out the outlines of the furniture in the room. She moved quietly across the floor to the bathroom and turned on the light. She pulled the door to within a few inches of closing, permitting only reflected glare into the bedroom. She glanced at the figure lying asleep on the bed and then at the clothes strewn about the floor. She picked up the clothing and deposited it on a chair.

She sat for a few seconds in another chair at his bedside, struggling with herself. Was it folly? She thought of Joe's words—"What can you possibly gain from it?" She shunted aside these disconcerting thoughts as she gazed at Baron's sleeping figure, strangely affecting her.

The covers had slipped to his waist, exposing a bare, almost hairless chest. His face was turned away from her, displaying the taped cheek. The urge to touch him grew stronger. For the first time since Enzo's death more than six years ago, the feelings within her allowed no room for conscience. Refusing to acknowledge the possibility of later regrets, all her thoughts were directed to Baron. "Oh! My poor Rick! I've made you so unhappy, and I can offer you nothing." She took a deep breath, her eyes gleaming. "Perhaps for one evening I can be the loving girl of your 'Roman holiday.' "

She started to undress.

After slipping into bed, she pulled the sheet to her shoulders. Sliding her leg across his thigh, she instantly realized that he, too, was nude. Savoring the sensation, she held his waist as she kissed him lightly on the cheek.

Baron knew he was dreaming. The warmth and solace that overwhelmed him could only emanate from a dream.

His eyes opened abruptly. The figure holding him was real. Stunned, he could only mutter "Lee!" without really knowing.

"Hush, my darling," she murmured, leaning on him to prevent him from sitting up. He rubbed his eyes, trying to focus on her. She remained silent, pressing her breasts into his chest.

"Lee! What's going on?"

She lifted her head to kiss him on the lips. "I'm here now . . . recriminations can wait."

"Christ, Lee! You picked one hell of a time to come back to me. I haven't . . ."

"Rick, darling," she interjected lovingly, "I know what you've been through. I understand."

Her flesh molded to his. A bewildered Baron placed a nervous hand across his eyes. She was the young, vivacious Lee of his memory. He drew in a breath sharply as her fingers continued their exploration.

Lee's actions were compelled by a memory no longer dim. With a deliberate movement, she stretched and reached down between his legs. Her breath became shallow as she felt him grow in her hand. Her returned lover was ready, and she was aroused beyond memory. She need wait no longer. Lifting herself from his chest, she moved down to straddle him. She heard Baron's gasp match her own as she guided him into union with her. Panting and eager, she leaned forward for his embrace.

Strange visions appeared behind Baron's eyes. He had to be hallucinating!

On her stomach with her arms outstretched, Lee was riding the crown of a massive wave surging toward him. As it loomed closer, the huge wave was going through the colors of the spectrum, excitement mounting with each stage. Blue to green, green to yellow—Lee's face more exultant as she drew closer—yellow to orange. Baron was about to explode. Through a fiery red bath, Lee fell into his arms. Engulfed in a maelstrom of ecstasy, his lips found hers.

For the better part of an hour, Lee had lain in his arms, occasionally touching his cheek and fingering his body. The smell of him lingering upon her, she reached down to touch him once more. It belonged to me first, she thought with some melancholy. Sighing deeply, she realized the reality in the last words uttered by Baron just before he fell asleep. "I'll see Riv in the morning, and then get back to work."

She kissed him on the cheek, fingered the stubble, then removed his arm from her shoulder. Sitting on the edge of the bed, she gazed at his bare chest, fighting the desire to stay with him.

She stared into the bathroom mirror after taking a shower. But for the shadows clouding her eyes, the face seemed fulfilled, leaving no doubts as to what she was abandoning. She saw his hairbrush lying on a shelf. She used it eagerly. It was his—a final sharing. If there were any lingering doubts in her mind, they were quickly dispelled by the vision of a crippled son and a daughter who was as yet unmarried. Her children would never think of leaving Israel. And for her to go thousands of miles away with a man who was forever traipsing around the world, well . . . She saw the face in the mirror, with its mouth turned down. "Don't you dare cry!" she murmured harshly.

Joe Green sat in a far corner of the lobby. His features were screwed in thought, displaying dissatisfaction. He glanced at his watch—11:30 P.M. Frowning, he looked at the late hangers-on, most of them military. Those in civies, if they were waiting for cabs, had a fat chance at this hour. How Paul had wangled a car from one of the news services was beyond him.

When Paul and Ralph had arrived at the hospital, they were unprepared for the sight of ambulances streaming in and out. Much later, they learned that wherever possible, civilian patients were being sent home to make room for the wounded. Inquiring at the desk, they were told that visiting hours were over and all visitors would be leaving.

After a few minutes of waiting dutifully, they caught Debbi and Joe coming down the corridor. Spotting them, Debbi ran forward, almost childlike in her exuberance as she explained Riv's injury and that he wouldn't have to serve in the army any longer.

"That's great," Paul said, accepting her hug. "But where's your mother-in-law?"

"Oh, she's at the hotel with Mr. Baron."

As Paul and Ralph exchanged bewildered glances, Joe grinned and handed them Baron's message.

Their eyes lit up. Overjoyed and extremely moved, Paul exclaimed, "Gosh, Dad! That's terrific!" Ralph beamed and merely said, "That guy can do anything!" The admiration for Baron was apparent in both men.

Debbi said, "Did you know he saved Riv's life?"

Ralph shook his head. "It doesn't surprise me one bit."

"Okay, that's enough for now," Joe interjected. "We have to get a cab."

"Uh-uh," Paul said. "I've got a car—at least until morning. And I've also got six reels of film."

Joe nodded, his thoughts in another direction. "Come, let's get Debbi home and pick up your mother."

Joe leaned back in the overstuffed chair. As he fished into his pocket for a fresh cigar, the latest wire from the networks fell out.

GOLAN FILM SENSATIONAL STAY WITH INTERVIEWS
NEW CREW ON WAY FOR FRONT ACTION SEND LAT-
EST ON BARON SOONEST POSSIBLE ALL ROOTING

Joe had shipped the Golan film to London for processing; from there it had been relayed home by satellite.

He crumpled the paper with a distasteful look. Rick wasn't going to like being replaced by a new crew. But Rick wasn't the only problem. He now had Mindy and Paul to contend with.

Paul's surprise announcement upon their return to the hotel had caught them off balance. In as calm a voice as he could muster, knowing that fireworks would erupt, Paul had stated simply that he was staying on in Israel—permanently. Mindy's elation with Baron's return evaporated instantly. Glowering, she looked from her son to her husband, unable to find her voice. Joe understood, even if she didn't, but kept silent.

Finally, she said, "And what would you do here?"

"The same thing I do at home—photography. What else?"

Exasperation showed. "And you think you can do better here than home?"

Joe interrupted. "It's late, Min. Suppose we discuss this in the morning." Paul shot him a grateful look.

Mindy turned on him. "Joe, there are times . . ."

"Min," he injected beseechingly, "please! In the morning?"

Joe held a lighter to his cigar, trying in vain to find one redeeming feature in Paul's decision other than Tovah. He thought Tovah was attractive and, recalling the events of the Golan, certainly level-headed enough to handle Paul. He smiled slightly, admitting to himself that the idea of Tovah becoming his daughter-in-law was appealing.

"Are you sitting up for me?"

Startled, he looked up to see Lee standing over him, her cheeks aglow, her eyes lustrous. He was aware of this almost immediately. He got to his feet hurriedly.

"Didn't you think I would?"

She nodded, smiling. "With an army jeep?"

"No, this time we can have our little discussion in style. A Mercedes."

Her smile dimmed. "Joe, there is nothing to discuss."

He gave her a meaningful look and then took her arm. "I think there is," he said quietly.

For the first time, she appeared unsettled.

Neither spoke until the Mercedes roared into life, Joe opening the conversation casually. "About Tovah, Lee. Does she have many friends? Boys, that is."

Mystified, she gave him a sidelong glance. The subject was totally unexpected. She replied hesitantly. "Yes, some."

"Any of them serious?"

Puzzled. "One or two—but not on her part. Why do you ask?"

Without hesitation, he told her of Paul's decision and of his own suspicions as to the reason. "Well, what do you think?" he added.

She gestured helplessly. "I don't know, I had no idea. Tovah never said a word. I can't even guess whether your suspicion is well-founded."

With Joe's attention drawn to his driving, they fell silent. The streets were deserted and, due to the blackout, dark and foreboding. Stopped at one point by a military patrol, he showed his press pass and was warned not to attempt going into East Jerusalem. Joe assured the soldier that he was merely taking the lady home, just north of Mea Shearim.

Crossing Jaffa Road, Joe jolted her once again. "What about you and Rick?"

She bit her lip. "What about us?"

Joe stopped the car on a narrow curving street, the engine still running. "Lee, I can read Rick like a book. I know marriage has been on his mind, even though he hasn't said it. Don't bother denying the feelings you share with him. I'm referring to the present—not ancient memories of Rome. What's going to be the outcome of your reunion? More bittersweet memories? What you're doing now will only make the future more difficult."

250

An overwhelming need to unburden herself prodded her toward willing confession. Within the sanctity of protective darkness, she decided that there was no one better than Joe to tell.

"Yes, I went to bed with him tonight . . . and it was as if we were both young again." She brought her hands to her cheeks, staring into the blackness. "How can I explain it? You, Joe, of all people, understood what Rick and I meant to each other in Rome. When I was told that he had died, I prayed for the earth to open up and swallow me. Yet, with Enzo's help, I managed to live a lifetime without him." She paused to catch her breath. "So now, with the specter of the past hovering over us, we discover that we have the same fascination as before. But Joe, the fact remains that we are not young and the situation is not the same." Joe groped for a reply, but failing, allowed her to continue. "Whether I love him or not, I cannot abandon my family merely to share pleasure."

So, Joe thought disheartened, even if Rick came to his senses and proposed marriage, it would gain him nothing. He looked at her, offering lamely, "He did save Riv's life."

"I've repaid him the only way I could."

Joe started the car forward, a despondency following him. Not really believing his own thought, he said, "Suppose Rick decided to stay in Israel?"

She shook her head. "That's beyond his thinking. But even if he did consider it, can you imagine the mental torture he would suffer not being able to tell Riv who he is?"

Nothing more was said until they pulled up at the apartment house. The night air was chilly with the portent of rain. Joe stayed her for another moment. "Lee, by your reasoning, would you suggest I persuade Paul into coming home?"

She didn't bat an eye. "For whose benefit? Yours or his?"

He laughed softly. "Thanks for nothing."

He walked her to the door. "Well, perhaps tomorrow you and Rick will think differently," he said.

Lee eyed him moodily. "Joe, I already know what tomorrow will bring."

CHAPTER 12

October 8, 1973

The shops were open, but except in an occasional supermarket, there was little activity visible. Wearing a baleful look, Baron halted in a narrow street to tighten the belt on his faded blue trench coat. The drab sky matched his sullen attitude.

About to move on, he became aware of an ancient synagogue nearby. Hesitating, he gazed at the sculptured stone windows. Then on impulse, he pulled the metal door facing him.

A short, dimly lit hallway gave off a musty odor. He took a *yarmulke* from a bin at the side of the doorway, set it upon his head, and walked to an archway leading into the main sanctuary. Standing there, he took in the Moorish columns holding up the curtained balcony reserved for women only. Anachronistic Orthodoxy, he thought blandly with no particular complaint. He scanned the interior, noting that although the morning service had finished, the pews facing the altar with its eternal light were still mostly occupied.

He spun about, alerted suddenly by the sound of a worn hinge grinding stridently through the hallway. A door had unwillingly glided open to his right. Before an unseen hand closed it, Baron glimpsed the room beyond, the scene bringing back vague recollections of something lost from his youth. Any one of the black-caftaned, pale-faced, Talmudic scholars leaning over the heavy, religious tomes in deep concentration could have been his father.

Frozen for a few seconds, he was struck by an uneasy thought. Unwittingly or not, the simple act of a door closing had imparted the feeling he had wandered unwelcome into an alien port. He shrugged and moved toward the outer door.

Replacing the *yarmulke* in the bin, he noticed the blue and white *pushka* above it. He pulled out his wallet involuntarily, fished out two lone twenty-dollar bills from among the Israeli pounds, and pushed them through the slot of the donation box.

In the narrow street once more, he took a deep breath. Walking toward Lee's shop, his thoughts inevitably reverted to his conversation with Joe that morning.

It was 9:30 when he walked into the dining room. He could almost hear his joints creak as he passed two waiters resetting tablecloths for lunch. Joe, seated beside a window, was the lone diner in the large room. The table had been cleared except for a cup of coffee. Baron could easily read the headlines of the previous day's *Jerusalem Post* in Joe's hands.

EGYPTIAN-SYRIAN ATTACKS HELD

Baron signaled to a waiter. "A pot of coffee, please, and the biggest cheese omelet you can make." Joe lifted his head, grinned, and got to his feet, greeting Baron with a bear hug.

He waved Baron to a chair, then sat down opposite him. He pointed to the paper, smiling broadly. "Not bad for two old cockers! We were there—the only American correspondents covering the initial assaults." He laughed. "You want to know the truth? I was never so scared in my life."

TANKS BATTLE AS SYRIANS PENETRATE GOLAN LINE, EGYPTIANS CROSS CANAL, ISRAELI PLANES MAINTAIN AIR SUPREMACY

Baron read it at a glance, then looked up. "We were damn lucky, Joe. All of us."

After a moment of silence, Joe said, "Mindy and Paul are at Lee's shop—working, believe it or not."

"I know. I've already spoken with both of them. Paul gave me a run-down on yesterday's episode at the Golan."

Joe glanced at his watch. Comparing notes would have to wait. His eyes averted, he asked, "Did you speak with Lee?"

Baron shook his head. "I also called Debbi at the hospital, but she doesn't have the vaguest idea where Lee is."

"About last night . . ." began Joe.

Baron cut him short, insulating himself against further questions. "Another time, Joe, please. I've still got to get my head straight."

Joe sat back. "Okay, it can wait, but you might as well know now. We had a heart-to-heart talk when I took her home last night." Baron failing to respond, Joe reached into a pocket for the cablegram.

Baron accepted the wire, wondering whether he was reading unpleasantness in the timbre of Joe's voice? He scanned the message hurriedly, then carelessly tossed it aside.

"Terrific!" he said tartly. "What does this mean? We're through in a couple of days?"

"Just about—unless you've other plans." Joe glanced at his watch again and got to his feet. "We can discuss it tonight. Meanwhile, I've an eleven o'clock appointment at the Knesset, and you have to call Colonel Stefan."

Outwardly, they were all business again. "What are you using for wheels?"

"Thanks to your tape, Stefan loaned us a jeep for the rest of our stay. Ralph's waiting for me right now. Look," he said, moving to Baron and placing a hand upon his shoulder, "I've got to go now, but we can discuss future plans tonight. Including Paul's decision to go into business here in Israel." Escaping from Baron's astonishment, he added laconically, "Later . . . tonight . . ."

His thoughts rambling, Baron took no notice of the heightened activity on Jaffa Road. Military trucks drove by, outnumbering civilian vehicles. In front of every coffeehouse and restaurant, groups had gathered, vociferously debating Israel's unpreparedness.

Stefan would have him picked up at 1400 hours in

front of Lee's shop. Perhaps after the meeting, he could wangle a lift to the hospital. Debbi had said that Riv was coming along well and was more cheerful upon learning of Baron's safe return. His thoughts constantly shifting, he then wondered where Lee was, and what was so important that she had to leave Mindy and Paul to handle the shop alone. Where was Dov Laslo? A troubled line creased his forehead as he thought of Laslo.

"Hey, Rick. Where you going?"

Startled, Baron spun about. Paul, stood in the doorway of Lee's shop, grinning. "Hey, Mac. Can I interest you in the hottest items in the Middle East?"

Baron shook his head absentmindedly as he was about to pass the store. Moving quickly, he took Paul's good hand. Giving the cast a perfunctory look, he remarked, "What some guys won't do for a decoration."

"Oh yeah! What about that?" He pointed to the tape on Baron's cheek. "You get that standing too close to your razor?"

Baron fingered it gently. "It *was* a close shave, at that."

Paul laughed aloud. "Christ, Rick! You always have to top me."

"Okay, enough of this stuff. Where's your mother?"

"She's inside ready to burst into tears when she sees you."

Masking his impatience, Baron pushed the door and gently prodded Paul back inside.

Paul barely made it out of his mother's way as she flew into Baron's arms. She kissed him hard on the mouth, then leaned back. "Damn you!" she exploded, her eyes tearless but moist. "You don't deserve a kiss from me! When are you going to stop playing 'Rover Boy'?"

Baron gulped air. "Holy Christ, Min! Is this the way you greet all your customers?"

She stood back, out of his arms, a quizzical look searching his face. Knowing her ever blunt manner, Baron returned her gaze expectantly. "You did see Joe this morning?" she asked. At his nod, she blurted out, "We're leaving on Thursday. Will you be ready by then?"

He tossed Paul a casual glance. "About as ready as your son." Paul stiffened, his expression unhappy.

"Then Joe told you that much?" Mindy said.

Baron unbuckled the belt of his trench coat. "Not in any detail," he said, taking out his pipe and tobacco.

Paul caught Mindy's glare. "Mother! Not again!"

"No, not with me," she stated harshly. "How about Rick? Perhaps he can be more understanding than your parents."

The door to the shop opened. A young couple entered and moved directly to a glass showcase displaying ornate silver and gold Yemenite jewelry. Mindy turned pleading eyes to Baron.

"You're the clerk," Baron said. "I'll take Paul into the back room." He looked at his watch—twelve-thirty.

A three-by-six-foot workbench was set against the far wall, the chassis of two stripped-down radios lying upon it awaiting repair. Radio tubes filled an upper shelf; a lower one contained boxes of resistors, transistors, and capacitors. This was Riv's workshop. The tools of his trade were neatly bracketed beneath the lower shelf.

Baron filled his briar, impassively ridding himself of disconcerting thoughts. He turned to Paul, who had seated himself at a small table at the other side of the room. Paul, his head bowed, glumly stared at his injured hand resting on the table.

"When was the seed of this idea first planted?"

Paul looked up, a knot forming in his stomach. Rick never did waste words. He wondered where to begin.

Baron seated himself opposite Paul, holding a lighter to his pipe. "Well?" he said.

Paul cleared his throat. "At the *kibbutz* in the Golan." He caught Baron's eyes studying him, then thought, What the hell! Give it to him straight. "It started when they put the splint on my wrist. All I had to do was listen to them. Most of them were younger than me, but they had a sense of purpose and a spirit that was contagious. I didn't know anyone there, but there were no strangers. They were all my brothers." Baron smiled. Israel did that to visiting Jews. "I don't know whether I'm making myself clear, Rick, but suddenly I felt *their* survival was *my* survival."

"And you decided right then and there that in order to survive you had to stay in Israel and go into business here."

Paul glanced at him hesitantly. Was it a question or a statement? "No, of course not," he said finally. "My motivation is more complicated than that. Back home, the struggle for life, liberty and the pursuit of happiness has

257

turned into just one big hustle with no true meaning except personal advancement. Here it's different." He paused, aware of Baron's penetrating look, then continued unabated. "Christ, Rick! I grew up in the last two days! I've seen them in action, men and women alike, hating war, yet accepting it philosophically. We were all scared, Rick, no one wants to die, but they never doubted that this is their promised land."

An embarrassed smile followed his brief speech. When Baron made no comment, he began again. "And Tovah —seeing her handle . . ." He shook his head. "She was the clincher to what I've been debating with myself about for the past few days." He saw Baron's questioning look, and thought—what the hell! "Yes, it's Tovah. She's a good part of it. I want to share this land with her." Avoiding Baron's astonishment, he lowered his head sheepishly. "I think I love her, Rick."

Baron's look didn't display his true feelings. Although he realized that Paul had truly grown up, Baron's only concern at the moment was in the latter revelation. Grasping at straws, he wondered how it would affect his own relationship with Lee. Without betraying his somewhat dubious elation, he said brusquely, "Well, don't say it as if you were ashamed." A tinge of crimson appeared in Paul's cheeks. Baron relented. "What does Tovah have to say about this?"

"I haven't told her yet."

"You haven't told her?" Baron's inner elation made a turnabout. "Why not? How can you make plans when you don't even know what direction you're going?"

"That's why I want to stay . . . to give it time. I know she feels the same way about me, but I need time to play it out."

Baron blew a jet of smoke across the room. "Who else knows besides me?"

Paul nervously rubbed his nose with his good hand. "No one. But Christ, Rick! That's why I'm telling you. I thought you might help!"

Baron grimaced. Help? How could he? If he raised a single finger on Paul's behalf, the others would take it as a selfish ploy to strengthen his involvement with Lee. He searched Paul's face, wondering about his own motives.

"All right," Baron said, keeping his emotions under cover. "Putting aside personal feelings, how do you intend to make a living?"

Paul grinned, sensing victory. He spoke eagerly. "The fashion industry is growing here. There's got to be an opening for an experienced free-lance photographer."

"And if there isn't?"

"A couple of doors down from here, there's a store for rent. It's a perfect spot for a camera shop."

Baron raised his eyebrows. He didn't want to believe it for a moment. Paul was too skilled to give up his camera. He loved commercial studio work and would drown in self-pity after a few weeks of vegetating. Baron shook his head in disbelief. "You'd give up commercial work to run a camera shop?"

Paul shrugged. "It would be a living, and"—he paused, measuring his words—"I thought Riv might like to come in with me. He's an expert with stereo, radio, and electronics. Did you know he's got an engineering degree? Until his father was killed, he worked on government projects. Frankly, Rick, I haven't asked him yet, but I know he'd go wild over the idea."

No doubt, Baron thought. Considering his injury, the idea alone would prove therapeutic for Riv. What kind of future would he have in his mother's shop after he returned from the hospital? Unable to get around, he would languish in his meager, radio repair work. As for Lee, he was sure Paul's offer would sit well with her. But Joe and Mindy? Joe—perhaps. Mindy—he wasn't that sure. Yet, looking at it from Mindy's angle, he began to understand Lee's attitude.

"Okay, Paul, assuming you're not being headstrong in your plotting, how did you plan to finance this venture?"

Paul's eagerness vanished. He answered slowly and hesitatingly. "Well . . . I have some money but not enough. I thought . . . perhaps . . . Dad might help me get started."

Baron gave him an oblique stare. "Look, Paul, I know what you're getting at. As much as I like the idea myself, I won't help you go against your parents' wishes. Is that understood?"

Paul felt defeated, leaning back with a sense of abandonment. He nodded without speaking.

Baron drew heavily on his briar, sending a cloud of angry smoke toward the ceiling. He was powerless to help. Paul was like a son to him, but he could do nothing but commiserate with the boy. Disheartened, a sudden thought struck him. "Suppose Tovah wouldn't object to coming to America," he said.

Paul remained forlorn. He shook his head. "No chance."

So much for that, Baron thought desolately.

"What's 'no chance'?" Mindy asked, parting the beaded strands in the doorway. Baron twisted in his chair.

"No chance of seeing Lee," he responded hastily. "I'm going to be picked up in a few minutes."

At a glance, Mindy took in Paul's despondency. Her heart burdened, she nevertheless stated resolutely, "I hope you've pounded some sense into him." She nervously twiddled an unlit cigarette in her hand. "Christ, Rick! You got a light?"

He held a lighter for her, saying, "Min, tonight—with clearer heads—we can discuss it more fully." As an afterthought, he added, "Have you said anything to Lee about this?" She shook her head, puzzled. "Well, I wouldn't. At least not until you've made a final decision."

She looked from one to the other, regarding their unrevealing faces. She settled on Baron. "What's going on that I don't know about?"

They heard the front door of the shop open.

"Tonight, Min," said Baron complacently. "Paul will explain everything." Angling his head, he sought verification. Paul wearily nodded agreement. "Min, you've got a customer." The conversation was over.

In the front of the store, Lee had just removed her raincoat and, acutely aware of Baron's staring, felt a blush creeping into her cheeks. Flustered, she walked around a display case to place her coat upon a chair.

Mindy didn't miss a thing, but judiciously didn't ask any of the questions cropping up in her mind. Instead she said, "Lee, we were getting worried. No one knew where you were."

Lee leaned on the countertop. It appeared casual, but in truth, it was to ease her churning stomach. "I'm sorry, Mindy," she said apologetically. "I should have left word, but I really didn't expect to be away this long. I've just

260

come from Dov. He's been helping me with my property in Rome. I've put it up for sale."

"Hey, Rick!" Paul interjected. "I think that car is here for you."

Paying no attention, Baron eyed Lee obliquely. "Any particular reason?"

She bit her lip, then nodded. "I'm breaking all ties outside of Israel."

Baron remained calm, displaying no reaction to the bomb she tossed at him. Inwardly, his world was collapsing. She couldn't have been more explicit. Lee was bidding him farewell. Why? Why had she come to him last night, offering herself in body and soul to share an experience that only true love could impart?

Out of the corner of an eye, he saw the uniformed man at the door. Damn! Not now! There were too many things to be sorted out. She had just come from Dov Laslo. Was he the cause of this latest "Dear John"?

"Mr. Baron?"

Baron nodded. "I'll be with you in a moment." He turned to Mindy. "Please have Joe pick me up at the hospital later. Afterward we can go over our future plans." He faced Lee. "As for you, *signora*, your shop is closed tomorrow. We'll have plenty of time to talk." With that, he stalked out with the Israeli soldier.

Following their departure, Lee stepped to the door and watched the car move away. She recognized Baron's inner turmoil. It mirrored her own. She twisted around, hearing Mindy come up behind her.

"Lee, you're a fool if you let him go."

Lee gaped in dismay. It was the second time in the past hour that those very words had been said to her. Unsettled, she recalled her meeting with Dov earlier.

Dov's apartment, one of many in a new block of ochre stone buildings, was only four streets away from Lee's shop. What should have been a ten-minute walk, she had dragged into an hour. Filled with self-doubts, she was finally in his apartment, sitting in an armchair opposite an old, scarred, wooden desk.

Dov Laslo lived frugally, despite the steady royalties he received from his books. The apartment, painted entirely in oyster-white, consisted of a bedroom, bath, kitchen, and living room. The furniture was functional and inelegant. A slight breeze from a half-opened window rustled a diaphanous curtain without disturbing the papers on the desk. Except for the papers he had been working on, the desk was orderly.

From the very beginning, it had been apparent to Laslo that the Roman property wasn't her prime interest. He had been aware of the clasping and unclasping of her hands and the nervous fidgeting that seemed to indicate that she was unable to express what was going through her mind. Tactfully, he had refrained from questioning her.

After meticulously collecting the papers and putting them to one side, he directed a benign look her way. Leaning forward, he rested on his elbows.

"Eleanora, suppose you tell me now the true purpose of your visit. This business"—he gestured casually toward the papers—"could have been accomplished over the phone."

She bit her lip, finding it difficult to speak. She took a deep breath, gathering up her nerve.

"Dov, do you still wish to marry me?"

Dov Laslo stared at her, not quite believing he had heard her correctly. A deep furrow formed across his forehead. "Eleanora!" he stammered.

Her eyes were level with his, but the tremor in her voice was unmistakable. "Yes, Dov. I'm asking whether you still wish to marry me."

After the initial surprise, Laslo dropped his gaze. He wondered why she was propelling herself into a marriage she didn't really want. He remembered his visit with Riv earlier this morning and how Riv, in the telling of his miraculous escape, had lauded Baron with unabashed enthusiasm. A cloud of suspicion passed through his thoughts. Could Rick Baron have been the catalyst in her sudden decision to accept the proposal made to her months ago? And if so, was he merely to be her escape from Baron? Not for a single moment had he doubted the existence of a nebulous bond between Eleanora and this American. Whatever it was . . .

Laslo lifted his eyes and studied her cautiously. "After all these months, Eleanora, why now?"

Lee looked aside, unable to face him, recognizing that

he was wary of her motives. She spoke softly, almost in a murmur.

"Dov, Israel is my home . . . but for my children, it is more than a home. No matter the circumstances, they will never desert. I don't doubt that they will survive with all of Israel, but for me, having to live through a fourth war here, I find the strain unbearable." She paused briefly, her voice trembling, and faced him once again. "Yet with all of this, I cannot leave them. You are strong, Dov, and I do think a lot of you. I know you can be the bulwark against my fears."

Laslo sighed deeply. ". . . Think a lot of you" lingered in his mind. "Eleanora, it is time for us to share confidences candidly. For you to reward me with marriage for being a good friend . . . would simply be too great a sacrifice on your part." He noted her chagrin. "There is also no need for you to feel depressed or even embarrassed because of my refusal. To be quite frank, Eleannora, you're too vital a woman, and I've become adjusted to a life of celibacy." Laslo knew he could never hold her in his arms while she conjured up visions of another man.

Lee's eyes misted. "You're a poor liar, Dov . . . and much too gallant."

Laslo shrugged, managing a smile. "Perhaps so, but if you want the real truth and a word of advice—you'd be a fool to let him go."

Lee sat in the back of the shop, sipping a cup of tea, preoccupied with the people shaping her life. With Laslo's rejection, her immediate reaction had been one of relief. It was curious the way everyone—other than her own children—seemed to be prodding her toward Baron. Unrestrained, she allowed herself to reflect on the previous evening and how she had loved him shamelessly.

Her hand trembling, she set down the cup, an irrepressible warmth flooding her. She got up hastily, brought the cup and saucer to a small sink, and rinsed them out. To repeat their act of love before his departure would only denigrate their love. *Their love*, she thought, a hand pressed to her heart. Dear God!

The cup fell from her hand.

Paul came running into the room, Mindy right behind

him. He stared at the bits of broken china spread over the floor. "Cripes! You scared the hell out of us! It sounded just like a gunshot."

Mindy took one look at Lee's ashen face and hastened to her side. "Lee, are you all right? Joe will be here soon, but he can pick me up later."

"No, no," Lee replied hastily. "Thanks, Mindy. I'm forever grateful for your help, but I've already imposed on you too much." She watched Paul gingerly picking up the broken pieces with one hand and placing them in a paper bag. "Leave it, Paul. I can sweep it up later."

Mindy went after the push broom propped up in the far corner. "What about the boys?"

"They're at a nursery just around the corner. Tovah will be here soon to bring them home."

Seemingly having an ulterior motive, Mindy told Paul to watch the shop. Leaning on the broom, she said, "Lee, you know our plans call for leaving on Thursday. Is there any chance you'll follow soon after?"

Lee seated herself at the table. "That's definite?"

"It is—unless the boys change their minds tonight."

Lee was on the verge of tears. "I'll miss you, Mindy, and all the others."

Riv's face lit up at the sight of Baron. Grinning, he spoke with genuine enthusiasm. "So the savior has decided to view his miracle!" He held out his hand.

Baron, taken aback by Riv's elated spirit, fought to control his emotions. Miracle! Which was the miracle? The creation of Riv or his saving? He forced a smile and took Riv's hand.

Savoring the feeling of holding his son's hand, he then said, "How's the leg?"

"In one piece—literally. I can't bend the knee." He noted Baron's sober expression. "But for you, it might have been much worse." The grin waned to a studious smile. "Is your so-called 'debt' repaid?"

Baron nodded in silence. Riv knew something. But what? Afraid to speak, he waited for Riv to continue.

"Mother has filled me in on your background. You're quite a man, Rick Baron."

Baron eyed him warily. "Just what has she told you?"

"Well, I know now that you meant a lot to each other at one time."

Baron tried to stem the fears within him. "That was a long time ago. Why does that make me 'quite a man'?"

Riv didn't appear to notice the tension building within Baron. He continued unabated. "Because of your relationship with mother, you risked your own life to save the son of an old friend." He watched Baron move to the window and, for a moment, wondered whether he was embarrassing him. "I realize now . . ." he added, "that was the debt you were repaying."

Baron saw someone get out of a car in the parking lot. It looked like Joe. He wiped a bead of perspiration from his forehead, then turning, regarded Riv. How understanding would he be if he knew the whole truth?

"Sorry if I've embarrassed you, Baron. It wasn't my intention. But what you did . . . I'll never forget it."

Baron fought the lump in his throat, then glanced at his watch. "Sorry, Riv, but I must leave. Business appointment. I'll drop in again. I've still got a few days left in Israel."

Baron waved Riv back when he tried to sit up. Stifling an overwhelming urge to embrace him, he took his hand. "Take care of yourself—I can't hang around to watch over you."

Riv watched him depart, his expression puzzled. Why did he get the impression that Baron was troubled? A frown appeared. He would hate seeing him leave. He wanted to know him better.

Baron met Joe coming into the lobby. He took Joe's arm and led him back outside onto the stone steps of the hospital.

Joe peered at him searchingly. "Rick, what is it?"

Baron swallowed and took a deep breath. "Just listen, Joe. Set them up with whatever they need. I'll split all costs with you, but they're never to know of my involvement. Make it look like a strict business deal. Riv—or Lee—would never accept it otherwise."

Joe nodded, extremely moved. Rick was as near to tears as he had ever seen him. "What about you and Lee?" he ventured.

Baron cleared his throat and reached into his pocket for his pipe. "Yes, what about us?"

Joe's manner altered abruptly. He retorted sharply. "Rick, you're running out of time. Why don't you stop horsing around and ask her to marry you? Since when have *you* refused a challenge?" Receiving no answer, he exhaled slowly and lowered his voice. "Rick, we have to leave by Thursday. We have commitments." Still no reply. Joe sighed heavily. "All right, stay on another week. I'll manage—somehow—until then."

CHAPTER 13

Golan Heights—October 14, 1973

Rick Baron had stopped counting at fifty. The rocky, desolate countryside was littered with the low silhouette Syrian tanks. Acrid odors from the charred bodies imprisoned in the scorched and shattered tanks permeated the landscape, trying the nerves of Baron and his three companions. Earlier, they had been told by an Israeli staff officer that at least 150 tanks had been destroyed when Israel had taken the offensive last Monday. In an engagement lasting five hours, they had knocked out two-thirds of Assad's guards, Syria's crack armored division, while losing only a dozen of their own tanks.

Baron sat in the front of the jeep, alongside an Israeli reporter who was driving. Seated uncomfortably behind them was a British correspondent and another American. Baron had realized, with some discomfort, that he had been offered the front seat because he was the senior member of the group. By at least fifteen years, he thought ruefully.

The Israeli correspondent drove at a moderate speed with orders not to pass the half-track leading them. The half-track was used to retrieve the wounded from the battlefields. In an earlier interview, the unit doctor told Baron how he had used up ten magazines in the mounted Uzi while rescuing the wounded during last night's battle.

Baron could appreciate his story since this was the same type of vehicle that had pulled him from the Sinai.

Along the road leading to Damascus, they passed through a deserted, mud and stone, Syrian settlement. Fixing the desolate character of the area, Baron saw scraggly fields of stone stretched beyond the horizon. The reporters wordlessly glanced at the brooding, impoverished village, respecting its somber silence.

They were twenty kilometers inside Syria when they heard the pounding of heavy artillery. After another two kilometers, they were stopped by Israeli soldiers. The British correspondent leaned forward expectantly.

"Yehuda," he said to the driver, "if they go into Damascus, will we be permitted to follow?"

Yehuda shrugged. "Damascus is still forty kilometers away."

The two reporters leaped from the backseat as Yehuda followed the instructions of a bearded Israeli soldier. Parking on the rocky terrain a few yards from the nearest British Centurion tank, he shut off the engine. About to leave his seat, he turned and regarded Baron who was filling his briar. "You look tired, my friend. Too many wars?" It was stated with respect for Baron's reputation.

Baron held a lighter to the bowl, sending a cloud of dense smoke into the noon light. Philosophically, he said, "Who decides when there are too many wars?"

Yehuda grinned boyishly. "If I knew, I would be a greater reporter than you." With someone hailing him, he slid out of the seat. "I'll meet you at the Command Post in a few minutes," he said as he departed. Baron waved him on, glancing idly at the impatient line of Centurions.

Baron sat there unmoved. His eyes were dark with the memory of the unforgettable events of last Thursday.

He had driven Joe and Mindy to Lod Airport before dawn. The farewells on the previous evening had been tearful for the women. Mindy had promised that she would visit again next year, then meaningfully offered Lee her hospitality should she contemplate a visit to America. Lee's answer had been a cryptic smile.

When they had astounded Lee with their "plan" on Tuesday, Baron had been almost certain she was weakening. Realizing the torment in her indecision, Baron was sure that with a few days layover, he could cajole her children into giving them their blessings. He had grinned optimistically, viewing Lee's bewilderment with Tovah's ecstatic acceptance of Paul's intentions.

His spirits soaring, Baron recklessly maneuvered through the hills of Jerusalem's outskirts. He had just two hours before he was to meet with other correspondents at the King David. From there, they were to leave for the Golan.

In anticipation of seeing Lee, even if only for a few minutes, he swept into Jaffa Road and headed for her shop.

Something was wrong. The shop was closed. A chill of doom passed over him like a tidal wave. He glanced at his watch, then jumped back into the rented Fiat. His face grim, he headed for her apartment, refusing to guess what might have happened.

A block before he reached his destination, he noticed black smoke rising from her street. The road was blocked off. He pulled over sharply, left the car, and ran the rest of the way.

Pushing his way through the crowd, he saw the remains of a military vehicle. The fire was out, but it was still smoking. Firemen were pouring water into the wreck. Unable to stem the little fears tugging at his chest, he shoved his way to the rescue van parked a short distance away.

Showing his correspondent pass, he took in the interior of the van at a glance. The sight of two strangers being treated for minor injuries flooded him with relief. Guiltily, he addressed the medic tending to them.

"Will they be okay, doctor?"

The medic nodded without looking up. "They're fortunate that the girl saw the bomb under the seat before it blew."

His heart skipped a beat. "What girl?"

"The girl they were picking up. She lives in the apartment house across the street."

Baron didn't wait for details. He sped around the angry crowd, past the soldiers guarding the smoldering wreck, and into the building.

He found Tovah, her face colorless, sitting on the living room couch. Her left leg was swathed in bandages from below her knee to her ankle and stretched out on a footstool. The doctor standing over her was speaking to Lee.

269

"The wound is not serious enough for a hospital stay, but she should remain at home for a few days."

Lee nodded, holding a hand to her mouth as if afraid to speak. It was at that moment that she became aware of Baron's presence. She stared at him, the shock of the event imprinted in her eyes.

Baron saw the look and the firm set of her chin that followed. His heart sinking, he knew that he had lost her. She would never leave.

The artillery had been pounding steadily at the low ridge line four kilometers ahead. The strong odor of cordite failed to penetrate Baron's senses; his thoughts ranged in another direction. The sun had passed its zenith, and he remained in the jeep, oblivious to the Israeli troops preparing for an assault on Sasa.

After several minutes of silent argument, the only conclusion he could reach was that his life—in whatever future was left for him—would be miserable without Lee. An additional thought preyed on his mind. Not only was he losing Lee, but he was also abandoning his son.

A Centurion tank clanked into movement and lumbered past his jeep. Baron looked up, angry with the interruption. He watched the metal monsters lined up on the road begin to move forward. Roughly emptying the bowl of his pipe, he pondered. "What am I doing here? Chasing an eternal war? Is this to be the sum total of my life? A reputation gained solely as a war correspondent? The Israelis at least had a purpose—what was mine?"

Struggling within himself, he dredged up the answer. His career had already consumed most of his life. Yet now, without Lee, it afforded him no sense of purpose. Suddenly, Joe's remonstrations became clear to him. Joe had already contracted enough TV commercials to last for a year. What else did he need?

He began to sweat. Could he convince her that he would give up all his wandering so they could spend the rest of their lives together? God! How he needed her! And the rest of the family! They were his family, if only for a few days each year. His pulse was racing. There was no worthwhile future without them. And Lee, dear Lee! To awaken each morning with her at his side . . .

He tried to think. He was committed to return to the

States in three days. A mere three days to convince her! He leaped from the jeep, searching for Yehuda.

He hadn't gone far before he spied the American correspondent, young and eager on his initial foreign assignment. He was running toward Baron.

"Where the hell were you, Baron? They're getting ready to close in on Sasa."

"I'm closing in, too," Baron stated, his spirits soaring. "I'm going back to finish the story of my life." Yehuda was coming up with the Englishman. "Is there any way I can get a lift back?" he asked him.

The puzzled Israeli nodded. "Yes, of course. There's . . ."

He stopped short at the sound of jets zooming over the horizon. "Run for cover!" he shouted. "They're Sukhois!"

In seconds, two planes swooped down on them, their guns raking a pattern along the road lined with tanks. The tanks rolled off the road like a string of broken beads with machine guns chattering at the soaring planes. Antiaircraft guns came into the fray, dotting the blue sky with black puffs.

The four newsmen selected the nearest Centurion for protective cover. In half-crouches, they moved around to the far side of the tank to await the expected return pass, holding hands to their ears to shut out the deafening racket.

They didn't have long to wait. Baron saw the planes flashing in the sun as they swooped in upon them once again. Realizing that they were in the direct line of fire this time, he dropped down, pulling Yehuda with him. The rain of bullets streamed down on their position like a banshee howl from hell. A sharp rock pushed against his chest as he burrowed into the hard ground.

He heard a loud explosion and felt himself being lifted by a hot wind. . . .

Lee hung up the phone and glanced at the clock on the wall. It was almost four o'clock; the days were becoming long and tedious. She and Tovah were alone in the shop and it had been a slow day.

Tovah, sitting in a chair with her cane beside her, studied her mother with exasperation. "Then you're really leaving for Rome tomorrow night?"

Lee nodded impassively, refusing to face her.

271

"And I suppose you won't get back before Wednesday," Tovah added.

"That's right. The shop is closed Tuesday. Paul will be here on Wednesday until my return. There will be no problem."

Tovah started to stand, then muttered a "damn" and sat down again. "Mother, running from Rick will not solve anything. Do you think we are all blind?"

Lee turned abruptly. "This does not concern you, Tovah!"

Tovah rolled her eyes in desperation. "Mama, I know what he means to you. I can see it in your eyes, your behavior, your every movement. You have a right to a life of your own. Your children don't need a permanent baby-sitter."

Nonplussed by Tovah's unexpected persistence, Lee snapped on the radio. The Israeli Symphony blared forth.

Undaunted, Tovah raised her voice. "I've discussed Rick with Riv, Mama," she saw her mother spin about, "and strangely enough, he wasn't even surprised." She lowered her voice compassionately. "As a matter of fact, he seemed pleased."

Lee's face blanched. "Tovah, you didn't tell . . ."

Tovah gestured impatiently. "Of course not! But Riv muttered something about an ancient Chinese proverb—something like 'When someone's life is saved by another, that life is forever indebted to that person.' Strange, isn't it," she said, now competing with the newsman that had just come on the radio, "that Riv should pick up on that particular proverb?"

"*—Sinai front stabilized—eight hour battle—200 Egyptian tanks destroyed—*"

Lee remained silent, her shoulders suddenly heavy. She had become unnecessary to her children.

"*—heavy fighting in Golan—about to take Sasa—*"

Tovah read her mother's expression. She leaned forward, distraught. "Oh, Mama! I don't mean to sound harsh or ungrateful, but knowing how you feel about this man, we would all be miserable keeping you from him. You're made for each other. Can't you see he looks upon you as a goddess?"

"*—two foreign correspondents wounded—*"

Both women stiffened.

"—one English, the other American, their identities as yet unknown—" Lee turned off the radio.

Tovah paled but kept her voice even. "Mother, he's not the only American in the Golan."

Lee muttered a tormented "Oh, God!" and moved quickly to the phone. Tovah watched her and worried.

Realizing an instant later that her mother was calling the airport for an earlier flight to Rome, she pushed the table away and labored to her feet.

"Mother, you're not going to Rome without waiting to find out!"

Lee turned on her, her eyes blazing. "I don't want to know! I don't intend to stand around the rest of my life waiting for bad news!"

Tovah stared at her, then sank back into her chair without replying. There was nothing more to be said.

CHAPTER 14

October 16, 1973

Lee paid the taxi driver and, seemingly at leisure, strolled into Piazza Navona. It had been years since her last visit, yet nothing had changed. Enzo came to mind briefly, the ache in her bosom increased, but the pain was not for Enzo. She stuck her hands into her coat pockets and moved slowly toward the Bernini fountain.

It was a typical autumn day in the Piazza—the air cool, the sun warm, and few strollers. Lee stopped beside the stone figures reclining above the rippling water of the pool, her eyes blinking away the mists that shrouded her memory. A picture of a girl waiting for her young American lover developed slowly in her mind's eye.

A gust of wind mordantly intercepted the old memory. Her eyes appeared troubled. She looked about forlornly, her thoughts reminding her, as they had ever since her arrival in Rome, that she had behaved like a fool. She had been shocked when her children tried to throw them together, but she realized later that their concern was strictly for her own happiness.

She watched two scraps of paper chasing each other in an eddy of wind. Poor Rick, she thought, always chasing, never catching. The story of his life, she thought bitterly. It had never been his fault. She fought the tears as she had been for the past two days.

She tried to swallow, but the ache in her throat persisted. Straining, she forced Baron from her mind and brought the business at hand into focus. All the papers had been signed and, by the end of the month, she would no longer own property in Rome. It was final now. She had closed her last road to . . .

Final, she thought. She had searched the morning paper for news of the fighting in Israel, but there had been no mention of any wounded correspondents. Nevertheless, she never doubted that he was alive. She would have known . . . would have felt something. . . .

Trembling unaccountably, she lifted her head to observe the people eating lunch nearby at the Tre Scalini. One more time, she thought, for old times' sake. She bit her lip. At least, she would have her memories.

Baron raced up the steps at the end of the narrow hallway, the familiar smells following him as he headed for the fourth floor. He couldn't believe it—the same apartment house, the same apartment!

His heart pounding, he knocked at the old familiar door, holding a hand to his chest.

No answer!

"Damn!" he sputtered, banging harder.

A door creaked open at the far end of the hall. He spun around to see a heavy-set, middle-aged woman staring at him. He spoke hastily. *"Signora, parla Lei inglese?"*

She nodded, smiling proudly. *"Si, signore."*

"Signora Moscati—do you know where she is?"

The woman frowned, then held up a hand. She shouted in Italian to someone in the room behind her. A man's voice replied, and Baron heard Piazza Navona mentioned.

Baron quickly crossed the hall to plant a kiss upon her cheek. *"Grazie, signora!"* he said to the stunned woman, then raced down the steps.

By the time he reached the front door, each gasp he sucked in brought sharp, jabbing pains. Forced to stop, he held a hand to his side, feeling the tape beneath his shirt that was keeping his cracked ribs together. A memento he didn't need, he thought with great impatience.

He waited for another minute, his pains subsiding, then stepped out into the small square. It was incredible. Other than the parked motor scooters replacing the bicycles, it was still the same. Focusing his memory, he found the small fountain where the inhabitants of the area used to fill their pails. The streets off the square narrowed into curving alleys, the light blocked by drying wash hung between the buildings.

Enough, he said to himself, moving at a brisk pace through the gusty alley. He was hoping for better memories to come. The street may be timeless, but he wasn't.

He hailed a cab on the Viale Di Trastevere and, settling into the seat, worriedly glanced at his watch. One o'clock. If he couldn't find her, what then? He had a ten o'clock flight back to the States that night.

He closed his eyes with Tovah's parting words burning in his mind. After the initial shock of seeing him and the small talk that followed, she had said ingenuously, "Don't waste any more time! Go after mother. You must be the one to take the initiative."

He left the cab, his heart beating like a schoolboy's on his first date. He was hoping that by some miracle, she would be waiting at . . . He shook his head, angry with himself. He was being immature and knew it. Why on earth should she expect him?

Standing by himself at the Bernini fountain, he had never felt so alone. Undecided as to his next move, he grew annoyed with the gusts of wind teasing his coat collar. Straightening his shoulders, he threw off the sense of defeat that was trying to mantle his spirits. He would try all the restaurants, one by one, until he found her. Determined, he headed for the Tre Scalini.

He peered through the potted plants protecting the outdoor tables. They were empty.

Undaunted, he moved past the tables toward the window.

He halted abruptly, almost frozen in mid-stride. There she was at a side table, holding a tiny cup of *espresso.* He opened the door and entered, his eyes never leaving her. As if a sixth sense was at work, he saw her lift her head.

Instantly, he knew he had won—they had won. Her eyes said it all. No questions, no pleading was necessary. Unbuttoning his trench coat, he took it off and draped it over his arm as he walked toward her.

Throwing his coat over an empty chair, he sat down opposite her. Their eyes never leaving each other, he leaned forward on his elbows. *"Io t'amo,"* he murmured softly.

Lee nodded, almost imperceptibly, a half-smile forming briefly. She didn't dare utter a sound.

"I thought you'd be waiting at the fountain," said Baron. Lee held a knuckle to her quivering lips. "I saw Tovah yesterday," he continued casually, "and it appears that we have a very understanding family." He held her gaze. "Riv will be home next week. I figure in about a month—say around Thanksgiving—you can be in New York."

Lee dropped her eyes, but he read her perfectly. "No. Riv never need know the entire truth about me. Since God arranged for me to play an important role in Riv's survival, I feel that that alone compensates for all the years I've lost."

To Baron, she seemed satisfied, yet puzzled. He smiled suddenly. "Thanksgiving—just as the name implies—a day for giving thanks to God." His smile widened. "Appropriate, wouldn't you say?"

Lee gazed at him, her eyes moistening. She reached across the table for his hand and brought it to her lips. *"Io t'amo,* my dear Rick," she said softly.

He gazed at her tenderly, his heart swelling with emotion. His voice husky, he said, "Lee, my flight's at ten o'clock. When do you leave?"

She regarded him for a moment, then got to her feet. He stood up, signaling for the waiter. He paid the bill. Leading her outside, he said, "Lee—your flight?"

She gave him a bright smile. "Not until eleven."

Baron returned her glance obliquely. What was she up to? He took her arm. Passing a *gelateria,* he said, "Some *tortufo?"*

She shook her head, looking at him strangely. "Let's go back to the apartment . . . where it all began. Perhaps with a little imagination, we can pretend we were never interrupted."

He felt a flush creeping into his face. He took her hand and placed it inside his jacket so that she could feel the tape wrapped around his chest. "You do pick the most inauspicious times, Lee."

A smile followed her initial look of concern. "I'll be very gentle, my darling." She entwined her arm in his, and began to laugh. She looked at him, and the laughter rippled from her lips.

Baron halted suddenly, staring at her in disbelief.

It was all there—the promise, the hopes, and the dreams to be shared. It was all there in her laughter.

Lee looked at him, a smile lingering. "Rick, surely I haven't shocked you?"

He returned the smile. "In a way, you have," he said cryptically. He took her arm in his again. "I'll explain someday."

A feeling of assurance and security followed him as they walked past the Bernini fountain. At the age of forty-nine, he had made a great discovery. The sound of dreams was not reserved for merely the young in love.